The Bone Thief's Tale

HELEEN DAVIES

THE BONE THIEF SAGA BOOK ONE

For Sarah.

Because you and I are more than best friends. We're like a teeny tiny gang on our own.

The Bone Thief's Tale

CHAPTER ONE
LYNNE

Way up on a dark mountaintop, I reached out and—*crack*.

I broke off the bone as if it were a rotten branch. Easy-peasy. Well, stealing has always been a piece of cake for me.

Smirking, I took a glance at all the skeletons and bones above me. Unlike the Topworld, the Underworld—*my realm*—had no blue sky. Instead, we had this filthy ceiling, looking like crumbled earth and shit, in a mashup with trillions of skeletons growing through it, piling up like my dirty laundry. I cringed as a rat climbed through an eye socket, looking at me with green eyes. *Oh, for skull's sake…*

But this mess of a ceiling meant money for me. Lots of money. Because I wasn't stealing just *any* bones. No. The one in my hand had this slight shimmer on its surface and that was what I was hunting for. The shiny dust hinted at the magic that laid dormant within some of these stinky bones. A dark power that made all kinds of wishes come true—assuming one were a witch. Which I was not.

Sighing, I turned the bone over, its light illuminating my

face from below. Sadly, that precious bone was nothing but another prize to sell to the Bone Queen. But I needed her Bloodcoins. Badly. Because stealing wasn't just a piece of cake, it was an actual cake for me. Chocolatey and fruity with a cherry on top.

As if on cue, my stomach grumbled, and I knew I had to hurry. I wasn't the only one almost starving to death in this bird cage of a world. And I still had a lot to do until we could eat.

After pocketing my stolen bone, I climbed down from the top of the mountain, where I was hanging like a spider monkey for a good hour while I harvested my ripe fruits. When I stood safely on a platform again, my hair tie broke and my white-ish hair whipped behind me like a flag.

I waved mockingly at the many skulls and without checking the void below, I jumped from the ledge—falling into a deep dark chasm. My skin tickled with sheer weightlessness and the cool air kissed my skin as my heart thundered like a drum.

I fell and fell, like a bird with clipped wings, until I sensed my friend below me, flying steadily through the thick and misty clouds. I stretched out both of my hands and braced myself for the hard impact as I crashed into my Sircha dragon, holding onto him with all my might.

"Hey, Soothie boy!" I laughed and patted his cold head. I could smell the Underworld on him—a dusty scent of death that clung to his scales for centuries now. My Sircha was dark enough that no one could see him, and big enough for me to ride. He was my little partner in crime—always waiting for me, flying underneath me with his leathery black wings, which were as long as six men in a row.

"You earned yourself some fine Rickelssack for tonight!" I said.

Soothie purred under my touch. Of course, he did. Rick-elssack was the most delicate meat there ever was. And thanks to the number of bones I stole today, we could afford it. The devil can take the hindmost, but definitely not me and my boys.

"You really need to stop being so reckless, Lynne." Something furry moved in my peripheral vision.

I giggled and made myself comfortable on Soothie's back, holding onto the sharp scales on his neck. "Stop being so boring. You'll get a bit of Rickelssack too, fine? Maybe then you'll stop being a pain in my ass, Bory."

"Don't be so rude," he squealed, shaking his blue fur and hopping onto my thigh. My other friend was a tiny Burlack, a feathery little bear that I could hide in my fist easily. He had really sharp teeth, so that probably wasn't a good idea at all.

"Was this the last bone on your list? *Please* say yes, Lynne."

"Yeeees," I said, pressing my legs harder into Soothie's back to navigate him where I wanted to fly next. "Good boy! Turn right now."

"Finally," Bory sighed. "I hate stealing from the Sacred Dead."

I rolled my eyes. "You don't say. Stop being a religious mother hen, Bory. We've been doing this for years and nothing has ever happened."

"It's never too late, Lynne…"

I snorted.

Bory was always afraid of everything and everybody. But he had a point. Those bones up there weren't just ugly to look at. They were also sacred and feared by normal dwellers below. But I didn't give a damn about normal. I'd rather be human, living in the wonderfully clean and nice Topworld than sit here waiting for the right death and starve as a punishment. Well, other Underworlders might also long for the upper world if they knew about it. But there's no way I'd just give up my favorite secret like that. It took me years until I found a passage through the bones, and I only told Bory and Soothie. No one else. And I want to keep it that way.

I leaned into the curve as Soothie turned left this time. He was a master of flying, which was necessary, since in the Underworld, everything was foggy. I couldn't see anything in this cloudy, yellow-ish soup except for some black mountain-tops sticking out under the fog. Thankfully, Soothie could.

"You need a mother hen," Bory said. "One day someone will find out what you're doing. And then you'll be in deep shit. I can't save you from the Tartaros, little girl."

I couldn't help but chuckle. Bory was so funny when he was angry. Sometimes I would intentionally look for something to piss him off. There wasn't much to laugh about in the Under-world, so an angry Bory was the highlight of my day.

He furrowed his dark blue brows, hopped onto Soothie's head, and propped himself up there like he was the king. Soothie growled in response but let Bory use his head as a lookout anyway. For better or worse, that was the only possible choice with Soothie. He was a very kind Sircha, and that was his problem. The thought twisted my insides. There was simply no room for nice creatures here.

"I knew it!" Bory squealed, folding up his puffy arms. "You have one last chance to tell me why we aren't flying to our queen right now!"

I grumbled, focusing on the mist before me.

It was obvious where I was flying to, and I was *so* not answering his stupid questions. No matter what some might say, stupid questions were a thing, and Bory asked most of them.

"Oh, for the Dead's sake! Lynne... you need to bring the bones to her, like, right now. She will kill you, knowing that you found them and didn't give them back to her. They belong to her now. You know what happens when you lose just one!" Bory stomped with one of his thick legs, making Soothie roar. If he had done that with another Sircha, he wouldn't have a chubby foot to stomp afterwards.

"Chill," I sighed and patted Soothie once again. "It will only take a few minutes and I've never lost anything."

"Oh no. No. No. No. Lynne. Please don't tell me that you're up to do *that* again?" Bory looked around, noticing that the trees were turning red already. He put two and two together and glanced at me again, eyes big as saucers. He finally got it. Wow, he really wasn't very smart, was he?

I held my hands up in mock defense.

Of course, I was up to do *that*. Did he even know me? It was Storm Day and I was so not going to miss it. It was my thing and I had to do it every year. It's not like I was going there for the first time today. It's more like the 12th time… and to be honest, I couldn't stay away from *him* any longer. I've already waited too long. 365 days.

"Lynne, do you even listen to me?" Bory's voice rang in my ear.

"No," I said, grinning at the frown on his face.

"Lynne! This is no good." Bory clicked his tongue. "Soothie, turn."

"Soothie doesn't answer to you," I said, worrying that I was already too late. It took me hours to get the Queen's Bones. What if I messed up this year and couldn't see him? My chest tightened and my heart began a steady thumping against my ribcage. But then when I finally saw a very familiar, reddish tower, my heart took another tumble and I let out a deep breath. We made it. I made it.

"I have to go, Bory. I *have* to."

I clutched Soothie's cold skin even tighter, ignoring my tingling fingers and toes. The closer we got to the tower, leaving all the black mountains behind, the worse the fluttering in my stomach became. I wished I could just blink and be there. I didn't care about much, but I cared for this day. For *him*. Which was a bit stupid—but whatever. I certainly didn't work this hard all year to survive and then not pocket my reward for all the hard work I went through.

When Soothie glided slowly towards the broken tower, my hands trembled. The tower was an old ruin made more or less of broken stone, perforated wood, and moss. It rose to frightening heights and was surrounded by the Black Sea.

Looking up at the tower's spire, I chewed on my tongue in anticipation. The roof disappeared completely into the skeletons in the sky, as if it had merged with them. It took me a long time to find the place, but when I saw this strange spike, I knew my life would change. This was my one and only passageway to another realm.

My way out.

When Soothie hovered in front of an open round window in the middle of the tower, I got off his back and quickly jumped into it. My fingers turned black with dust as soon as I touched the charred, ice-cold stone. Earlier, when I didn't have my precious Sircha, I climbed up the stones by myself and tore my nails to get to this window. It's much more comfortable this way to be honest. Pure luxury. Even if I liked to climb and jump from buildings to distract myself from boredom.

"Be careful, Lynne!" Bory called after me, wriggling on Soothie's top like a rattlesnake.

I put my hand on my hip, piercing him with my dark brown eyes. "I love you, you sweet mother hen. But I'll be back in no time. You can have a little chit chat with Soothie while missing me."

Soothie growled in annoyance, and Bory gave me the look. The *do-not-mess-with-me* look. "Soothie can't speak, and you are going to be dead soon. But not the good kind of dead!"

"You'll be okay," I said as I turned, my chest glowing from the knowledge that my guys always had my back, no matter what. Maybe some would say that animals or monsters couldn't be considered family, but Bory and Soothie were mine. Period. "I'll be right back. You won't miss me for long, I promise."

Bory mumbled something, but I had already made up my mind. There was no going back. Storm Day was my day.

To be honest, I wasn't exactly proud of myself for being this addicted. After all, I wouldn't call myself a person who liked to show emotions, but everyone had a vice, right? Mine was this man from another world. My stomach fluttered the moment I saw him in my mind's eye. Hell, he was the most handsome creature I knew.

Like every other year, I ran up the spiral staircase which filled the entire space in the narrow and dusty tower. I knew the way by heart and although it was always dark in my world, it was even darker in here. It was as if I had to step through a barrier before getting to the Topworld. And yet, I could walk there with my eyes closed.

My steps echoed throughout the building and my heart pounded with excitement, so fast that I could feel the pulse beating up to my temples, pumping in my veins.

Sighing in relief, I opened the door that allowed me to cross from my realm to the humans', the wood rattling beneath my sweaty fingers. I stepped through like I belonged, like I was human. But their world had knowledge ours didn't, and that knowledge was very forbidden to my kind. So, I had a penchant for bad things… sue me.

Once out, I walked a few steps on the lush grass, grinning at the gentle midnight breeze on my skin and the autumn colors in the trees. In my world, the grass was brown or yellow-ish, the earth black as soot and the trees broken. The only natural light we had came from glowing lava that broke through the crust. Sometimes the volcanos hurled their sparks into the air. That was the normal, down there.

But up here, everything was green, soft, and smelled so good. I halted for some seconds and took in the familiar, sweet scent. Fresh wood. Water. The sweetness of hundreds of flowers I couldn't even name. The corner of my eyes filled with unbidden tears, and I reminded myself that I needed to hurry, blinking them away. I was already late and every second I had in this world was worth its weight in tons of Bloodcoins. So, buckle up, silly goose.

Shaking my head, I went straight to where I thought I would find him. He was always in the same place, every year, at the same time. Before I met him, I used to wander around, touching everything, and collecting objects from this world that I was still guarding in my cave with all my might. My human treasures. Every time I went back to the Underworld, I had thousands of questions in my mind. What was this world called? Was it really called the Topworld? Why were there no bones in the sky?

As if I had to check whether the dark blue sky was still there or not, I looked up. Briefly. Yes, it was still there, and the bright spots were there too and on the far right was this crazy monstrous circle—very white—which illuminated the whole world. That thing was amazing! Once I spent a whole Storm Day just looking at this ball in the human's sky. My neck hurt like hell the next day.

But everything stopped when I saw *him* for the first time.

At some point—I can't remember when exactly—I had noticed him kneeling behind a bush in front of one of these big stones, putting flowers on a mound of earth, his face all dangerous edges. I had no idea what he was doing, but I thought he was sad. So sad...but from then on, he was always there.

Every single year.

Just like me.

But he couldn't see me. My kind was invisible to humans. Pity? That's an understatement. I would give everything to finally talk to him. To ask him about his world and how to use all the objects I collected.

And there he was. For a brief time, my heart stopped before palpitating in my chest like a bird that wanted to free itself. I stopped dead in my tracks. Just looking at him gave me this little tickle in the pit of my stomach. Oh, skull. I missed him.

Like always, I stood behind the stone he was kneeling before, so I could see him up close. The stones here were big but not round, more like… square-ish. There were orange and red flowers and candles everywhere, flickering lights lighting up his handsome, sharp face from below. He lit his candle and put it into the mound of earth in front of him. His dark brows furrowed, and his full lips pouting.

Carefully, I peered over the stone as if I would somehow distract him if I got too close. Silly, I know. But the closer I got to him, the more my heart fluttered and the air between us became electric. Bory would have laughed at me. Up here, I felt different. I wasn't this brave, heartless girl like in the Underworld. I was vulnerable.

Closely, I examined him from top to bottom. His light blue eyes, his wavy black hair… he'd changed his hairstyle over the years, but this year some black hair strands hung down onto his forehead. Overall, he had changed again. How did that even work? Unlike him, I had hardly changed at all. I was still as tender and pale as ever, looking like 16 instead of 20. When I first saw him, he was a boy—not quite a man yet. Looking at him now, he seemed like a completely different person. A grown man that could woo me with a blink of an eye. Back then he was thin, small, with dark rings under his red-rimmed eyes, wearing torn and strange clothes. Okay, today he still wore strange clothes—nothing like us Cave Town dwellers. We wore normal leather tops and loincloths. But today he had something else, a different kind of fabric. My clothes were scratchy and rough. His seemed as smooth as a courtesan's butt.

Anyway, he was a man now. Tall, well-built, with a light musky scent but… the most special thing about him were his light blue eyes. His skin was darker than mine. But that wasn't hard. I was so pale that it actually was kind of a problem. Even my hair was white-ish. In the Underworld, it was unfavorable to have light skin and hair like mine. Light skin could be seen much too well in the dark, and that was very bad. The darker the skin, the better one could hide in the darkness.

I tilted my head and looked at him closer now. He just knelt there and gazed at the mound of earth in front of him. When I first met him, he used to cry. Today he only clenched his hands into fists and bit his lips. But he was hurt. I felt his pain every year—deep and unbearable. As I leaned over the stone in front of me, my heart took leaps in my chest. *Oh,* I wanted to touch *him.* Just a little. What would it be like if he could see me? Touch me? Would he like me as much as I liked him?

His chin dipped and his lashes fluttered down. Those ridiculously long lashes. I stepped closer and a wave of goose-bumps broke out over my skin. I lifted a hand and imagined how touching his hand would feel like—

And then there were whispers behind me.

I winced, turning around on the spot, catching my breath. Voices? There were never any voices here. No one else was ever here but him. High on adrenaline, I checked the woods behind me and stumbled back, trying to locate where the noise came from. As if I knew that nothing good could come from it, I ran through the grass, past the softest trees and bushes, and finally found two men behind some other stones. Dark figures, hiding themselves from my sight.

"Is he still doing that?" a man said, making me prick my ears. "Stupid. How is someone like him so vulnerable…"

The voices blurred. *Argh,* I needed to get closer. As I tried to make out the silhouettes, I saw they were wearing something over their heads. A kind of hood. I narrowed my eyes.

"It was hard for him," said the other one, a much younger voice.

I went even closer, stepping over some branches. If Bory saw this, he'd kill me for sure.

"Rio has always been awfully nostalgic," said the bigger one.

I widened my eyes. Was that his name? Rio? How interesting. At last, I had a name for the man I was marveling at for years. Rio... what a beautiful name. Well, it was funny, but also beautiful. For over a decade, my crying boy finally had a name...

"He still visits her every year. What's the point, huh? She's dead," the younger one said.

"Exactly. And when will *you* kill him?"

I twitched—the moment stretching between us. What? Kill him? Kill Rio? *My* Rio?

"Soon. I have a plan."

I sucked in the air between my teeth.

"You should have. You know what happens if you don't. You *must* kill Rio," the older one said.

Whether I wanted it or not, at that moment something inside me screamed. I buckled and got tangled up in one of these bushes I was hovering in. Stupidly, I fell headfirst onto the grass and my leather pouch popped open.

"Damn, my bones. For skull's sake! Damn it." My fingers scurried over the lawn, trying to find my bones between the stalks and the prickly bushes. What the skull was happening? Since when did I twitch? Was this fear?

"Did you hear something?" one of those Topworlders said.

I paused, as if I had been hit with an arrow. Could Topworlders hear me now? What the skull was wrong with today?

I picked up all the bones as fast as I could and ran back to Rio. Why? I didn't know. I had the need to warn him. Absurd. Totally idiotic. As if I was responsible for him.

But once I got back to him, I noticed he didn't have a clue about anything. He didn't seem to have heard any of this—didn't even know there were others. Rio still kneeled in front of the mound, seeming to be praying for something.

But if these strange men could hear me, couldn't Rio too? I swallowed and took another step closer to him until I was right in front of him. I twitched my fingers but they spasmed.

"Hey!" I croaked, stunned about the sudden dryness in my throat. I should facepalm myself. After all these years, this was the first thing I'd say to him? Hey?

But I got no response anyway. Of course, he didn't hear me. He never did. Those men probably didn't hear me either, I just acted like a chicken. And because I was a very silly chicken, I tried again. I knew I didn't have much time left. It's always the same pattern, and soon the Underworld would want me back. But today didn't really seem like a day of wisdom—at least not for me.

"Rio. This is what they call you, right? Someone wants to kill you! Rio! Can you hear me?" I waved my hands in front of his face. "Rio?"

Just when I wanted to take a step further and somehow pull him away, he looked up. Right at me. The blue of his eyes even put a glistening diamond to shame. I blinked and reminded myself that I should hurry. My fingers curled inward, making me almost drop my bag of bones again.

But when his eyes pierced mine, I didn't know whether he really looked at me or rather *through* me. It was only a short moment, but it was an intense one. My hands felt useless, my movements slowed, and I squeezed the leather pouch hard and all at once my heart hit rock bottom.

The pouch. It felt so empty.

. . .

I OPENED MY BAG AND——NO.

I was right.

A bone was missing. How could that happen? It was my greed. My skulling greed for new things, for a man I could never have. I turned, my hands shaking like I was wet and cold.

Whenever I was in this world, I felt as if I had an invisible thread tied around my waist, keeping me near the tower. This thread always pulled on me at some point and I couldn't help but go back into my realm. Even if I wanted to stay up here, I couldn't. The Underworld wouldn't allow it, and that's exactly what was happening right now. The thread pulled me back to the tower that was now edged by dark clouds and from within, a swarm of crows descended in an inky swirl.

My stomach dropped.

I would die.

The queen would kill me.

I tried to resist the pull and pressed all my physical strength against the invisible power. Taking another step forward, I fought the undertow. I put one foot in front of the other, as slowly as if I was walking in deep mud and tried to go back to the place where I dropped my bag.

I had to find the bone. I simply had to.

Just as that eerie power was pulling me back home, I saw Rio get up. He walked a few steps and picked up *my* bone, glancing at it with raised eyebrows.

In that heartbeat of time, everything around us darkened.

He stole my queen's bone.

And with that, the man I believed I loved for years turned into my enemy.

CHAPTER TWO
RIO

Englewood.

I stretched my neck, trying to free the lingering tension from last night. That day always drained me— or better said, the memories did. To distract me, I looked at the newspaper in my hands, scanning its headlines.

Man shot. Restaurant robbed. Woman killed.

There was always some shit going down in Englewood. All neighborhoods had issues. Even if you thought you lived in a safe one, you never truly knew. One had to see for themselves, Chicago style. I was no longer surprised of who lived among whom. You could get fucked, killed, shot randomly anywhere you went. No one was safe from stray bullets.

"Boss?"

Someone knocked from outside.

"Come in, if you must," I grunted.

My bodyguards, called Slappy and Punchy, opened the door, pushing a skinny white man in. At the sight of him I immediately sat straight in my chair, looking at him with big eyes. I was irritated for a few seconds, then I let my look freeze over again in my typical poker face. As a gang leader, you can't show your feelings. Never. Unless you have a death wish, then it's fine. Nothing easier than dying.

Punchy's dark brown hand patted on the guy's slim shoulder, giving him a short sign that if I needed my best man, he'd be there. The tiny man stared up to him, meeting dark eyes and a sharp, trimmed beard. His gaze lingered on the tiny scars scattered over his neck and jaw. The old man swallowed, apparently knowing all too well that Punchy wasn't the kind of guy who liked to be fooled. His eyes flicked to Slappy, a shorter guy with a red bandana and hazel eyes.

Smiling proudly, I signaled my bodyguards to leave.

Once alone, I rocked in my chair. "What the heck are *you* doing here?"

"Rio—" the man started, and I shot up.

"Don't come into my house and call me that ever again. *Ever*. Do you understand?"

His gaze dropped and he played with his sweater.

I SAT DOWN AGAIN, the newspaper rustling between my fingers. "What do you want?"

"Your… sis—They need money," he corrected himself.

"I just delivered."

"They need more. R—they need more supplies for the school. It's very expensive. The school." He played with his fingers, avoiding my gaze.

"That's why I wanted them to go there. Remember?" I hated to be reminded of my family. My three brothers and two sisters. All of them in rich bitch fancy clothes, getting what I never got. Thanks to their sugar brother. I rummaged in my cupboard drawer and threw a fat wad of cash right in his face. The old tad staggered back, struggling to catch it. Of course, the money dropped on the floor.

"Goodbye, have a nice day," I said. "Never show up here again. It's the 21st century, we have phones."

Seconds later, Punchy opened the door and pulled the man outside, granting me an understanding glance. I sighed in relief and allowed myself to relax. That bastard. How dare he just come in here? In case they run out of money, I had a hundred cell phones and numbers where they could contact me. He was only supposed to come in person in case of real emergencies. Fucking idiot. For a second, I thought something happened to my family. I cracked my knuckles and stretched my neck once more.

There was another knock and Slappy poked his head in again. Thanks to his bronze skin, the white shirt beamed behind the slightly opened door gap.

"What?" I asked, breathing away the thought of losing someone I loved again.

"Boss," he started.

"Speak, man. Speak." I rubbed the bridge of my nose.

"*He's* here," Punchy said, his head popping up above Slappy's. My giant was almost two heads taller than Slap.

I grinned back. Finally, some good news. "I'll meet him at the bar."

They were just about to close the door when I called out to Punchy again. He stopped dead in his tracks, looking at me with big puppy eyes.

"Punchy…Rolex and Balenciaga shoes? Seriously? What'd I tell you?" He really wasn't the brightest bulb in the box.

He screwed up his face and tried to hide his expensive shoes behind the door, that brickhead. "We shouldn't… show off, boss?"

"Greed, Punchy, is the beginning of the end. They all got caught for fucking too many women, bragging about their gold, and trying to be giant brokers. Cut the bullshit. Buy yourself some Nikes and stop with the gold watches. Keep that crap in your dump."

Punchy lowered his eyes and nodded. "Yeah, boss, all right."

"Hope it is. Told you a hundred times already but there's not gonna be a hundred and one. Remember that."

Then he was gone, and I couldn't help but facepalm myself. No wonder so many people in this business got fucked. Other gangs practically revealed themselves to the cops, screaming, *I am a drug dealer, lock me in.*

Yeah, Punchy wasn't the smartest. Never had been. High school was too hard for him, so he dropped out. So, what? Degrees were not a must-have here. But common sense was, and Punchy didn't have that at times. Wearing gold chains and bragging in front of pretty ladies? He might as well be carrying a big sign saying he sells drugs and makes thousands a day. I liked fancy clothes and stuff just as much as anybody else. But we had to lie low.

That was also the reason why I didn't wear tailor-made suits and didn't buy the most expensive ones either. Brain, man. Brain for the win. It might not make any difference for our clients which brands we wore or not, but for the cops and their spies? They could smell avarice, money laundering, and men throwing their drug money out the window.

We were the Chicago Loops. The most powerful gang in the state, and we could only stay that way as long as we didn't act as stupid as the others who had all the fast money going to their heads.

As I strolled down the stairs to my club, it was already so crowded that the idiots were lining up outside. I grinned and saw dollar signs instead of eyes on every one of my guests. Just leave your money and drink my watered-down liquor, and I'll wash my dirty money with you.

And there he was.

I smirked. He was so obvious, sitting alone at the bar, surrounded by dancing and kissing twenty-somethings. All drunk or high. Hopefully none of my morons—but no, they knew that there was no such a thing as a high salesman in my gang. I made sure of that. Controlled enjoyment of alcohol and cigarettes, that's it. One had to decide for many things in life and whoever wanted to belong to my gang earned the money of his life but also had to live with many rules. Otherwise, he had to go to another turf, to one of the four other gangs in Chicago. Life was always about choices. Bad or good, we decide it ourselves.

I saw that the others kept their distance from *him*. That's good. That's what I liked. Things going smooth, like clockwork. My club had the most famous DJs, rappers from Chicago, and once in a while some straight from LA. We were famous for good music and beautiful women who shimmied around the poles and gave horny guys a lap dance.

His dirty suit and nervous foot made me smile. Then, he seemed to notice that I stopped and pinned him with my eyes, since he turned and gave me a skeptical look, scratching his head with a bloated hand. The man got stuck on my white Nikes and then looked at my hands, which I had casually put in my pocket. What was the fool thinking? That I was just walking around here with guns because I was afraid of him? On my turf? I'm safer here than the President on his porcelain toilet.

"Oh, what an honor," I heard Fox purring as she slid down from the pole next to me, giving me a kiss on the cheek. The scent of flowers and honey invaded my nose.

"Fox." I grinned, pretending I didn't care about the man anymore. Such important men hated nothing more than to be found unimportant.

I leaned against the S-shaped dance stage and looked up at Fox, shades of pink light dancing in her beautiful face. She elegantly turned on the pole and, as always, threw me off balance with her curves—or at least she thought she did.

"How is it going?" I asked and my eyes flitted over her as she slid down the pole again, taking my face in her soft hands. Red nails sliding over my heated cheeks.

"Good, since my shift's almost over, even better if you'd join me later," she purred, caramel eyes pinning mine.

"Stop it," I said, knowing she would kiss me again. Her look was anything but innocent.

"Just for fun. Hm?" She smiled like she always did and kissed me. I grinned into her lips and slightly bit her lower lip.

"Addicted much?"

"Maybe."

"Told you to be careful." Turning away I wiped my mouth with one hand and devoted myself to the fucking prick again. Fox sighed but I didn't care. There was no way I would jeopardize my plans for a chick. She should know better by now. Looking at him, I wondered why he aroused pity in me. Was it the way he sat there like a wet blanket or his moaning fear of us because he was outnumbered, feeling different? Oh, poor, fat, rich guy. Try walking in my shoes just for one day. You won't even make a mile.

"God bless you, governor," I said and sat down on a barstool next to him.

Cherry smiled at me from the bar and brought us two whiskeys—not the good one, of course. The governor stared a tad too long at her, at her Bantu Knot Out hairstyle…the way she dyed her pretty curls, the upper half a bright pink, the lower half black like the night. I glowered at the governor, telling him to stop bother my friend and best bartender. He glanced away and she disappeared.

"Should you really put the name of God in a mouth like yours?" he said, glancing at me, freezing at the sight of my eyes.

They put him off track—a totally normal reaction. An Italian guy with eyes bluer than some Scandinavians was odd, yeah. I got them from my mother. My dad, a gang boss, fell for a Swedish prostitute and the rest was history.

I took a sip of whiskey. "Should *you*, Mr. Jenson?"

I had to hold back a laugh when he hesitated to try the drink. True, I'm killing a governor who may have been none other than Vernon van der Volt himself—or maybe not. Who really knew that?

I took a sip of whiskey. "Should *you*, *sir*?"

"WHAT DO YOU WANT, *SIR*?" I asked, casually returning Fox's smile.

s not.

"Spare me the courtesy," the governor spat as he spoke. His baldness was already advanced, and his mustache yellowing. By the look of his fingernails, he needed more calcium and the wedding ring on his thick finger actually made me feel sorry for his wife. A little bit, anyway.

"I'll tell you what I want. I want to report you to the police," the governor said and took a sip of the whiskey.

I chuckled and paid no further attention to him, but watched Fox rub her back in a snake-like line along the pole. Her black, straight hair fell down like a dark veil.

"What are you going to report? That my club is doing well? Then off you go. Spread the word."

I heard Cherry giggle and pulled my lips into a slight smile. That girl was so smart. She knew exactly what I was doing. She tried to hide her grin while polishing glasses next to the sink.

The governor rubbed his knee, his nostrils flaring slightly. "Don't fuck with me. The club is just for money laundering and nothing else. I can bust you for drug dealing, weapons trafficking, recruiting minors, hustling, and serving alcohol to minors."

"Really? That surprises me. I don't do anything that's not legal, sir."

"I call the police." He emphasized every word.

I raised my eyebrows and leaned back. "And tell them what? The cops can't do shit without proof, Jenson. You should know that."

What an idiot. Who made a deal with threats? I'd love to get up and let Punchy pull him out right now, but I had to do what I had to do, right?

"I'm ignoring your lies now and gonna offer you something, and if you're wise, you'll take it," Jenson said. "Give me 30% of what you make with C-Wax."

"C-Wax, governor?"

He sighed and drank the whiskey all at once. Then he looked at me, and his right eye twitched. "Don't fuck with me!"

Cherry stopped polishing the glass and glanced at me, asking silently if I needed her. She was always so protective— but so was I and I would never endanger her.

"Easy, Jenson. Easy," I said, and Cherry continued polishing. "Remember where you are." Threatening a gang boss in front of his followers was never a good idea. Down here all good and bad came because of respect. If he got in the way of me and my reputation, I would lose my patience. There was always another election and another chance for a new racist governor.

"You know who brought C-Wax to the United States," he muttered. "Don't play dumb. I know you've been selling it for months. You have contacts to van der Volt."

"Van der Volt? Never heard of him before," I said, sipping some whiskey and playing with it in my mouth. This guy knew nothing. Not everyone could prove an IQ of 140 points. In fact, only 2.5% of the population could, and I was one of them. Poor governor. He had no chance against one like me.

"I'll just try to ignore that now. So, 30% and you are

immune. You can do whatever you want but you will have the support of—"

"—a corrupt politician. Sounds great."

He winced. "Does it sound great to have the police rolling in here, huh?"

"I wouldn't know what they possibly could find, governor."

"Well, well, well, they would certainly find the boss of the Chicago Loops and his million-dollar empire, wouldn't they?" The whites of his eyes suddenly turned slightly red. "They would also find the key to a new synthetic drug called C-Wax and a way to make gold out of nothing."

"Sounds like a fairy tale to me."

"Ah please," he growled, licking his lower lip. "Just because they can't prove anything doesn't mean they don't know who you are. People talk."

"Always have," I said, shrugging it away, and called for Cherry. She gave me another drink, the good whiskey this time.

"Yes, that's why my help would be good, don't you think?"

I pretended to think about the shit he had said and shook my drink slightly, watching the waves of liquor grow in my glass. He didn't know what he was getting into, but I did and that made me all the happier. Fish on a hook.

"Suppose I wanted to expand, and I needed investors," I started, grinning at his stupid face. I just had to say one sentence and he already showed me how much he wanted my money. "Then you'd definitely get 5%, not 20%, not 30%. Ten is already too much for *your kind* of investment act."

"That—"

"—is my final word."

"Will you at least introduce me to Vernon van der Volt? You're the only one who seems to have any contacts," the Governor of Illinois said. Suddenly his expression was all soft while he tried to lean into me. The ass kissing mode.

"You want to hear something crazy?" I said, finishing my whiskey and watching Fox and her beautiful legs dance.

"Rumor has it that *you're* van der Volt, governor. Why do I have this awkward feeling that you're just making this deal with me because you want to make a double fortune on your new awesome drug?"

The governor snorted and spat some of my whiskey on the bar counter. I wasn't the only one giving him the evil eye now. Cherry was mad, too and that bothered me even more.

"You gotta be kidding. Of course, I'm not *van der Volt*. Nobody knows who he is. Though you most likely do."

"I only know a guy who knows another middleman of his. Volt never shows," I said.

"They say your *guy* is a good friend of yours."

"I can only tell you what I know," I said dryly. I didn't want to think about the one year I spent in high school for preppy kids on this fucking scholarship.

I did well without them, anyway.

"My contact met one of van der Volt's men while on vacation in the Netherlands. There they took C-Wax together. Now Volt is here, selling his stuff in the US. That's it."

"Can't you tell me the name of your contact then?" he said, way too eager for my taste.

I leaned into him, piercing him with my eyes until he swallowed. "You're so smart and know everything, don't you, governor? Contact him yourself then."

"We have a deal," he stuttered.

"The deal is limited to immunity and money. You and I will never be friends and contacts are limited to them."

I got up, thanking Cherry.

"Good day, governor. Thank you for investing in my club. We'll soon be thinking about a franchise. My salesmen will contact you."

"When?" he asked, turning for me and watching me as if his momma was just about to leave him.

"When I say so."

On the way out, I grabbed Fox by the hip, pulling her off the pole.

"My shift isn't over yet," she giggled.

"I'm giving you time off now. Blame your legs."

I still had a couple of hours until I had to meet with some salesmen. Since my head still spun around the strange bone I found the other night, a little distraction was perfect.

CHAPTER THREE
LYNNE

"You did what? *What?* No. No, no, no. No. I—"

"Don't you say *I told you so*. I swear to the Dead I will kill you right now. Don't you dare!" I screamed at Bory, well aware that I took all my unwarranted frustration out on him.

I had come back dead quiet and asked Soothie to fly us to my cave. Immediately. No questions asked. Of course, Bory sensed right away that something was wrong with me. Very wrong.

He had known me since my Drop and he was smart enough to let me think in peace before asking questions, but after I paced around in our cave, he finally dared to ask me what happened. And I exploded. The words came out of me like a dragon's fire breath.

The sweat tingled down my face and my whole body shook. Oh, I messed up. I really messed up. My stomach twisted and I might puke now. This day had to come, hadn't it? Bory had been right. Oh, Bory had been sooo right to warn me. I sank to my knees and buried my head between my legs. Somewhere, I heard Soothie howling, but I couldn't deal with that right now.

I didn't usually act out. I was Lynne. Courageous, reckless, and not to be rattled, but now my penchant for bad decisions had caught up with me. That was it. My life was over. Just like that, I broke all the rules that were cherished in my world. Over a crying Topworlder…over a skulling man.

"She is going to kill you. You know that, right?" Bory said.

Now he was pacing too, a tiny blue ball of fur with trembling wings running circles in my barely lit cave. The poor thing didn't have anything to sit on. I usually slept on the floor with a little fire, curled up next to Soothie.

But Bory was the spoiled one. He slept in a small chamber in the Bone Queen's castle, and it was way prettier there. He was used to having actual rooms and furniture. But people like me didn't live in such fancy buildings. Dwellers like me—the poor ones who weren't really useful or important to anyone—lived in the outskirts of the Underworld and were ready to die as pet food. So, this cave was the best I could offer.

"I know," I screamed back at Bory, trying to stop my damned shivering but then Soothie whimpered again. I turned to him—my stare cold as ice. "What is wrong with you? What Sircha feels empathy at all?"

He howled in return, and I felt like the worst and guilt twisted my face. I shut my eyes, and a sense of doom beat the air, a feeling I've never knew before.

I went too far because I always did. Whenever I felt cooped up, I lashed out without thinking about consequences. Well, have I ever thought about consequences at all? No, but maybe I should have.

I sighed, biting my lower lip. "Sorry, Soothie. I didn't mean to hurt you."

Soothie growled once more but I knew he would forgive me. He was one hell of a softie. That was the reason I had to save his life in the first place. His dad had nearly bit his head off—just because he was not like them. Soothie was not as big as a dragon like his conspecifics, and he was not mean, not aggressive, thoughtless, or a killer. He was my little cuddle Sircha, and I hurt him because I messed up and was me…

"Guys." I lifted my gaze, feeling like shit, my eyes heavy like a ton of stones. "I'm sorry."

"You should be!" Bory screamed, folding his puffy arms and showing me his scrunched-up face.

I ran my fingers through my white-blonde hair and looked at him with my eyes wide, a slight pout on my lips. My asking-for-help-face. I knew he hated it when I used it, but a few seconds did it for him.

"Ugh, why do you never listen to me? You are so naïve! It was about time you messed up. You always go there although it's more than clear that Underworlders should not go to the Topworld. Why do you think there's no official passage up or why normal dwellers do not know about the world above? Because *no one* should! Not only do you steal sacred bones for the most insidious person ever, no, you also sneak into the Topworld. Now what? You broke a contract with the Bone Queen, girl," Bory screamed. Something in the tone of his voice penetrated.

It was hard to stomach but yes, I did cross the queen. Everyone knew the three rules of the Bone Queen and only a fool would mess with them.

One: Every dead bone belongs to her. Two: Every deal one makes with her must be fulfilled. And three: Messing up rule one or two equals death. If I was smart, I wouldn't have made a deal with her in the first place. But, I was hungry for a lot of things, and I had a gift—or was it a curse? Not so sure anymore.

I could feel magic, and I was the stealthiest thief, even though my skin was snow white. It seemed I was the right fit for the Bone Queen and her agenda. No one really knew what she and her sister really did but everyone feared them, even more than her brother, the Shadow King.

Once I saw the Bone Queen look like a walking skeleton. On that day, her magic was low. I could only see her flaw for barely a moment, and then she looked as beautiful as ever. I always imagined she needed the bones' magic as some kind of sustenance, to be able to use magic herself. The three rulers of the Underworld were as old as stone, so making herself younger with all the bones would fit. I wouldn't want to walk around looking like a corpse either.

When the Bone Queen came up to me and offered me the job of my life, I didn't need to think twice. Of course, I agreed. Why the skull not? Maybe because this decision was going to cost me my neck now…

Bory lowered his gaze, his voice dropping an octave. "She doesn't know mercy, Lynne. Everyone messing with her rules awaits death. But not the good death. You won't suffer in the right way. Do you even know what that means for your soul?"

I swallowed at the sight of him. I had never seen Bory like this before, not with this concerned glint in his eyes.

"I know," I sighed, my voice suddenly dry. "I'll lose my soul."

The only goal an Underworld dweller had to reach was paying for bad deeds from a previous life. All souls who made the Drop down here had to be punished. That's why we lived—our only purpose. Depending on where the soul landed, one could guess how bad his soul had been. I landed in the Outskirts, so I was as good as insignificant. I must have done something bad, but it wasn't that bad to care about, according to the Shadow King's thinking—not that I had ever seen him. He only consorted with the bad souls, or if he liked a Dropper and wanted to fuck them. The most unpleasant place to be in the Underworld was the Tartaros. Only the worst of the worst souls landed there.

Each ruler had an important task, so that the rulebook of the Underworld was preserved. The Shadow King regulated how the souls were divided, or so it's said.

The thing was now, if the Bone Queen killed me—just like that—I wouldn't atone for my bad past, and my soul would be damned. Therefore, I would never have the chance to be reborn or redeemed. I had to probably serve as a shadow slave forever, something even I feared... So, hope of redemption through repentance was the most important good in my world and I was about to lose exactly that.

"Okay. Plans. Anyone?" I said.

"You're asking me for plans?" Bory screamed. "I told—"

I jabbed my finger at him. "Don't you dare!"

"Hothead!"

"What was I gonna do, if you had your way, huh? Stay here and rot like the others? Starve until some creature falls into our cave hole again because everyone else is too scared to hunt properly? Of course not! I will not spend my life waiting here to be eaten by something bigger to atone for my sins. I don't even know what my sins were and I'm not stupid like the other Cave Town dwellers, just doing what others tell me."

"Have you ever thought that maybe the others are not stupid, but actually smart? You have a death wish, girl. Stealing our sacred bones, making contracts with the Bone Queen, and visiting the Topworld once a year. Pff. All I can say about that is stupid, stupid, *stupid*!"

My nostrils flared and I was trembling again, clenching and unclenching my fists. This little creature always managed to get under my skin. If it were anyone else, I'd have punched them like crazy right now.

Since I said nothing, he went on. "What now? Are you done with messing up your life?"

I turned away, staring at my shelf, my treasures. There were all the things I had collected over the years and didn't even begin to understand. Funny clothes, silver things, big things, small things. Was it my curiosity that led to my recklessness? My need to know more about this other world, this human realm? The wish of being someone else?

I closed my eyes and cold sweat slicked my brows.

"You really should be grateful," Bory started again. "You had it good. Nothing easier than being a Cave Town dweller. You wouldn't have to suffer long, and you could just do your time. Just that. Easy. But no, you had to look for adventures and excitement, fun or who knows what! What's next? Will you be going to visit the Blood Queen to ask for her help?"

I stopped.

The Blood Queen?

I turned around again, literally feeling my eyes getting bigger and bigger now. The Blood Queen! Of course, why hadn't I thought of that idea myself? She could do something about it. Who else but her?

Bory cupped his little mouth with both hands. "Oh no. Oh, no, no, no. What did I just say? Why am I saying such things to you? You are not seriously considering—Lynne!"

Bory was hopping towards me now, shaking his head. But life was good again! Skull consequences, I would dig myself out of it. Of course, there was always a solution to my problems.

Full of adrenaline and confidence, I jumped past Bory, ignoring his calls. Then I hugged Soothie and promised him everything would be all right again and that he'd get tons of good meat soon. He growled back at me, knowing that I was up to something bad.

"What the heck are you doing now?" Bory yelled after me, trying to follow. But I was way ahead of him. When motivated, I could be fast as lightning. As I climbed down the rocks in front of my cave to reach the path into the village, I bowed my head and grinned at Bory.

"Stop asking stupid questions. I'll make a deal with the Blood Queen."

"No—I can't believe it. I can't!" Bory croaked, now accelerating to catch up with me. "I won't let you do anything stupid again. You'll end up in Tartaros and I can't live with that. I've grown fond of you."

"Poor thing," I said, jumping over another rock.

"You know," he said, breathing heavily while he wiggled after me, "one day, you'll regret all the deals you've made. I swear."

"I won't."

"Lynne!" Bory squealed, jumping down the big rocks as well. "Don't go to the Blood Queen, please."

"Relax, I need to visit Malachtit first anyway," I said, noticing the torches lighting up my face. The only source of light we had in Cave Town were the countless torches that some poor drip always had to light. I don't know who had to do that, but they were always burning. Always.

"What? Why?"

"I need his… powers," I said.

"You are one crazy girl!" Bory said.

"Maybe, but at least I am not normal and boring."

"I wish you were," Bory sighed.

I narrowed my eyes. "You don't."

As I scurried along with Bory on my heels across the small bridge and the black river flowing throughout our caves, I could not help but whistle. I knew I could fix everything again. For a moment I really thought I would give up my ghost, but no. I could fix this. For sure.

Cave Town was deep down in the Underworld, somewhere no one cared about. One day a thousand years ago, a poor dweller dug hundreds of caves out of sheer boredom. I could understand if one didn't know what to do with his life here anymore, but that was a bit too much. Despite this, there were some places where the scenery could look quite beautiful though, with all the waterfalls pouring down. In Cave Town, we were protected from the outside world and could live even longer and wait pointlessly for a good death, starving while doing so. *Wonderful, just wonderful.*

So, Cave Town had many aisles, marketplaces where everyone sold their stupid things, and home caves. *Lots* of home caves carved into the sandstone walls. Some of them were creatively decorated with furs, stones, and of course, torches. My cave was nothing like that. I completely lacked the creative streak.

I crossed another one of the many bridges that led to some other corners of Cave Town. We had a lot of bridges. Like, really a lot. They were above me, under me, next to me. There were so many that I was not even sure if I had ever stepped on every bridge. Below me I could see the white tents of Cave Market. Everything you could think of was sold there. Jewelry made of horns, games made of stones, music instruments out of wood, clothes made of leather…

Then I was hurtling down Gamestreet. That's where all the game caves were, logically. Since cave dwellers had nothing to do, most of them loved to bet and get rid of their trash. Nobody here had many Bloodcoins; they were a rare commodity around these parts. Whenever someone did have one, it was stolen—usually by me.

"What are you up to?" I heard someone ask.

At first, I thought the voice wasn't talking to me, but I turned right and looked into the green eyes of Marlina. Her skin, always fawn, had some freckles that splattered around her cheeks and her dark hair was short, almost reaching her chin. I knew her since the Drop. Unfortunately.

"I had no idea you would be interested in me, Marlina," I said.

Bory sighed, climbing up to my shoulder. He didn't like Marlina either, but who did?

"Of course, I am. Did you manage to catch another beast?" she asked, glancing behind me as if I carried food wherever I went.

"Beast… right. No. Sorry. No luck today."

All the dwellers thought I was hunting when I wasn't home. They really didn't know a thing about me, but always wanted a piece of my catch. If they only knew what I really did all day. Most of the time I sold bones to the queen and bought some critters with the Bloodcoins and devoured them with Soothie and Bory. But sometimes I gave it away and let the cave dwellers snuffle. They loved me for it, but it seemed to have gotten out of hand lately. They literally expected me to bring them food every time I saw them. What am I, their Cave Mom?

"Guess you need to find some food for yourself, Marlina," I said, smirking right into her face. As I was about to turn, she dared to stop me, holding my arm. "Are you out of your mi—"

"You probably don't know what the other dwellers say when you're gone but if you don't bring us food regularly, we'll rob your treasures. We know you're hiding something up there," Marlina said, gritting her teeth.

I pressed my lips into a thin line. Oh, that was so typical. Cave Town dwellers always preferred the easier way. Instead of getting their own food, they wanted to threaten me. Not with me, Marlina darling.

"You forgot one teeny tiny thing. You'll be torn apart by my dragon before you can say Sircha," I answered, jabbing a finger at her. "Aren't you all scared of a bad death? I understand death by beast isn't considered desirable, is it?"

She trembled and bucked, like she always did when facing me. Cave Town dwellers were so frightened by beasts, it was obnoxious. Such stupid religious beings. They were so blinded that they didn't even know how real Sirchas acted. They were so different from the other Underworlders. I understood why everyone outside mocked Cave Town. Normally, all the Underworlders wanted was to find good death, but not the cave dwellers. No, they wanted to starve here and *wait* for a good death. Wait until they became dust.

They were so afraid of dying the wrong death, that they even started hunting with holes in their caves, waiting until a beast fell into the hole, and only then did they finish it with a manpower of twenty. They were that brave.

I thought they made up those rules about the bad death, because according to cave dwellers, *every* death was bad except when the Shadow King himself granted us death and salvation. But that was unlikely to happen. Cave Town dwellers certainly didn't care about him not paying them any attention. They worshipped him like a god and feared the queens like demons. I believed that losing the soul was bad, and that's why I had to go now.

"I gotta get going. Marlina, nice catching up with you." I approached her. "Next time you touch me, I'll hit you where it hurts."

As soon as I was a little further away from her, Bory snorted. "Boy, she's got guts."

"Bullshit. I spoiled them too much. When we solve our problem, they won't get anything for a few weeks. Spoiled cave dwellers are the worst."

"Our problem?" Bory muttered.

"Yeah, you're here, aren't you?".

"Fine." He looked away, and the silence stretched between us while I hurried to Mal's cave. Then, Bory cleared his throat, saying: "I am curious what Nana thinks of Marlina talking that way."

"Don't mention that woman," I said.

"She raised you…"

"Great, but I didn't need *her* to be brought up," I said a tad too brashly. "And she's a religious fanatic. Give me a break."

"Yeah right, acting all cool and unbothered again, huh? Why does she always get the biggest animal and get to decide with whom she shares? You love her, but she hurt you back then. Admit it. You have a heart."

"I do not. So, shut up now and don't talk when I'm with Malachtit."

"As if I wanted to talk there…"

As I PUSHED AWAY the many curtains hanging down in front of Malachtit's cave entrance, a strange smell invaded my nose. It was a mixture of holm oak, cedar wood, and animal skin. His scent.

"Mal?" I asked, walking carefully. With Mal, you never knew what to expect.

His cave was barely lit, and the few flickering lights made the walls look orange. There were furs of all colors everywhere. He had to be somewhere between those layers. I glanced around. He had many herbs hanging from the ceiling to dry, so he can make ointments with them.

Where was my best friend?

He was pretty much the only one that fit that description. Except Bory and Soothie, of course.

"What? By the Death, Lynne!" I heard his voice first and saw him underneath another man at the far end of his cave.

"Oh, for skull's sake, Mal," I said, turning away and blushing like hell. That was clearly something I didn't want to see at all. Even Bory squealed and covered his eyes.

Of course, he was with a man, doing only the Dead knew what. I covered my eyes with one hand and waved with the other, so that he noticed I was in a hurry. Then I heard an annoyed grunt, a smacking that sounded like a kiss, and a rustle. I didn't dare to look yet.

"Can't you announce yourself properly?" Mal grunted, tiptoeing towards me.

"You probably wouldn't have heard me anyway, busy as you were."

"You can uncover your eyes now, sweetie, he is gone."

I did and immediately regretted it.

I hated cave men. They loved to be naked and show off.

"Can you throw on some furs, please?" I said through my fingers, my skin burning.

"Are you afraid of my best piece?" he teased.

Bory puffed. I was still looking away, but I knew he was smiling widely. Mal was one hell of a kinky bastard. But then I heard a hustle and a bustle, so I thought he had finally put something on, and dared to turn around and look at him.

Mal had gray hair, although he was the same age as me. Time was odd here. Since I knew that the Topworlders aged faster than we do down here, I have often wondered how time worked. Since my Drop, I may have aged four years, but Rio had aged about ten years, or even more. He changed in front of my eyes while I was still looking the same. I was a girl, he a man, although we both were kids when I first saw him…

Mal had gray hair like the elders which he had twisted into long dreadlocks, falling down to his hips in spite of the pony-tail. He always looked like he'd ran a mile, an everlasting tinge of red under his terra cotta skin.

"Was that another court dweller? I thought you were going to quit it with these guys," I asked curiously, stepping on the many furs.

"Well, it's difficult. I kind of have a type. Addict and so on," he said, straightening a skin on the wall.

Mal was the closest to being like me. Except he sought

danger in other ways, mostly between the legs of men belonging to the Blood Queen's court. Nothing good could come from there, but he also wanted to stand out from that dreary village that meant nothing to anyone. I could understand that. The feeling of wanting more, wishing to be more.

Mal laid down on a pile of skins, running his hands through his locks.

"What do you want?" He pretended not to be interested, but I knew him better than that. He was always as curious as I was.

I tilted my head. "Maybe I just wanted to see my friend?"

"Skull. You always want something."

"Well, he's right," Bory muttered, and I shot him a glance.

Okay, he was right though. Since I didn't live with Nana anymore and worked for the Bone Queen, I stopped coming to him to waste time. I had more important things to do now. Here and there I let him talk me into drinking some Deadtime or Ashwater, but that was it, unless I needed something from him, like now.

"I need your… special gift, Mal," I admitted, feeling my stomach twitch.

In no time he sat upright, looking at me with his tawny eyes. No smirking anymore. Yeah, I was good at that, confusing cavemen. Bory started to get restless on my shoulder now, all nervous again. Maybe I should be too, but, I wasn't.

"*What* did you do this time?" Mal asked.

"Why—ah. Forget it. Can you just help me, *please*?"

"No. You know that I am not using… *that*. Ever."

"But I said please." I grinned.

"I am not doing it. It is *sacrilege*," he said, folding his arms.

"Oh, come on!" I snorted. "Since when are you a religious dweller? I really need you, Mal. I might die a bad death… I messed up. Really messed up."

His eyes grew bigger than saucers. Now he seemed to understand my urgency.

"By the Dead, Lynne. What have you done?" Mal said, his voice still serious.

"Okay," I said, slumping down next to Mal. "But you can't tell anyone. Otherwise, I'd have to kill you."

"*Tell* me," he said, gritting his teeth.

"I kind of made a contract with the Bone Queen and skulled it up. So… I broke rules number one and two."

"You... did… *what*? Are you kidding me?"

"I wish, but I got better things to do than that, don't you think?" I said, folding my arms.

"No idea what you've been doing lately, to be honest. So, when you're out—you're doing work for her? Is that what you do?" he said.

I made a face, looking at my hands. "Kind of."

"By the Dead, Lynne."

"Can we skip all this, please? Let's just pretend you've been busting my balls for hours now telling me what I should have done instead, okay?" I urged. "Because I'm running out of time. We need to hurry. So, are you willing to help me save my soul? I will be in your debt, of course."

He sighed, falling backwards on his fur pile again. "Lynne… you're skulled."

Now it was my turn to sigh. Why couldn't anyone here just once do what I wanted? Like I don't already know how messed up I am.

"How should I help you?"

I shrugged. "I'll make another deal. This time with *your* queen."

"Oh no. Lynne…That woman is even crazier than the Bone Queen! You can't just—"

"*Your* queen is the only one who can help me right now. I have to," I said.

"First, she's not *my* queen," Mal said, "I just help her out to earn some Bloodcoins, and maybe hook up with some of her servants and courtiers. That's called a job, Lynne, not a commitment. I'm not doing stupid things like you are. No deals. That's the one rule you need to follow. I always thought Nana taught us well."

My stomach tightened. Why is everyone mentioning that woman today? "Well, it seems there are more rules than just one to follow here and you know I—"

"—yeah, you hate rules, and look where it got you," Mal grunted, sat up and glanced at me as if I'd just dropped from above. "Lynne, this is no joke. It's not like last time or the hundreds of times before that. This time you really messed up. The Blood Queen will only make it worse. Maybe you should consider just—"

"—dying?" I yelled, not believing what he'd just said. "I wouldn't give a shit if I died right now, Mal. But the Bone Queen is going to *take* my soul. That's worse than dying."

"Then at least you're afraid of something for once," he said, with a grain of truth, for better or worse.

"Told her that myself," Bory sighed.

I wiggled my toes. "Oh, could you both just shut up and start helping me instead? I will fix it, promise."

The utter silence between us stretched but at some point, Mal punched the fur he sat on and said: "Ah, damn it. What do I have to do?"

I took a deep breath before I spit it out, "I am going to give your queen the one thing she wants the most."

I tried to hold Mal's stare, but my stomach turned, and I quickly glanced to the floor.

"What? You can't give her *bones*. Every bone belongs to the Bone Queen," Mal said.

"Not every bone, only the *dead* ones. My bones are alive, so I will give her one of my own," I said, leaning into Mal, more than ready to bag the shit out of him if needed.

Bory and Mal simultaneously hit their foreheads with a hand.

"Are you out of your mind?" Bory squealed.

"She is," Mal said.

"Bory, shut up, and Mal, maybe, yes. But please just use your gift and cut a bone out of me, preferably a bone I do not need. I don't care which one and I don't care if it hurts. Just do it. Please." I put on my puppy look, knowing it was unbeatable.

Mal sighed again, rolled onto his stomach, and punched his furs with his hands like a kid.

"Why?" he mumbled into the pile. "Why do I have to be friends with you?"

"That's a question for later. Mal, please, I need to go there. Like, now," I said with an extra whiny undertone.

Mal glanced at Bory, suddenly shooting dagger-like glances at him. "Shouldn't you be looking after her? You're really doing a great job, man."

"Hey, she is uncontrollable. Don't put this on me."

Before I could say something stupid, Mal stood up. "Okay. I am helping you. But I want Bloodcoins."

My eyebrows draw down. "How many?"

"Three."

I dramatically threw my hands up in the air. "Wow, what about a friend's discount?"

Three Bloodcoins was a horrendous price. With one coin alone, I could feed them all for a year or even longer.

Mal gave me his wicked half smile and I felt a knot tightening in my stomach. Hell, I hated that stupid grin. "It doesn't matter, Lynne. You might die anyway. Wherever you go, you won't need your coins there."

I bit the inside of my cheeks. He was right, but I was a

greedy thing. I loved everything I collected, and I abso-bloody-lutley hated not to be right. "Two."

"Three," he repeated.

"One."

Mal widened his eyes. "Lynne… it's not your place to bargain. You're skulled if I don't help you."

"Okay, " I shrugged. "You made a point. Out of generosity and because I might die, I'll say: two."

He sighed. "Fine. You are a pain in the ass."

"It's called smart." I smirked. At least he made it cheaper by one Bloodcoin.

Mal shook his head and closed the curtains. He fanatically checked all the openings and made sure that no one could see what was going to happen any minute.

He turned, staring at me, with his feet fidgeting like an eel. "Okay. Like always—"

"I am not telling anyone, " I interrupted him. "If I do tell, you can rat me out too. Forgot that?"

He rubbed the bridge of his nose. "No, but—you know. The powers I have are… shameful."

"I know, Mal. Get over it."

By the Dead, this man had some serious complexes. Okay, healing in the Underworld was not a cool thing since everyone—except me—wanted to die. But damn it, he could use some power. Magic! It was cool, kind of.

Worse, his wounds kept closing by themselves. Whenever Mal hurt himself, he had to hide as soon as possible. Self-closing wounds were so not good down here. It was a coincidence that I knew about his strange gift at all. One time we were practicing throwing the javelin and I hit him in the leg but instead of developing a cool scar or wound, the cut closed right away. No signs of injury remained. Creepy. Saying that my jaw dropped to the floor would be an understatement.

But this time he could help *me*. I really didn't know how to cut out a bone and still be able to walk or use my legs afterward. Plus, it had to be an unharmed bone, without debris, perfectly cut out. I was such a clumsy person that I was sure to splinter it. But Mal wasn't—he was able to witch it out of my body, or whatever.

"Just make sure we can't see anything afterward. I want to keep my beautiful limbs," I said. "Oh, and when you're done, you need to bring me into the Blood Queen's court. I know you're allowed to visit her anytime, my precious healer."

"You are crazy. Like, really nuts," Mal hissed.

CHAPTER FOUR
LYNNE

To escape the dreary everyday life, Mal took a march of over four hours every three days to the Blood Queen's court. Even if he told me he was working there, I knew he was attending her dances. Nobody could fool me. Mal even wore the clothes of the Blood court from time to time, all in secret. I've seen him in them twice, and it was never good when I knew someone's secret. I always found a way to use it for my own good.

Since such a long walk was too much for me, Soothie flew us right to the Blood Queen. Funny thing: Mal was really afraid of heights. He clung onto me like a monkey, whimpering and praying to Stix.

At least I had something to laugh about after the ordeal he had inflicted on me. I didn't ask him to tell me which bone was missing now, but according to the pain I felt, he had taken a bone from my right leg. I honestly didn't want to bother about it too much. Everything was fine. I wouldn't miss this small bone. Not at all. Mal had mastered his power so well there was no sign of his magic on me. He was extraordinary, and I had a living bone for the Blood Queen that did not belong to the Bone Queen, since she solely owned the dead bones. *Yay!*

Everyone knew that getting the Blood Queen's audience costed and I was certain that mine would cost even more. I was a simple Cave Town dweller, and practically non-existent to the big players. So, I needed sharper methods: the thing she wanted most. Bones. The Bone Queen hoarded them all and left none for her poor baby sister. Why, I didn't know. Everybody kept secrets, if they were smart.

I hopped down from Soothie's back. "Why do you even have ball gowns from the Blood Court?"

While feeling funny in this blood-red, monstrous thing, I straightened it with my hands. I had never worn such a dress before. It made me feel so…ladylike. Usually, I wore leather underpants, a loincloth apron over it and a leather top. And now I was wearing a red something that tied off my breasts and covered all my skin, leaving no air behind to breathe. There was no running or sweating in that for sure. So, why would someone wear such kinds of dresses? *Voluntarily?*

"I like to wear them. Sometimes," Mal confessed.

I raised my eyebrows and looked at him. He had really changed over the weeks in which we didn't have much to do with each other. My stomach churned, and I felt sorry for not being there for him, for not knowing what he must have gone through. I checked out his outfit of the day. Mal wore long black leather pants now, and a white tunic with fitting boots. We never wore boots…

It wasn't that I didn't know that there were other clothes than the ones we wore in Cave Town, but I never really wanted to wear anything else, or better said I never had the possibility or the money to. While stealing bones, I often saw courtiers or dwellers of other Underworld villages and wondered why they didn't wear skins or fur. That seemed to be a Cave Town thing. I flew around a lot, so I could tell which fashion belonged to which court, but no one dressed like the Topworlders.

I stared down at my wrapped-up body. "This thing fits you, Mal? No way. It's like trying to wear Bory's clothes." I wasn't tall, but Mal was. So, how would he fit into that dress? I shot him a glance, but he shrugged it off.

"It doesn't fit, but sometimes I like to wear it or pretend to. Stop staring at me like that. I have a thing for court fashion! I'll hit you if you don't stop staring at me," Mal said.

"Um, sorry. I just…I'm sorry I wasn't there for you. I could have helped you find the right dresses or…" I sighed. "We need to buy a bigger one for you. You'll wear it way better than me for sure."

He paused, as if thinking about what to say in response to my apology. But just as back then, he preferred to avoid the unpleasant topics and grinned, running a hand through his silvery hair. "I will, when I finally get your Bloodcoins."

"Oh, I never pay in advance. You know that."

"Those dresses are expensive like hell and the one you're wearing was a present from a lover," he said, looking at his shiny boots that must have cost a fortune as well. Whatever he did at the Blood Queen's court, it couldn't be much better than what I did for a living.

"Hm. Maybe I'll give you three Coins then. You really need better dresses than this one. It's horrible."

"Wow, how generous of you," he laughed.

"If I survive this, we'll go shopping. Ha, Nana would get a heart attack, seeing you in Blood court fashion!"

"As long as I don't look as stupid as you, everything will be fine."

My grin dropped. "I really look stupid, don't I?"

"No. Just let me fix your hair. It'll give them a fright when they see you like this."

I sighed and let him touch me. Mal strained my hair with

his fingers and fumbled in his jacket pocket, went back to my long white mess of strands, and put my hair up with a hairpin.

"Ouch! What are you doing?"

"Hold still. That's how the ladies here do it," Mal said, still working on my hairdo with one hand while trying to hold me still with the other.

"As if I were a lady."

"No, but at least this way you seem a bit like one. Done!"

With a skeptical frown on my face, I tried to feel what he did. My hair was now put together into a big dumpling, held in place with a needle. A strand of hair fell across my forehead and reached my chin.

"And? How do I look?" I grinned, spinning on my feet.

Mal laughed, tipping his head back, reminding me of the good old days.

"Wow. Is it that bad?" I asked, swallowing while his eyes widened.

"No. If I were into girls, I definitely would bang you."

"Okay. I'll take that as a compliment. So, let's go."

I was about to leave when Mal grabbed my arm, pulling me towards him, his glance determined. "You need to behave yourself in there, Lynne. I don't know about the Bone Queen, but here at the Blood Queen's court, we do things by the code, okay?"

I didn't reply and avoided his gaze. This guy and his know-it-all attitude.

His lips thinned. "You don't look anybody in the eye, you let me do the talking and you stop speaking as loud as usual or acting foolishly in any way. Don't attack anything in there, don't steal anything for the devil's sake, because I don't want to lose my soul, too. Do you understand?"

"Yeah, yeah, I got it," I said, baring my teeth and nodding towards his hand, still grasped around my wrist. "I'm only gonna steal things, no one will know."

Mal gasped. "Lynne!"

A laughter bubbled up in my throat, and as Mal understood that I was just teasing him, he grumbled.

"This is way too serious to make jokes about it, girl. I'm not going in there unless you know how to behave yourself."

"Yes, mother. I will behave myself. So, move your skulling ass!"

He let go of me and I could have sworn he mumbled something under his damn breath. I tried to ignore whatever it was, patted Soothie on the way and followed Mal to the bridge.

"Stop this sourpuss face," he said, offering me his arm. "You'll scare the guards."

"I'm too charming to scare anyone," I snarled back, hooking into his arm and trying to relax my face. Not so easy, considering I wanted to bite Mal's head off.

The bridge led over a big gorge and as I looked down, the Mother River of the Underworld beat high and thick waves. They were black, playing with the lava that sneaked its way into the river. A glittering mix of red and black shades.

The lava cast an orange light on the huge black castle that finally appeared in my line of sight. Unlike the Bone Queen's court, this castle was pompous, almost ostentatious. The big, pointed towers of blue-black stone were so high I began to wonder if I could steal some bones in the sky from the ceiling up there. Probably not. Some towers only seemed to be high and were not in fact.

"I don't have a good feeling about this at all," I heard Bory whimpering from my pocket.

"Stop whining in there," I grunted through my teeth.

"*Psht*, idiots," Mal hissed, walking with his head held high. "The guards. Not a word now."

I let him lead me to the huge gate made of iron bars. The cold wind made me shiver. Everything smelled of sulphur—like rotten eggs. The normal wonderful smell of our world.

Two men in blood-red leather armor waited for us, looking like someone pissed on their shoes.

"Codeword, dweller?" one of them said with a scratchy voice.

I lifted my head to do a quick scan over the guards. The one in the front looked like a horse with all kinds of yellow teeth sticking out of his deranged mouth. The other was small and chubby, like a weasel. Both fairly simple to fight. I wondered how these two got their jobs.

"*Im ta sikil e ne,*" Mal said.

I looked at him, my eyes widening. Holy hell. Since when did he know the Old Language? Questions formed so fast I had to bite the inside of my cheeks while my mind tried to figure out which one to ask first. How deeply involved was he in the Blood Queen's affairs? I narrowed my eyes at him and although he seemed to know I was bursting with curiosity, he didn't so much as blink at me. It seemed like I wasn't the only one here with a sacrilegious hobby…

Mal stared at the guards with an equally grim expression. They checked us carefully, but something Mal had said to them must have worked, because the little one of them nodded to the door.

"Go. You have two hours. Then you must leave," the Weasel added.

Horsey was nodding as well. So off we went.

I blew out a long breath and kept on strolling inside the castle.

Without saying one more word to me, Mal dragged me through a tunnel, and we entered a vast courtyard with a huge well in the middle, decorated with dragons and drawings of bleeding souls. Everywhere around me were grey stone brick walls with arcades, more tunnels, and round windows. All the corners were covered with large sculptures representing the prophecies of the Nine Kinds of Good Death, carved from blood-red marble. My stomach turned. This place reeked of death.

He pulled me through the crowds as if he did that every day. As if he was one of them, and not an ordinary Cave Town dweller. This court was so different from my queen's. She liked it all pale and white. There I fit better. I hardly got noticed with my skin and hair. Here, I felt like a colorful dragon, totally out of place and much too bright. Strange that I felt even more uncomfortable here than at the Bone Queen's court. There I never wore the Bone Fashion, but I felt more welcomed than here. I wondered how they would have reacted if I'd worn my loincloth? *That* would have been funny for sure.

"So, we're just walking in there now? Or how do we do that?" I asked, trying not to stare too much at the passing Blood courtiers. They all had strange hair. Some tied it up into a hairdo that looked like a snail or a tower. Others had hair nets that held rolls of hair and braids in place.

As we passed, their eyes felt like daggers in my back, twisting with each step we took.

I couldn't help but stare back, at the jewelry in their hair, the crystals around their necks, the gold on their wrists. Swallowing, I pushed through one cloud of perfume to the next—it was like a swirl of different scents, one sweeter than the other. When a young man walked past me, winking, I actually blushed. Wow, give me a dress and I act like a damsel in distress.

"Stop looking at them like that," Mal said, stiffening up.

"No need to be rude," I hissed back.

"Your middle name is rude."

"That might be true."

Mal giggled but quit right away when he met someone, making me halt jerkily. I looked into the light brown eyes of a thin, very old man. His face was covered with wrinkles and his glance pierced me as if he knew I was a thief. A sinning thief. I avoided his gaze, not sure where to look at.

"I request an audience with the queen," Mal said firmly.

"Finally. She's been waiting for you for hours," the man said with an empty voice, sounding like he already was dead.

But how could we be late?

"Tell her we're sorry. We're in her debt and will pay back the wasted time," Mal said without hesitation.

I squinted my eyes. What the hell was Mal talking about? How can we be late to a date we haven't even made yet? The queen didn't even know I was coming here. Or did she? Well, she was a witch. Skull. Witches were weird.

The man cleared his throat. "You can tell her that yourself. Follow me."

THE HUNCHED MAN took us into dark halls. I almost dislocated my head because I was so busy admiring this strange furniture and decorations. The Bone Court had a completely different theme. There was nothing there, but furniture made of bone, white stone, and white fur. This court was made of even more strange things. I had never seen anything like it, and I loved it. Somehow, it reminded of some objects I found in the Topworld.

All the rooms were so crowded. Chandeliers shone above us, with thin long candles, and the black marble glittered in the pale candlelight. My stomach dropped. Those candles reminded me of Rio. It was because of him that I was in this stupid situation after all. I wondered what he was doing, though, and if this guy had already killed him. Hope not. I needed to scream at him at some time because he stole my bone. Or the Bone Queen's bone—whatever.

"She's waiting for you," the man said and vanished like a ghost. I looked around, but he was gone.

"Wow. That one is awkward," I said, a tad too loudly apparently, because Mal winced.

"Stop it. He heard you."

"So?"

"Ah, forget it," he grunted. "Go in there now and hope she'll be up to helping you. I'm out."

I gaped at him. "What do you mean *you're out?*"

"You're on your own now. I'm definitely not going in there. A friend of mine is dancing in the hall, and I'll join him. Come to me when you are alive and finished your skull."

I watched him stride down the dark hall, his fancy shoes striking the marble floors in a rhythmical way, leaving me behind looking as dumb as a doorknob. Wow, what a friend my Mal was.

"Unbelievable," I muttered and fumbled into my dress's pocket. Bory was hiding somewhere in there.

"Ow! What are you doing?"

Ah, there he was. Soft and fluffy like a baby bird. "Come out. If Mal won't go in there with me, you have to. Sit on my shoulder."

"No, it can't be, can it?" His chubby cheeks twisted into a smile, one that I didn't like at all. Satisfaction. "Are you *scared?* The great and fearless Lynne is scaaaared?" he said, not hiding his sarcastic undertone.

"Shut up and sit," I snarled, placing him roughly on my right shoulder. "You're in this as much as I am."

"In what way? You have to take the blame yourself, madam."

"I don't think your charming queen will be all too happy when she hears about what had happened. Didn't she create you to look after her belongings in the first place?" I said, pinning him down with my dark eyes.

51

He fell silent for a few seconds and swallowed eventually. "Indeed, but as you can see, I'm not good at it. I befriended you and look where I am now."

"Right. That's why she'll punish you if this doesn't work out. So, give your best in there."

I straightened myself, trying to pull myself together. Fear was a natural reaction and could be overcome. At least that's what I've been telling myself since day one. Not that I was often afraid, but my soul was at stake. That was a huge thing, even for me. Maybe it was a good that I felt fear for once…

Taking a deep breath, I pushed the ancient and heavy door open, which led me straight into the Blood Queen's chambers. No matter what the old geezer had said earlier, she wasn't waiting for me as urgently as we were told.

I came at a bad time.

Very much so, because the queen was kissing someone with full pelt and just as I was about to rush out again, ashamed like hell, I felt her splashing a glass of some kind of liquid in my face. I managed to breathe in once and then everything went black.

"WELL, well, well. What do we have here?" a lovely voice purred.

When I opened my eyes, I found myself sprawled in a chair. A very soft and velvety one. Confused, I checked my body and noticed that Bory was sleeping on my thighs. As I held my fingers in front of my eyes, I saw blood on them. I jerked up. The Queen had splashed blood on my face…

My eyes widened, and found her standing across from me, leaning casually against the wall.

The almighty Blood Queen of the Underworld.

She wore a red robe and was playing with the ivory-colored ribbons of her cord belt, while checking me out more than I liked. The queen had fiery red hair, waterfalling down her back, and a pout that she curled into a cold smile. Hell, she was beautiful.

"I'm sorry my welcome was so stormy, but you saw something I couldn't let you see. It's over now. Don't worry. All is well," she said with a voice that reminded me of fingernails scratching down the walls.

Now that she mentioned it, I noticed my memory was gone. I knew I had talked to Bory, but from the moment I walked through that door there was nothing left than scraps of memories. But…she was kissing someone…and I had forgotten his face. Skull. Actually, I had forgotten everything about him. His body. His voice. His looks. I narrowed my eyes, scanning her slightly concerned eyes. Seemed like somebody didn't want me to know her cuddle buddy…

I stood up and placed Bory carefully on the chair. My little guy couldn't handle the spell as well as I could. Then I quickly assessed my surroundings and found myself in a huge hall. The floor and walls were covered with red velvet and everywhere were golden mirrors, chandeliers, black plants, as well as the smell of myrtle and smoke. But in the middle of the room stood a big black fountain filled with a dark liquid right up to the edge. My stomach twisted into a tight knot. That was blood. I swallowed and noticed that the queen was following my gaze.

She smiled and ran her long fingers along the edge of the well, let her index finger slide in and licked the blood off as if it was a sweet nectar she couldn't resist.

"You're late. I thought you'd be here much earlier. It's not very smart to say my name out loud. It's easy to get into your head then, sweetie." The queen winked.

Well, there it was. Witches were so creepy.

"But why, Lynne? Why did you come to me at all?" she asked, leaning against the fountain, staring me down.

I shoved a hair strand away from my sweat-dampened face and chose my words carefully. "I'm sorry I wasted your time, your Highness, but I need your help. Of course, I will pay according to your wishes. If I may, I would like to propose a trade."

My last words came out fainter than I intended to.

But dealing with the Bone Queen had taught me a lot in my young years. One was not allowed to talk to queens as one usually spoke. I may have been foolish, but not unreasonable, and certainly not dumb. Every word could be my last or be used as a weapon against me. If, in the presence of aristocrats, words were phrased incorrectly, the wording decided about the rest of one's life.

"A trade you say?" she purred, licking her lips as if she wanted another taste of the blood. "If that doesn't sound intriguing. You may speak about it."

"I-I've brought you a bone," I started and stretched out my hand, opened my fist and presented the bloodstained bone to her like on a golden plate.

Her eyes glistened when she saw it, but I noticed she was pulling herself together. Waiting for the sake of strategy. The queen didn't want to show how much she lusted after this tiny piece, but I knew. Oh, I knew.

Smiling, she took a few steps back and leaned against the velvet wall again.

"I'm listening," she said, lighting forking across her eyes.

"I am willing to give you one of *my* bones. It's alive, belongs to no one and can be yours, but I need your help. A magic spell of yours." Something in my chest wrenched and my heart beat so fast, I could feel the pulsation up to my throat. I hated the shaking that overtook my knees. I tried to hold them still. Revealing my nervousness to her wasn't a good idea.

The queen nodded. "Magnificent, but before I agree, I need more information. What will my spell grant you, sweetheart? True love? Endless youth? Beauty? A day with the King?" She picked at her nails while rattling off those stupid wishes.

I shook my head. Did others come here for such idiotic dreams? What nonsense to wish for. What about Bloodcoins or endless food?

I took a deep breath. "No, your Highness. I've broken a contract with your sister and am about to lose my soul. I need your help to save me from it."

She frowned a little, scanning me again as if this information gave her a new picture of me. "That's a pity, my love. Unfortunately, I cannot interfere with my sister's machinations. My hands are tied."

"I—I know that, your Highness, but I want to make up for my mistake. I was in the Topworld and—"

She raised her eyebrows. "You visited the Topworld, you little cave dweller?"

I nodded.

"Interesting. Very interesting."

Even though she seemed a little off track, I had to try my luck and rushed forward. "I lost one of your sister's bones there. Please conjure that bone back for me. I'll give you mine in return. That way you wouldn't interfere with your sister and save me. I beg you, your Highness."

She sighed again and beckoned me with her long fingers to the fountain.

Something in her eyes had changed now, making my heart beat even faster. Sweat gleaming on my brow. I silently prayed to Stix.

Oh, it was maddening.

Would she help me? What would I do if she didn't? Go to

the Bone Queen and get myself killed on the spot? I hadn't even said goodbye to Nana…

She tilted her head and a veil of hair slicked back, revealing a sharp-edged face with ebony eyes. "Here. Cut yourself and drop some blood in my fountain." She held out a knife to me.

At first, I hesitated. The knife was dirty and covered with old blood, forming crusts and her look was way beyond trustable. But then, what did I have to lose? I had nothing left. This was my last resort. In my position, I could only win.

Gritting my teeth, I took the knife, cut my palm, and winced at the little sting on my skin. While my blood trickled into the well, the whole fountain lit up. It was so bright I turned away, covering my eyes. In the Underworld, there was no light at all, so I was not used to such brightness.

"What—" I coughed.

"Mhm. Aha…" she muttered.

I tried to open an eye, forcing myself to recognize something and begging the blurred view in front of me to become clear again.

"There we have it. Oh, no. What a shame," she continued. "You dropped your bone at the graveyard…"

I shook myself, as if reminding myself to stay focused—to pay attention. With burning eyes, I turned and watched her bend over the glowing fountain with one hand gliding through the pool of blood. Her face was lit up from its light and her hair seemed to blow in a slack wind—one that I had no idea where it came from. I stood there like I was rooted to the ground.

For the first time I could see real magic.

I almost lost myself in admiration, forgetting why I was here, how bad my situation was. The power...what energy…I wanted to rush to her and throw myself into the pool, but I held myself back. How wonderful it must be to work with such power. What she could do…what influence she could take on this world…

She narrowed her eyes. "Well. That's tempting, my dear. More than tempting."

"May I ask what you mean, your Highness?" I dared to get closer, the tip of my shoes touching the well.

When I wanted to slide my finger over the edge, she glared at me, and I quickly pulled back. Skull. What was wrong with me? Did I really have a death wish?

"I'm so sorry, your Highness.''

"I'm afraid I can't get that bone back for you. It already belongs to my sister, and her magic is in its fibers," she said, offering me a sad, kind smile.

Oh, no. Did that mean I was a dead loss?

"So, you are trying to tell me you can't help me?" I stuttered vaguely, focusing on my breathing, because I might lose it in no time. The tight dress didn't help either.

"Did I use those words, cave dweller?"

I shook my head, sweat sliding down my back.

The queen lifted her dark brows and looked at me as if I were a game board, ready to play.

"No… your Highness?"

"I said I'm not able to bring your bone *back*… but *you* are," she simply said.

I coughed and tried to put her words together into a meaningful sentence, but I could not.

"How?"

"If I can't bring the bone back to the Underworld, I'll just have to bring you to the bone," the queen mused. "I'll send you up, you get it and come back."

I gaped and quickly closed my mouth again. She was capable of that? Was she skulling with me? That wasn't punishment at all! I longed to be able to go there and live like a human.

"Sure. I mean, of course I will. Here's my bone!" Naïve as I was, I stretched out my bone to her and she took it, grinning.

My grin faded. Damn it. I was a fool, wasn't I? "Is there a catch, your Highness?" I asked.

"Of course." She chuckled and took a long look at my bone. She seemed very pleased and had probably already thought about what she was going to do with this piece of art.

"How long does it normally take you to work through my sister's list? Oh, don't frown like that, sweetie! Do you really think I don't know what you do for her? Of course, I do... So, how long?"

I tried not to show her how confused I was at this very moment. I had to jot down a reminder that I didn't like witches. Not at all.

"Two to three months. After that, she starts asking," I said.

"Well then, you have some time to waste. Good thing Earth time runs differently."

"What time?"

She ignored my question and went on. "You have 99 Earth days to find and return your bone. Is that all right with you?"

My mouth dropped. 99 days? "Yes, of course."

"Good," she said. "My sister won't know you're gone. That's hardly a period of time for us down here but darling, you know I don't do anything without getting something in return."

My breathing turned uneven. That smile on her face. The wicked light in her eyes.

She already got my bone. What else did she want?

"I know your bone is wonderful, but it's just about to pay for one spell. That's obvious, isn't it? With this, I am merely taking you to the Topworld. But I also have to bring you back again and maybe even distract my sister a bit. That costs, my dear. That costs. You owe me three times."

My stomach sank. What more could I give her? I was a skulling cave dweller. I had nothing. I was a nonentity!

"Oh, sweetheart, don't lose your mind. So, you still owe me two favors since you already paid one with your bone. No big deal. I'm a nice woman. I'll offer you another deal, all right? I've been looking for—" She glanced sideways and suddenly it seemed some degrees colder and goosebumps rose on my skin. I made another mistake…

"—a way to return an artifact from Earth back to me. So, your little problem comes in handy. Lucky for you! I need a book back. It was a gift from a penitent lover of mine, and he foolishly took it back to Earth—what an idiot. Anyway, you can bring it back to me again and settle a debt with it."

I let out a deep breath. All right. One more stupid thing to collect didn't make any difference now, did it? I was a thief, so stealing didn't matter. Plus, I had so much time anyway. And how hard could it be to find a book?

"Of course, Your Highness. I'll find it."

"Oh, wonderful!" She giggled, rubbing her hands. "It's great we are so united already! This is going to be extraordinary. I can sense it. I won't bother you with more details now. As soon as you are settled up there, I will send you a message about how and where you can find the book. I have to…well…pull some strings first." When the word string flitted across her full lips, a slight shiver came over me.

I bowed my head, trying to breathe away the rising lump in my throat. "As you wish, your Highness."

"Oh, and then there's just one more debt to settle. You know what? I'm in a good mood right now. I'll make it easy for you."

I hung on her lips and couldn't wait for her to tell me her last condition, but in that moment Bory coughed and woke up. I apologized to the queen and ran to him.

"Bory? Are you all right?" I took him into my hands, rubbing my thumbs over his puffy arms.

"Yes, yes," he coughed. "All well. Oh, by the Stix! Lynne, the Queen! Behind you!"

"Oh, I know." I giggled and carried him to the fountain. "We've already worked out a plan to fix everything. It's amazing."

"Skull. That doesn't sound good," Bory whispered and climbed up to my shoulder, making himself comfortable again.

"It is. It's great. You'll see," I said.

"When you say words like *amazing* and *great*, it has to be terrible," Bory winced.

"Your Highness, please forgive me but my friend means a lot to me," I said and returned to her. "How can I repay my last debt?"

She smirked and that sinking sensation came over me again. Hitting me like slap.

"Passion," she said. "I want you to *kiss* the man."

There weren't many moments when my heart almost slipped into my pants, but this was one of them.

"Please—what… your Highness?" Apparently, I lost the ability speak.

She flashed a lupine grin. "Oh, dear. Don't act so innocent! I've seen all of it. How you looked at him, marveling at his tawny skin, the stunning blue eyes. So, I want you to kiss the man you visit year after year on Storm Day."

"You were meeting men up there? What? Lynne! Marveling? Looking? Blue eyes?" Bory choked, but I didn't have time for that now. I waved him off and turned my attention back to the queen.

Was she totally nuts? How should I kiss Rio? Well, he had the bone and was a looker so maybe I should see it as hitting two birds with one stone but… should I steal the bone, kiss him, and run away? Why would she even want that? What was the point of all this?

"It's a little trickier than just kissing him, my dear. I want *desire*. I want real pleasure and for the man to have feelings for you."

I took a step back, catching my breath. Could she hear my thoughts?

"He must want you and melt with lust when he sees you and then, yes, then you must kiss him and that's exactly the emotion I want to feel on my lips. The magic of a first kiss. Well then, you've got it. If you manage to collect these three things, you will save your soul."

"Lynne," I heard Bory whisper in my ear, "that's too much. Don't do that. Maybe we can find another way... please, I—"

"I agree," I said in a firm voice. There was no other way.

"Oh no—" Bory cried.

"Wonderful," the Queen said and threw the bone in the air, only to catch it again. "Oh, there's one more thing."

I sighed. Not again. "And what is it, may I ask, your Highness?"

"You won't be able to talk up there. I can't risk you telling a soul about the Underworld. I'm sorry but I don't want to get in trouble too. And don't try to write or draw about it, the pencil will crack if you try."

I swallowed.

How was I supposed to wrap Rio around my finger without my eloquence, or even look for the bone and the book? It was a fool's errand.

"I never said that it would be easy, but this is about *your* soul, isn't it?" the queen said. "You're going to have to work for it, sweetheart."

"Is this all, your Highness? I'll get the bone, the book, kiss the man, and then I'm free?"

The queen nodded. "Of course."

"What if she doesn't make it?" Bory asked, his voice dropping to a whisper once he looked the queen in the eyes.

She smiled at him, making his wings tremble. But I was impressed, because it must have cost Bory a lot to ask that for me. I loved this little blue fur ball of mine.

"Eternal slavery," she said without moving a muscle.

I choked at that. "What?"

"Darling… I can't send you up there and risk my neck. If my sister gets wind of this, I'll have her on me. Of course, I don't want that. So, if you screw up even one of your chores, you'll not only risk your soul, but you will also have to serve me until forever. You'll become a shadow slave, only living for me."

My knees shook. Hell, I felt so dizzy. Staggering back, I crashed into a wall. The sweat was impossible to hold back now. I was skulled. Officially. Totally skulled. Sorrow, pain, guilt, and regret filled my lungs until the lack of air almost choked me.

"Just return the three things, Lynne. Then you're free. It's very simple. A book, a bone, and a kiss in 99 days."

I tried to breathe more evenly, slowly inhaling and exhaling. Now the fun's over. Eternal slavery without my soul? Could it get any worse? There was no rescue possible from that. That was the end and I suddenly realized there were lots of worse things than death.

"Oh, come on, my love. With your looks, it'll be a cinch."

The queen laughed and sauntered towards me. I had to take another controlled, deep breath to avoid collapsing.

She drove an elegant hand through my hair. "With this mane, your beautiful eyes, and this body of yours, the kiss will be nothing. Not even worth talking about. He'll want you the minute he sees you. After all, he's a man. They're easy. And the rest? You're a master thief. This task is made for you, and you won't be alone, of course. Bory will be by your side."

"I'll … what?" Bory croaked.

I avoided his stare, my stomach dropping. Now I dragged him into the darkness as well.

"Of course. She'll never make it by herself, she needs you as an advisor. The cars and buses… oh, it's best not to start at all—all right. So, here we go."

Before I could recall anything, I felt that she sprinkled me with blood again.

Oh, I was so done with those witches. When all this skull was over, I'll never ever make a deal with one of them again. I would earn my Bloodcoins by hunting. Yep, I had sunk so low in so little time.

"One tip, Sweetheart. Find the Baron, he will lead you to success. I have put a spell on you, and it will automatically take you to him."

CHAPTER FIVE
LYNNE

" I didn't dare ask earlier, but what the hellhounds are you wearing?" Bory said.

All right, ever since the Blood Queen excused us, I've been mad. I was in such a bad mood that neither Mal, nor Bory, or even Soothie could have said anything to me without risking their head. It was all too much for me and I didn't like the feeling. I liked being in control of everything and now I had none.

I was in a world I didn't know—which would have been wonderful under any other circumstances—and I had to kiss Rio. The queen's other demands didn't bother me that much but this *kissing* thing. It's not that I didn't want to…his looks have always intrigued me, and I fantasized about it for years. But I was nervous enough already with all the other stuff on my plate. Just thinking about kissing him stressed me out.

When we were in my cave, I was looking for my treasures, which I had collected year after year on Storm Day. Luckily, one day I found the dress I was wearing now, made of a silky fabric, looking utterly garish. It was in a color that I had never seen before. Some lips were dyed like it, only this color was much more intense. It was short and showed quite a lot of my breasts but hey—if that was the usual Topworld dress code, what could I do about it?

"Well, Bory, they seem to be wearing this here. I have to fit in. Otherwise, I'll attract attention. Didn't you learn anything from Mal and his Blood court? Hey, wait! Didn't the queen say that I can't talk here?" I asked.

Bory squeezed his eyes together, they were still a little wet. I never thought he would like Soothie so much one day that it would be so hard for him to say goodbye. Even Mal seemed to have a queasy feeling when we said goodbye. I hope he used my Bloodcoins well, that he bought himself a stupid dress with one and gave the others to Nana, as promised. She needed the money for the children, and I could be sure that she didn't spend it on anything but food and other essential things. As hard as it was for me to say this, Nana was a good soul.

"Maybe she has forgotten?" Bory asked, still thinking about my ability to speak.

I gave him a look of disbelief. *As if.*

"Okay," he started again, "maybe you can just talk to me, but nobody else. They can't see me, so it would make sense. I mean I can have an effect on them and their world, but I'm invisible to humans, just like the wind."

I looked around. Usually, it was the best day of the year for me to be here in this world. I collected things, stared at Rio, and thought about what kind of person he might be. How it would have felt to be his…

"I still think your dress is weird. The last time I was up here, humans wore something different. They weren't this pink," Bory said.

"Pink?"

"The color of your dress is called pink."

"Of course, they're wearing that. Why else would I have

65

found this, then? Don't bother, Bory. We've got to go. So... how does this work now?"

"Didn't the queen say you'll have a locator spell on you? You must know which way to go."

I grunted. "The queen apparently talks shit—oh, or not."

At that moment a strange force pressed me in the back, as if an invisible hand was pushing me forward. I stumbled awkwardly and felt my bare feet touching the soft grass, giving me goose bumps.

"I think the spell works," I whispered and let myself be pushed in one direction.

"All right. Then... off to see the Baron," Bory said, looking behind me with a concerned glint in his eyes.

I tumbled across the grass. It would have been so beautiful. This pleasant air, the smell of those plants, the chirping little animals in the bushes and the bright spots up there in the sky. I hated that I couldn't enjoy it.

I came to a big gate, and I braced myself for whatever was about to come my way. It was a swing port made of iron bars, with many small stone flowers. I sucked in the air. Never ever have I been this far away from the tower.

"They have a funny way of decorating things," I said, holding myself upright and trying to hide my nervousness.

Bory glanced at me, a frown line creasing his blue face. He noticed my uneasiness, knew that I started to regret all my wrongdoings. Damn it. Stubborn as I was, I looked ahead.

The invisible hand kept pushing me further and further until I stood on a cool stone path.

"What's that?" Then something shot past me, and I took a step back. "And that?"

Bory huffed. "It's called a street, a concrete road, and those things that drive are cars. They drive on highways as well."

"Wow, can I touch them?" I asked as solidly as I could and tried to run, but that skulling invisible hand seemed to be holding me back, just like a leash. "Are you kidding? What is this spell or a babysitter?"

"Luckily both," Bory said. "You're not supposed to run here! They're not animals you can pet. They'll hit you. People sit in there and get taken from one place to another."

I stopped wiggling around like a kid and took a good look at the street. It was gray, with many lights and different colors that illuminated it. "Oh, it's like a coach then?"

"Yeah, something like that, only without horses. But please, Lynne, be careful around them. It's no joke. They are very, very strong."

The hand pressed me further again and I stumbled forward, my eyes overwhelmed with all these new impressions. The street was treelined, and everywhere grew strange long poles with a light on them. On the opposite side, there were big, square buildings towering above us.

"What is that? Over there?" I pointed at the lights, trying to slow the push I got from behind.

"These are houses, people live in them."

"How many live there? Twenty?"

"No," Bory laughed, "usually only one to four."

"Why?" I wondered. "Are humans so tall? Or are they fat?"

"No, they just like space. A cave of their own."

"Ah, that's understandable." I didn't like others that much either.

We continued, but I stopped again at a pole with three different lights.

"This is a traffic light, and a crosswalk, " Bory said with an annoyed undertone. "We have to wait here because the cars have to stop so we can cross."

I snorted and realized that people were actually sitting in those cars. As I became more attentive and looked inside the machines, I noticed that people stared back at me. One of them even made a turn because he was so distracted by me.

What was the problem? Except for the different gender, we looked totally the same. Two hands, head, feet. Why was he looking at me like that?

"What's their problem?" I asked Bory and stumbled across the crosswalk, gazing into another car. Big white eyes fixed on me, the man's mouth slightly opened.

"I don't know," Bory thought aloud. "Maybe you should've put the shoes on after all."

"No way," I sighed and was glad to be back on the sidewalk thing. "Those sticks are so high and uncomfortable! I can't walk in them. I tried."

"People like to wear heels. Maybe it's weird that you don't have any."

"Those guys didn't have any either, so what the hell? I don't care," I muttered.

It went on like this for half an eternity. We walked and walked, or rather I stumbled and stumbled. This annoying hand was like a blunt knife and the place where it pushed me forward gradually started to hurt. Apparently, I wasn't allowed to take in this new world at the pace I wanted to, because that stupid thing didn't let me stop and stare anymore. It constantly pushed me around. No time to waste, I guessed.

Bory taught me that the light pole things were called lanterns and supposed to illuminate everything, like torches. People were apparently bad at walking in the dark. It made me smile. How would they do if they were in the Underworld? We didn't have a ball of light—ahem, a moon—that made everything bright. For me, this was enough light. Again and again, a car like the ones I saw before drove past me. Some even slowed down so that they could look at me. One even called to me, but I had no idea what he was saying. Another one whistled. Strange, these humans. Really odd.

I mean, in the Underworld we had to be careful where we were going, too, since we had to watch out for the wrong death.

The biggest danger for us was getting killed by accident because a soul made the Drop. They just fell like a slimy lump. *Boom.* Then they lay there and sometimes they just hit a poor drip that was wandering around. You never knew when another soul was gonna make the Drop. It could happen anytime, or even several times a day, so you should always pay attention to where you go and what kind of noise you hear. But with time I could hear quite well when one was falling. Some funny souls even tried to get hit, but that didn't work out, of course.

As soon as the souls had made the Drop, they were divided into the appropriate zone according to the gravity of their sins. This was done by means of the Bloodcoins that were hidden under their tongue. After the Drop, the Soulmaster read the inscriptions and knew where to put the soul for the right amount of suffering. That was the Drop and that's also why we didn't have all too many Bloodcoins. We had to steal them from the souls.

AFTER WHAT FELT like hours to me—I had lost my sense of time at some point—I found myself in a park. Here, the lanterns were broken, flickering like fireflies in the settling darkness, and, in the corners, several men waited for something. *They wore* some kind of *hoods*, so I couldn't see their faces, but their heads popped up the minute I stepped into the park. It seemed to be a human thing. This weird staring. Suddenly, I felt utterly naked, standing there like rooted to the ground under the *cone of light* from a shaded *lamp, as if* it *wanted to* announce my arrival.

"Go on," Bory urged. "The men frighten me."

"I can't," I said honestly, taking a glance over my shoulder,

"I don't know where we should go. I've lost my connection."
Where the hell was that strange hand?

"What?"

"Hey baby," a dark voice purred from behind.

The cold crept down my spine.

I wanted to say something, but I couldn't. The only sound I made was a silent croak. *Skull*, I said to Bory and realized I wasn't actually talking but yet I could communicate with him. It was like mind-speaking.

What is happening?

"Go! This doesn't feel good, Lynne."

I know, I said to him, still puzzled over the fact that I could talk to him without moving my lips.

"Cat got your tongue, baby?"

I whipped my head around, taking the stranger in, but his hood cast a deep shadow on his face.

"What are you looking for? Are you working? Need a customer?"

I gaped at him and he twisted his lips into a wide smile, snow-white teeth gleaming from under the darkness. I caught my breath, stumbling back two steps.

He gripped my upper arm. "You know you're not allowed to work here. Don't you know that this entire district belongs to the Loops?"

I narrowed my eyes. What were the Loops? District?

Bory, what is he saying? I asked through our mind-connection, not letting the man out of my sight for even a second.

"I don't know," Bory said back, and I realized that this man could neither see nor hear Bory.

"Oh yeah, you're a hard nut to crack." He laughed, dragging me backwards, where it was even darker.

I gaped and swung at him, but he caught my hand in flight. He surveyed me and my words sounded hollow in my mind. I wanted to scream at him, hit him, punch him but I didn't want to hurt him. Bory said that humans were weaker than us, that we had a kind of Underworld strength within us—a strong power. So, I didn't want to make a fuss and wasn't even sure what will happen if I accidentally hurt him. Would I get punished? I had no clue who was in charge in this world and what the rules were.

Hey, I yelled but nothing came out, I screamed in a void.

"Take it easy," he said softly, and I noticed my heavy breathing. His eyes brushed me slowly from head to toe, traveling appreciatively over the flimsy gown I wore. "I'll pay you. You're making me horny, babe. There's nothing like you here." The guy snickered and pressed his hips against me, making me feel *how* horny he was. My hand fidgeted under his grip, not willing to settle and my jaw clenched.

Why? What did I do?

I tried to fight back and hit him with my fist. But he grabbed my other hand as well and stopped me right then and there. I could use my Underworld strength, but humans seemed so fragile…

"What?" he said, stopping my train of thought. "Are you a hooker or not? What are you doing here? Searching for Baron?"

Hooker? What?

Baron? Yes! The Baron!

I nodded very clearly, trying to slow down my breathing.

"Then you're in the right place. Back there." He pointed to a huge building with a sign and flashy markings. When I looked closer, I noticed these signs even made sense. Was that another spell? Some help from the queen? It said SPIRITS. Ghosts? I was a ghost, kind of…

A hot hand slid down my shoulders and I froze. He *groped* me.

"There's our club, babe. That's where you'll find him, but don't you want to stop whoring afterward? We could do a quickie, huh? I just earned some bucks. You sure need some." He leaned in and purred into my ear.

I felt the bile rising in my throat and I flinched as his rough hands felt me up. I fought for any kind of trickle of air down my lungs, desperately trying to breathe. I screamed, but no sound came out—just a rattle that sounded frightened even to my ears.

Then I fought, pushing him away with both palms and—h

e dropped dead. He fell before me, blowing up a swirl of dark leaves.

I blinked and stared

, shaking my head at the sight of the man on the ground.

"What have you done?" Bory squealed.

"I, I, I—" I stuttered, backing away, feeling the hair prickle on my skin.

Was that me? Had I just killed him? Oh *skull*, yes. I did.

Dazed, I stared at my hands. They were shaking like aspen leaves. Actually, my whole body shook.

"Take it easy," Bory whispered, touching me with his fluffy paws, shivering as well. "Take it easy, Lynne. We'll…we'll work this out."

I nodded, more as a matter of habit.

My palms. They did that. I killed a man with my bare hands without using a weapon. He wasn't the first man I ever killed, but—by the Dead, he certainly was the first one I killed just because of a touch. Why was I even able to do such a thing?

I kept staggering back until I bumped into a tree. Then a feeling of suffocation struck me, and I pressed myself against the rough bark. I couldn't catch a single breath.

Bory patted my face. "Lynne. Pull yourself together. This isn't you."

I nodded again, rubbing at my temples. I had just killed a human. Just like that. Like my hands were pure poison. Why hadn't that damn witch told me about my killer hands? Suddenly, anger was boiling inside of me, taking over every fiber of my body. That damned witch.

"Lynne," Bory said again, "come. Go. Go to this club. That's where we find the Baron. I suppose he can tell us more. Lynne, wake up now!"

I exhaled sharply, and eventually managed to move my feet. He was right. We had to go on. I concentrated on breathing, stepped over the dead man and didn't look back.

The other men didn't seem like they had noticed anything. Some casually lit something. Others were leaning against a tree but everyone was looking at *me crossing the park*. This time, however, I did not return their gaze and instead sped up my walk. All I wanted was to reach this building. Find the Baron. Nothing else. Hopefully no one came towards me again. Please. I didn't want to kill them too.

"All's well, Lynne. We'll work it out," Bory said but his tenseness told me he wasn't so sure anymore.

"Yes," I exhaled sharply, lying as well. "Yes. It's all good."

When I arrived at a red glowing door, a man stood before it, crossing his arms.

"Hey Barbie," he sneered, his eyes lingering with a glint of amusement on my cleavage.

I cringed.

Why did they all address me by B-names? *Barbie, baby, babe?* What was that about? Was that some human way to let me know I was a woman or... oh, screw it. I tried to say something again, and of course, it didn't work. By the skulling Dead. I loved to talk. I usually talked too much, and now I couldn't get a word out. I sounded like a dragon baby when I tried.

"What are you looking for? Want to see the hustlers?" He looked me over, his smile dropping. "Hm, where else would you go? You're lucky I'm here today. Come."

No. I stomped. I didn't want to leave. I wanted to go to the Baron! This was so not working out for me here.

Bory, what is he doing? I said to him while the man took my wrist and dragged me away. Afraid to touch another human, I let him drag me along, trying to keep my fingers away from his skin.

Bory frowned at the man. "I think they mistake you for a woman that sells her body for money."

What?

"He means prostitutes. It is a profession where people earn money for having sex. A sex worker." *Oh, skull.*

The huge man was still dragging me behind him until the Spirits Club came to an end and a new building started. There was another sign above the door, and it shone red... actually everything here was red and... pink. Like the color of my dress. All right, maybe I shouldn't have worn it.

The sign read PARADISE GIRLS.

He opened the door and pulled me into this so-called paradise. But w

ell, paradise was not what I would have called it. In here it was even stranger than outside. I could not stop gawking at it. Everything was pink. Really everything. Even a plant. It was so bright in here that my eyes hurt. Just when I had somehow gotten used to the shrill colors, a woman turned the corner, or was it a man? I narrowed my eyes and watched the feathers on the dress moving while they came towards us.

"Punchy?" they said, and I stared at their face. Their skin was a russet, reddish brown with pink cheeks and hair that looked like a beehive. "What the hell are you bringing me this time?"

The voice reminded me of a man in drag, like Mal. Oh, he would have liked it here. But I couldn't think of my best friend. I had to stay focused.

"Punchy, what is this? White trash? A kidnapped girl? Did the princess get mad at her parents and ran away?"

The huge man, apparently named Punchy, shrugged. My eyes bounced back and forth between the two.

"I don't know. She's not talking. Hey," Punchy said and shook me.

I jerked, hiding my killer hands behind my back.

"Barbie. What's your real name? Do you *understand* me?" He spoke louder now, making me wince and praying that he didn't force me to touch him. "Are you Russian?"

Again, I tried to say something, but of course it didn't work. Why did I still try?

"Is she mute?" asked the one in feathers.

Punchy shrugged again. "Diva Dee, I have no idea. I'm sorry. She wanted to come to you, I think. Look at her, what else could she be but a hooker? Here, in Englewood… in that thing? She probably won't be the daughter of a regular Karen."

Diva Dee huffed and smiled, staring back at me. Between his eyebrows, however, wrinkles of tension stood out. It definitely wasn't a face one would cross. "Well, the Baron has to approve it. You know that nobody's allowed to work here without his permission."

When Diva Dee said Baron, I jumped slightly. Yes, that's exactly who I wanted to see. I looked at her with big eyes, nodding and desperately trying to signal her that I wanted to speak with that guy.

But Diva Dee's gaze got stuck on my breasts.

"Hmm, something exotic wouldn't be bad. Some of our clients like slim. Barbie Girl. Sounds good. Sounds like cash. Can you dance?"

I looked at her again. She twisted her lips.

"She's a cutie." Punchy smiled sheepishly.

Diva Dee grunted at him and grabbed me by the upper

arm, yanking me away from Punchy. "You know the rules around here, kiddo. Go drool somewhere else and make an appointment with Baron. He's gotta check her first. Come on, sweetheart. Let's go put on some normal clothes. Why are you so dirty and why in the world would you wear a cheap negligee and walk around in Englewood on your own? Did they force you to work in this? Did you run away?"

I blinked several times, screwing up my face.

"Well, don't worry, honey. Not everyone can be a chatterbox like me. But whatever happened, it's over now."

Diva Dee moved further into this pink monstrosity of a house, and we passed several pink doors with flowers onto it, coming to a staircase. While I let her drag me forward, I looked over my shoulder, watching Punchy standing in the door frame. He still seemed to be trying to figure me out. Oh, what did I get myself into…

CHAPTER SIX
LYNNE

"And she's mute?" whispered Cherry to the other one, whose name I think was Cheetah, a big, curly-haired woman.

"Mhm. She didn't say nothin', did she?" whispered Cheetah back.

I sighed. Like I couldn't hear her. Diva Dee asked me the same questions a hundred times and then found me either hopeless or moronic and took me to a room upstairs. It had a bed with extremely soft blankets—all compared to my cave, of course—and like Bory told me later, even cushions. Fluffy things I could put my head on! I've never slept anywhere but on my stone floor. It was a simple room, with a wardrobe, a desk, and a lamp, and yet it was the most beautiful room I had ever slept in. My first real room.

While I marveled at it, four women came rushing in. They wore patterned, tight trousers and just as colorful tops. They all talked to me at once and tried to do something with my hair—no idea what they wanted to be honest.

"Can you write? Maybe that's how you can tell us your story," a slim woman named Mallow asked. She was exceptionally beautiful, with inky, straight hair and a golden skin like the fiery glow of sunset. I had probably stared at her for too long because she curled her lip and blinked.

I cleared my throat. Of course, I could write but what should I tell them? I couldn't tell them anything about me, the queen made sure of that.

Bory, what should I do? I asked through our bond, *smiling oddly at Mallow.*

"I'm already thinking it over," he told me.

"Children," I heard Diva Dee, who suddenly stood in the doorway.

In her hand, she had two cone-shaped glasses with—how could it be otherwise—pink liquid. I had chosen the dress all wrong. But really, how was I supposed to know what they wore in this world? I didn't have such patterned pants, and the loin-cloth would have been totally wrong too.

"Leave her alone, girls." Diva Dee pressed herself through the now embarrassed wall of girls. "You can see how scared she is. Who knows who she is running away from? Here, Barbie, take this."

I frowned in curiosity, staring at the drink she held out to me.

Shall I drink this, Bory? It looks funny, I asked him. *I don't want to be poisoned.*

"Oh, I think it's fine, just a drink. Something alcoholic. Like Ashwater," Bory said, still assessing those girls.

Oh! I grinned. That I needed.

Now I hurriedly reached for the glass and forgot all about manners.

But Diva Dee laughed.

"I thought so. Whatever you've been through today, drinks are always good."

I smiled and drank. It was pretty good. I couldn't taste any alcohol, it kind of burned a lot more downstairs, but it was delicious anyway.

"This is a Cosmo, honey," Diva Dee said.

"Don't you know it?" Cherry asked, a very young woman with a deep sepia colored skin. She had curly hair, the upper half a light pink and the other black light the night. Her nails long and green.

I shook my head and Cherry sucked in the air. "Oh my gosh. She doesn't know Cosmos. Where are you from? What brothel did you work at?"

"Now leave her alone," hissed Muffin, a curvy woman with short hair and tight curls.

"We *have* to ask her," hissed Cherry back.

"Yes, we sure have to," Cheetah buzzed in.

"Girls." Now Diva Dee was getting loud again. "That's enough, now. Candy?"

"Yeah?" A small, petite white woman with red hair answered. She hid behind Cherry.

"Why don't you bring some Cosmos for everybody?"

She nodded and scurried downstairs and came up later with a tray and some more drinks.

Diva Dee sat down on the bed next to me, the girls still staring at me as if I were some sort of attraction. "We call ourselves Diva's Girls," she said, and took a sip. "We work at the club, owned by Baron. If he hires you, your life will change from now on."

"He's really good," Cherry said and drove a hand through her hair. "All we have to do is dance, nothing more. No touching. Otherwise, the Loops come. You can even get your GED and start over. Like me. I am going to—"

"Shut up, Cherry," Muffin growls. "No one is interested in your stupid plans."

Cherry sticked out her tongue and folded her arms.

"They're protecting us and helping us get on the right foot again," Mallow said, patting Cherry's shoulder and glaring at Muffin. "You just have to give them a little bit of your profit. That's all. They are not like other gangs. They really help women."

"I'm sure the others told her the same thing," I heard an alluring woman's voice.

I raised my head and noticed a tall woman with an hour-glass figure and a long, black ponytail. Her skin was a dark umber and absolutely flawless. No pimples or scars. I glanced at my fingers, at all the white scars there…

"I'm Foxxy T, for short Fox," she said and waved at me. "Hi."

I smiled and waved in reply. Oh, I hated that I couldn't speak.

"And that's Belle," Fox said, pointing to a girl behind her with lots of black pigtails. Belle waved at me too. Then I sighed again. What was I doing here? I've never been in a room with so many girls. I wondered if this was such a good idea after all.

"You'll probably make us a lot of money." Cherry grinned and immediately was struck in the ribs by Mallow.

"Stop it."

"What? It's true. She looks like a pop star."

"And you're sure she's not an undercover police-loving bitch or something? What is someone like her doing here? In fucking Englewood?" asked Fox, who was still leaning in the doorway.

I narrowed my eyes at her.

"Fox," Diva Dee hissed and stood up. "Let the boss decide that. We don't make decisions here."

"That may be so, but if *we* don't want her here, then she has to leave," Fox replied.

Diva Dee looked at me for a long time then but at that moment Cherry patted my knee and I flinched.

"Don't worry. She is like that with all the new ones. Right

now, she's the best of us and just afraid you'll take her customers away. Something that was bound to happen at some point."

"Watch your fucking mouth, Cherry," Fox snarled.

"Don't start things if you can't handle the backlash." Cherry curled her lips, and I sucked in the air between my teeth. That girl looked like an angel, but she surely could fight for herself.

Fox opened her mouth, but Diva Dee held up a hand and said, "Okay, girls. You're going to your rooms. Now. The party is over. We'll see what tomorrow brings."

The girls sighed, said goodbye to me and went outside one by one. When there was none left, Diva Dee turned to me.

"I want you to understand something. If some cop sent you, you're dead. I don't want to scare you. I just want to give you a chance to reconsider your decisions." She paused and I had a feeling Diva Dee had given this speech many times before. "This is a good place for girls who took the wrong path, we are a community and share this house with love. Got that? This is no place for cops and their snitches. If you need help, you may have found the right place. So, think it over. "

I nodded.

"Okay, whatever. Get some sleep, sweetie," she sighed and pulled her lips into a smile again. "Argh, I hate having to give that speech every single time, but I have to. Forgive me."

And then she was gone.

"AND NOW WHAT, Bory? I just wait to meet this Baron? We're only losing time here. Shouldn't I just go and find him?" I stretched out on the soft bed next to Bory.

"No, I'd rather not, Lynne. We'd better follow their lead.

Who knows what else they'll do to us? You're safe, and we're close to the Baron. That should be enough for now, don't you think?"

I wriggled my toes. "I hate it already! What if they won't let me go again?"

"Well, in case of emergency, you'll have your strange power."

I glanced at him. He couldn't be serious, could he? " I don't just kill humans at random. They can do it themselves."

"You're not this squeamish at home," Bory yawned and tried to make himself comfortable on our bed.

"Things are different back home."

"Come lie down and rest. We're going to see the Baron tomorrow. Who, as you know, is supposed to help us. After that, we'll look for Rio. That kiss for sure is the easiest part of our mission."

CHAPTER SEVEN
RIO

"Come in," I said and saw Fish, grinning stupidly as usual.

God. I really hated that guy. Then Punchy pressed in behind him, wearing a foolish grin on his face too. What was going on?

A few seconds later, I knew why they were looking like that. Someone could have knocked me down with a feather when I saw *her*. All I could think of at that moment was… sex. With her. Everywhere.

Admittedly, not a smart thing to think about. Still, she triggered those primal thoughts in me, whether I wanted her to or not. It was the kind of thoughts that just happened. Images that buzzed around in your head, that you wanted to get rid of, but they kept coming.

So, there she stood, long white-blonde hair, curling around her waist and dark brown eyes. God, she was beautiful. Her glance had something vulnerable but also so sensual that I had to force myself not to look at her any longer. Of course, the idiots would only grin like that if they had a girl in tow.

The most beautiful girl I've ever seen.

She stepped out of Punchy's shadow, returning my gaze and opened her eyes and was… shocked. Totally thrown off balance at the sight of me. I opened my mouth and wanted to ask her what's wrong, but my damned eyes flitted over her body once more. I couldn't do anything about it. Fuck. Literally. I was fucked.

"Eh, Boss?" I heard Fish stammer at some point.

I glanced at him for a few heartbeats. How much time had passed and how long had I been staring at her like a complete idiot?

"Yes?" I asked and could have hit myself in the same moment. What was wrong with me? I don't say yes to a question.

"She's the girl Punchy found yesterday…" Fish tried.

"What?" I said, like my mouth wasn't connected to my brain anymore. I shook myself and got up. I wanted to be near her, but luckily, I gathered my wits again and stopped at my desk, leaning against it. Her gaze hardened and somehow it seemed as if it was just the two of us here, us and my dirty thoughts.

"Boss?" Fish repeated.

"I am thinking," I growled, trying to find a way out of this situation.

I haven't felt this paralyzed in a long time.

"She can't talk…we think. Maybe she's in shock. Or something. I've heard that it affects the voice. Sometimes," Punchy babbled.

"Her name is Barbie," Fish said.

I raised my eyebrows, never taking my eyes off her.

She pinned me with those dark orbs of eyes, her mouth slightly opened as if she were surprised to see me, too.

But her name wasn't Barbie. For sure. Her pout told me she was as annoyed with them as I was. Somehow, she reminded me of the movie *The Last Unicorn*. It made me laugh. Alba loved that movie. One of the few happy memories we shared. Damn, why was I thinking about her now? Of all people?

"Her name's not Barbie," I said, and she nodded.

"We don't know what else to call her," Punchy said and shrugged.

I hummed and approached her.

As I came closer, she took a step back, like a shy deer. But her gaze was not timid, no, she was ready to fight. Her eyes glowed with fire. Like a wild cat. I smiled and my stomach took a tumble the moment she did the same. Like a wild cat. I knew she had a rebellious side, intriguing me even more. I widened my smile into a grin. She was a rare treasure that I wanted to own but she also was the kind of treasure no one could own.

"She wants to work at Diva Dee," Punchy said.

"Are you a sex worker? Hustler?" I asked.

She shook her head, still looking up at me as if I were a ghost.

"Why do you want to work there then?" I said.

She didn't answer and then Fish, the idiot, went up to her and grabbed her by the wrist.

"Talk, bitch," he hissed, and I felt the anger building up inside of me.

"If you don't get your fucking hands off her right now," I said and *a deep rumble* emanated from the back of my throat, "I'll give you a mouth shot with everything I've got."

Punchy narrowed his eyes and stepped between Fish and the girl—or young woman. These days you could never be so sure. Some looked so young and some rather old.

"All right. She wants to move in with Dee, fine. She can, but we need dancers. Can you dance on a pole?" I asked, swallowing down the rage I had for Fish. That fuck really needed to leave my gang.

She hesitated and I knew she wasn't a stripper either. She probably thought about how she could tell me that. Fuck, what was I supposed to do with her now? Why did she even want to move in with Dee? I couldn't just give her a job because I… well…because I liked her at first sight. I couldn't. I wasn't a fool after all.

"Is somebody after you?" I asked, closing the space between us.

She didn't flinch this time. Our eyes locked, giving me a mischievous glint that made my knees buckle slightly.

Man, her eyes.

I tilted my head, taking in her delicate face, stopping myself from touching her. Instead, my eyes flitted over her little nose, the high cheek bones, and her sweet chin I wanted to curl my fingers under, lifting her face to meet mine. I halted, catching my breath and stepping away.

She looked so familiar. Have I seen her before? I've never had this feeling before, it was like I knew her from somewhere.

She blinked several times. Still no answer. What was she afraid of? It clearly wasn't me or my position as a gang leader. But before I could think about saying another word, stupid Fish came and grabbed her, one hand on her wrist and the other on her ass. He pushed her against the wall, and I lost it, just like that, as I watched her in pain. The thought of her being parted from me let something primal rise in me, something I thought dead and forgotten.

"Speak! When the boss says talk, then talk! Know your place, woman!"

I was about to punch him senseless, but it was already too late. There was a loud thud, and he was on the ground at my feet.

He actually dropped dead.

Like a fly.

Punchy screamed, sounding like a five-year-old if you asked me, and my eyes rushed to her. She looked over her shoulder back at me, swallowing, shaking her head and hiding her tender hands behind the back. Her hands… she touched Fish… causing him to… die? What?

"How? What did you do?" Punchy cried and waved his hands in front of his face as if he wanted to shoo her away like a wasp, panic visibly rising inside of him.

I glanced back at her.

Just looked at her and her eyes told me volumes. She didn't want to kill him, but he was pushing her, and it was her touch. She killed him with her bare hands… but it couldn't be. No one could do that. There must be a trick, something she did while I was distracted, thinking about her rather than watching her like I should have.

Punchy screamed again and then I yelled at him, "Shut up Punchy, for fuck's sake. Get out. I got this."

"What, I—Boss! What are you doing with… *her* now? What if she's a threat? She could kill you." His blood drained from his face, and I think he needed to throw up. Well, not on my floor, man.

I pointed at the door. "Get out, she won't do anything to hurt me. Don't tell anyone what happened here," I said and swallowed down whatever feelings had built up inside of me.

Punchy nodded and ran. I made a mental note to remind myself that I would laugh at him later.

When I had closed the door, I walked towards her and reached out to touch her wrist, but she recoiled and staggered into a corner, shaking her head again and again, looking down at Fish.

I didn't know why, but I was certain she wouldn't hurt me. Maybe it was foolish, but I wasn't afraid of her. The incident with Fish was unintentional, it had to be and let's be honest, if she wouldn't have hurt him, I would have.

I looked her up and down, searched for hidden weapons, signs of previous fights, body language that might tell me something about her plans, but there was nothing. She was like a blank page. I definitely had to take her fingerprints from Fish later and have her background checked.

As I was looking at her, hundreds of questions ran through my mind. What was she up to? Did she kill him on purpose? What kind of trick was that? It had to be a trick or an accident. She can't just kill a man like that. That wasn't possible. All odds were against it.

Then she was breathing hard, starting to realize what she'd done. She leaned forward, her black top stretching, and my gaze lingered on her rising and falling chest and traveled down to her tight jeans.

PULLING MYSELF TOGETHER, I held up both of my hands, showing her that I wasn't about to tell anyone what she just did. "It's all right," I said—not knowing why. Nothing was all right at all. She could kill people with her bare hands within seconds. So, it was more than fitting that she was afraid of me knowing. Nevertheless, I tried not to take advantage of her fear —very unlike me to be honest. I somehow had the urge to protect her, although I didn't even know her, wanted to say something, comfort her. But all that I came up with was blaze.

I hated Fish, so his loss was probably a gain, thinking of his stupid actions, but why didn't I start to shout at the girl? Well, her skill seemed to be something of use. If she really could kill men like that, I needed her. I needed my own assassin— someone that could move as silent as a wraith. I had to find out how she did that. I had to keep her.

Her wary gaze didn't change, and she swallowed again. I came closer to her and took her wrist, pulled her towards me and made her take a step over Fish.

"It's okay, calm down. You're safe with me."

I led her to my desk where she could lean against it, take a deep breath. In such situations keeping a cool head was everything. After her breathing normalized, she looked at me once more. Her mouth was slightly open, her saucer eyes wet, and her little nose rosy. She couldn't have been an FBI agent. No, she wasn't a spy.

"No one will know," I said, nodding at Fish. "He just disappeared, don't worry."

She nodded and ran a trembling hand through her long hair. I wondered if she'd dyed it like that, but her roots didn't look like it. Strange.

"What kind of trick was that?" I asked later.

I wanted to touch her hand, examine it but she backed away, as frantic as before and I stopped pushing her. I had to be gentle, I couldn't afford to scare her away. Apparently, she was afraid to touch people now. Great, new neurosis incoming. I sighed and went to one of my bookshelves. I knew my way around with difficult people, so I had an idea.

"Here, put these on." I held out a pair of white gloves to her, elegant ones that would go up to her elbow.

She narrowed her eyes and looked at her shoulder before taking the gloves. As if she had to ask her shoulder first. I grinned. Well, there definitely weren't many like her. If she had been in the city for a while, she must have attracted attention. An easy one for my eyes and ears. I would quickly find out who she was.

She took the gloves and put them on. Every move she made was so sensual, I felt goosebumps rising on my arms. She admired them as if she had never seen gloves before in her life. Bizarre. I curled my lips into a crooked smile.

Once she wore the gloves, I did something that was probably fucking stupid, but I took her hand and touched my chest with it.

She jumped back, eyes wide open, alternately looking at

her hand and the body part of mine it touched. I knew she was trying to talk but I was sure now that she couldn't. She opened and closed her mouth like a sweet guppy. She really was mute then. Surprising me once again, she swung out and gave me a slap. A fucking slap!

I blinked.

She blinked, realizing she did something wrong again.

At first, I did not know what to do but then she tried again, and I caught her wrist. She wouldn't get away with it twice, no way.

"Girl, you know who I am, right?" Her breath caught in her throat.

We stood so close I could see my own reflection in her eyes. "You can call yourself lucky we're alone." I let out a sigh. Shit.

She grunted and pointed to her hands and then to Fish.

I huffed, now she was mad at *me*? *I* should be angry, not her. "Well, now you can touch me without being afraid. Touch anyone," I added quickly. "You still should be afraid of me when it comes to touching my body, though." God. I was talking shit. What did she do to me?

She shook her head and didn't go for my poor flirting attempt. It has been a very long time since I last tried to really flirt.

"Aren't you going to tell me why you're here?" I asked, still rattled.

What a bold girl. To prevent myself from staring at her like a fool any longer, I sat down at my table.

I leaned back, assessing her. How she stood there across from my desk. The way she cocked her head. She seemed to be very athletic, though it didn't show much, but I knew she had to be strong. The way she searched my office with her gaze told me she was looking for something specific. It was no coincidence that she was here. Oh no, she had planned it. Her motion was very casual. She was sexy but in a different way than Dee's girls. She didn't know it and she didn't know how she could enhance that bonus, how she could make me sweat even more. She couldn't be a dancer, probably not a prostitute either; her look was too innocent, too ignorant of what she could do to me with her eyes alone. I had to teach her a few important things first, but she'd undeniably help me with my plan.

It seemed as if she was as finished analyzing my room as I was studying her. At least for now. She showed me with her hands that she needed to write something.

"Of course," I said and put a piece of paper and a pen on my desk.

She came closer, bent down, and wrote.

All I could see now was her white-blonde hair, spreading like rose tendrils on my wooden desk. Oh, and her scent. Fruits and something smoky. I couldn't get it right, though.

A couple of minutes later she gave me the note. I grinned. Her writing was far from beautiful, but I could read it.

I am not a prostitute! I'm looking for a bone. You picked it up some time ago and took it with you. I need it back.

Okay now, I was completely blown away. I had to read her note twice—a two-liner! She was here for a bone? A fucking bone? I mean, I had actually found one. An utterly weird one. I visited Aria—like always—and then I heard strange noises and found a dark gray, undoubtedly human bone.

I was more than aware that this bone was not normal. I took it with me to find out more about it but forgot until now. And now she was here for it? For that clearly not normal bone?

I leaned back, playing with the note. "Why do you want it?"

She shrugged. She wouldn't tell me.

"I don't have it anymore," I said, wincing in a playful way.

Ah, and there it was. The shocked face I wanted to see. Proof that she desperately needed the bone and that I had her now. Well, darling, you really shouldn't show me anything like that. I suppressed a spiteful smile. "That means I don't have it *here* anymore, I have it elsewhere." I smirked at the want in her eyes.

Her face changed instantly, but her breathing was still rapid, showing me her nervousness, like a mouse did before the cat got it. Just as I thought she was indeed incredibly talented I was almost sorry to admit I wouldn't just hand the bone over to her. If I were a good person, I would give it to her, of course, but sadly I was not.

If I can take advantage of something, I do.

Unfortunately, she told me three things today that were essential for me: she was dependent on the bone and therefore on me, she had a deadly gift, and she could probably fight—even without adding her beauty as a weapon, it was enough. All in all, she was unfortunately exactly what I was looking for throughout the last twelve years. After I already considered alternatives that were not half as good as her, she just stood there like a meal ticket. Who should I thank now? As a Catholic, I probably should thank God. So, thank God for this useful gift.

Now I couldn't help it anymore and smirked.

"I'll give it to you, don't worry," I said. "But only if you will help me with something in return."

Her gaze hardened immediately, and she placed her hands on my desk. Again, she tried to say something, but it wasn't possible. Of course not. Then she looked at me with such curiosity that all I could think about was how I could make her feel like that all day long. Vicious much? I guess.

Her expression asked: *Why? What do I have to do?*

"I have a purpose. A pretty big one, and I need you to help me achieve it. Don't worry, you don't have to do much. Just work for me for a few weeks. I help you, you help me. Simple."

She raised her hands. *What do you want me to do?*

"No hustling, I promise. I want you to become a gang

member. You can leave after the job is done. I'm gonna give you some jobs and after that, you'll get the bone as a paycheck. What do you think?"

Her eyes hardened. Yep, she hated me right now, really hated me. I knew that she was not an easy girl to work with. Oh, and I liked that. Yes, I liked her wild side. She was a perfect fit for my team, my own personal killing machine and no one would ever look at her like this.

"You'll get anything you want. Food, clothing, a roof over your head, as much money as you want. Not a thing missing. I tell you my price, and you tell me yours."

She sighed and tore the note from my hand.

All right, I had to work on her attitude. She wasn't supposed to treat me like that in front of the others, but I'd manage. A couple of minutes later she gave me the note, glancing at me with cinder in her eyes. Oh, I'd see that look in my dreams tonight for sure. I smiled and glanced at the sheet of paper.

I don't have much time. Two months. At most. Then I must go.

I nodded. "All right, then. We'll work it out. Ah, and don't get me wrong, if you mess up, you won't get the bone. And don't go searching for it, my men will rat you out and then you're screwed, darling." The minute I said it, I knew I was going to have trouble with her. With treating her like a regular gang member…

She hesitated, thinking hard but eventually she nodded, put her hand out to me and I shook it. We had a deal.

"I would love to ask you for your name, but we have a lot of rules here. So, here's rule number one: No real names. We operate with codenames, nothing else. We will call you Barbie, if that is all right or do you want to be called something else? You can choose."

She shrugged.

"It's for safety only. So, Barbie it is." I stood up and nodded at Fish on the floor. "I have to go now... clean up after you. But this'll be our little secret, okay?"

She nodded again, crossing her arms. Oh, she really was a wild thing.

"As much as I find your rebelliousness appealing, you have to pull yourself together in front of the others. Anyone who violates my fundamental principles, I must punish to spread fear. Is that clear, Bone Thief?"

She furrowed her brow, as if something I said made no sense. But before I could start over, she nodded again. Fine. It fitted all too well. But what were we? A match made in hell?

"Privately you can spank me as much as you like, but as soon as there is a third person, consider who I am. I cannot protect you if you do not follow these rules."

She rolled her eyes, making me laugh out loud. Twice already.

"All right. We'll let the others think you're one of Dee's girls for now. Just pretend a little. Don't leave her house, or when you do, do it incognito please. I want to keep your identity hidden as long as possible. We'll have her teach you a few things and I'll come up to you in a couple of days with your first job details."

She sighed but nodded again. Good girl.

"Oh, and your story? What shall I tell the others?"

She wrote something down again, letting me glimpse her pointy nipples. No bra? Dear god, she really was a walking weapon.

Think of something. Surprise me.

Her eyes lit up as she gave me the note back, biting her lower lip. We exchanged glances for a minute too long and then I pushed aside the thought of throwing myself at her. Rarely, but sometimes there were people who caused this kind of sexual tension without having to do anything for it—and damn. She was one of them.

And I didn't need that right now.

I grounded some important rules for my gang to make sure we were as successful as we can be. I, too, had to abide by them. No sex between gang members. When we work, we need to keep a cool head and as soon as sex came along, one of them wouldn't work properly. People committed to each other would fear for one another, care for each other's well-being, and therefore they would not be good for an operation like mine, not good for operations with guns, drugs, and killing. So, I had to put her body and that damned mouth out of my mind now. After all she was just a woman like any other.

CHAPTER EIGHT
LYNNE

I swore, pacing in Dee's room, which apparently was mine now for an indefinite time. "Did you see that, Bory?"

That man was Rio. My Rio... the Rio I saw crying on a mound of earth every year and now... now he was a gang boss who didn't even bat an eyelash when I killed a man with my bare hands. My skin tingled in an uncomfortable way, and I rubbed my arms, clenching my teeth. This was insane. Rio couldn't be a gang boss, he couldn't. I had imagined him to be different and—

"Are you going mad again?" Bory asked, tilting his head and looking at me with his eyebrows drawn together. He opened his mouth to say something but then thought better of it and closed it.

"Yes—no. I mean, that was Rio, Bory. The man I see every year... or watch over. Skull, that was him..." I scraped my hair back and forced out a laugh. That couldn't be, right? Rio couldn't be that cold... could he? Why was Rio the Baron, and why didn't the witch say a thing about it?

Bory's eyes widened, suddenly putting two and two

together. "Oh, Lynne. No. No, no, no! That's the kind of men you like?"

"No," I said, raising my voice. "I never knew him, I just… I never did anything—"

"By the Dead, *the* Baron? The guy you stalked is *the* Baron?"

I grunted, making a face. "I wasn't stalking him, he's just always there when I'm here. That's it."

"I cannot believe this," Bory said, throwing his blue, chubby arms up in the air.

"Me neither," I sighed, and suddenly felt hot. I pulled at my top, trying to get some fresh air under it.

"This can't be a coincidence," Bory said again. "You see him every year and now the queen sends you to him and he doesn't give you a skulling bone he found on the floor? This bone can't mean anything to him. Something's wrong."

"Oh, yeah? Tell me," I said, rolling my eyes.

My feet twitched as if urging me to run back up to Rio and skull him. What was he thinking? I had to work for him to get the bone? I shook my head, suddenly very aware of my rigid muscles. All these years I had imagined him as a dream-man, idealized him… my face, ears, and body felt like a burning stove now.

Rio had hit me with his personality. I wished he was as I had imagined him. Bones meant nothing to him and still, he refused to give it to me and now I had to stay here, work for him. This couldn't be happening—he just couldn't be that heartless. I hit the air with my fist and accidentally pulled down a curtain.

"Great. Now we can't darken the room anymore," Bory said.

"I've survived the light today and will survive it tomorrow, " I sighed.

"Oh, but you almost died because of that light. Already forgotten?"

I rolled my eyes, trying to fix that shitty curtain again, but it wasn't easy since I've never even seen such a thing. But no, I certainly did not forget what impact that light had on me this early morning. That sun was terrible. My eyes were used to the dark and here everything was bright and lit up.

What humans called daylight was insane. I thought the moonlight was strong but the sun! Holy skull. The whole day, my eyes were reddish and watery. It took forever until my eyes adjusted to it. Cherry asked me if I'd cried and thought it was because of Fox and her harsh comments the day before. But someone like me was not going to break over such trifles.

Bory drew out a sharp breath. "You're just going to have to play along, Lynne. He is like he is, get over it. What choices do we have? Your soul is at stake, we can't just say, *that's it, don't meddle with us, asshole.* You'll end as a *shadow* slave. You realize that, right?"

I almost laughed about him saying such bad words. "Yes, you're right…" I mumbled back, falling onto my bed. It was so soft that I sunk in and didn't want to get up ever again. "But how shall I kiss a guy like him, Bory? I can never woo a man like him."

Bory hopped onto the bed, propping himself up next to my head and giving me his lecturing look. "Did you see the same thing I just saw? He was about to take your pants off, girl."

I narrowed my eyes. "Not at all. He just liked that I had killed that guy and that's horrible. He's dangerous. I saw it in his eyes."

"You don't have to marry him, Lynne. Just lure him in and then kiss him. Afterwards we steal the bone and are gone for good."

I nodded, wanting to like Bory's plan but all I could think about right now was Rio and that he wasn't the guy I wanted him to be all those years. I rubbed my wrist, as though to erase his touch I still felt on it. What was I even thinking? Of course, he wasn't like I wanted him to be. I was dreaming—a naïve little girl. He wouldn't immediately take me in his arms, kiss me and treat me as if we had known each other for decades.

Because we didn't. Only I knew him. But no, not even that. I imagined it. I had this vision of him and had an embarrassing crush on that skulling version of Rio. All I thought I knew about him was pure imagination. I wanted to be swallowed by the ground right now.

"How will our precious queen tell us where we can find the book?" I asked, trying to push away the thoughts about him. About his face. His skulling handsome face.

Bory shrugged. "In some strange way, I'm sure."

"I hate witches."

"So do I." Bory snuggled up against me and I thankfully leaned into his touch.

I was skulled.

UNFORTUNATELY, it didn't get any easier for me over the next few hours. Rio apparently gave Diva Dee some creative information about me and really did invent a story. All it got me was Diva Dee looking at me with puppy eyes and feeling sorry. So, there was another question for me to ask. What the hell did Rio tell her?

She kept saying that she couldn't believe it and that she would certainly help me with everything in her power.

Well, it was my fault to be honest, but I just couldn't come up with a decent explanation. Once again, it was good that I couldn't talk. In this world, it was pretty easy to make people believe a lie. After a while, they answered their own questions and just concluded something.

It was somewhat hilarious—but well, not really. Diva Dee

didn't understand at all why I didn't know how to dance or seduce men—even flirt, as if flirting was equal to breathing. I never had a man in my life, how the heck should I know how to lure them in? Or what they even like?

I spent my first hours getting used to the many girls. I've never been in such a small space with this many people before, especially same-gender ones. I was more the type of woman who preferred the company of animals. I just couldn't establish real conversations with most people. Somehow, I was different. I didn't like to be protected, didn't give a shit about how I looked, and was desperate to put the stupidest ideas into action.

That was one of the reasons Nana, after raising me and protecting me like the mother hen of all mother hens, threw me out of her home. There weren't many kids in the Underworld, and I was lucky Nana had found me and I grew up in Cave Town. Children were scarce in the Underworld, and they were highly traded. The wildest stories were told there. Unfortunately, I didn't appreciate the protected environment. So, it came as it should have come.

Later that day, Dee made me watch the girls working at the club. I had to wear a brown wig and wasn't allowed to interact with the guests. The clothes they gave me were also very subtle. A black dress without a neckline and I even had to wear a jacket over it. Everyone else in the club wore almost nothing. Apparently, the Baron gave this odd order. Cherry told me he demanded that I wouldn't be touched by any other men—whatever that meant.

Cherry soon became something like my shadow. She was cute but somehow scary, because she seemed to follow wherever I went. Sometimes I didn't even hear her and then she just appeared behind me. I lost count of how often I flinched because of her.

I learned that Mallow was something like Cherry's personal lapdog. So, it was always me and the two of them. Granted, I liked those two a hundred times better than Fox who seemed to *really* hate me, down to my very blood. No matter where I went, she'd shoo me away or snarl at me, just like a dragon would.

"You don't belong here," was all she'd say.

If I was in the Underworld, I would have shown her who was the stronger one, and that was definitely me. I could fight creatures she couldn't even imagine in her wildest dreams. I could fight men if I wanted to, and I could stand up to her— hell, could easily kill her with just one touch. But I was not in the Underworld, and I was no killer. They didn't solve things here the way they did in my world.

Here they wore colorful clothes, they smeared shades on their faces, on their toes, fingernails—generally there were a lot of colors here—and one thing I learned quickly, they didn't say what they thought. Luckily, I couldn't talk. In retrospect it was a real blessing. I would have done so many things wrong.

My first days here consisted of observing and learning how this world worked. I almost got run over by cars three times but only almost. Bory nearly decapitated me each time after that, mainly because I was not allowed to leave Dee's *paradise*, but I always snuck out the window when it got dark. As if they could lock me in while leaving a window unlocked. I observed how people did simple things, how they ate, washed themselves and yes, how one went to the toilet here.

They had their own room and sat on a throne to take a dump. That made me crack up. Humans couldn't do their dump outside. No, they needed their own room, one for each of themselves, to do *that*. Actually, they needed a room for everything. To sleep. To eat. To wash. For their hobbies, for cleaning supplies…

They also had a kind of picture that moved. They could have knocked me over with a feather when I saw it for the first time. All the girls sat in front of the picture in the afternoon and watched a man who chose his mate among a bunch of other girls. The one he liked got a flower. It was weird. Maybe it was like a mating process, and that this is how humans found their beloved. Cherry was obsessed with the guy. I think his name was Bachelor or something. Another culture, clearly.

I only saw Rio casually passing by here and there. Sometimes, he was at the club checking on something. But each time, when we were in the same room, it didn't take long for our eyes to meet, and I'd lie if I said it left me cold. The opposite. The moment his sapphire eyes pierced mine, I stopped breathing for a second or two. He actually took my breath away. Shame on me.

It was strange to see him, the way he did things, handled his life. He sometimes yelled at people, rebuked them. He clearly was the boss here. Of everyone and everything. Still, it was hard for me to be afraid of him. I felt I knew him better, as if we were closer, but of course that was nonsense. I didn't know him, and I wasn't allowed to be led into anything other than that. All the feelings of security I had when I looked at him weren't real.

All these years, I had given him some character traits he didn't even have, dreamed about a man who only existed in my mind. That he didn't give me the bone, even though it was worthless to him, had hurt me. Hard to admit, but it did. But what the hell did I think he would do when he saw me, when I begged for the bone? That he would see me and recognize me, like I did? That he would love me? I was young, but I couldn't believe how dumb I've been. How should he recognize me? That man had never seen me before. I could not have been more than a ghost to him, invisible as the air. I was nothing to him and that was exactly what he had proved to me that day and ever since.

All of it made it hard for me to want to seduce him. I didn't want this kind of Rio at all. I didn't want that cold, calculating man who apparently dealt with really bad things.

While I was analyzing during the day, I was observing during the night. I'd watch the girls flirt with men, get them hot, and walk away just as they drooled. Behind the bar, the girls put on shows, they threw up their glasses, and danced on the bar, while pouring liquor into glasses or the guys' mouths. Then there was a stage and three girls—mostly Cheetah, Muffin, and Fox—danced on poles up there. They were spinning around and doing the most incredible things. I knew right away that I couldn't dance like that, for sure. Other girls went straight to the men and danced on their laps until they got a boner and then they left. I hoped that I didn't have to do that but according to Dee, the Baron gave clear orders that every man had to stay away from me. One time, I noticed him watching me while he had a business talk at the club. His eyes didn't leave me for a second. Later I guessed it was because a man tried to talk to me. Punchy led him outside at some point.

On the third day, Diva Dee decided that Cherry should teach me how to dance. For this, Dee had a—as she called it—studio in the attic with mirrors and bars on the walls. Cherry glittered from top to bottom as she led me into the studio. I had learned quickly that Diva Dee's girls were divided into two groups.

There were Cherry, Mallow, and Cheetah. This group talked to me and helped me whenever they had time, so I apparently was part of that group now. The other clique was of course led by Fox and included Muffin, Candy, and Belle. They were Fox's personal puppets, or so it seemed. And if Fox said that they should treat me like shit, well, then they did.

Cheetah, however, was lucky enough to be so impressive and loud that they didn't dare to do anything wrong to make me disappear. They definitely were planning something, but I didn't care. Not that I was afraid of the chicks, but I didn't want to go all berserk and smash their skulls. They were like annoying little creepy-crawlies. I tolerated them.

"You'll see," Cherry said and stretched before me, "everything will be all right. The boss must have a lot of faith in you, investing so much."

I raised my eyebrows and watched her put one foot on the bar and then bent down to the other one. I was in pain just watching. Why did she do that again?

"Oh, you don't know?" Cherry asked. "He pays your rent and everything. Fox is so jealous."

Of course, she was. Fox was one hell of a bitch.

"Well, you may not know this, but Fox and the boss have got this little thing going on. I don't think it's anything serious. The Loops have this stupid rule that they can't date the women in their gang, so sooner or later they end up with one of us, Dee's girls."

Great, so I'm not allowed to have anything to do with Rio? I was labeled as a gang member and not really one of Dee's girls. I wasn't even allowed to work at the club, just sipping cocktails and learning from afar how to seduce disgusting men. At first, I thought this could be helpful, since I needed to woo Rio anyway, but Dee's girls knew so much more than me, I wasn't sure how much I could implement from what they've taught me. I was so immature in comparison. Many of Dee's girls had to learn early to play with their charms. I didn't even know I had charms until recently, or that I could be found attractive in a sexual way. In Cave Town, only men hunted and I didn't fit the stereotype of a cave woman at all. So, I never really got into flirting and just spent my time with Soothie and Bory. I didn't have to grow up in the Underworld—but maybe it was about time.

I looked at Bory. He sat in the corner with his eyes closed, sleeping. Wow. What a help, once again.

Cherry sighed, stretching her arms this time. "Fox thinks she's got the boss hooked, but I don't really think so. She doesn't like the fact he's sponsoring you. He never did before.

We all had to afford the living by ourselves, work and make money. But I think it's great. Finally, someone's showing her that other girls matter too. Not just her."

"Cherry," Diva Dee buzzed in the doorway and we both flinched. She wore a metallic dress today, shining like a star. "What did I tell you about bitching?"

"Sorry," Cherry muttered, lowering her head.

"You girls always need a reminder, don't you? Well," Diva Dee said, putting a hand on one curve while pressing a finger at something in the wall, "we're gonna show you some moves now. The boss wants you to dance and move your body properly. Although it shouldn't be lap nor pole dancing. Honestly, I have no idea what he wants, girls."

Then I got the shock of my life.

Something was booming from a corner and a woman was singing! The sound was so loud I had to hold my ears.

Dee turned off the noise immediately and ran towards me, the clickety clack of her heels following her.

"Sweetheart! What's the matter with you?"

"Barbie?" Cherry squealed, hugging me. "It's just music. What's the matter? You got an earache, sweetie?"

I breathed fast and looked at Bory for help.

He rushed up, suddenly very awake. "It's music. Only it comes from speakers, like things that play it by themselves."

Music? I told him through our bond. *Music, my ass! It sounds just like Mal drumming on pots!*

"Now, cutie, I know you've been through a lot, but we've got to get this going. You know, at some point you should start making some money for us. Whatever the boss wants from you, you need to deliver," said Diva Dee and went back to the Hell Machine.

My heart was still beating fast, and I forced myself to relax again. I glowered at the machine. Music? Pfft, they had no idea about music. Nana's scratchy singing voice was a hundred times better than whatever came out of this box.

But of course, Dee dared to turn it on again and when it played, I closed my eyes for a few seconds. I could feel this music in my whole body. Everything was vibrating. The whole floor. Every second that went by, there was one knock, then a high-pitched voice sang. There were too many instruments. It was too much and I couldn't hold back a wince.

Then Cherry took me by the hands. "You know," she said softly. "Dancing is what I love most about this place. The loud music! Then I can dazzle everything. The guys. All of it! I'm having fun, and you've got to make it work. Fuck the others. Feel the beat, baby."

Feel the beat? Yep, I did, with all my pores. That music wasn't for the ears, it was apparently for the skin, or don't ask me what it was for.

"Show her the steps, Cherry," ordered Diva Dee, who leaned against the doorframe now, watching us intently.

Cherry nodded, grabbed me by the hips, and I flinched. What was she going to do now? "Well, you must always move slowly. Round movements are good, they emphasize your butt and breasts. Try to feel the rhythm and move to it. Look."

Cherry was circling her hips now, squatting down and swaying with every single body part. My eyebrows shot up to my forehead. I should do *what*? How? It seemed like her hips were kind of loose, and what she was doing with her butt was beyond me.

"Come on!" Cherry laughed, grabbing me by the hips again.

She tried to move my body to match hers, and suddenly it was just too close for me. I didn't even know her. Not really.

"Don't be so stiff. What are you? British?"

I shrugged my shoulders. No clue what that was, but she misinterpreted my gesture.

"Oh, you are? Gosh, too bad you can't speak! I love the British accent, it's so sexy!" Cherry laughed and tried to make my stiff hips go round. "Do a hollow-back, sweetie."

I glanced at her. *A what?*

"Look," Cherry pushed her back out and then back in again. "Like a snake."

I sighed and tried to imitate her. Skull, what was I even thinking? We just didn't do that sort of thing in our world. Why should we? We had court dances, which were enough. Sometimes there was a party, and a real person would sing and play real instruments—no devil machines.

"When I graduate," Cherry dreamed, throwing her hands over her head. "I'm gonna go away with my sweetheart. I swear. It's going to be amazing!"

I smiled. I kind of liked Cherry. "Are you making any progress?" Mallow asked, who stood next to the devil's machine now, of course. Where there was Cherry, there was Mallow.

"Yes." Cherry grinned and pointed to my hip, which gradually began to do something else rather than just sway back and forth jerkily.

"Moderately," mumbled Diva Dee.

"No wonder with the music you put on," Mallow sighed and tied her shiny hair into a knot. When another song came on, she came towards us and showed me some other moves. I couldn't help but laugh. The two of them were really a fun duo.

"You've got to do it this way." Mallow laughed and showed me something she called twerking. Yeah, that was really something. I'll probably never forget that. I'd dream about her ass all night long, but not in the good kind of way.

Bory giggled and looked away embarrassed. The class went on for quite a while. At some point I wanted to see Diva Dee's face when I thought I had made progress, but she wasn't there anymore. She must have figured Mallow and Cherry were enough, which I guess they were, and then, I laughed. Even though hell froze over, I laughed.

"So now turn and then jump," Mallow said, showing me how the—well, how the *pirouette* went. I shook my head. That was really too much. For what in the world would I need a pirouette? To jump in a man's face so he would know I'm interested?

"Come on, it's fun!" Cherry laughed and showed me the move again. I rolled my eyes and tried. All right. Why not? It's all screwed up anyway.

Then jumped, trying to make a turn like her but unfortunately in that exact moment I saw Rio in the corner of my eye. There he was, leaning against the door, his ankles crossed and a smile on his face as if there was no tomorrow. I nearly dislocated my head looking at him and then it happened. The most embarrassing thing ever. I stumbled and fell to the ground at full speed. Skull.

Lying on the floor like a dead fish, I closed my eyes and ran my hands over my face. When Cherry rushed over and asked if I was all right, I nodded but hell, I was not. On top of that, I heard him laughing and I couldn't help but give him an evil look. How dare he laugh at me like that! Son of a witch.

"WELL, THIS IS... PROMISING," Rio said, still chuckling.

"Oh, that's nasty, Boss!" Cherry said, helping me up and visibly trying to hold back a grin.

Damn it, my cheeks felt so hot I feared they'll burn up soon.

"She was doing pretty well before you came," Cherry tried to save the day.

"Mhm, sure." He grinned in that skulling way of his.

Oh, I really could punch him in the face right now. Like *really*. How in the world was I supposed to kiss a guy like him? Did I have to feel this stupid feeling that the queen wanted me to? Because that was so not going to happen. He was trouble and nothing more.

"Go to the club, girls. Your shift is about to start," he said. His eyes focused on me, like a predator's eyes and my mind stopped spiraling around. Suddenly all I could do was look back at him, into his handsome eyes. I realized I had never seen him smile before and he was striking. When I saw him smile, I fell into a daze and a peculiar heat flared in my stomach.

"But, Boss, we're supposed to train with her. Dee said—" Cherry tried, obviously disappointed that she had to go. She really did have a crush on me, didn't she?

"I'll handle it," he said, seemingly ignoring the astonished looks of Mallow and Cherry, who stumbled outside after a few seconds.

Meanwhile, I had crept into a corner and tried to avoid his gaze, the reality of my situation beginning to dawn on me.

"How are you?" Rio asked when they were gone, his eyes suddenly blazing and *his deep voice* curling inside of me, making my knees tremble.

Okay, I shrugged, surprised by the simple question.

Would I finally get one of his ominous assignments today?

Okay, I shrugged.

"Wonderful," he said, striding towards me.

"So, listen. A week from now, you and I are going to an event—" He glanced at my feet, as if I'd just stepped into his personal space although he approached me.

"—and I want you to seduce a man there. I'm gonna give you some more info on what he looks like and what exactly you need to do. Don't worry, you just have to flirt with him, nothing more." He took a deep breath, and I noticed him folding his fingers into a fist. "I want you to distract him, put him on the wrong trail. Are you okay with that? If you don't like it, I—"

I raised my hands, nodding, showing him that this was fine with me, but honestly, it all depended on how I had to glamour said man. If I had to twerk, I was out.

"Well," he said, still fixing me with his damned eyes, "you're gonna get a beautiful dress from me and you have to be elegant, extravagant. I need a weapon that nobody will recognize as such." Now he was getting closer again. I held my breath.

"The man is an easy target. He likes blondes." He paused as if he hated what he wanted to say next. "So, how do you get his attention?"

He stopped right in front of me, then stood silently still for some time.

Damn, his stupid eyes. It reminded me of a portal, all these different shades of blue…in contrast to his olive skin, it was so skulling special.

"You smile at him first," he said, holding my glance, a few shiny black strands of hair falling on his forehead. "Gently. Go ahead, smile at me as if you were shy, vulnerable."

I squinted my eyes.

Was he seriously teaching me how to seduce that guy? Definitely not an everyday thing. I sighed but did him the favor. I lowered my eyes and opened them again, batting my thick eyelashes, smiling shyly. Right into his face. But it wasn't just my eyes that sparkled at that moment.

Then I looked away and grinned again as if I found the situation funny. He took a deep breath at that. My stomach fluttered. I wanted to hear that sound again.

"God," he muttered under his breath, biting his lower lip. "Very good. That's how you do it. With that look you'll get him on the hook and after that, you talk to me or Punchy. I don't know yet who's going to accompany you. Pretend you don't care about this man after hooking him. Wake his hunting instincts. Smile like that once more, darling."

I didn't know why, but when he said *darling*, my whole body tingled and all the nights I had wished for him to be this close to me, to talk to me and smile at me, flashed before me like lightning. I exhaled with strain and took a few steps away from him, grinning and playing with my hair.

He twisted his lips into a crooked smile. "Yeah, start playing with your hair, give him a furtive look here and there, and then leave. To the bar, to me, he will follow you."

Apparently, we were playing a game right now, so I joined in, my skin still tickling from head to toes. Slowly, I walked challengingly to the other end of the room, as far away from him as I could.

There was a glint in his eyes and… damn, I liked the way he looked at me. The way he assessed my body while I walked, how his gaze lingered for a bit too long on my hips, my ass. Suddenly my back arched naturally. This time I didn't need Cherry to do it for me. Once I felt his gaze on me, my body did it on its own and then reality hit me hard. Because deep down, I still wanted him to like me.

"If he's with you—" Rio said, his voice echoing back in this huge room.

When I heard his footsteps I turned, pressing my back against the wall. Now, I was the one looking him up and down and I wasn't shy at all. I looked closely at every single body part he owned.

He wore black trousers and a hoodie, one of thousands of words I had learned from Bory. The white shoes flashed towards me with every step and the hoodie showed me exactly how many muscles he hid under it. I put the desire to undress him aside. What was wrong with me? Was it only me that felt this tension? Was that all part of the strange game we played or real?

"—then you turn your back to him, lean against the bar as if you didn't know he was approaching."

I turned around again, noticing my breath speeding up. Damn…I didn't even do anything, but my heart was racing like hell. I even got goose bumps once he stood behind me, and I could feel his breath on my neck. One second, I was hot, the other I was boiling. His hot respiration tingled down my wet skin and I closed my eyes, feeling his presence behind me. "You'll lift your head up and smile at him over your shoulder," Rio whispered behind me, just a hand's breadth away from me.

I did and glanced at him over my shoulder, my chest rising and falling due to my heavy breathing.

"Then he says something like, *hello beautiful* and you smile anew, no matter what he said."

I smiled and there was this glint in his eyes again, making me catch my breath.

"Touch his arm. Slowly, and then you take your hand away again. As if the touch had been purely accidental. Instinctual."

I hesitated, tilted my head, and turned, touching him gently on his forearm. Somehow, I had the feeling I had gone too far but it was exactly what he wanted. I had no need to worry, since I always wore the gloves now but still…Rio glanced at my hand that casually caressed his arm and then back at my face again and I was lost, *looking up* at *him* with a lust in *my* eyes that I couldn't wipe away.

"Let him talk you up," he said, his voice dropping to a whisper. "Touch his arm again and again, as if it were unintentionally. Laugh when he jokes, play with your hair, and let him take you out. Pretend you like what you see. Once it's done, you leave."

And just like that I turned around—slowly—never letting him out of my sight and walked back to the other side of the room again.

While striding, I looked over my right shoulder and

smiled at him. The one smile he liked best and he came towards me again as if he was no longer in control of his feet.

"Good. Just like that. Keep doing that. You'll drive him crazy."

I went to the other end of the room, fighting *the* tingling sensation building *up* and sending lightning bolts *through my* body. "Go outside. Step on the balcony. There will be one at the event. You need to go somewhere private."

I went to the mirrors.

"He'll follow you," Rio said, coming for me. "Because by then he'll have taken the bait, and when he's yours, this time, show him your front."

So, I turned and leaned against the bars, pressing my back into the soft wood once more, watching his every step. It felt like a dance. Even more so than the ones I did with the girls before.

His look flitted over my body as if he hadn't planned it and had to blame himself for not stopping. But he did stop, right in front of me. He was so close that I could feel his breath on my lips. "He will try to kiss you, but you won't let him. Push him away. Don't worry, you'll wear the gloves. Push him away, darling."

I poked him with one finger, and he smiled, took both of my hands and showed me that I should push him hard. I did, trying to not show him how dizzy his touches made me feel. He pretended to stumble back because of my push and quickly took my face in both hands.

I stopped breathing for a second.

His scent wrapped me up like a veil. Oak moss, ambergris, and musk. I would have recognized him among thousands and of course it reminded me of all those years when I cowered behind that gravestone, staring at him. How many times did I wish I knew where he lived? What kind of a man he was?

What his wishes, dreams and fears were? Too often. So often that the truth about him almost overwhelmed me.

"Then you bend your head down," he put a finger under my chin and positioned my head gently into the way he desired, "and look at him from bottom to top. Yes, exactly. Just like that. Give me the big eyes. God, your beautiful."

He focused on my lips. "Yes, *that's* how you'll look at him. As if there is no one else for you."

I swallowed. Was I looking at him like that? No, *of course* not.

"Don't, don't stop. With that look, you put an envelope into one of his pockets, and go. He'll ask you what's wrong, but you'll point to his coat pocket."

Rio then closed his eyes as if he had to rethink something, licked his lips and walked away from me as if he had to recover from something.

"That's all you have to do. Seems like you're a pro anyway. So, is that all right with you?"

I nodded, still breathing heavily.

"Fine," he said and swallowed too and I watched his throat moving gently.

"There are some black clothes in your room. Please go and put them on now. I need to find out what you can do. We'll meet outside the club at 10 pm."

I squinted my eyes together. *Why?*

"You have good back muscles, which makes me think you can climb. Let's see how good you are at it."

Oh, his smile told me he was up to no good.

CHAPTER NINE
RIO

Parkour.

I've been doing it since I was ten. Back then I didn't know that some would later do it to make cool YouTube videos. No, that's not why I jumped off bridges, climbed up fire escapes, or searched for emergency exits in my city that no one knew. I ran for my life, that's why I did it. But now I did it for the feeling. All for the feeling. The whole neighborhood became my playground.

At some point I knew exactly where every tree was, when which railing, or staircase came. Today I didn't have to think anymore. I ran. Free. Free from everything. I jumped down everywhere, not because I was thoughtless, but because I knew everything around me like my living room. When I ran, I became one with my surroundings.

I found paths that nobody in my hood knew. Escape routes that saved my life when another gang was after me, when the cops had found me. Even if I wasn't doing it for months, I could get on the walls—anytime and anywhere—as if I have some kind of muscle memory. Compare it to bicycle riding: we hop on the bike and immediately know what to do.

Doing my job, I couldn't feel the same adrenaline high. Not anymore. Sometimes my life felt like a blur, a dream. I knew that I was always on the verge of danger, but it felt wrong. Parkour didn't.

"You ready?" I asked her.

She stood in front of Dee's club like an angel in black. But she certainly was no angel. Unless she was a fallen one.

She nodded, straightening the climbing gloves that I gave her.

Barbie was still afraid to touch people without them. So, I told Dee that she had some kind of neurosis, and she should make the best out of it. As if she was contagious, what bull. The thing with Fish must have had a realistic explanation—otherwise it was not possible. As if she could kill anybody with her hands just like that.

"Well. Try to keep up then. Won't wait for you."

It was all a gamble, the thing I did tonight. Navigating urban spaces with a non-traceur. But what if she was one? I had to find out. The way she moved, the way she assessed her surroundings. Barbie was no dancer, that I knew. She had a different view on the music's rhythm. She felt it, but not the way Cherry or Diva Dee wanted her to. Her body was used to other things and maybe she was willing to use pavements more as a guideline than a rule. Perhaps. They say parkour is about fear management.

Was she a fearless one too?

While running and jumping over a park bench, I saw a fence in front of me, gripped it automatically and launched my leg on the same side as my placed hand, jumping down without thinking. Parkour was not about figuring out. It was rather about feeling. Running, jumping, balancing, climbing, and repeat.

I hopped over another railing and rolled over to reduce the force of impact. Immediately, the adrenalin rushed through my heated body. That's what it all was about. That feeling.

As I turned, I saw her jumping down the stairs too, landing on the ball of her feet like a cat in her own territory. Her body worked like a spring when she hit the ground, but she didn't allow her legs to bend below 90 degrees like a newbie would. No, she knew that it would slow her down. Crouching forward, she absorbed some impact with her delicate hands. She knew the importance of basic landing.

Yes, she was a traceuse. I knew it.

But her movements were different from mine, they were more instinctive than trained. I did the typical jumps, but she did it as if it was in her nature. She had not learned it but lived it and it made me smile proudly.

As if it was completely normal to move like that, she stood up. Her chest rose gently, and I forced myself to look away. Away from her daring curves. When she showed me how she'd seduce that asshole, I almost lost it. I couldn't explain it, but I wanted her from the moment I saw her, as if she had put a spell on me.

She cocked her head, fixing me with her dark eyes. Like she always did. Stubborn, brave, challenging. Her hair shining all white under the dull light of the streetlamp.

"Where did you learn this?" I asked, trying not to get too close to her. It threw me off balance, and I didn't like that. I couldn't like that.

She pushed her chin forward as if to ask me where *I* had learned it.

"On the street, darling."

Me too, her eyes said.

Man, how I'd love to know who she was and where she had come from. Something told me she wasn't from around here. She couldn't be. Some of her facial expressions and gestures were truly otherworldly. As stupid as it sounded, I had never

117

seen such a woman before. Not just one with her looks, but her appearance, her underlying traits.

"Come," I said, without going into any more detail.

Sometimes it was just better not to pay too much attention to what was going on around me. Tonight, it was all about running. Being free. Just once.

So, I ran again, but this time she was not behind me but next to me. I tried to ignore her radiating warmth, the sudden flashes of her sweet scent, and I kept on running until I got to the building I was searching for. I jumped and climbed and climbed, all the way up. Since the wall was made of bricks it was an easy one for me to master.

When I looked at her over my shoulder, I saw she followed my train of thought quickly.

I grinned and climbed further up. As I rammed my nails into the cold brick cracks, I smirked. They were an incredibly good base, and the windows and beams just made it easier to heave my body upwards. After a few minutes, I was at the top and felt the cool Chicago air burning on my cheeks. The smell of burnt wood and smog was mixed with the damp, fresh smell that was still stored in the concrete, even hours after it rained. Behind me, I could see the light reflecting on Lake Michigan. Beautiful. Chicago has always been way more beautiful at night.

When I turned around, she was already sitting on the other end of the roof, staring down at the Gold Coast of Chicago, the rich kids' neighborhood. My eyes widened and I blinked several times. How could she have overtaken me? Had I been so engrossed? She certainly was no ordinary girl. Well, I suspected it before, but now I knew for sure.

"So, you can climb as silent as a wraith, huh?" I asked, sitting down next to her.

She grinned.

But I knew she could do more. What else would she show

me? I was so curious. Dollar signs glittering all over her face.

"Here…" I rummaged in my backpack.

As I gave her a box, she raised her eyebrows but took it anyway. She already trusted me, and my stomach dropped. It was never good to trust a man like me.

"It's a cellphone. So, you can text me, speak with me when you must."

She stared at me, dazed, and did the little thing again, looking to her shoulder. Was that a tick?

"It's safe, don't worry. No one in my gang uses traceable phones anymore. So, no one can eavesdrop on you, no matter who you run from."

She winced and I could tell by the look in her eyes that she was really running away from someone. But who? Was she from another turf, the Black Crowns, the Taipans, the Roosters?

No matter what, whoever harmed her would feel my wrath.

She didn't seem to be impressed by the smartphone and stuffed it into the small bag I had given her. Then she looked ahead, to the city of Chicago. Glowing from afar. Huge and unpredictable. She glanced around as if she was seeing it for the first time in her life. The orange, warm light of the many rows of houses below illuminated her face and made her eyes light up with sheer enthusiasm.

"I've already saved the most important numbers: mine, Dee's, and Punchy's. You can check out the girls yourself but make sure you're always available when I need you to be."

She said nothing, even her face was expressionless now.

I tilted my head, trying to read something in her face.

What was she thinking about?

"Are you ever gonna tell me where you're from? What you need the bone for?" I asked, watching her slightly furrow her brow. Then she turned to me, holding my gaze and shaking her head with a slight pout.

A fuzzy feeling in the pit of my stomach emerged. "Well, at least I know now." I tried to hide my disappointment and stared at the rich houses bellow.

"So, you see that lighted house straight ahead?" I pointed at it. "That open window there?"

She nodded, looking closer at it.

The home was one of the many row-houses with tiny front gardens. The streetlamps barely lit the sleeping street, but she nodded. Lucky for us, governor Jenson had no curtains and lots of old-fashioned big and white Victorian windows. Freaking fool. I could see everything.

Right now, the governor of Illinois was sitting on the toilet playing a game on his iPad. Well, that made me smile. If he played Candy Crush, I'd laugh out loud, for sure.

"There's a picture in the office on the second floor... the first window on the left, can you see it?" It was a van Gogh, a lesser known one but still an original self-portrait of the red-haired painter. I didn't really like the impressionistic style, the many visible brush strokes, and the ordinary subject matter made me roll my eyes. When it came to works of art, I preferred expressionists or cubists, more extreme and offbeat. Nevertheless, the van Gogh was worth a lot to me.

"You need to steal it for me."

I heard her gasp and turned away from the red-bearded painter. She touched her throat and studied my face.

I tried to show no emotion, pretending to be cold as a stone, although I hated to ask her to steal for me. "Do you think you can do that?"

Barbie shrugged in indifference, as if it weren't even a job for her, like she was used to such questions. Was she a thief? Could it be? Was that why she could climb like a wild cat and ran from seemingly important people?

"Have you ever stolen anything?"

She tipped her head back and laughed and I joined her. Oh

well, then she really knew her way around. My instincts never betrayed me.

"How good are you? Can you do it unnoticed?"

She smiled once more, rolled her eyes, and nodded.

That's a cinch, her sparkling eyes told me.

I smiled. "Alright. I'll tell you when to steal it. I need to plan it properly first. Before that we have to do other things, remember the route we took." I pointed to his bathroom. "You'll enter from there and don't worry. That neighborhood is neutral. It's not owned by any of the Chicago gangs. It's where the preppy kids live."

She looked at the route for a second or two and seemed to already know how it worked. My interest increased with every glance. Did I just stumble on an ace thief? Just like that? Ready to work for me without a way back?

"The idea that you can't tell anybody anything reassures me immensely," I said, simply because I didn't want to go back yet.

She made a face and played with her fingers.

Normally I would stand up now, go home and work. But something held me back. I wanted to talk to her. Funny, given the fact she actually couldn't.

"Do you need anything? With Dee, I mean. You want me to get you anything?"

She looked at me like she was studying me. What was she seeing? Something about her was uncanny but I just couldn't figure her out. It was like I knew her. Did I? No. I didn't.

She had no need for anything or anybody, so she shook her head.

"That thing with your hand, that was just a coincidence, wasn't it? Has that ever happened to you?"

She studied her hands and sighed.

I winced slightly. My question made her uncomfortable. Then she took out the note and pencil from her backpack and wrote something down. I wondered why she didn't just take out her new smartphone. After all, it was ready. I even charged it. Funny. Me all caring.

I'm cursed. If I ever touch you with my bare hands, you will die. Everyone will.

I read it and was about to laugh when I saw her eyes. Deadly serious. Did she really believe that kind of stuff?

"Oh, come on. There's no such thing as a curse."

She shrugged like she didn't care if I believed her or not.

"Barbie, it's just not possible. Did you press anything on Fish that would kill him point blank, like in Kill Bill?"

She looked at me like she didn't have the faintest idea what I was talking about.

"Well, you know, the movie. Kill Bill," I said.

She shook her head and my eyebrows shot up in disbelief. She didn't know the movie? "Where did you grow up? On the moon?" God, or maybe I was just old.

She didn't laugh.

"Sorry but you just can't kill people by simply touching them."

She tore the note from my hand and wrote something down again.

If you'd rather be stubborn, okay, go on. Don't believe me even though I'm telling you the truth. But if I touch someone, they die. Every time. So, I am not going to do that for you. That painting? I'll get it, don't care. But my hands are a no-go. Okay?

Huh, she was funny. What would I give to hear her say that paragraph out loud? At that moment I imagined her voice. What did she sound like? Was her voice high-pitched? Melodic? Deep, smoky? I didn't know and probably never would. But the way she spoke or well, wrote to me was really refreshing. She was smart. Witty and bold and probably didn't know all the stories about me or our gang. If so, she wouldn't talk to me like that.

A girl like her wouldn't normally dare to come near me, or

even look me in the eye. When they see me, they try to avoid my glance and pray I don't follow them. Well, I liked her way of challenging me. Maybe I shouldn't, but I did. So, I grinned and indicated to her that we were leaving.

"We'll see about your hands. But it's better to use your little trick more than once."

She shook her head as if she didn't agree.

When we had firm ground under our feet again, I thought of something else and grabbed her wrist, stopping her from running home.

"Barbie. One more thing. Did you learn how to defend yourself? From men?"

She looked at me for a few seconds. She often did that, as if she had to translate my words first. Then she nodded.

I took a step back. "Try it. On me."

She raised her eyebrows, shaking her head.

"You're wearing your gloves, stop being a chicken. Try and defend yourself against me. I need to know what you can do. *How* I can use you. If you need a babysitter or not."

She grunted and folded her arms.

"Fine, you don't want a babysitter and I don't want to play one. So, show me what you can do." I smirked. "What if I want to steal your backpack, huh? What do you do then?"

I walked up to her and tried to rip the strip of the backpack off her shoulder, but she blocked and spun around me. All of a sudden, I found her on a completely different side. I laughed, impressed. "You're fast, I've seen that in your little dance lessons, but are you strong as well?"

I jerked my wrist from her grip. She crouched and surprised me by popping back up, driving her knee into my gut. I swung at her, but she caught my arm and twisted it behind my back. Fuck, that really did hurt. Then she was behind me and had me into the headlock. I chuckled.

"Barbie, I *am* stronger than you. I could grab you and

throw you on the floor. Don't try me."

She smiled above me, her sweet scent wrapping me up. We locked eyes, and all at once I was very aware of her body. Her perfect body touching mine. We just stared at each other for a few heartbeats, her eyes telling me she was indeed faster than me and would never let me outdo her. I wriggled out of her grip.

"All right, I like that you can fight back. But I will always take the blows aimed at you, understand?"

The moment I said it, I realized something. I went too far. I told her I don't want to be a babysitter and there I was. Caring for her—although she wasn't even in danger. How would I react if she were? I had to be clear in my head and I was no longer sure if I could handle it when she was with me. I stepped back, suppressing all the feelings her sudden closeness caused me. "Do you know how to use a knife?" I cleared my throat. "In case the little trick with your hands doesn't work?"

She pushed her chin forward again and I didn't need a translation. *Yeah*, she knew how to handle stabbing weapons.

"Good. Shoot. Can you shoot?"

She winced, apparently not knowing what I wanted from her.

"Guns?" I pretended to have guns in my hands and shot at her with my index fingers. "Pow, pow."

She studied me as if she wanted to find out if I'd gone nuts and bananas. Then she shook her head, irritated by my gesture. She had no clue about guns…but weapons? Honestly, where the hell did she grow up?

I turned around. I had to go home, distance myself from her. "Punchy will show you. You need some basic skills. Around here, everybody carries a gun or two, and there's always a pair of knives in our underpants. But I'm impressed. You'll be a terrific addition to our operation. I have no doubt at all." At this point, I only doubted myself.

CHAPTER TEN
RIO

"Are you ready?" I asked as she got into my car.

She shrugged and so I just drove off.

She was always a bit reserved at first when we didn't see each other for a while, but it was better that way. Although avoiding her wasn't as easy as I wanted it to be. After that parkour session I had to rush home and lay hands on myself…that night I swore I was going to avoid her, stay away because I couldn't let her cloud my brain. The following weeks were too important to mess up. So, I was going to send Slappy today, but couldn't in the end.

Weak? Yes.

Whenever I thought she was just a woman like any other, she aroused my interest anew. Just like her background checks did because they revealed nothing about her. Nothing at all. Her fingerprints simply did not exist, nowhere. She had never had a passport made, never been to a doctor, to a hospital, to school, to an airport, or whatever. It was like she didn't even exist, as if she were a ghost. I took her fingerprint, not just a photo, her individual fingerprint…that was weird.

I mean, technically I was dead too, but if the FBI or the

DEA ever got my fingerprints again, that was it. Then they knew that I didn't die when I was eighteen like I made them believe. So, how could she not have a fingerprint or even a tiny bit of evidence that she was alive? To delete the documents from the police database or archives was one thing, but to delete oneself from the minds of the people, so that there were no photos or any proof of being in this world was quite an achievement and I had to find out how the fuck she had done that.

But all of it meant I could make her be any person I wanted her to be. She was a nobody. To protect her perfectly unknown face, I asked her to wear one of Dee's wigs today. She chose blood red.

I needed to buy her some clothes today to shape the identity I wanted her to have, make her come alive. It intrigued me more than I wanted to admit. So, today the Dutch Beauty arrived in Chicago, bitches.

I drove us to one of my favorite outfitters, one who was regularly supported by the Loops. Meaning that there would be no blabbering, as hush money was the best kind of money.

As we entered, my tiny friend Leonardo was already grinning broadly, sliding the yellow glasses over the bridge of his broad nose. I didn't come often, but when I did, I left him a fortune.

His shop was a blend of Victorian architecture mixed with a modern style. A collection of dark wood, iron, and sculptures that could be called either art or rubbish, depending on the judge. The smell of old furniture, polish wax, and vanilla was everywhere, and I couldn't help but smile. This man knew me from the start. From the very bottom.

Inside, Barbie was allowed to take off her wig, making Leonardo almost freak out with joy.

"Oh, I have so many dresses for you waiting to be tried on!" he squealed.

When he took her measurements, he babbled away without even trying to take a breath. She looked at me as if she was planning on killing me. Ha, I knew she wanted to do something else. She wasn't into dresses at all.

Well, darling, not everything is all beer and skittles.

"We need a dress for Friday," I said as I saw her nostrils flare and grinned sheepishly. "Leonardo, I need three ball gowns and two rich ass looks. Can you do that?"

He nodded. "Oh, I can do everything with her!"

Leonardo pulled Barbie into his backroom, where he had the special clothes for his best customers. I waited in one of the blue velvety vintage chairs that stood right by the entrance, preparing myself for a good show. I'd love nothing more. Although I maybe didn't look like it, I had a preference for decent clothing and color-coordinated looks. I probably got that from Alba. She never went out without being styled from head to toe. But in my everyday life, I wore clothes that didn't stand out, in which I would be stereotyped and judged by first sight. A hoodie, jeans, sneakers in the colors of my gang: red, black and white. *Pride goes before destruction, and a haughty spirit before a fall*, was my mantra, stolen from the Lord's words.

But that didn't mean I didn't have other clothes in my closet. I only let people see what they wanted to see. A club owner, who slowly started to invest his profits in real estate, shuffling more money year by year. Living the American Dream. Not a millionaire controlling drug sales in Chicago. Although I was both.

"Doesn't she look like an angel?" Leonardo cried, tiptoeing on his tiny feet, making me smirk.

But damn, when she came out, I had to exhale a long breath. She was wearing a black dress that clung to her pretty curves, making me think of a lot of stuff I didn't want to think about. Or maybe I wanted to but knew that it was more than stupid. I pressed my lips together and curled my fingers into a fist. There was no such a thing as love or belonging for a man like me. Never.

"Turn," I said, watching her closely.

She rolled her eyes, whirled, and showed me her back. Assessing the tiny strips of her dress, the high stilettos, the heart-shaped decolletage. I drew out a long breath before pressing a fist to my mouth. I was fucked.

Yes, that's how the Dutch Beauty would perform. Like this and no other. I nodded at Leonardo in an appreciating way, glad about the opportunity to stop marveling at her and thank God, he disappeared into the back with Barbie in tow. I needed to calm down. Since when was I this weak?

Taking another deep breath, I checked the clock, realizing we didn't have long until Z-Mexx should be finished with the appointment with the governor. I knew that the bastard would make more deals, it sucked for him that I had my eyes and ears everywhere.

"You need to see this!" I heard Leonardo before I saw him.

I lifted my eyes and Barbie came out again, shyly at first, but she straightened the moment she felt my gaze on her.

Leonardo opened her ponytail and straightened her hair so that it fell over her right shoulder. This dress was red, and I was sure she would be remembered by everyone who saw her like that. Perfect. It was perfect. She was perfect.

"Oh, I have a coat to match," Leonardo said, clapping and walking away, leaving Barbie and me alone.

She looked at me now, her hips swaying with every step while she strode towards me. I curled my fingers into fists again. Fuck. She had learned quickly, I had to give her that. Tilting her head, she stopped right in front of me.

Do you like what you see? her eyes asked me.

Yes, mine told her.

She came closer until she stood between my legs, the silky fabric of her dress rubbing against my knees.

"Barbie," I said, not sure what I wanted to say but I had to keep her away from me. My mind already tricked me, telling me that I could fuck her once. Just once. Telling me it wouldn't matter and help us to get rid of the tension. But thank God I knew better, knew there would be feelings after. Sex clouded the brains, made everything worse. It was a tale as old as time.

She lowered her gaze, and her gloved fingers stroked my arm. I leaned into the chair and our eyes locked. When she bent down, I took a breath and Leonardo screamed for her.

I silently thanked him.

God, I was weak.

AFTER LEONARDO SHOWED her some more variations, he went back to the fitting room and put on a killer business outfit we chose for her.

"Leonardo," I said with feigned kindness, leaning against his counter and watching him writing the bill. He made a mistake while counting the prices, but I didn't care, I would have tipped him generously anyway. "You play golf with the cook from Big Al Cortez once in a while, don't you?"

Leonardo's smile was nipped in the bud, and when he looked at me, his mouth was hanging open.

"Baron, sir," he stuttered. "I—I would never say anything about you. Ever! I wouldn't know what to tell them! You only buy clothes from me. Nothing else."

That was the point. A cook could see a lot more than his boss's dress size. It was strange that Cortez hadn't fired his chef long ago, considering who he was hanging out with. But as I said, for some of them money was everything, so everything else seemed less important. Capitalism always affected the brain at some time. Therefore, they didn't even give a shit about the mouse in their own house.

"Of course, Leonardo," I said, giving him a smile that showed him my teeth all too well. "I would never say it was any different. It would be a shame if something happened to your business or your boyfriend, wouldn't it?" I picked my nails. "What's Philip doing again? He likes to paint, doesn't he? Pity if he couldn't do it anymore…"

Leonardo seemed to take my hint and nodded one too many times for my taste. That's why he was my outfitter, because he was easily scared. I didn't even need to do something. Threatening him was more than enough, even if I was bluffing. I grinned at the beads of sweat along his long forehead.

"Well, finally some common sense here. So, take this." I placed a generous wad of bucks on his counter and saw Leonardo's throat jump at the sight of it.

"This, this is far too much, Baron," he said, shaking his head. "I can't—"

"No, not for your service, Leonardo. It will never be too much for that. Besides, I think you deserve a second floor here, don't you think?"

His breathing became faster, and he looked at the bundle once again, trying to count how many bills there were.

"If you go golfing with your cook again…do you think you could let something slip a little, just a little?"

I stared him down. His eyes and mouth twitched, and I feared he was about to lose it any moment. So, I gave him a few seconds to gather his wits and glanced over my shoulder to the fitting room, seeing Barbie's slender ankles underneath the red curtain, brushing against each other as she stepped into the skirt. My mind played me again as I saw her standing behind the curtain. Naked, brushing her hands against her thighs, moaning because of me—

"No, Baron," stuttered Leonardo, making me look at him again, stopping my stupid thoughts. He still didn't understand what I really wanted from him. "I would never—never do that!"

"Even if I asked you politely to?"

Leonardo held still, trying to find out if I tried to trick him. It wasn't so far-fetched. However, I sighed and started again. "The woman in the back is known as the Dutch Beauty. Why don't you tell your cook that she just walked into your little shop and bought some really expensive dresses? Nothing more. Just a teeny tiny bit of information. Of course, you're not mentioning me—just her. The Dutch Beauty, you understand?"

I pushed the money a little closer towards him and raised my eyebrows expectantly. Slowly but surely, he nodded. When Barbie came out of the fitting room, prepped in a pencil skirt, with a white blouse and high heels, I looked at him once more and knew he wondered who she really was.

"The Dutch Beauty," I said firmly and beamed as he reached for the money. Like I said, whoever had money here was king. It's very simple.

Later, when Barbie and I were sitting in my car again and had a long drive ahead of us, I explained the next job to her.

"I'm gonna drop you off in front of the row house we creeped on last night, you go to the door and wait there until a man comes out, you pretend you didn't expect him, look startled and then when he's gone, you'll leave too. All right?"

She looked at me with a deep scowl on her face.

"You don't have to do anything else. Just this. Walk, look, and leave. Easy, isn't it?"

She rolled her eyes but nodded. Luckily, she didn't ask for anything else. I couldn't have told her the reason anyway. At the stage we were at, I couldn't take any chances. No confidants.

As we arrived at the Gold Coast neighborhood, I asked Barbie to get out and walk towards the governor's house.

I drove on, watching her in the rearview mirror. She hesitated at first, but then she went straight to the house with the snow-white facade and the bushes in the tiny front garden. The street was tree-lined, with big, black lanterns and the trees themselves fenced with fancy iron railings. Everything was clean and looked after.

Normally Jenson commuted between Springfield and Chicago two or three times a week, because the governor actually had to live in the governor's Mansion of Illinois, which could not be surpassed in decadence. But since Jenson's wife didn't want to move away from Chicago and he had unfinished business here in town, he split up. Something seemed to be up with the mansion in Springfield though, because until now there was hardly a governor who really liked living there. Maybe it was because they all had too much money to live in a city like Springfield. Who knew?

When I turned into the alley, I parked my car on the side and waited, wondering when the time would come when she would ask me why she had to do these strange things for me. There would be some more jobs like that, but she didn't seem to care for what I did. So, I was curious when she would start to.

Then I saw a little boy from the corner of my left eye and lost it.

CHAPTER ELEVEN
LYNNE

"What does this guy want from me, Bory?" I asked, stomping angrily in the direction of the side street where Rio was waiting for me.

Bory shrugged. "Looks like you're a pawn in his game."

I snorted. What was the point of running into an old dude who looked at me as if I were a ghost after our encounter? Which, theoretically, I probably was, but still, it didn't make any sense. How was that supposed to be a job?

"I wouldn't give too much of a skull about it, Lynne. If that's truly all you have to do, then who cares? It's an easy job, don't you think?" Bory said. "We need something easy right now."

"Easy," I grunted. "Who knows what I'm really doing here, Bory. Fortunately, I don't care about humans that much. Although, I'd like more information about his objectives, what if his machinations hurt others?"

"Nah, I don't know. Maybe you shouldn't stick your nose into his things all too much. Just do what he wants, try to lure him in all the while and take advantage of the moment. After, we steal the bone from him, search the book and return home,"

Bory said, trailing after me. I grinned a little. He looked so funny in this human daylight. A bright, little, blue furry ball, hopping on a street.

Even though I depended on Rio, I wasn't so sure if I really had to go through with everything. Just like that? He could at least give me an explanation of what he's planning, what I was being used for.

Rio and his world confused me far too much. I didn't even have time to take a proper look at these beautiful houses here, how cute the little fences and trees were, the colorful flowers which started to sprout. It was *so* nice here.

"I know you all too well, Lynne. So, I'll say this only once," Bory started. "You have to enchant him, Lynne. He must want to kiss you. So, for your soul's sake, try. Please try it and don't mess it all up again, let's just do whatever he wants and use him. We don't have much time left. I wouldn't stress this much if it weren't for you!"

I sighed. "Yes, Bory. I know and I love you for it. Did you see how he looked at me at Leonardo's? I almost got the kiss, I think."

"Yes, you did great, but I'm not sure if the time is right, if we got what the queen wants," Bory said, hopping over a manhole.

Enchanting him was difficult.

I tried at that weird clothing shop to charm him like Cherry and Fox did with all the men in the club. For a moment I was sure that he liked it, that he wanted what he saw, but nothing happened. Nothing. As usual, we just looked at each other and Bory was right.

So, how did I get him to feel that desire that the queen wanted?

Maybe it was a dead end.

Of course, I could have pressed my lips against his. But what if he didn't feel the emotions the queen wanted? I was scared and backed away. What if I'd kiss him and he didn't want it and never would after? I had to wait for that moment, the moment of lust, and it was not there yet. So, what did I have to do to change that? I really didn't know, mainly because I wasn't very motivated either. I wanted to kiss the Rio that I'd imagined all these years, not this brutal—

Maniac!

Yes, this man was a maniac! When I turned the corner and saw him, I knew that kissing Rio was going to be the hardest thing of all. There he was, pressing a little boy against the wall. The boy cried and trembled under his rough grip. I clenched my hands to fists, storming towards him. Rage boiled its way up into my throat and I struggled to take a deep breath.

"Lynne, what are you doing? Stop!" Bory shouted after me, but at that moment I didn't care about anything.

I only cared about this boy who needed my help. Children had always been special to me. Maybe it had something to do with the fact that I had ended up in the Underworld as a child —a very rare circumstance—or perhaps because I helped Nana raise the stranded children. I don't know.

In my world, children were special, important, and above all, to be protected. So, even with the best will in the world, I couldn't watch him traumatize this little boy any further. Since I had no weapon at the moment, the only option I had left was to take off my shoe and hit him in the back of the head with its heel. And that's what I did, at full pace.

Rio cried out, dropped the boy at once and turned around with his fist raised, his jaw clenched, and the brows furrowed. But when he noticed me, his frantic expression changed to curiosity. He immediately lowered his fist, glancing at the shoe I still clasped like a weapon. Rio's breathing turned noisy, and his eyes cold, hard, and flinty.

"What the fuck?" he said, holding his elbows wide from his body.

Without thinking I raised my shoe once more, threateningly, and shoved myself in front of the boy.

"I," Rio started, rubbing the back of his head, and searching for words. When he drew his hand towards his face, it was covered with blood. Yes, my punches were never weak.

"There will be consequences," he spat.

I wasn't sure if Rio talked to me or the boy, but he tried to push me away, gentle but still. I reared up in front of him like a mama bear defending her cub. Rio's look hardened at my behavior, fingers flexing and veins throbbing in his temples. I knew he was checking all kinds of scenarios in his mind right now and none of them ended well for me. But I refused to back away, even as my heart shattered into pieces in my chest.

I held his gaze, showing him that I wouldn't let him see or hurt the cub anymore.

His expression grew stony. "Well, now you are hiding behind her. Brave one, aren't you? Real brave," Rio said to the boy but his eyes never mine. "Get out of here, and if I catch you again, I'm going to visit you at home myself."

I felt the boy trembling behind me, so I turned and stroked the back of his head, giving him a smile. He was so slim. His skin a light bronze, and his hazelnut eyes thanked me for saving him.

The boy forced himself to smile and then ran away.

Before I could turn back to Rio, my feet were lifted from the ground. Rio swung me over his broad shoulders and slapped my ass. Not gentle at all. I wanted to cry out at the sting of pain, but his hand lingered a second too long on my body, sending a wave of heat through me. I closed my eyes and the pain I felt seconds ago mellowed into a sweet delight. When he took his hand away, I quickly suppressed any hint of pleasure.

That skulling bastard.

He dragged me towards his car, and I tried to scream, but I

couldn't make a sound. Of course, all attempts were nipped in the bud. Then I freaked out and drummed with my fists on his back.

"Try this once more, Barbie," he said with a deep voice, his touch firm on my lower legs, "and I'll do things with you that are far worse than the mess you got yourself into. A lot worse than spanking your fucking nice butt."

All I wanted to say to him now was: *Try. Try to be worse than the Blood Queen, you arrogant skullhole.*

THE NEXT TWO days I didn't see or hear a thing from Rio or the Baron or whatever. I must have really pissed him off. Bory scolded me for hours at Dee's for my stupidity, but I didn't care. It was just not OK what he had done to this kid. I had to do something.

Only later had it occurred to me that I might have skulled my plan. How could I kiss him now? I couldn't bring myself to do it…never.

So, instead of battling with Rio again, Punchy and Slappy —apparently the only guys Rio trusted enough to work with me instead—stood outside my door and abducted me. Well, not really abducted, but they took me in one of those cars and drove away. Like usual, no one told me where we were going.

Punchy glanced at me through the rearview window, shifting in his driver's seat. Apparently, he hadn't quite forgotten the Fish accident yet. He treated me differently from that day on. He flinched when I touched him, shivered when I neared him, like I was some kind of poltergeist, or worse.

They took me to a place they called a shooting range and put a *pistol* in my hand. I learned how to pull the trigger and oh boy, those things were legit. Luckily we didn't have them in the

Underworld, or things down there would be worse than they already are. Well, somehow, I thought it was a shame too. I could have threatened everyone with this kind of weapon. I should steal one and take it with me.

As soon as I had the pistol in my hand and knew how it worked, I couldn't stop grinning and bounced from one foot to the other. Punchy told me that it was called a 9mm pistol and had a hand grip on the side to eject the magazine. There was something in it that was called a magazine and I learned how to fill it and lock it in place again. Amazing.

Then Punchy showed me how to secure the pistol and I had to do it hundreds of times. Lock, unlock, lock. He lectured me over and over again on how dangerous guns could be and if I couldn't secure it properly, it could just fire without me wanting to. So, I always had to secure it. To get the weapon ready to fire, I had to pull the slide to its rearmost position and release it to chamber a round.

"Now try to align your eyes with the sights and the target. But be careful there's a recoil," Punchy said, holding my back as if I were going to fall backwards. Oh boy, that thing really was incredible, and I loved it! It was dangerous and so was I.

I wanted to try and shoot these signs at the shooting range all day long. At the beginning I was so bad, I couldn't hit anything, stomping like a toddler and then, when I hit a target for the first time, I jumped and hugged Punchy, who of course pulled a face. Idiot. I glanced at him the same way as I felt, and he forced himself to laugh. He assured me that it was only because of my scary hands.

Scary hands? What a big baby that mountain of a guy was.

Afterward, Punchy took me back to Dee and told me he had to collect the money from all the treasurers of all the hundreds of gang cells and wouldn't be able to accompany me tomorrow to the shooting range. So, it would just be me and Slappy. Great. I liked Punchy—despite his exaggerated anxiety

—better than Slappy. A lot better, actually. When I found out Slappy was with Cherry, my jaw nearly dropped. Slappy and Cherry? Terrible! Slappy barely talked and all he did was frown like a dwarf.

In the evening I had to go to the club with the girls as usual. I wore a pink wig and a short white dress and sat at the bar, bored like hell. As always, I wasn't allowed to interact with the people here and had to watch the girls work over and over again. At some point I knew what was going on here. In the back room they sold things that didn't seem to be legal, the alcohol was diluted down with water to make more profit, and the aim was to make the men spend all their money.

Then things got worse, because Rio came in, with a man in tow, who he probably forced some kind of deal on. Our gaze met the moment he set foot inside the club, but this time, I shot daggers at him. Unexpectedly, he twisted his handsome lips into a wide smile, making me scowl even more. He really knew how to make my blood boil.

"Barbie," Cherry leaned over the bar counter towards me. "Don't punish him like this."

I gave her a confused look. *Punish?*

"I know what happened. Slappy told me you protected a boy from Baron, or tried to," she said with her light, calm voice. Her doll eyes immediately put me at ease. I don't think anyone could look at Cherry and be mad. She was kindness personified.

But what else did Slappy tell her? Did *the boss* tell her he had violated a kid?

"You might want to know that this boy was about to rob a house and fire at innocent people…"

What? I furrowed my brows, looking at her. *That was a little kid!*

Cherry sighed. "In Chicago, even kids do terrible things, Barbie. Especially boys without a father or a person to talk some sense into them. The boy is twelve. A lot of kids start a lot of shit at that age. The boss had seen what he had in mind and cut him down to size. His father was a Loop, so the Baron had to do it. You know, he sometimes seems brutal, but he's not, not really. He's the best thing that could have happened to us. To all those kids in the Loops' turf. He set up so many places where they could go and play instead of doing stupid stuff. He wants to make a difference for them."

Could that be true, or had Rio brainwashed her?

I glanced over at the table where he was sitting. Punchy and Slappy were right behind him, his protectors, counselors, and oldest friends. He shook his head, disagreeing with his counter-part. Then Rio seemed to sense that I stared at him and looked over his shoulder, right at me. The blank expression on his face faded as our eyes locked. My heart skipped a beat, and I quickly avoided his damned eyes. If only my whole body didn't tingle every single time he looked at me.

"He may have done some fucked up shit, but he has a good heart, Barbie, and he seems to like you. Give him a break, huh?"

I gave Cherry the benefit of the doubt. I didn't care if he was good or bad. For Hell's sake I was an Underworlder. We were *all* bad! But I had made so many bad decisions lately, that I was starting to question myself, my thinking, my actions, my morality. But it was probably not the right time to develop a conscience, was it? Plus, it was hard to resist a bad boy who was a good man.

Cherry gave me a drink and I gulped it down.

Why was it suddenly so important to me what Rio was doing, what kind of man he had become? I couldn't care less!

More deaths? Piece of cake.

Substances that made people dumbstruck? Whatever.

Still, I was kind of... foiled. Disappointed at what he had become. I was angry because I wanted him to be a good man despite all of this skulling dichotomy and I was angry at him for not being that way, angry at me for wanting him to be different.

But was it really my place to judge? No.

I wasn't allowed to judge at all. I had already killed two people in this world.

"If the boss hadn't taught that boy a lesson," Cherry pulled me back on track, staring me down with her dark eyes, "he might be in juvie by now, so get this straight."

I nodded, watching my fingers clasping the empty glass.

I wanted to like him, I really did. Maybe I wanted to like him too much, and that was the problem after all. I checked on him again, as he was gesturing strongly and giving the man an envelope. Tomorrow, I had to do the second job for him. I had to do what we rehearsed in Dee's studio and slip the same kind of envelope to another man.

So, what was in it?

Money?

But for what? Was this how he made his crimes disappear?

A few hours later, I went up to my room and played with the cell phone that Rio had given me a few days earlier on our nightly trip. Cherry had to show me how the thing worked. Neither Bory nor I could figure it out.

But writing on it was even harder. At first, I watched the girls and the gang members using their phones. Everybody had one of these in their pockets, and they wrote with their thumbs. So skulling quick! It was maddening. So, the other night, Cherry had seen me with this thing in the afternoon, fumbling like an idiot and hissing at it. She laughed when she realized that I didn't know how it worked.

"Of course, this is new to you." She grinned and sat next to me on the bed. "You don't have anything like that with the Amish, do you? Strange growing up like that, huh? Well, not that I had it any better or anything. Oh, forget what I said. It was rude. Sorry, sweetie! Shall I show you how to use it?"

Again, I couldn't understand what she was saying. *Bory, what are the Amish?* I'd asked. He'd shrugged back.

Bory loved Cherry. Apparently, she smelled special and sweet, and he loved her scent. Whenever she was with me, he would stick to her side. Creepy guy. Fortunately, she didn't notice her suitor.

Cherry had explained everything to me. Like really all of it. She'd talked so fast I had to concentrate really hard. This phone thingy could do so much and there were some things I had to ignore... pictures, videos... What the skull? I'd asked her to show me how to write, that had to be enough for now, maybe I would check the rest like internet and streaming sometime, but not yet. At the moment everything was too much anyway. It was a total sensory overload. Everywhere I looked there were new things, words, phrases, looks, colors, sounds. Most of the time I stood there with my mouth hanging open.

And tonight, I was playing with my phone, trying to under-stand it better and then, oh skull, then I did a thing.

"Oh skull. Oh skull. Bory!"

"What, what? What happened?" he squealed from the food of my bed, where he already had curled up, ready to fall asleep.

I dropped the phone immediately. How could that even happen? I did nothing! Just held it!

"What did you do?" Bory asked and hopped to the smart-phone on the floor. "Oh."

I buried my face in my hands. "Yeah. I wrote him a letter. Rio! What should I do now?" My heart was racing and the way Bory was looking at me right now, all the blood must have been drained from my face.

"Well, at least it makes sense," Bory tried, still reading my text. "And it's not called a letter but a message. You wrote *hi*. Good one."

The blood drained out of my face. "Hi? Skull! Bory…"

"It could be worse. You could have sent him a stupid photo. It can happen, so relax."

I rushed up, walking up and down my small room. What was I even doing here? I was so out of place! So skulling out of place!

"That thing!" I yelled, pointing at the phone. "Let's throw it away now. It's the devil himself."

Then there was a ping and Bory and I were both standing there as if struck by lightning.

"Skull," we said simultaneously.

I rushed back to my smartphone and huddled over it. My hands started shaking and I stared at the glowing thing, my mouth dry as the desert.

He had written back.

You miss me? So, no brooding anymore?

My heartbeat immediately sped up

"Bory, what do I do now?" I said, staring at the message, fingers trembling and nausea threatening to overtake me. Skull, I really didn't know what to think anymore. *Miss him?* What made him think that and what was that stupid picture next to his text?

"That's a *smiley*, Lynne. I watched Cherry using them like emotions. There are a lot of symbols for a lot of variations. But be careful, the large purple vegetable is a symbol for dick!"

"Bory!" I hissed.

By the Dead, these humans were awkward. "Stop talking so filthy. I won't send him something like that! I won't use such *smileys* ever!"

For sure not. Not if they had such meanings. I just needed to kiss him, nothing else.

"Won't you write him back?" Bory asked, all nosey again.

"No, of course not. What was he even thinking? Missing him."

"Lynne, you need to attract him, forgot that?"

I grunted.

Skull. That was so skulling stupid! All of it! Everything I had to do here. Maybe I should just quit and go back. Perhaps being a slave to the Blood Queen wasn't that bad at all… Ah, who was I kidding? That was the worst thing ever. Stepping out of my comfort zone meant more to me at the moment than ever before.

After five minutes I was still holding the cell phone in my sweaty hands, walking up and down my room. Bory's eyes were following my every step.

"What am I going to write him back, though? What is this all about? *Do you miss me*, my ass. What an idiot. I don't even know him—how can I miss him?"

Yeah, I was babbling and Bory smiled at it. I really wanted to punch him in the face right now. Such a stupid grin.

"Maybe he's flirting with you, Lynne? He likes you. Already told you that."

I snorted.

Bory held back another grin. "Hmm, maybe write something like—"

I waved Bory off and decided to write the truth.

I just pressed the wrong keys. Don't flatter yourself, I wrote.

Then I was about to put the phone down when I got another message. Wow, those things were fast! It was creepy. Like a spell.

I don't know where you're from, but hi sounds exactly like 'I miss your sexy ass' to me, he wrote.

What? I dropped the phone again.

"Stop that," Bory squealed. "You're going to smash it!"

I ignored my little furball's outburst and spoke to him instead. "What's wrong with him, Bory? I don't get it."

Bory read our messages and smiled again. "Well. Flirting. I told you so."

"I hate it when you say that." I quickly grabbed the phone again and started typing.

Don't you have that stupid rule that says you're not allowed to flirt with me? I'm a gang member. Forgot about it? I wrote.

Who's talking about flirting, darling? You miss me, not the other way around. I didn't text you, did I?

I was puffing. That son of a witch!

Maybe I miss your face but that's about it, I wrote back.

Liar, he texted.

Fine, your butt is okay, too. The corner of my mouth kicked up.

My abs feel bullied, he wrote with a winking smiley.

Erm, what? "It doesn't make sense, really. That guy's insane," I told Bory but didn't look away for one second from his messages.

They're arrogant. Just like you. I wrote back, faster this time.

Okay this one's on you, but I guess it's about time to say sorry, don't you think?

For what?

Your dirty mouth and hitting me with a fucking shoe.

Not going to happen, creeper, I wrote back. Arrogant bastard.

Yeah, flirting was definitely my thing. By the Stix, shouldn't I lure him in and not drive him away farther? I facepalmed myself. I was a mess. But he triggered such aggression in me. He was obnoxious. I really had to change my tactics, or I would never get the kiss.

My phone buzzed and I looked at his message.

You're the creeper. You miss me even though we've only known each other for a week, he wrote.

I don't miss you. Didn't you realize you were the reason I left the club today? Doesn't sound like missing you to me, I wrote back. Okay, okay, I would change my tactics tomorrow. Today was skulled anyway.

The way you looked at me today told me everything. The way your eyes searched me in the club. No need to deny it. But I am glad that you came to your senses again, Rio wrote.

Likewise, Baron, I wrote back.

Fox will bring you your dress tomorrow. Sometime in the evening. Come to me when you're dressed. Need something nice to look at.

Oh no, not Fox. Not her!

Good Night, Bone Thief, he added.

Good Night, Baron, I wrote back.

But I had anything but a good night.

Now I was more awake than ever and decided it wasn't a night to sleep. My thoughts wouldn't leave me alone. Again and again, I remembered that I still didn't know which book I had to bring back to the queen. I thought about the envelope I had to give to that unknown man. And last but not least, I thought about Rio flirting with me today. He *was* flirting! Sending me kinky texts and kinky smileys!

Eventually, I found myself climbing out of my window. I decided I had to do something. Just something. I hated to wait for the Blood Queen and the days that went by without me doing anything went to my head. So, I ran back to the cemetery.

Honestly, it was a bummer for me to learn the place I visited each year was something like a human burial ground. It was so strange that humans buried their dead. I guess, that's how they must have found their way to us. People buried their skeletons and at some point, there were so many that they piled up on our ceiling. It had to be that way, right? There was no other way to explain it. Maybe the Bone Queen had more to do with it, because I had no clue how there were magical and non-magical bones.

Anyway, I found out there was no way back into my world at all. There was no tower anymore. It was gone. I thought I would just climb down the tower into my world, ask the Queen about the damn book, and climb back up again. In retrospect, it was better the tower had vanished. But it was only on my way back that it occurred to me time was different in my world. If I'd managed to climb down, I'd probably have disappeared for weeks from Earth's perspective! When would I get smarter? When would I stop doing such reckless things?

I had no possibility to visit the Underworld, unless the Queen herself summoned me. Neither I, nor Bory, who fortunately did not notice my stupid attempt, could go home right now. I had no choice but to wait until she felt the time was right to tell me what book to look for and where.

Great, that was just great…

As I walked and walked and thought about my life, another stupid idea came to me. I could check Rio's office and see if I found the bone there. But when I was already standing in front of the club's front door, I turned around and climbed back up the facade to my open window. Eventually, I thought better of it. I wouldn't search for the bone, because I still needed the kiss first. Baron had to be sure he could trust me and stealing from him wasn't exactly the way I could achieve that. I needed that kiss, then I could get the bone and eventually focus on the damned book.

CHAPTER TWELVE
RIO

"Punchy, what you gotta do when you collect money?" I asked him, leaning back into my black leather chair, and staring at my best men.

"Check it?"

I nodded, clenching my hands briefly.

Between my desk and the door into my office lay twenty open gym bags with all the money from our turf. The neighborhoods we owned. The gang had a hierarchy like any other system. At the top was the Chairman, which was basically me —not quite but almost. The real Chairman of the Chicago Loops had been in prison for 12 years and operated from there. My mentor. I visited him twice a year so as not to cause a stir. The rest ran over corrupt guards, of course. Everyone had a price, you just had to know how much or what they wanted.

Under me were my senior officers, Punchy and Slappy, then came junior officers, who ruled over the lieutenants of the neighborhoods. Sometimes all the officers met, which was the much-quoted board meeting.

The lieutenants were little gang leaders themselves, mini bosses under my control. They had their men, foot soldiers, drug crews, tenants, shop owners, and so on to guard and control. Then there were the kids; the little fuckers we called Slylords, 15-year-olds were Midgets and from 17, they were called PeeWees. The latter were always the ones that worried me the most. Those fuckers and their hormonal brains, as well as the relentless greed for money and a better life. Mostly, it was them who made bad decisions.

I used to be one of them myself, so I knew how uncontrollable they were. Always onto some shit, causing their high school teachers and parents heart attacks. We tried to control the PeeWees but that only went so far. Eventually, some of them would snap, and of course the lieutenants were responsible for their shit-magnets, but if nothing worked, I had to use force. I was the one everyone had to kneel in front of, and these kinds of men and kids always needed a demonstration. That's the way it worked around here.

In total, I was the leader of 75,000 gang members throughout Chicago. We were the most important gang next to the Black Crows and had control over 67 community areas. That's an impressive number, wasn't it? Especially when you consider that there are 220,000 people in gangs in Chicago in total.

"I don't even have to look at this shit to know that we're exactly $123,450 and 30 pennies short, Punchy," I said, trying to ignore all the numbers in my head for now.

Punchy bit his lip.

Normally the treasurers of each set had to count the outturn of our drug and gun trafficking, but since so much was missing, it could only mean that one of the treasurers had a hand in it. It was probably a PeeWee. It was always one of them. Although I sent the young ones to the church where we had a priest educate them to be halfway normal individuals, they were mostly reckless, or had girls and other things in mind than doing what the board, or rather I wanted them to do. Little fuckers, like I said.

At some point someone always thought it wouldn't be noticed if a few bucks were missing at the end of the month. If you made millions, how many were a few thousand that could change one's life? Well, I saw everything, I was calculating everything. Numbers and my brain were my gift. I never missed a thing, so I knew exactly how much they owed me without wasting time to use a calculator.

This month it was the Far Southeast side, the Far Southwest, the Partial Southwest and parts of the Northside that were due. That included protection money, drug and gun money, and of course taxes. In the said neighborhoods, I had 573 sets of 30–40 members and 22,920 foot soldiers in total. So, I should have more money in front of me. I was $123,450 short.

Not much for a gang boss but a lot for the community, because we needed the money not only to fill our bellies and buy gold chains, but to invest. To buy more freaking public housing projects back and expand. To turn this shit into something useful, something the people could live in without getting diseases.

I don't want to appear a saint or say that my actions would save all these people here—I am doing bad things all day long —but I truly knew that some kids would have a better life than I had thanks to my gang and that really made me sleep better. But, yeah, it was an excuse.

We certainly were not the good ones here. Not entirely. For some, maybe, but not for those who bought our guns and drugs and died from an overdose or gunshot afterward. But who were the heroes in our story?

The cops? No, they weren't the heroes in this story.

We were all in this shit together. But now the question was, what did we do with it? What kind of choices did we make?

Well, I had one goal and I've been seizing it for over 20 years now. So, for me, the facts were important, and those bastards stole money from me and our community. So, now they had to pay. With their lives.

"You know what to do?" I asked Punchy.

He nodded, still ashamed.

Man, that guy shouldn't be a senior officer. But I didn't trust a lot of people, and in my position, it was better to stay low, to duck. I only let the ones near me who I'd known my whole life and trusted them with mine. Those were Punchy, Slappy, and Anwyn. The latter stood behind me, still and stiff as always.

"All right, you go right down to the neighborhood and beat the shit out of him—if he doesn't listen, tell him it's his lucky day, cause I'm gonna kill him myself. Get the money, bring it to me, and oh, Punchy?"

"Yes, Baron?"

"Did you spread the word?" I asked.

"Everything," Punchy said.

"Did you meet the hooker I told you to?"

"Clarisse? Yeah, told her all of it."

"Good. So, we might hear something of it tonight. Very good, Punchy. Then start to spread the rest of it."

"Yes, Baron."

"Slappy?" I asked, raising my eyebrows. "How bad was Barbie at the shooting area?"

"Not bad at all," he said, running his hand through his long afro hair. "She can aim. Needs to practice but well, maybe tomorrow she'll shoot better than even you."

I grinned at that. "Good. Oh, speaking of the devil. Hello, Barbie."

Everyone turned to the door, shocked that she dared to just walk in here like that. She didn't seem to realize what she had done, and it didn't matter, it was different with her. I was different with her.

Anyway, her appearance made everyone in the room stop thinking. Including me.

Her hair was curly tonight and fell wildly over her bare shoulders. The dress was perfect. I knew it. It was the black one that almost took my breath away at Leonardo's. Damn, it suited her like a second skin. Her full lips and fingernails were painted red, and I felt the hair on my skin rising in unison.

Did only I have a kink for red nails?

Clearing my throat, I tried to block out the feelings that were coming up inside of me at that exact moment. The thoughts I had when I was staring at her breasts, at her lips, at her beautiful face, imagining what she would look like when I would tear said dress off her body and touch her with my aching hands—

Then she smiled.

She knew I was mentally undressing her and fucking her with my eyes. As I ran my thumb and index finger over my eyelids, I cooled myself down mentally. It was my own fault. There was a reason some didn't let women in the higher ranks of their gangs. Not because they weren't good, but simply because some men couldn't control their dicks. It was a tale as old as time. But it was never the women's fault, it was ours. Men like me.

A category I never thought I'd belong to until now. What a shame. After all, that was the reason she was here. To get at the throats of men like that and punish them. Taking a deep breath, I pulled myself together, nodding at her.

"Nice job, Barbie. This will have exactly the effect we want. Punchy, Slappy. You are dismissed."

They left, and I was glad that my voice seemed cool and disinterested again. That's the way it should be. That's what a gang leader was supposed to sound like. Not consumed with lust, like he wanted to fuck a woman he doesn't even know in front of his members. That wasn't me.

"Meet your date. Any," I said to Anwyn, pointing to my best friend behind me.

At that he stepped out of my shadow, greeting her. As usual, he was not impressed at all. I sometimes wondered if any woman could ever throw him off track, because in all those years I never met a single one. So, I supposed not. Maybe this was also the reason I let him be her date tonight. Not Slappy or Punchy.

"You can trust him," I said as she gave Any a mistrustful look.

"Of course. Whom, if not me," he said and ran his fingers through his blonde hair that used to hang down to his fore-head. She looked up at him, making me grin. Any wasn't as tall as me but still taller than Barbie.

But Any was a good man and yeah, I was jealous of him because of that. But I knew my weaknesses very well, and that was my secret of success. Exactly because Barbie affected me the way she did, I decided not to go to the event with her tonight, but to send Any. The one friend I had since that one year in high school, who I went through hell with at the age of fifteen. No, I didn't want to think about Aria. Not today. Still, I could see her right there in front of my eyes whenever Any was standing next to me. They just looked too much alike. After all, she was his little sister.

It was better to send him. Today, there would be too many people who could otherwise expose me. Of course, there were rumors about my position, but since K.C. was still in jail, operating and starting rumors, everyone assumed he was still our leader. Wrong assumption. I had stolen his throne long ago.

"Oh, honey. Don't look too disappointed that I won't be your date tonight. I'll be watching from afar, checking if you do everything right. Don't worry." I winked at her and knew this sentence would upset her.

She glowered at me.

Fuck. I was starting to like it.

I turned to my best friend. "Any, you're not gonna get foot soldiers this time. You're on your own. Nobody knows her and her associates, and I'd like to keep it that way, so take a different route than usual. Pick up a coat at the bar downstairs. Fox has the other stuff too. Take it and cover her well."

He nodded.

"You know what to do?" I asked.

"Sure," he said and sauntered towards her.

I watched their meet and greet carefully.

She was different with him. I pulled my eyebrows together and wondered. Why did she act so reserved in his presence? That was odd. I guess, Barbie didn't like him at all, but did she know him? Usually, Any was the type of man that everyone loved. A troubled mother's dream, as I always called him. Even my abuela loved him and she was a hard one with rich people.

"Don't bother too much, Baron. We'll work it out." Any put his hand on her back, and when she turned around, I noticed how low-cut the dress was. I took a deep breath. Unfortunately, I knew exactly what she was going to do tonight and the mere thought that she would look at this man the same way she had looked at me was enough to make my heart race. Of course, it meant nothing. I was just possessive over my belongings, that's all. Unfortunately, she didn't belong to me though and I hated it.

Suddenly, I remembered I had to take my damn pills.

"Don't disappoint me," I said as a goodbye to them and reached into my drawer, searching for my pills. But Barbie's damn bone was blocking the drawer. So, I wriggled it out and put it on the table. Then I winced, because she was looking at me through the door gap, raising her eyebrows at the sight of the bone. Our eyes locked, and she grinned slightly, closing the door.

Great.

So, now she knew where I kept the shit. I really wasn't myself around her anymore, was I? She was a sly one. All right, so I had to hide it somewhere else. What a waste of time.

I'll do it before I give the governor of Illinois another visit.

CHAPTER THIRTEEN
RIO

I cowered on top of the roof of a building that was right across from the opera house, using it as a lookout and watching the queue of all these noble people rushing to their performance. Of course, Z-Mexx, the Black Crowns' leader, was right in the middle of it. Neither he nor his girl, one of his many girlfriends, were interested in the performance of *Carmen*—a good opera when the conductor was decent. Today's conductor was, so at least Barbie could see something enchanting.

They stood out from the crowd. None of them had hair as fair as Barbie's and Any's. There were some blondes down there, mixed in with the many colors of hair that looked like colorful balls to me, but those two were so bright that they shone like two flashlights. Apparently, they had still not made friends, because Barbie kept her distance and didn't so much as look at him, although he kept talking to her.

She glanced at her shoulder even more often than she did when she was with me. This shoulder tick of hers slowly but surely got to me. I wanted to understand it...

I told Diva Dee that she had escaped from the Amish and

was looking for a hiding place now. All right, maybe I added a few more things. But she was so weird, my story really could fit. Fox told me she knew nothing. As if she really was from another world.

She tilted her head, and I started to like my job for tonight. I could watch her, without interruptions, enjoy her beauty. I remembered Fox telling me that the TV almost knocked her off her feet and Cherry had to help Barbie with the phone. She even was afraid of the elevator, the microwave, the stereo, the light—everything. Barbie didn't even know how to cook on the stove, turn on the shower, or even flush the toilet…

She would never admit to anyone that she didn't know these basic things, but Fox watched her and gave me information—almost too faithfully to be honest. I knew she was jealous because I gave Barbie too much attention, but how could I not be interested? Barbie was an enormous question mark. Always.

And now they went in. I put the black hood over my head and prepared to wait, a bit sad that I couldn't see her any longer.

Operas were long, but they would only have to stay until the intermission, the most important part of tonight. Gang leaders like Z-Mexx loved to distinguish themselves and pretend that they belonged to the better breed, among the people who preferred to go to the opera rather than hang around in front of the television. It was all for the reputation, wasn't it?

I knew Z-Mexx would use the intermission for making deals, trades, and plans and the Chicago Loops were playing mice tonight.

Barbie and Any showed the ticket collectors their cards and went inside. Any offered her an arm, and she took it reluctantly, but she did. Was it my imagination, or was she much warmer with me? I shook my head—that was not important at all.

157

Now they handed in their jackets. The men were already turning around to see her, and I smiled, yeah, she was a knockout.

I had to give Cherry a raise. She actually taught her how to walk in high heels. I could hardly look away from her swaying hips. And Z-Mexx took a bite out of it, too. The gang boss was big, filled his tux out pretty good and had olive toned skin. He drove a hand over his bald head. His brown eyes scanned the crowd and eventually remained fixed on Barbie. Everyone knew he had a weakness for beautiful women. More than others, to be clear. He wanted them all and believed just because he now had all the money in the world, he could get them, collect them like *Pokémon*. Men like him were high and mighty, but they were careless. Eventually the system ate them up. Tonight, I was the system.

Barbie looked over her shoulder now, pretending that Any had fucked up and couldn't entertain her. She smiled at Z-Mexx instead. In that moment, I clenched my fingers into fists. Thank God I wasn't in there. I would have screwed it up. Definitely. If I were in there, I would have flirted with her and I guess she would have flirted back at me, brainwashing me with her smile. We would have forgotten about Z-Mexx and I would have shown her the whole opera, just to see if she liked it…oh, I would love to do all of this now.

But Any was with her, and he did a perfect job. She didn't care about him at all, everything he said seemed to annoy her, and it was just the way I wanted it. Z-Mexx already felt he had to save her. Oh, even I felt it. He watched her like a hawk, staring at her ass as she went up to the hall to look for the row she was sitting in. His gaze followed her everywhere, and I couldn't help but grin. Everything was as I wanted it to be and then I did not see her anymore and my neck tingled with uneasiness.

The show began.

All I had to do now was wait for the break.

So, I looked down, observed my surroundings, and examined this part of Chicago I had to share. One block to the left were the Black Crowns. One block to the right were some of my men, selling drugs for me. I didn't know their names, but thanks to my memory I knew the faces of all my 75,000 gang members. I knew a lot of names too, but some of them just did not interest me. You had to earn names and for me, that also applied vice-versa. Those down there didn't seem to interest me very much—although, oh, shit.

I narrowed my eyes at a guy.

Down there was Prawn, a PeeWee. One I had under my radar. Not good. Did he have to be there today of all days?

I reached for my gun, sighing as I found the damn thing. Well, if he screwed up today, I'm prepared.

BECAUSE THE ENTIRE opera went on for three hours and more, I watched my men and their crews dealing C-Wax instead. Doing that I couldn't stop my brain from calculating how much they were making while waiting; 437,320 dollars. That wasn't bad.

C-Wax was expensive. We had to dig that shit up every week. Van der Volt insisted on hiding his goods in lakes and each time it was a different one. Never take any chances, that was his way. Good one, though. So, he delivered the stuff and some of my frogmen had to bring it back up and cook the shit before selling it. That costed, oh, that costed. But expensive was not bad. The price almost made it more attractive and therefore everybody wanted it, but only we had the contacts.

A monopoly.

Naturally, van der Volt had already been in contact with

the other gang leaders—he wanted to become rich as fuck like everyone else—but they were not ready to make a deal with him yet, so, my gang had it all. Five times already, other gangs had stolen our goods. They got tips from rats.

So, they had a bit of C-Wax to sell, but they didn't have the contacts that we had—that I had—the contact that linked to van der Volt, but that's exactly why border areas like this were always dangerous. Foot soldiers could be captured, goods could be stolen from other gangs, or other gangs could start shooting at us.

A drug war.

A term that everyone here knew and feared. Gangs used to fight over cocaine for centuries and now it's C-Wax, way stronger than coke. My job was to keep the monopoly and make sure that no one got to van der Volt.

Then I saw her again. God bless all those houses with glass fronts. They were everything for spies like me, but of course, I wasn't there just to be a voyeur. No, I was there to make sure my investment doubled my profit and Barbie was doing exactly what I wanted her to do. She was a natural and Z-Mexx was so on the hook. Oh, and her smiles were enough for me to... to get jealous?

No, they... Hell, no, I couldn't think about her that way. She was a weapon. My gun and nothing more. So, it didn't matter how much she flirted with Z-Mexx at the bar right now. I needed to distract myself, ignoring my tightened muscles and the annoying burning in my chest. That's when I heard a scream.

I whipped my head around, searching for Prawn. The fucking PeeWee was fucking up again. My crew was yelling at another crew of Black Crowns and then they pulled out their guns in a side street. I sighed, clenching my fists, and asking myself why. Why were teenagers such a pain in the ass?

Well, I too was one selfish kid back then, and what did it

lead to? Aria was shot and killed. My father thought of himself as a god and what did he get?

Hell.

Climbing down again, I tried to be as fast as possible. I held on to the window frames and was glad when I could jump off a balcony and hit the street.

The idiots had already started shooting at each other. Just as I was running towards them a dull shot roared in my ear and made the hair on my neck rise. Immediately my body stiffened, and I sprinted faster, my pulse racing.

Even though I hated guns, the shooting itself wasn't my problem. It was the cops who were attracted by it. Everything that was going on down there right now would come back to me and my community.

We have some principles. One of them was to keep disturbances to a minimum, because disturbance put cops in our business, and that was bad for sales. The fewer cops, the more profit. So, what was happening in front of me right now was not okay. I had to stop it.

I limbered up my shoulders and neck. Ready to fight. Some of my idiots sat in their cars and shot out of them randomly, elevating my pulse even more. Prawn stood ducked behind a parked car, shooting over his head. With a rapid pounding in my ears, I passed the first PeeWee, punched him in the face and watched him stumble.

"Get out!" I said.

At first, he wanted to fight back, but then he recognized my eyes and my face and ran.

That's my boy. I got to the next one and rammed him into the wall too. An edgy feeling running up my heated skin.

"Back off. Understand? Fucking back off," I said through my bared teeth.

The kid with long dreadlocks nodded, shaking uncontrollably with a trembling lower lip. He stunk of fear and his eyes widened at the sight of me.

Grabbing my gun, I cursed the fucking thing under my breath and pointed it at the other boys.

"Get away! It's the boss!" one kid yelled at the others and a couple of cars drove away, making me sigh in relief. But another shot made me straighten up again, checking the street. On the other end, the Crowns were still firing at Prawn. He ducked behind his car and fired tremblingly at the Crowns, not knowing where he was shooting at. A red bandana hung loosely from his head, his letterman's jacket was torn, and his pants were already covered in blood. Two other PeeWees hid beside him, glancing over the car's edges and advising him with even more stupid ideas.

I panickily searched for a way to get to them but I was no fool. No way was I going to run into open fire.

One of the Crowns shot and hit Prawn's car window, which shattered and distributed thousands of glass particles. Prawn and his friends stuck to the ground, fingers shaking and adrenalin flowing. One of them squinted past the rear and saw that one of the Crowns was storming towards them.

The fire stopped for a short time, and I ran to Prawn, the beating of my heart pounding in my ears.

"Get out!" I yelled.

All of them turned around.

They pressed themselves up, one stumbled over his own feet, but they ran towards me and tried to escape. But then the blue lights came on. We all froze in place. The Crowns stopped in the middle of the street, considering whether they should flee or continue firing. We all looked at each other for mere seconds, then the Crowns drove away.

When Prawn tried to run past me, I grabbed his collar and dragged him into the alley I came from, running away with him from the crime scene and his car.

The high-pitched police sirens became louder and louder, and then, when I thought us safe, I pressed him against a wall, feeling his anxious breath on my skin. As the blue lights flashed past us, they brightened our faces.

"You damn fool!" I hissed, pistol-whipping him in the stomach. "Wasn't your lieutenant's lesson enough?"

He was whimpering now. I felt delighted as he mourned and my fingers twitched, urging me to punish him more.

"I, I—" he stuttered and tried again. "That Crown fucker stole my girl."

"And then you start shooting in a pedestrian zone? Yeah, that's the solution, good choice!"

He swallowed.

I pressed him further into the wall, smirking as he winced. "Somebody could have died, and then what would we have done, huh? Everything you do sheds light on our community. I'm not telling you to shit on that girl, you hear me?" I pushed him further into the wall and had to hold back, so as not to hit him with my gun.

"That's not the way to solve it, though. You could have taken an innocent man's life just because you can't accept the truth. Either she wants you or she doesn't. If she wants someone else, accept that. She won't love you just because you're on a rampage. Fuckin' hell!"

He was still shaking under my fingers.

"Now run," I hissed. "If you don't report for duty with your lieutenant tomorrow, run further. Run to another state, because God help me, I will find you."

"Y- yes, sir… " he said and as soon as I let go, he ran for his life without looking back.

I sighed, relaxing my hand.

My blood pressure was fucking high right now. How come nobody here could take anything seriously when it was said normally? Damn it!

I went in the opera's direction, carefully staying in the shadows, in case the police checked the area, but I guessed that they'd have enough to do with the PeeWee's.

Actually, I promised to meet Any and Barbie in a side street behind the opera, but I didn't meet them there, but five gang members of the Crowns. They probably didn't know who I was, but they saw my gun. That and the obviousness that I wasn't one of their members was enough to open fire again.

I cursed, ran, and fired back while stumbling. And then—at moments like this, when else?—I realized I hadn't taken my pill after all. My heart was pounding so hard because of my thoughtlessness. I first thought it was the adrenaline rush but no. I forgot the pills! The bone distracted me. *Barbie* distracted me.

Fuck.

I suddenly couldn't breathe.

I gasped, clasping my chest and staggering to the nearest tree to hide, blinking at my blurring vision. I was only a few yards from the point where Any had parked his car. I pressed my back against a tree and although the shooting was ringing in my ears, I felt my heart racing. Everything was pounding in my head. Grabbing my chest once more, I noticed that my legs gave way. I was trembling, shivering, and I couldn't breathe. Fuck. *I'm dying. I'm dying.* That's when I saw Barbie and Any standing ten feet away and Any had a gun on me.

I hit the hard ground, and all went black.

CHAPTER FOURTEEN
LYNNE

I knew he was no good and bless Stix I had followed him. He wanted to go to the toilet even though we had an appointment with the Baron. I didn't trust him and went to the meeting place at the appointed time anyway. I didn't want to wait until he took a piss. Thank Stix! There he was. *I have to go to the toilet*, my ass!

Any was none other than the guy I saw on Storm Day, talking about killing Rio. At first, I had my doubts, but now, I was sure. He wanted to kill Rio and that's why I had lost my bone back then, because of him. Any was the reason for all of this, and right now, he was pointing the gun at Rio, who suffered from I don't know what and had crashed to the ground.

Everything inside me was filled with rage and I just wanted to kill Any. I wanted to strangle him with my bare hands, spit on his face, kick him to the ground. I've been wanting to do that all evening. All that shit he had been whispering in my ears —because I knew that man was a walking lie and I hated him for it. Didn't Rio say he was his best friend? I was shocked when I saw him.

Although I was not quite sure about my feelings for Rio, I knew I was on his side. It was Rio and me against Any. Even though Rio may not have been the one I wanted, he meant something to me. Enough that I'd always save him, and I would make that decision over and over again.

So, I didn't have to think long and picked up a rock, walking towards Any. Bory, who was following me everywhere, screamed behind me but I didn't listen to him. Not this time. That tight skulling dress was bugging me, and I couldn't move like I wanted to, but I hit him right in the head, making him grunt. Apparently not hard enough, because he was still able to turn around.

"What are you doing? We must protect him. The Crowns!"

I tilted my head and narrowed my eyes, as if saying: *Oh, please, stop lying.*

He didn't want to rescue Rio but kill him! I knew it. He'd promised somebody he was gonna kill Rio—and okay, maybe I was just skulling it all up again but so be it. I knew where Rio had the bone, and yet I still wanted to save him. I could have just rushed to him, kissed him goodbye, stolen the bone, and searched for the queen's book. But I couldn't do it.

Instead, I shot daggers at Any, trying to keep my breathing even. I held his stare as he touched the back of his bleeding head, giving the gun in his hand a considering glance.

A moment of inattention and I took advantage of it.

I punched him in the face with the stone, grinned at his wince and stole the pistol from his hands, leaving a cold feeling in my stomach. Without hesitation I pointed it at him, my glance determined.

"Don't do anything wrong," he said, still in a grasped voice, utterly surprised as he raised both his arms, showing me that he was weaponless know. "He needs me, and I don't want to kill him. You have misunderstood. I wanted to protect him… from the Crowns."

I grunted, knowing that this was total bullshit.

But he was right about something.

In my peripheral vision I saw two men approaching us at this very moment. Crowns indeed. I winced and just when one of them raised a gun, I shot before they could count to five. Of course, I hit the guys. In archery, I was an ace and even though those pistols were worlds apart from the weapons I was used to, it all came down to aiming, and I had to save Rio.

Right now, Any was looking at me with his eyes wide open, then he glanced at the ground, at the two bodies lying there. My toes curled in my heels as I watched him. Any hesitated at first, but then finally ran to Rio.

I let out a deep sigh and watched him carefully carry Rio over to his car. I slumped into the backseat, staring at Any as he put Rio next to me. With one hand I still pointed the gun at him and with the other I helped him put Rio's head on my lap.

When Any was done, he raised his hands, bowing his head slightly and showing me that he was no threat. The gleam in his eyes turned into sorrow. "I'm gonna drive. Is that okay with you? We can't stay here. Either the police or some more Crowns will find us. "

I nodded and let him close the door.

I stared down at Rio, stroking his short hair and checking his body. There was no bullet wound, but he couldn't breathe and was sweating heavily.

"Just kiss him now, then you're done with him, and we'll get the bone," Bory urged behind me.

Are you really that heartless? I told him, catching my breath as Rio leaned into my touch. I couldn't leave him like this, and I had promised him to help. To run away just like that… I didn't even know if I could fulfill my deal if I kissed him just now. Would he be able to want me, to desire me in his current state? I guess not.

167

Bory hummed and crawled into the passenger seat next to Any, glowering at him as well.

"Reach in his pocket and find for his wallet. He has pills in there. Anxiety dissipators," Any said, looking at me through the rear-view window.

Cold, green eyes.

I narrowed my eyes at him and tried to mimic a question: *What do you mean?*

"Well," he huffed and drove away like a madman, "he's having a panic attack, can't you see that? He's been having them since he was…fifteen, it's chronic now. So, get the pill. Also, put your hands on his heart. It'll calm him down…why are you looking at me like that? I've known him since we were kids."

I swallowed, braced myself and leaned over him. His hot breath heated up my chest and the goosebumps rose on my skin. I reached into his pocket, carefully. Yep, his ass was tight. I bit my lower lip as his body tensed and pulled out his wallet, opened it and searched for said pills. Oh, by the Dead, I found it.

I took it out of the plastic-packaging and tried to push the pill into Rio's mouth. Any made a jerky turn, pushing us to the right and Rio slid on top of me, taking my breath away. I startled as one of his hands was somewhere it shouldn't be.

Moaning, he woke up, his face pale and his eyes wide open—shocked as he saw me. He looked at my hand when I brought it to his mouth again and calmed down when he recognized the pill. My stomach dropped. So, he really had panic attacks. A badass gang leader who jumped from rooftops like a cat struggled with anxiety?

Rio still couldn't breathe, so I made short work of him and stuffed the pill into his mouth. Any quickly handed me a water bottle over the driver's seat. Hastily, I opened the screw cap and lifted the bottle to Rio's mouth, and he gulped down the half of it. Then his eyes fixed on mine, and he brushed a knuckle along the inside of my knee. My cheeks turned red.

"Thanks," Rio coughed.

I opened my mouth, but Any interrupted me: "We'll drive to the only place you feel safe."

Without realizing it, I started stroking Rio's forehead again, and he closed his eyes, leaning into my touch.

"Those are mighty hammers," Any explained, still driving like he was deranged. "They calm him down very fast and make him fall asleep. But watch him please, those attacks could lead to real heart attacks. He had one before and I don't want him to have the second one today...or ever," he quickly added.

I glared at him.

Maybe he didn't wish him a heart attack, but rather a bullet in the chest. Oh, I would definitely watch that so-called best friend.

ANY TOOK us to an area that was quite different from what I had seen of this city before. I could see huge mansions everywhere, grounds filled with green grass, and tall, well-decorated streetlamps. Everything was brightly lit and seemed peaceful and so clean. There were no people standing in the corners, or any sales going on. I could just see enormous house after house after house.

Then Any stopped at a white mansion with lots of illuminated big windows and a spacious driveway. We shouldered Rio together and brought him in. The woman who opened the fancy door for us immediately started yelling at the sight of Rio and spoke in a language I didn't know. All I knew was that she talked incredibly fast and gestured a lot. "Madre mía! Madre mía! Rio! Madre mía!" she kept repeating.

I didn't have time to admire the enormous house, because Any and I had to haul Rio up the stairs, puffing like two walruses. But what I could see out of the corner of my eye was wonderful. Everything was shiny and expensive. Did Rio live here? Was this his house? I knew that he didn't live at the Club, but this was… a bit too family-oriented for a guy like him. And who was that woman? She looked like she was my age.

My stomach dropped.

Was she his wife? Did Rio have a wife?

As we walked along a corridor, I saw a door open, only a crack. But it was enough to see a little boy in pajamas standing there and looking at me with big brown eyes. As he saw Any, he beamed but before he could say anything to the little boy, the woman came crashing up from below, yelling at the boy. He nodded then and crept back into his room.

"Ai, Rio," the woman muttered, opening another door for us and we threw Rio on the bed.

"Get his sweaty clothes off and... yeah, Reina, I'll be right there. Stop bitching now," Any hissed. So, the woman was called Reina and no, she was not amused at all. When Any used the word bitching, she threw a picture frame at him, but sadly, the prick ducked in time. Pity.

He simply rolled his eyes and turned to me. "Be right back."

I nodded and sat down, straightened up next to him on the edge of the bed, staring him down.

For skull's sake, what was going on today? First this skulling mission, then the opera, which was really great, but instead of admiring it until the end, I had to let Z-Mexx drool on me. And then? Then everything escalated and I just couldn't figure out what Rio was suffering from or why he even was suffering.

I straightened up next to him on the edge of the bed, staring him down. I asked myself if it was my fondness for this man that brought me here, eventually. It was my fault for being here, wasn't it? All mine and no one else's. Bory has been telling me for years to stop my thoughtless actions. It was reckless coming here with the bones, all that time ago.

But on that damn day everything had gone wrong. Nana had discovered me stealing another Bloodcoin and had given me a look of contempt. Her disappointment felt like a knife stabbing me in the back. Of course, I couldn't let that go. No, I had to fight back, tell her off, and of course I was too late for anything else afterwards. I was a hothead, even though I didn't like to admit it. It wasn't Any's, nor Rio's fault, but my fault alone.

I stroked his short hair again and only noticed it when it was too late. *Damn*, I smiled. What made him so special? Why was I so taken by him that a simple death threat startled me so much that I lost a bone? I never lost a bone once in my life and I didn't even care about death. I didn't care about anything! I was an Underworlder, so showing sympathy for a dying man made no sense. Usually, I wouldn't have batted an eye.

Yet here I was. In another world, interwoven in the greatest skull ever, stroking a man's hair who I shouldn't even trust with my little finger. He was sleeping peacefully, though making my nerve endings tingle and my mouth dry. His long, thick eyelashes met his high reddish cheekbones, just like a fan and his lips seemed to be so soft... I swallowed. All right, he looked gorgeous. Skull it.

"Take his sweater off, Lynne," Bory grumbled. "He's soaked through."

I snorted, glaring at him. "Oh, now you care."

Somehow, I was afraid of skin contact now. Not because of my creepy hands but rather because of him. I didn't know why, but touching Rio was no easy matter for me. I had to overcome that sense of doom to manage it. Funny, considering I was a Cave Town dweller. Actually, I shouldn't mind that. Not at all. Cave Town dwellers banged like rabbits.

But the thing was, I minded because I was different. Sighing, I pulled the hoodie over his head and winced. There was still another layer to take off...his T-shirt.

"What's the matter?" Bory asked, hopping next to Rio.

Even though he wanted to leave him alone a few minutes ago, Bory was looking at him with quite a bit of concern now. He probably didn't care about him but more about finding out how I felt for him. Son of a witch.

"Lynne, you're not afraid to take the poor guy's shirt off now, are you?"

"No," I growled. "Of course not. Just let me do it and stop talking."

Of course, I wasn't afraid. I just didn't want to have the feelings that his naked torso could possibly—most certainly—provoke in me. I didn't want them. Not a single freaking emotion.

Ignoring Bory's look, I sighed once more, took action and pulled the skulling shirt over his head. Gently, I led his hands through the openings and when I saw his tanned, muscular torso in front of me, I swallowed. Yes, there they were. All kinds of feelings at full pelt. Hello, freaking feelings I do not want.

I bit my lower lip. Why me?

"Don't start drooling yet." Bory laughed and well, maybe I had overdone it, but I hit him with my palm, and he fell off the bed. My blue furball tumbled down, did a somersault, and looked at me with his lips pressed into a thin line and a certain tightness in the eyes.

I just shrugged. "Stop bothering me."

"You like him." He brushed his fur and folded his arms, scowling me.

"No," I growled back.

"Of course, you do. That's why you didn't want to leave him behind when you could. This is more than just a soul-rescue-mission for you, isn't it? Why have you been watching him all these years, Lynne?"

A rage was boiling inside me. I flexed my fingers and turned away from him. Why did he always have to confront me? I liked ignoring my feelings—no, I actually loved ignoring them! And yes, I liked Rio. And now what? I would never be able to do anything with those feelings for him. I'd never... I lived in the Underworld and he lived here. So, I just had to forget whatever my hormones were doing to me right now.

Grinding my teeth, I picked up his blanket and flung it roughly over his bloody attractive body. I wanted to go somewhere away from all this mess. But before I could have yelled at Bory for making me confess my stupid feelings once more, the door opened and the woman from before was standing in front of me. Her eyes were red, swollen, and watery. As she looked at Rio her expression hardened, but I could sense that she loved him very much.

"Here," she said and pressed a few clothes into my hand. "Pajamas."

As she ran her finger through her long brown hair, I examined her. Her skin had an olive-tone and she was beautiful, overwhelmingly beautiful.

"Do you need a second blanket?" she asked, still looking at him.

I frowned. Why did she ask me if I needed another blanket?

"You will sleep in here, won't you?"

I furrowed my brow, shaking my head violently. By the Dead, those humans tended to assume too much!

"She can't speak and she's not with Rio, Reina," Any said, rescuing me.

"Oh," said the woman and looked at me very closely now. "No?"

Any shook his head, but she didn't seem convinced. So, I

173

shook my head too but with a genuine facial expression, showing her that I really meant it. Rio and I were nothing. Nothing at all and never would be.

At that moment Rio grabbed me by the wrist; his touch gave me a tiny jolt. Wincing, I turned and—skull, that touch was intense. He was still asleep but was probably dreaming something.

"Oh, yeah. I see," Reina said, looking at me with raised eyebrows. "Anyway. You can sleep here or in the room next door, our guest room. I'm Reina, Rio's sister."

Oh, that was... interesting. I saw no resemblance at all. None! How could they be brother and sister? Was that kid hers or Rio's? Or even another brother? I had so many questions right now, but Reina looked at Rio one more time, shook her head and left.

"Good night," I heard her say, and then she was gone.

"Anything else you need?" Any asked me.

I shook my head.

"I'll sleep at my place, it's a few houses down the road, but I'll call tomorrow. So, good night, Barbie."

Pfft, as if I cared where he sleeps. I was glad he didn't sleep here and try to kill Rio again. Still lost in my thoughts I sauntered to the toilet, put Reina's shorts and shirt on and brushed my teeth. Then I tried to sleep, but I couldn't. My head was spinning, my heart was hammering, and no position seemed good enough. I was worried about Rio having a heart attack. What Any had said in the car had scared me.

After Bory fell asleep, I went back to Rio, but I didn't want to sleep in his bed. So, I went back to the guest room just to look after him again three minutes later. Then I started to pace around the hall, admiring the photos. I found out that four people lived in this house. Reina, two boys, and a little girl. She looked less than five years old, nothing more. I noticed that there were no photos of Rio and sometimes there was an old lady pictured. They all had brown hair and looked very much alike. Maybe they were all Rio's brothers and sisters, but why wasn't he in the photos? So, were they Reina's kids then? But what was Rio doing here? Why did Any take him to his sister's?

I tried three times to fall asleep but just lay in there like a fish in a sardine tin and went to Rio to check his breathing once more. I found him alive and happy every time. Oh boy, I acted like a mother hen, didn't I? Yet his illness frightened me. Panic attacks? It was really unfavorable that he just happened to have them randomly. What if he was in the middle of a fight? What about when he drove a car?

I crouched down next to his bed and at some point I must have fallen asleep, because when I woke up, he was no longer there but I was *in* his bed. The moment I woke up, I stiffened and spread my fingers like a fan against my breastbone, breathing heavily. After gathering my wits, I ran to the guest room and yelled at Bory, who was still asleep, snoring like a bear.

"Wake up!" I picked him up, shaking him a little.

He slowly pressed his eyes open, looked at me, and yawned. Yeah, he had a big mouth and it looked like his teeth were still intact.

"Where's Rio?"

"I don't know." Bory yawned again, chewing on his tongue.

I dropped him on the bed and rushed downstairs without even looking at myself in the mirror first. Once down, I was relieved to hear his deep voice. But then I realized he was talking in the same language as his sister, and I didn't understand a thing. Nothing at all, and they were screaming at each other.

"Don't worry," I heard a child's voice.

I turned on the stairs and saw the boy from yesterday, still in his blue pajamas. Big green eyes stared back at me. His dark hair grew into his forehead, messy like a bird's nest.

"That's normal. They yell at each other and then they like each other again."

The boy couldn't have been more than eight years old. Because I didn't know what to do, and I didn't want to go into the kitchen either, I sat down on the stairs and the boy sat next to me.

"Rio has never brought a girl home before," he said. "What's your name?"

I indicated to him that I couldn't talk, and he nodded in disappointment.

"Too bad," he said.

Then, the little girl from the photos came as well. I couldn't help but smile when I saw her. She was as sweet as those donuts I tried the other day. Big, dark beady eyes and a tiny doll in her arms. Her brown hair was slightly curled. The doll sparked my interest, though. It was skinny and had long blond plastic hair. It reminded me of something. The girl's dark brown hair on the other hand went straight down to her chin.

She waved at me—a small, uncertain gesture. So, I waved back and before I knew it, she was sitting on my lap, smelling like strawberries and cotton.

"I'm Raquel," she said, playing with my hair. "You have the same hair as Any!" I tried not to roll my eyes when she said his name.

"Oh, and I'm Rafael," said the boy, and told me something about a man who was like a spider—or was he a spider? A spider-man? I couldn't understand. Anyway, sometime later—after a lot of yelling—Rio stormed into the hall with Reina in tow. He saw me with his siblings, stopping in his tracks and raising his eyebrows. As if the sight of me being there didn't fit at all.

"Good morning," Reina said with a chirpy voice and a light accent. Her expression was hard and not as friendly as she tried for her voice to be. "I heard you're both staying here until tomorrow. It's Raquel's birthday. She's turning five today."

I widened my eyes at that and rocked Raquel on my lap, leaning into her to show that I was excited for her. Although we didn't have birthdays in the Underworld, I knew the importance of this human festival day, thanks to Cherry. Her mother had turned 55 and she had taken me with her. So, I learned everything about loving mothers, cakes, and what it is to grow up in a neighborhood like Cherry's. It was very different from the one we were in right now.

"Yay! You stay," Raquel laughed, grabbing my cheeks with her sweet fingers.

"I—" Rio growled, and Raquel immediately went dead quiet. She looked at him, her lower lip trembling. I could tell she was disappointed. She was used to it, though.

"—look forward to your party," Rio finished his sentence.

He didn't seem to actually want to say this at all, but he did. Then he pointed at me. "Talk. Upstairs."

I was about to put Raquel down when Reina clicked her tongue. "Ai, Rio! I just made pancakes! Let her have breakfast first, why do you have to be so rude?"

Rio snorted. "She—"

"—will eat first!" Reina snarled.

Well, I was hungry, and I didn't like Rio's tone either, so I preferred the pancakes.

It was a little strange, though, to sit at the table with everyone, especially with Rio, puffing like a dragon in his pajamas. I found out that all of them indeed were Rio's siblings. But the middle kid was missing because he stayed at a friend's place.

"Don't you think he's with a girl? Sounds more believable at his age," Rio said and swallowed another piece of pancake. He would have been a good caveman. He probably could swallow a whole Sircha if he wanted to.

"I guess so," Reina replied briefly, taking a sip of orange

juice.

They were still fighting, but with their eyes this time.

"Reina—" Rio said, and then his sister started scolding him again in Spanish, as I learned.

After some time, she switched back to English. "We all know what it is like to raise children, Rio," she said with a lethal undertone. "Not just you! Ricardo changed diapers during the night. He's careful. Trust me, just because he sleeps there, he won't do anything stupid."

"Okay. Good," Rio said, throwing the napkin on his plate. "If you say so."

"Don't give me that look, Rio!"

Embarrassed, I tried to look elsewhere and noticed Rafael pick his little sister up off the chair and leave. Apparently, he knew what to do when their big brother and big sister fought. I would do the same, but it seemed a bit rude and disrespectful, so I just sat there and tried to get the dirt out from under my fingernails. Bory hid away somewhere and I couldn't even blame him.

"You haven't been around much the last few years, have you?" Reina hissed.

"I was there before that," Rio spat back. "It's thanks to me that you have this standard of living."

"Oh? Do we? Just because of you? I'd be long gone if they weren't so little! I could do whatever I want to, but no, raising them is apparently my job, a lesser one compared to yours, the almighty working man, huh? Aren't you an angel walking on earth!"

Rio shot up and held on to the table, clenching his fingers. "I raised you and Ricardo, Reina, from fourteen on and never stopped caring. So, go on! Tell me something about childcare." Rio held her stare and once she glanced away briefly, he sat down again, looking out of the window. "Fucking go to Europe or wherever you want, if you hate it so much here."

Reina snorted, throwing the cutlery on her plate. The loud bang made me jerk a little. "No. I am not like you. I won't abandon them. Ever." Her dark eyes focused on her brother.

I suddenly felt like all of this was getting much too personal for me to hear. I should leave...

"Remember who's paying for breakfast here, Reina."

Reina shot an angry gaze at Rio again. "Yeah, then remember who's here for them 24/7. Who they accidentally call Momma during the night when I kiss their nightmares away, and who forgot it was Raquel's fifth birthday!"

They were staring at each other. Ground, can you please swallow me up now?

But Reina caved first. "Ai! Your present is in the closet, wrapped. You can thank me later, prick."

Rio didn't say anything, just stood up, and simply nodded at me. Well, if that's not the universal sign for follow me... but anyway, I was happy that their awful conversation was finally over for now. When I ran after him, I saw Raquel and Rafael behind the living room door, hiding. I smiled at them and was glad they smiled back. They had surely overheard every single word.

Then I looked up at Rio. He was so tense. Stiff like a pillar. I followed him into his room where he reached into the bedside table, opened a pillbox, and took another pill. Afterwards, he took a deep breath and let himself fall backwards onto the bed, rubbing his temples.

"You shouldn't have seen this," he finally said after quite some time.

I pulled a face and realized there was a mirror opposite me. Shit. I looked pathetic. Dark circles under my eyes, messy hair, and I must have spilled maple syrup on my shirt... Oh, great. I tried to freshen up myself a little but stopped immediately when he pushed himself up on his elbows, pinning me with his blue eyes. His glare went to my bare thighs and yes, Reina's pants were small. Instinctively, I crossed my feet. Rio glanced away.

"No one can know I have a family, Barbie—okay. Wait. This feels wrong. Can you please just tell me your name? You know mine now, and I—I need to know yours. Maybe we're crossing a line here, but we already did, so…"

He tilted his head, suddenly worrying I would say no but that sounded like a good idea, and I didn't want to be called Barbie any longer. It was a silly name. So, I quickly got my mobile phone—by now I was faster at typing than at writing with a pen—and typed my name. He smiled when he read it.

"Lynne," he said, smiling as he said it, dragging out every syllable. "I'm trying to keep this top secret. A man who's got something to lose eventually will lose it all, you understand me?"

I nodded. Yeah, I knew what he meant.

He was afraid his family would get killed just to get at him.

"That means no one can know about this. Rio Renero is dead, Lynne. I was—"

He seemed to think about whether to tell me about it or not. So, I quickly typed a message on my cell phone.

I saved your life yesterday. Don't you think you can trust me by now?

"Trust? There is no such thing in Chicago. But yes, you did save my life yesterday. Thank you."

He looked at me for a long time then and I could feel that he was really grateful. So, I smiled back, typing another message.

You would have done the same thing. My ass did it to you.

He laughed when he read it.

"Pretentious, much?"

My cheeks burned. No, but I knew how he had looked at me in that dress last night.

"All right. I was in prison for a long time and when I got out, I worked my way up the Loops to provide for my family and give them a life, a chance I never had. Well, I also did it to achieve some selfish goals. It's not easy to just leave once you got the wheel spinning, but... I wanted revenge above all."

I made a face. *Revenge?*

"I need to return some favors," he said, glancing at his feet. "I know they say, that the wise ones let life happen to their enemies, but I go by a different saying. Ever heard the proverb: *The axe forgets, but the tree remembers?*"

I shook my head.

"Well, it means that I won't let Karma happen to those fuckers who wrecked my family, my life. I will be Karma instead, Lynne." Rio said with a stern voice that made me shiver. Serious. He was bloody serious.

Suddenly, the room seemed to get slightly colder, and I felt the hair on my nape rise in unison. He held my stare, probably checking if I caved once he told me the truth about his plans. But I didn't so much as flinch.

So, he continued.

"I faked my death eight years ago. There is no Rio anymore. My name is Baron. I severed all connections to the Reneros. I even let an old geezer adopt Reina and the rest to be able to legally care for them and be sure that my drug money never affected them. That means you can't tell anyone about this."

I made a face. How the skull was I supposed to tell anybody anyway?

"You still can communicate, Lynne," he said as if he had just read my mind. "You can write, type, paint. I don't know. The fact you can't talk is the only reason I tell you anything about myself at all right now. Nobody knows this but Any, Punchy, and Slappy, and they only do because they grew up with me. Do you understand how important it is that you don't let anything trickle through?"

He looked up at me, his arms resting on his knees.

Hell, I saw Raquel and Rafael with his Spiderman in front of my eyes and yes—I understood. Suddenly, all of Nana's kids came to my mind as well. I knew what it meant to care for someone and fear for them. In the Underworld a lot of people wanted to have a kid, and they were traded for even more than Bloodcoins. Mostly, the rich court members wanted kids as a pet, to pretend that they were a family or use them as their slaves. I tried to save the children but couldn't save them all. So, I nodded. I knew how to protect dear ones and just like that I kneeled before him and took his hands in mine. No one would ever hear the slightest thing from me about his family.

I even wanted to tell him about Any at that moment but suddenly I wasn't so sure anymore if he did want to kill him after all. What if I really misunderstood the signs? What if he was trying to save him, not kill him? Maybe there was more to it, and I simply didn't know. My gut told me something else, but I decided not to tell him for now, to keep it to myself and try to find more information. I could still keep an eye on Any, and that certainly didn't mean I had to like him, because I never would.

"You're probably wondering how I ended up selling drugs."

I nodded, glad he finally told me something about him.

"My mother was Swedish, my father South-Italian. I have her looks, but my father's bad traits, he was a gangleader and had unfinished business. I needed to take care of it at a young age. Unfortunately, my mother died when I was one, so my father's new wife and her mother—my abuela—adopted me, raised me. Therefore, I'm Catholic, my first language is Spanish, and I celebrate Mexican festivals and customs. But I don't belong anywhere. Not really. I'm no Latino like my siblings, not European like my parents…and to some, I'm not even american enough thanks to my Italian face and my different mother tongue. So, I guess, I'm a mess."

I shook my head. What should be wrong about him? I just

didn't understand. He was the most attractive man I had ever seen and the language he spoke to his sister attracted me even more. So, he certainly had no problems because of it, or did he? What could anyone not like about his skulling great mix? Then, he took another pill, and I looked at him questioningly. It bothered him, though.

"Anxiety reliever," he admitted, biting his lip. "You're learning a lot about me, aren't you? I've been haunted by my past since... since I was fifteen, and my current job doesn't make it any better. The pills help but I forgot to take one yesterday. Usually, I get by pretty well but...I need to be at a certain level and when I forget to take the pills and have to do something I hate, like handling guns, it happens. I always think I'll die. My feelings are eating me up inside." He sighed. "Man, I can't believe I'm telling you all this. I'm rambling."

He laughed a tad too loud. I could tell that it was simply because he felt embarrassed and didn't know what else to do. Then he got up and his foot fidgeted. Why was he suddenly nervous like a hellhound? I wondered what else he kept from me, or all the others?

My eyes followed him as he stopped in the middle of the room, looking right at me and oh, all I could think about was how handsome he was. His eyes were light blue, not just blue like the human sky, no, even brighter. Like the stars that I never saw down below, like a little glimmer of freedom in a body that seemed so locked up.

"You realize if anyone finds out about this, you're gonna die, don't you?"

I knew he told me the truth. He wanted to play down the harshness of his words, but he meant it. There was nothing above his family.

"I have to accomplish something really big, Lynne. Until then, everything must go like clockwork."

I nodded. Didn't I have the same problem? My soul was at

stake if I messed up. If things didn't work out like I wanted them to. We both knew very well what could happen if one of us screwed up.

"All right, then," Rio said. "We'll stay here tonight, if that's all right with you, of course. I can have Any drive you back, if you prefer, but I think the kids would... love it if you stayed."

He lowered his gaze, avoiding mine, as if he was suddenly afraid that I didn't want to stay here. That I wanted to go and leave him here alone. But I nodded anyway and showed him I really wanted to stay. I tried to convince myself that it was only to finally kiss him and fulfill the contract. Oddly enough, there was more to it, though.

I never really had a family, rarely anyone in the Under-world did, except the rich ones who were pretenders, but I didn't have a found family either, no people I wanted to have around me. Except Soothie, Bory, and Mal, of course. I was all by myself and somehow it felt good not to be alone right now. Cherry showed me how nice it could be to be in a place that you shared with people you loved, even if you didn't have much.

"Lynne," Rio said and came closer, "will I ever know where you come from? Why you are here?"

I hesitated but thought the better of it and shook my head. He never would. Even if I wanted him to know, I couldn't tell him. There was no way.

"Well, I have to accept it then," Rio said and played with the ties of his pajama bottoms, making me feel a certain tingle in my stomach. "I'll keep some things from you and you from me. Sounds like a deal."

As I RETURNED to the guest room, I smelled a scent. Myrtle and smoke. All my muscles tensed as I rushed to the door, pressing the handle with ice-cold fingers. The room was dark, pitch dark but the window was open. Everything screamed *magic*. I shut the door and placed myself against it, trying to keep anything dangerous in and everything I cared for out.

"Well, well, well."

When I heard the Blood Queen's voice, I winced and searched the dark room. My eyes were used to the bright world now and I saw nothing for a few seconds until she raised her elegant hand and made a tiny ball of fire dance on her fingers. It hopped from the left to the right. The faint light illuminated her face and gave me a close look at her smirking mouth. There was nothing but pleasure on her face.

"I can't stay long, darling," she purred. "Normally I'm not allowed to be here, but thanks to your bone I'm capable of a lot."

She walked up to me and her emerald green dress swung gently around her thighs, showing me her hour-glass figure. Then she shot forward, and raised her hand, showing me a smothering fire between her fingers. I staggered back, looking at her other hand. Bory. She had Bory and he was unconscious!

"Leave him alone," I gritted through my teeth.

"Oh," she grinned, and looked at Bory. "Not so fast. I'm just here to remind you why you're here."

I swallowed and felt the sweat run down my neck and my stomach tightened. "I know that, your Highness."

"Apparently not!" she said, but then she relaxed her face noticeably and crackled her neck. "You must kiss him, not stare him to death!"

"I—I know… your Highness!"

"Then make it happen, you need forever, and I'm bored. You know what's at stake, don't you?"

I nodded and tried to push the lump down my throat.

The Blood Queen smiled, shook her head, and came at me. The fire shot from her hand, leaving a trail of smoke behind. She then grabbed my throat with her cold fingers and pain shot through my whole body, as if she had stabbed me with thousands of tiny knives. I felt the stinging everywhere. The heat rushed through me, and I had a sudden need to scratch me everywhere at once. I screamed, but my cry died at my throat when she put an image in my head. She forced herself into my mind as if it were an open door for her.

Shadow slavery.

It was pitch black again, it stank of sulphur and rotten eggs, and I was naked, stripped of my body—only a shadow remained. I felt nothing but pain and was doomed to do the lowly work for the queens and the king. Sewing clothes out of blood and shadows and ashes. Making food from embers, dust, and dirt, to transform them with stolen magic that was not supposed to be used by shadows. The magic rushed through my body and ate me up until there was nothing of my shadowy body left and then…

It started all over again. Working and being eaten up.

Pain, all I could feel was eternal pain.

When she let go of me, I sank to the ground, breathing heavily, crouching on all fours on the floor trying to breathe, trying to get some fresh air again, but my lungs felt as if they had thousands of little glass shards inside.

"That's what's in store for you, sweetheart. So, don't play around and do your duty. You don't have much time left, and I *want* my book."

Then I heard her turn away from me and exhaled the breath I was holding in. "Oh, I'm taking Bory with me. He'll bring you the information you need as soon as I locate its damned place."

CHAPTER FIFTEEN
RIO

L ynne was here. With my family.

And that was all I could think about as she sat in the pink sandbox building towers with my five-year-old baby sister and her little friends. She could communicate with the children in a different way. With kids, she didn't need to speak, because it was all about her eyes and her contagious laugh. I could hear the kids giggling every so often, and I wondered how she did it. What did she do to make the children laugh like that? So, every time, my eyes flicked to the sandbox, and sometimes, our eyes met. She was playing with me even more than before. But did this game mean what I thought?

Reina looked at me more than once and I knew I was smiling at Lynne. Adoring her. God, I was stupid. My puppy-eyed sisters talked me into staying here and jeopardizing my dream, and I let her. Meanwhile, all hell was breaking loose in Englewood. Yesterday's shooting caused severe internal conflicts. I had to yell at Punchy and Slappy on the phone three times already. My muscles were tense and my neck stiff, but Reina was right. I had to be here for my little sister.

The rest went like clockwork, thank God. Any told me that

Z-Mexx leaked yesterday that he knew van der Volt was moving to Chicago. Once they knew where he lived, gang leaders would probably contact and blackmail him and therefore, I had to do something. But right now, I was giving pink presents to my sister, laughing as she blew out the candles, and singing her birthday song. Was I the same man today as yesterday? No. Today I was Rio and I hated being in this skin once again. Living with this guilt. I preferred being the Baron these days.

But something else set my nerves on edge.

It was Lynne seeing me like that and me not even trying to stop her. There was a rule that no one in the gang could get involved with each other, and the rule was not taken lightly. It made sense. I was already afraid for her when I thought about all the things I still had to make her do.

How would my stupidity affect the project? The day of days? The one day I had been planning for fifteen years now? Maybe I should let her go, give her the bone, and tell her off. But when I saw her sitting in the sandbox in the white dress and the long blond ponytail, grinning at me like a nymph, a naïve thought came up: *grab her and run away with her.*

I snorted at my dumb thoughts and drank the martini all at once, glad at the faint burn in my throat. Of course, Reina saw it and glanced at me reproachfully. She knew me like the back of her hand, but instead of saying anything, she poured me another martini. Oh, I couldn't even be angry with her.

She had three degrees from Chicago University and the opportunity to do her doctorate in Europe. Her dream. But what did she do? She cancelled because she had to take care of our brothers and Raquel. Their mother and my stepmother, Alba, had died because of our father. Because that prick let slip her identity, just like he did with my mother's. Eventually they all had to die, when the other gangs found out that my dad had a family and enjoyed pancakes on weekends, in the middle of a drug war.

Abuela raised us, because my father had been on the run since I knew him, but abuela was old. Eventually, she also died after Raquel was born.

I only cried for two people in my life: Aria and my dear abuela.

When my mother died, I couldn't cry because I didn't know. I was one year old, and after that I only knew my mother from photos and an album with Winnie the Pooh on the cover. I had to protect my family, more than anything else. That's why I felt like I was burning up in flames while enjoying cake with my loved ones. Not because I didn't want to be here but because I shouldn't.

Something warm hit me and I looked down at my feet, smiling. Raquel hugged my feet. I picked her up. She always missed me the most. I squeezed her tightly, smelling her strawberry scent.

"Eres mi pequeña querida, ¿lo sabes, cierto?" I said to my baby sister, telling her she's my little darling. And yes, it felt good to speak Spanish again. It was a different feeling to speak my native language. Like freedom. It was easier, even though I spoke English without any accent. Spanish was what my heart spoke. The language of my dear abuela. She was probably scolding me from heaven right now because of the job I had.

I grabbed the little silver cross around my neck and prayed to God, she would forgive me. I had to do it, for Aria at least, and make up for the bad things I've done.

Reina did everything to give Raquel the best day of her life, and I was proud of both of them. Raquel had so many friends, all of different backgrounds and statuses, and that's what I wanted for everyone. Including the kids at Englewood. I wanted everyone to have that chance, the best possible health care, education, and welfare. Even though I couldn't give

Raquel and Rafael any parents, I could make sure that they could get any education they wanted, and they could choose their job and not be forced to do anything for a living.

I rubbed my nose against Raquel's, and she laughed, high pitched, and started to tickle me. I tipped my head back and laughed with her, noticing the glance Reina gave us, smiling only with her eyes though.

I took in Raquel's dark eyes and was glad she wouldn't have to grow up in a Robert Taylor building like me and Reina— where the urine from the apartment upstairs leaked into the bedroom. She wouldn't get beaten up because of where she came from. My only way out was selling drugs; it allowed me to have a cell phone or go to the movies like the other kids with normal parents—like the kids in the movies we always watched on TV. The world was an open book for my siblings, ready to be read.

"Did you enjoy your day?" I asked Lynne as the evening came to an end.

The children had all been in bed for a long time now and only the adults were still in the garden, drinking a few night-caps. She sat alone in the white wooden pergola. Several different roses overgrew it and a small fountain in front of it rippled gently while she sat on an iron chair, pondering. She stared at the moon and thought about something. Something serious.

She was beautiful. The moonlight lit up her hair, and her eyes shone towards me, pinning me. At the sight of her I hesitated, with two drinks in my hand, and just like that I realized *why* I approached her now. I couldn't do that. No, I couldn't always picture her in my bed, under me and looking at me like that from below. No, I couldn't. I was fucking up everything I'd spent years building. The stories were always the same, and I read enough to know what was coming for me. All the heroes failed when love was involved and yet I still stood next to her.

This was my downfall.

"It was a nice day after all, wasn't it?" I said, giving her the drink.

She didn't seem to mind all those drinks at all, as if she were used to stronger ones. She nodded and started to write a message for me with her phone. Fortunately, she didn't see me staring at her cleavage while doing so. My cheeks burned.

Your siblings are great, she texted me.

"Yeah. They are."

Thanks for letting me be part of it, we do not celebrate birthdays, she wrote.

I narrowed my eyes at her. Where the hell don't people celebrate birthdays? "Lynne, what country are you from?" I couldn't forget about the strangeness that enveloped her, the feeling of otherness when I looked at her.

She smiled faintly, staring at the moon again.

There was a sinking feeling in my stomach. I'd never know, right?

But there had to be a way to find out where she came from, there had to be! Was she really Amish? Or had she been locked in a cellar for years? My skin tingled with impatience, and I wanted to push her further, make her answer me, but I stopped. It was not my place to ask. I had plenty of things I couldn't tell her, so I needed to let it go or find it out by myself instead of torturing her with questions that obviously hurt her. "We're leaving in the morning for the club. Punchy will get us."

She nodded again.

"Do you want to do something stupid?" I asked, and suddenly her lips curled up into the dirty smile I was so fond of.

THAT NIGHT, we climbed to the roof of the tallest church in the suburbs. I had packed up a bottle of wine, which we drank like it was totally normal to do so on a roof in a rich ass neighborhood. But I felt comfortable up here, and so did she. Up here, the lanterns lit up all the mansions down there, the pools seemed to be small turquoise puddles and the little garden lights like fireflies.

We sat, talked—well, she wrote—about stupid things until the sun came up. Of course, I often thought about how it would be if I ripped that stupid dress off her body. I also saw more than two times under her dress when she climbed the wall. And yes, something was stirring in my pants too.

And then, Lynne asked me why my dad or Reina's mom didn't look after the kids.

"Well," I started, staring over the many different shaped roofs in front of us, "my father is a selfish bastard. Back then, just before I was born, he was the boss of an Italian gang. They were the strongest gang back then… The Loops were small and not very important. My father became greedy, acted like he was a god and believed himself to be one. Then he was betrayed and before the cops came and took him away, one of his so-called friends and senior officers robbed him, stole his money, and killed my mother. Then they almost killed me just out of spite and envy. My father rescued me, took me to the woman he had on the side, married her only hours later and disappeared into prison for a few years. At some point, he broke out and dragged his wife Alba further and further into his shit. Then Reina and Ricardo were born."

I swallowed, needing a break.

Visualizing my past always made my pulse race and my fingers twitch. But I wanted to tell her, I needed to tell someone and therefore I left my comfort zone. "My father couldn't make it back to the top as he'd always promised. None of the gang leaders wanted him anymore because he was so arrogant and full of shit. In prison, he told the cops too much about the other gangs to get cigars."

Lynne was typing on her cell phone, her brow slightly furrowed.

He sold out his friends for cigars?

I nodded. "Some people do it for less, and my father is a weak man."

What about Raquel and Rafael? she wrote.

I shrugged. "Alba became a drug addict and let my father persuade her to run away with him. They left us with Alba's mother and didn't return for years. Abuela was always more than a grandmother to me, she was the only real mother I ever had, but she couldn't speak English until the end of her life, so we only learned English in kindergarten properly."

That's intense, she wrote.

I was so glad she didn't write that she was sorry. Only then did it occur to me that she probably knew how I felt and was therefore wiser than to pity me.

"When I was fourteen, my middle school teacher made me apply for a scholarship, because I stood out, you know. I read a lot, didn't have to learn as much as the others and simply knew every word she'd told us. Because of that, I was allowed to attend a much sought after private high school in fall."

Thinking about myself back then made me laugh. I had all sorts of ideas about how great my future was going to be, because I was granted a scholarship. About the chances I had of getting into a school like that after I graduated. Well, it never came to that.

"Wanna hear something stupid?"

She looked at me as if to say: *of course!*

"I see numbers and letters in colors. My brain couples sensory perceptions to each other, which makes it easier for me to remember everything imaginable, to calculate numbers that many wouldn't even try without a computer. I remember words, patterns, and languages more easily than anyone else. It's called synesthesia."

Lynne raised her eyebrows and typed something again. *What colors does my name have for you?*

"Shades of red and white."

She grinned, frowned slightly, and asked what my father had been up to.

"I transferred to high school and barely a year later Alba and my father, led by drugs, left again and didn't come back for years. Abuela had to raise us, but she didn't have many opportunities to keep us afloat. She cleaned when we slept, but it wasn't enough."

As I talked about it, I noticed my breathing was speeding up, my chest rising and falling heavily. What Alba and my father had done to us was still bugging me. Being here with Reina and the others triggered all the memories.

"I noticed that some of my old classmates suddenly had more and more money and so I met the gang leader of the Toxic Taipans, the Mexican gang. He took me in because I spoke Spanish, and I started as a drug mule. Alba and father returned after several years, introducing us to Rafael. Some years later she gave birth to Raquel. Shortly after, Alba got shot and father disappeared again, leaving his children behind once more. We didn't need him anymore, though…Once I got out of jail, I made more money than he ever could."

If I ever see your father, I'll kill him, she wrote and made me smile.

"But only if I'm dead. He's mine to end."

She nodded. *Deal.*

I wanted to top off her glass, but I slipped and stopped just below her alluring gaze, letting my eyes search hers. Our noses touched, giving me hot flashes throughout my body. Her lips were so close, I could bend down and kiss her. Closing my eyes for a second, I felt her hot breath on my lips and pulled back.

My heart raced in my chest, awareness and desire on its highest level.

I couldn't let this happen. As soon as I'd touch her lips, I'd fuck her. There was no way back and if I did, it was all fucked. Women reacted with strange feelings after sex. They confused happiness with love and such feelings didn't exist for people like Lynne and me.

"We have to go, it's getting late, " I said, my stomach sinking when I saw the disappointed look on her face. But it was better, for the both of us.

WHEN I LAY in my bed, I couldn't stop thinking about our little nose rub. Wrapped up in my black satin duvet I remembered she had fallen asleep here beside me yesterday. On the floor. She watched over me.

I took my mobile and texted her.

Are you thinking of me? I wrote, because I thought of her.

I knew it was far-fetched to assume she thought of me too and maybe a little provocative as well, but as far as I knew, there were two ways to get a woman's attention. Either you gave them what they wanted, or you made them angry. I was a proponent of the second premise, because there was nothing hotter than a woman who didn't know if she wanted to kiss or kill me.

The world doesn't always revolve around you, idiot, she wrote back.

I laughed.

Man, I'd love to hear her voice just once. Know what it sounded like. The way she'd say my name, the way she'd yell at me, the way she'd whisper something into my ear. I imagined her voice melodic and soft with a slight accent.

Asking yourself if my eyes have undressed you today? I wrote quickly.

I don't have to ask myself that question. I know the answer, she wrote.

Do you? Tell me then, I wrote back.

Your eyes have never done anything but undress me. Quite curious what I look like underneath, Rio?

There it was again.

My name. Hundreds of questions were bursting through my mind right now. Did she emphasize the initial *r* more than others? Did she roll the *r*? Did she draw my name long or was it sharp and short? Purred?

While rereading her message I smiled. Yes, she was right, but she was no better; that's why it was so grossly negligent what we did right now or the whole weekend itself. We were glancing at each other, touching each other slightly as we passed, trying to get near. That was the sort of attraction that worried me. I had to stop it but still, I wanted to go into her room and undress her, touch her breasts, her belly, her butt. The three Bs at last. My body ached for her and I wondered why I had such feelings. Was it the primal hunting instinct deep inside of me that made me want her so badly? The wish to fuck her once? Or was it because of that feeling that I've had since I first saw her? That I knew her from somewhere…

Good night, Bone Thief, I wrote.

Good night, Baron, she texted back.

I forced myself to stop now. It was better that way.

CHAPTER SIXTEEN
LYNNE

After Punchy had brought us back the next morning, Rio's and my little vacation was over. Those two nights with his family had been like a dream I never knew I had. If only I could have stayed longer and explored this world by myself.

Rio had not been at the breakfast table in the morning. I only saw him when Punchy picked us up. Even though his texts let me think he wanted me, I was too anxious to go to his room and try for the kiss. I did try at the roof, and he clearly didn't want to kiss me.

For the love of Stix.

I wondered if it was some kind of trick, like playing hot and cold with me, or if I had written something wrong yesterday. Why did I always mess things up? I needed this kiss, the queen had made it more than clear. Simply thinking about her gave me the shivers. For a person who's never been scared before, I've been pissing my pants a lot lately and my time was running out.

The whole trip back, Rio calculated some numbers with Punchy—or rather told Punchy something he couldn't quite grasp—and talked about his business. Drugs, sales, weapons, borders…

When we were back in Englewood, Rio shot into the club without even looking at me. After all we had experienced in the last forty-eight hours, the honesty we had shared. How dare he treat me like that? Somehow, I felt closer to him now than before and yet he treated me like one of his foot soldiers. I wanted to hit him with my shoe again. Yeah, that was a good feeling.

I didn't have time to think deeply about his rejection or that Bory still wasn't back, because Cherry, Mallow, and Cheetah were already waiting for me, arms folded, brows furrowed and asking hundreds of questions.

Why and where I was with the boss, what I was doing with him, why I was wearing different clothes and why nobody had heard a word from us since Friday.

I shooed them away and went up to my room to find none other than Fox herself waiting in front of my door, blocking the entry like a beautiful stone figure. She crossed her long black legs, making me wish to be that tall too. She wore hotpants and a white top that showed her big breasts.

Fox said nothing to me but watched my every step, her eyes flitting over me from top to bottom. I tried to ignore her, going straight for the door handle but her look pierced me like a knife, and I felt her eyes like daggers on my skin. Fox was hurt, that I could tell, and I knew she wanted me to pay for it. She waited for me to give me a message. Oh, I received it, thank you. She thought Rio was hers.

I stopped and nodded at her, trying to let her know that I didn't care about what she thought and slammed the door in her pretty face.

Later, I learned that everyone talked about that the boss had taken me on holiday to fuck me. I knew that I was not allowed to tell the truth under any circumstances, but I couldn't let them think such things as well, right? I wasn't his personal whore after all.

So, I wrote them a little about the opera, the shooting, and that we had to hide until things calmed down, emphasizing the part that we didn't sleep with each other or even kiss. No romance at all. That seemed to be enough. Although the girls continued to ask questions, which I answered partly with truths and partly with lies. Cheetah later fetched me and Cherry some drinks, and we cuddled up in the living room, ignoring Fox and her lapdogs.

But it felt so strange. In the short time I had been here, I felt more comfortable than all these years in the Underworld. Although I knew nothing about this world, deep inside I felt as if I really belonged here. As if I had been mis-assigned to the Underworld.

When Cheetah and Cherry had to prepare for their shift, I found myself dancing on the bar with them, with alcohol bottles in both of my hands. Well, okay, the evening had escalated quickly, but we had fun and the girls brought Dee some pretty good money. So, everything was good. Of course, I had to wear my pink wig and wasn't allowed to talk to any of the men—not that I could anyway—but I had more fun with Cherry and Cheetah behind or on the bar anyways than I would have had if I really had to work like the other girls. That was hard-earned cash, it really was.

"WAKE UP, PARTY GIRL!" Slappy cried the next day.

I cracked one eye open and saw him waiting at the end of the bed.

"If you can drink, you can work," he said, pulling me out of bed. *Oh skull*, I'd forgotten I had target practice again today.

Oh, I missed Bory. Since Saturday night I couldn't really talk to a soul and that hit me pretty bad. So, to stop thinking about my situation, I got up, did what Slappy said and went with him.

I spent the next three days with Punchy and Slappy at the shooting range and it went so well that Punchy was now not only afraid of my hands but of me as a person and that was so funny. If someone saw the two of us together, they'd think I must be afraid of Punchy and not the other way around. He was at least three times the size of me. His look was always grim, his eyebrows constantly furrowed, but Punchy was a softie with a penchant for songs sung by women and cheese-cakes. Oh, he was a sucker for cheesecake. We often had to stop at a bakery and because he was embarrassed that he liked that stuff so much, I had to get him his large Frappuccino and a cheesecake.

"Van der Volt will buy a house here, in the area. I heard," Slappy said to Punchy as we drove home from the shooting range.

"Pssht," Punchy hissed, checking me through the rear-view window.

He still didn't trust me and didn't want me to overhear any important conversations. *Silly bear.* I rolled my eyes, checking my cell phone for the hundredth time. I've been waiting for texts from Rio for three days, but none came. Unbelievable how addicted I already was. I constantly looked at Rio's profile pic in my messenger and zoomed in, gazed at him, sighing.

Was he playing with me?

I guessed.

Still, I wanted to see how far his games would go. Did they go as far as mine? We were both players. I needed that attraction, and I had to make him want me, really want me, but the more we went in that direction, the worse it got. It didn't feel right and day after day I hated the Blood Queen even more, especially now that she was keeping Bory down there, for whatever purpose. I needed my little friend. I really did but time was different in the Underworld, and I knew that mere seconds lasted days on Earth. I wouldn't see Bory for a long time...

But the question of what role I played in Rio's games was constantly on my mind, and I needed Bory to sort it out. He always told me the truth, if I wanted it or not, he was my needed voice of reason.

So, the question was, if Rio and I were on the verge of cheating on each other, or if he did have something else in mind? For my part, I didn't want anything else but to get the things for the damned queen, and yet every minute I looked at my phone I could have thrown it out of the window because I had no message from him, asking myself why he wouldn't talk to me. Why he didn't want to see me.

"Barbie? Please?" Punchy smiled at me, and I realized he'd stopped.

To our right was the Pie Factory. I smiled back.

Again, Punchy? I mimicked.

He shrugged. "Barbie, I even said please!"

"The fuck, Punchy? You're getting fatter and fatter!" Slappy growled, staring him down.

"Hey!" Punchy grumbled, he hit a weak spot of his and I glared at Slappy. "Everyone loves something to cuddle with at night."

"Yeah, a little. Boobs and all, but not your swimming tires!"

Before it got out of hand, I slightly hit Slappy's back and got out of the car. They always had to pick at each other.

"We'll wait by the parking lot, Barbie," Slappy said through the open window as I crossed the street.

By now it really had become a habit, Punchy the old sweet tooth.

When I queued up in front of the cash desk, clasping my clutch, the man in front of me grinned at me. He had short black curls with a few white strands neatly decorating his head. His skin was a soft amber and matched his honey *brown* eyes. He certainly was a looker, so I grinned back.

A little flirting hurt nobody, right?

"Well? Cake or coffee?" he asked.

I smiled again, stroking back a strand of hair. At moments like these I really hated that I couldn't talk. So, I just shrugged.

"Shy girl, huh? I'm Farid."

Then he wanted to shake my hand and clumsily pushed the clutch of my hand. It fell on the ground and the seal sprung open, spreading all my things on the floor. Skull!

Farid and I were both ducking for my things and suddenly we both froze, glancing at my stuff. At *it*. There was a small plastic bag. Thanks to Rio, I knew exactly what kind of bag that was. C-Wax. Right in front of us.

Yellow, glittery stuff.

How did it get in *my* clutch? I had nothing to do with that and I didn't want to! Rio had told me all about the drug and that he didn't want any of the gang members to take it. Did Fox smuggle it into my stuff? That would fit, and a flyer from an art auction was in there too. Reacting quickly, I grabbed everything and ran out.

"Stop!" Farid yelled after me.

He pushed himself through the gawking people, following me. As I pressed the door open in panic he started shouting. "Stop! Police! Get the girl!"

From my peripheral vision, I saw him holding up his police badge. Rio informed me that I had to flee as soon as I saw that thing. Skull. Of course, Farid was a cop! What else? I had such bad luck. A handsome guy in a bakery smiled at me and then it turned out he was a cop! I frantically looked over my shoulder. He was still on the hunt for me, running. Fortunately, I was faster. Jumping over benches and trash cans, I ran down the street, squeezing in between all the people that strolled around.

But just as I was about to check for Farid again, I rammed into another man. Not my day, huh?

He was coming out of the doctor's office that had aroused my interest while driving by before. The sign said, *'Psychotherapy, Dr. Meinhard'*. Punchy had explained to me that this was a shrink, but I didn't know what that was either. So, he simply had said that these were doctors, who talked with people. Not that I understood why one should pay people to simply talk to them.

But out of this very doctor's office came a man, with snake eyes and a dark suit. He grabbed me, holding me with a firm grip. Panting, I looked up at him with eyes wide open, checking if Punchy and Slappy could see me and help me. But they were still far away, probably arguing about cheesecakes and some musicians called Rihanna or Ariana Grande.

"Come," the man said, glancing at the street and pushing me back into the building with the *Psychotherapy* sign on top of it. The man saw the cop too and squinted his eyes at him. Then he followed me into the building, and we were both standing in a stairwell, staring each other down with pure curiosity.

After a couple of seconds, I managed to wriggle out of his grip, wondering why the hell he stared at me like that, as if he saw a ghost. Then I checked the door again and could see through the milky glass that the policeman was running in the wrong direction. *Phew*, that was close. Freaking Fox. Skull her.

Skull her for doing such a thing. She probably wanted Rio to find it, assuming we would hook up or something like that. Him thinking I took drugs would definitely screw everything up for me.

"Where did you get this stuff?" the man asked me.

He had an accent, a little like Reina but much stronger. His eyebrows were as thick as his thumb and his gaze hard as steel. His nose was big and his eyes snake-like. Green like poison.

When I didn't answer, he tore the C-Wax out of my clutched hand, smelled it and then grabbed the flyer, frowning deeply.

"Have you made contact with van der Volt?"

I didn't move.

If he knew *that name*, he must have been working in the drug scene too. Could that be a coincidence? In Chicago there lived a lot of drug dealers, I knew that, but it still was a little awkward to meet a guy who asked *me* about Volt within seconds of meeting me.

He shook me. "This man who's after you. A cop?"

I nodded. At least, that's what it seemed like. He grabbed for my wig and pulled it down, his eyes widening as he took in my white-ish hair.

"Those fuckers," he said. "You were at the opera the other night. A girl like you can't be mistaken for anyone else."

He knew me from there, then. I looked at him closer now and remembered him too. Yeah, I had seen him at the opera. He had talked to Z-Mexx, but they weren't friends, their meeting was rather unpleasant but they seemed to talk to each other about something important. As always it was about one man. From afar I thought I had heard the name *van der Volt*, and now I was sure.

"I'll keep that, " he quickly pocketed the C-Wax. "Stay safe, the others are out looking for you."

I arched my eyebrows. *Who was looking for me? Why?*

But he was already gone. I remembered the address of the doctor's office and ran to the parking lot, not wanting to stay here another second. I didn't put on the wig again, just in case the policeman was around the corner.

"Man, what did you do, Barbie?" Punchy sighed, taking me and my heavy breathing in as I finally reached them.

"Where's my cheesecake?"

My mouth fell open at that. I was so mad I gave Punchy the middle finger and okay, I wasn't usually this grumpy with him, but what I was going through was just too much. His skulling cake was the last thing I could think about right now. Worst of all, I couldn't discuss any of it with Bory later to find a solution. For skull's sake! Of course, Punchy and Slappy were anxiously waiting until I wrote them what had just happened.

"Shit," Slappy said. "We gotta tell the Baron."

"But my cheesecake," Punchy grumbled.

"Drive! Idiot!" Slappy screamed, punching our driver and this time I didn't mind at all.

WHEN WE GOT BACK, Slappy accompanied me to Diva Dee's and Punchy went straight to Rio. My fingers were itching. Oh, I wanted to text him so badly, especially after my skulling day. I started to pace around in my room again and then—just like that—he stood there, leaning at my closed door, ankles crossed, and his arms folded.

"How are you?" Rio acted as if he hadn't been ignoring me for days.

I shrugged. Was that really what he wanted to ask?

"Pick up your cell," he commanded.

I grunted at his tone. I had no other choice but to grab it, because I couldn't skulling talk or scream at him. Nevertheless, I showed him that I was not at all happy with the way he spoke to me. Over the last weeks I quickly learned how important facial expressions and gestures were and even without speaking, it was very clear to him that I was anything but in good spirits.

"What happened at the bakery?"

His tone didn't get any better nor did his scowl, but I texted him what I had already written to Punchy and Slappy. However, I left out the part about the C-Wax. I wanted to deal with Fox myself and didn't want him to think I was buying this stuff from some dealer.

"That was it?" he asked as if he knew I left something out.

I stiffened at that and pressed my lips into a fine line. Why did he ask me that? Did he put it into my clutch or did Fox tell him about it?

I gave him a challenging look.

Apparently, that was the wrong answer. He took a step away from me, checking me up once more.

"Rumors say you know van der Volt. You don't, right?" he asked as if he weren't so sure about trusting me anymore.

I snorted and shook my head vehemently. No, I didn't know that freaking man. Why was everyone asking me about that stupid skull?

"Maybe it's the light hair. They also thought Any was my contact. Totally wrong. Maybe that's the way people here imagine the Dutch." He shrugged his shoulders and looked at me once more.

I narrowed my eyes at him. What the hell did he want from me?

"Well, you and I have a very simple relationship," he then said with a serious undertone, and I became very attentive.

Oh, did we?

Was it simple to climb into dizzy heights together, was it simple to write kinky messages, was it simple to undress each other with our eyes, was it simple to save each other's lives and at the same time make them harder than necessary? My gaze asked him all these questions and he seemed to understand but didn't even bother to think about it for a second.

"There's an event in a month," he said, ignoring my angry look. "Van der Volt wants to settle in Chicago. To avoid the stress of dealing with the gang bosses, he wants to sell his C-Wax formula at an auction to the highest bidder and retire with a shitload of money before it's too late. In doing so, he wants it to become someone else's problem. That's where we come in. We want the problem, and until then, I need you. Then you leave for good, okay? Never return, no looking back."

I caught my breath.

I didn't see that coming.

I knew we'd part soon, but the way he spoke to me right now was different. Cold. This man in front of me was not the same man who smiled at me on the roof under the stars, touching me again and again as if he had no control over it. What had I suddenly done?

Taking some steps back, I tried to nod at him, pretended not to care. I felt my lips quiver slightly but demanded it to stop. That left me a week to find the book. Alright. That was possible, a bit risky, but possible. I would kiss him goodbye, somehow, hoping it would be enough and then I would find the book. Assuming that Bory could tell me where to find it after all.

Then Rio pulled me out of my thoughts by showing me a piece of paper, an ad. It was the same flyer I had in my clutch at the Pie Factory. He pinned me with his deep blue eyes, probably feeling my uneasiness draping over the room like a quilt.

Did he really put the drugs in my bag? Or was that flyer also another message from Fox to tell me she was one step ahead of me? By the Dead, maybe it really was for the better to just disappear in four weeks and never see anyone here again.

Rio closed up the space between us, his eyes still fixed on me. I looked up, suddenly well aware how much taller he was. If I had gone closer, I could have put my chin into the hollow of his chest and he could have easily put his head on mine.

"Tomorrow we're going to a party," Rio said then, casually, his long lashes touching his cheekbones like a fan.

I was so glad he said something. Anything. I could hardly stand the silence. Even though there was nothing I could do to fill the silence acoustically, when we really talked with each other, it felt like I was talking, filling the silence in a peculiar way. I would laugh, wink, twist my eyes or change my gaze, type sweet nothings into my cell phone, and gestures. Now I just looked at him, and he looked back. Neither of us said what's really on our minds, what that weekend did to us.

Not wanting him to know how disappointed I was about how cold our relationship had gotten, I simply nodded, staring at his hands. The hands that had touched me hundreds of times already. Whatever. Let's go to another stupid party.

"Punchy will give you more information later. Stay in here until then and try not to party too much at the club and get off on drunk men."

I narrowed my eyes at him. He muttered the last part of the sentence, but I could hear it quite well.

My eyebrows shot up.

"Stay in," he said, and I could swear his nostrils quivered.

I opened my mouth but before I could croak anything, Rio stormed out of my bedroom.

I turned around, punching a wall.

That son of a witch. What was he even thinking? Me getting *off* on drunk men?

At that very moment, Bory showed up in a corner, black smoke all over the room. I forgot about Rio and shot to the window, closing it and pulling all the curtains. Bory coughed, waving his puffy arms in front of his face. After I checked everything, I ran to him, taking him into my arms and squeezing.

"Thank the Stix, you're back."

"I missed you too. The book is at an auction, according to the Blood Queen, I don't know where and—" he babbled, and I quickly interrupted him.

"—Shhh, Bory, slow down. I'm so glad your back!"

"Yes, me too but Lynne," he squealed. "We run out of

time. We have to find out what auction she meant and—"

"Oh, I know exactly what auction..." The very skulling auction Rio was talking about just seconds ago. It seemed everything was about to go down on that stupid day then.

I put Bory on my bed and slumped in next to him, telling him all about the C-Wax, what happened at the Pie Factory and of course, about Fox and how cold Rio was towards me now. How I messed it all up again...

"Everything seems to be connected," he said, "but I think the queen wants to help you. She watches you in her blood well, so watch what you say."

Swallowing, I glanced at the floor as if I could scold her with my eyes through it. Stupid witch.

"You must know," Bory said, "the queens can sew threads together and affect people's lives in a certain way. I think the Blood Queen did that with Rio and you."

I huffed, raising my eyebrows. "She did what?"

"Each person has a white life thread that represents the life-span of that person. They have fractures, fissures, depending on how life goes. Some lives are longer, and some are shorter, or they're even cut off by someone in the Underworld, tampering with their lives, which means that life is ending. Once the souls enter the Underworld they get a new thread, a black one."

I ran my hands through my hair. Things were getting worse and worse. So, the Topworld and the Underworld were even more intertwined than we knew, than we dared to suspect.

"I fear there is a reason the Blood Queen isn't allowed to get bones, Lynne. She is tampering with your bone right now. With it I have the feeling she gets very powerful. I think she witched the book to the auction, because you already planned to be there, because Rio and you talked about it. I think it is strange that she wants it that much. She will even help you bring it back. Maybe we shouldn't bring the book back..."

Suddenly, my nausea hit me like a punch right into my face. I knew nothing about her magic and only a little about the Bone Queen's. What if all we did was an even bigger fault than the one I made?

"So," my voice dropped to a whisper, "you think we shouldn't bring the book back?"

Bory shrugged. "We have to. I won't let you die."

My eyes watered a little at that. He could be such a sweetheart.

"Oh, Bory." I hugged him again and pressed a kiss on his forehead. He tried to wriggle out, but I needed to hug him a bit more. I felt so alone.

As soon as I let him go, he straightened out his feathers. "I assume she strung the threads of Rio and yours together, Lynne. So, you are linked to each other. I don't know if it's true but with all this skull going down it makes sense. There has to be a reason why you met him each year on the cemetery...we have to bring the book back, but we have to be cautious and maybe stay away from her after we brought it back. I don't have a good feeling about this."

I nodded and made a mental note that I will stay in Cave Town and do everything Nana wanted. Something was off, clearly and I was so out of this bullshit.

"But this auction rings a bell," Bory said, and I showed him the flyer Rio gave me. He studied it with a deep scowl on his face. "It's the largest art auction in Chicago and I guess you're right. That's where we're going to steal the queen's book from. Then, or better, before, you kiss Rio, and we get the bone. If it's necessary, we steal it as well. But we have to do it after we got the kiss because that guy won't feel a thing if he ever notices you stealing from him. After, we leave, without looking back. Okay?" Bory's glance was determined.

Whatever he saw in the Underworld frightened him even more than before. He was dead serious now.

I nodded. We had to be careful. "But we have to be well prepared, Bory."

"I've got a plan, Lynne."

I laughed at that. Even when he was miles and miles away from me, he was more productive than me. "All right, what do you know about the book so far?"

"Not much, but I overheard her talking about the name. The Book of Silva."

"The what?" I squinted my eyes.

"It's a tiny ancient book. I need to find out more about it, though." He touched his chin and rubbed it thoughtfully.

"No, don't stick your nose too much into it. We just steal it, no matter what the skull it is, and then we forget about everything."

Bory gave me his annoyed look. He hated nothing more than me being thoughtless. Reckless. Sadly, for him, I was almost always thoughtless.

Then Bory shrugged. "I don't know why she needs it, but we have to get it, otherwise you—"

"I know, I know! Yes, we'll steal that skull, just stop the admonishing. I really got it by now."

Bory noticed me tensing up and so I told him about my weekend. Of course, I left out the flirting with Rio, which was none of his business. But he was particularly sensitive when I told him about what was happening just right before he came back to me.

"Did you ever think that maybe Fox got the drugs and wrapped them in the flyer so no one would see? It totally looks like you stole drugs from Rio," Bory said after some thinking.

I went back to the moment my bag split open. The flyer was wrinkled as if someone had squeezed it, as if that person wanted to hide the drugs. "Yeah, I already thought about Fox, but Rio acted disappointed when I told him about the cop running after me. It was like he wanted me to mention something else…what if he waited for me to tell him, what if this was a test? A trust test?"

Bory let out a deep sigh. "Let me see what I can find out. I'm invisible, remember? I can spy on them easily," Bory said.

"I don't care that Fox hates me, but she must not screw up my mission."

Bory nodded and then gave me a small brass box. I looked at him questioningly.

"I had a moment to visit Mal and Soothie. Everyone's fine. Once I told Mal what you do here and what kind of scary weapons humans have, he made you a healing ointment."

"He didn't." I laughed and opened the little box. It was as big as my thumb. When I loosened the little lid, I smelled a strong mint-like ointment. Wow. He must really be worried about me if he voluntarily used his gift without any threats.

"It closes all kinds of wounds. Just be careful that no one else gets their hands on it," Bory said.

"That's helpful."

"Oh, and Soothie misses you!"

"Ah." I almost cried at that but of course, I didn't, I never cried. "My poor Sircha! I miss him so badly, too. How is he doing?"

"You know him, he hates every minute that you're gone," Bory said, sighing.

We spent the whole evening in my room, sitting on the windowsill, watching the humans and laughing at them. It was good to have my little friend back. He made me feel less alone. We talked, laughed, and at some point Bory fell asleep at the foot of my bed and I laid awake, staring at the ceiling.

How long had I been here? Almost two months.

I was running out of time but all I could think about at that moment was Rio. What was that crap about me getting off on drunk men? We were just having fun at the club, with the other girls. So, what was his problem? The thought that maybe he slipped me the drugs didn't leave me alone as well. Eventually, I was so restless that I picked up the phone and texted him. Well, I shouldn't have, but I did.

What was that about today? Why are you so cold to me?

It took a while to get anything back. For a moment, I thought he would simply ignore my message, but in the end, he texted back. It was late by now, and he was probably already in bed too. Wherever that was.

You're in my gang, that's why, he wrote back.

The vibration of my mobile phone made my heart jump, giving me a jolt.

This weekend didn't seem like I was just a gang member, I messaged.

Then you misunderstood something, he wrote.

My stomach dropped. It hit me harder than I wanted to admit. He couldn't be serious, could he? A man can't just twist and turn like that overnight. No way. I decided to provoke him. I had to coax him out somehow, to find out what really was going on, and calculate my chances with him.

I don't think I would have misinterpreted the looks you gave my ass, I typed and pressed send, closing my eyes and fearing I went too far.

He wrote back quickly this time. *How about the looks I gave your boobs?*

If you mean the drooling, yes, I noticed that too.

My phone buzzed only seconds later. *If I could see you naked, I'd probably drool even more.*

As I read his message, my ears felt hot, and I typed back without even thinking about what I wrote.

Getting off on dirty talk, aren't you? my text said.

My fingers trembled slightly.

I had to get out of my comfort zone for this, but I needed to know if he was playing another game right now or if we were on the same page.

The way you get off on other men at the club? Maybe, he wrote after quite some time. Oh, skulling Stix…

I wasn't hitting on other men, I typed and grunted, pressing send.

Punchy sent me a video of you, you did, he wrote with a winking smiley.

Punchy did what?

Would you have preferred that I threw myself at you instead, boss? Touched you? Rubbing myself along your body like you were a pole? I wrote.

Okay, I didn't know why I was so upset.

But why did Punchy film me and send it to his boss? Did he do that with all of Dee's girls? Certainly not. That was unfair, I was just dancing, not minding anyone but me.

Nothing came back for a few minutes, and I got so nervous that I wiggled my toes and started to pace in my room again. I glanced at his messages every single second. Was my last text too provocative?

Oh, I walked a fine line, didn't I? He didn't write anything back and I waited over ten minutes. The longest minutes in my life.

So, I sent him another one. *I don't know why you even care. About what I do at the club.*

The club is my business, Lynne. I told you to stay undercover, he wrote back immediately.

I made a face, sticking my tongue out, quickly feeling stupid because he couldn't see me anyway. So, he didn't fall asleep or throw the phone ten feet away then.

No one could recognize me in this stupid wig, with all that make up! There is something else going on, Rio. Do you get a hard-on controlling me like that? I wrote, my heart pounding like crazy.

No, but maybe I get a hard-on when I see you and that is my problem.

The corner of my mouth kicked up.

I can do something about that, I wrote back without thinking one bit about what I just texted him.

Oh, by the Dead.

Did I actually write that? I squealed, and ducked under the cushion, embarrassed at myself. A moment later my phone buzzed once again and at first, I was too afraid to check. What if he didn't want me to help or what if I didn't want to help?

But then I did read his text and my nipples got pointy as if someone had pushed a button. A very certain someone…

Maybe sometimes I get turned on just by seeing your name popping up my phone. That's what I call a problem, you're fucking with my head, his text said.

Um…was it just me or did it get hot in here?

Maybe one of us is in the wrong bed then and that's the problem, I wrote, my eyes sticking to the screen. I realized that at that moment I wished he would walk in and kiss me.

I don't want you to touch someone else, Lynne.

My whole body tingled, and I bit the inside of my cheeks.

Why? I dared to ask. Every second I had to wait was one to many.

Because I get jealous when others take my place, he wrote and just a blink of an eye later another text followed. *I think I should stop texting you now. You shouldn't be on my to-do list at all.*

What if you're already on mine? I shivered when my thumb hit send.

I waited impatiently for the three bubbles to pop up to tell me he's typing but they didn't, and I sent another text, hoping to keep him talking just a bit longer.

Why do you think we shouldn't text?

I sighed in relief *when the three bubbles popped up.*

Well, are you smiling when you read my messages?

Yes, I texted him.

That's why, darling. Have a good night, he wrote, and no message came after.

215

CHAPTER SEVENTEEN
RIO

The shooting outside the opera house still caused problems for my gang. The cops were asking stupid questions, and my tenants got afraid. Not good at all. Exactly the sort of thing we tried to avoid. So, I spent the whole morning shouting at Prawn's lieutenant, making it clear to him he had to control his foot soldiers better and make sure they did what they were told.

When the lieutenant disappeared from my office, I knew that Prawn would probably not survive the day. But I didn't care. Thanks to him, we could forget about six corners, and had to find a new safe place to sell. Not easy, because all the hoods and streets in Chicago already belonged to a certain gang. I would have died because of that PeeWee, if it weren't for Lynne, and that certainly couldn't be tolerated. Lynne—who was costing me my head right now—had saved my fucking life.

Yesterday a truckload of raw C-Wax arrived. My men had to bring it up from a remote lake and cooked it up in abandoned warehouses at the end of Southside. Besides, the first part of the payment to the damned governor was due, and I gave Punchy the job. He was the tallest of my men, perfect to scare others.

After all the hundred kinds of shit I had to do today, I straightened my tie, put on a watch, threw my jacket over my shoulders and waited for Lynne in my car. Slappy picked her up and made sure nobody could see her face. I straightened myself as I saw two figures approaching my car, Lynne was hooded, covered like I wanted her to be. She was my ace card and the reason why everything needed to go like clockwork.

Slappy opened the door for her and the minute she sat down, her compelling eyes met mine in the rearview mirror. Last night's texts flashed by in my mind once again. I knew by heart every damned message she'd typed, and given the look she just gave me, she remembered them too. Then we fucked each other with our eyes again. She had pinned up her hair and was showing me her naked neck, making me want to bite her between her nape and shoulder.

Within seconds, I would have taken her clothes off twice and nailed her in my back seat. Not gentle at all. Only when Slappy closed the door with a loud thud, could I take my eyes off her and forgot about the daring images in my mind. Her naked body pressed against mine...I pushed the clutch and shifted into first gear to start my precious pitch-black BMW.

Once I drove ahead, Slappy trailed us with a few other men. The top priority in Chicago was to arrive with backup. That's why we found a whole entourage when we parked outside the gala, and I knew there were at least as many armed men as there were cars waiting in that huge parking lot right now. A crew for every gang boss or henchmen in there. I was armed too; the gun pressing against my back frightened and reassured me both at once.

Tonight, several hostile parties were present.

During a drug war, the kids were fighting in the streets, shooting each other and regulating it with fists. The big fish handled it with such shitty events. We made contracts with politicians, businessmen, all the corrupt assholes in this city, and tried to play each other with mind games. Besides me, two other gang bosses and the governor showed up at the gala.

But I had already won because Lynne was *my* date. She was my most profitable investment. When she got out of the car and dropped her coat, I tried not to look at her, knowing that my mind would trail off if I did. She wore the purple satin dress that was cut in a V at her cleavage and fitted at the waist, and it was damn hot. Up from the height of her belly button, the cut was A-shaped. My jaw dropped a little when I took her in.

She had pinned up her hair and was showing me her naked neck, making me want to bite her between her nape and shoulder. My desire grew stronger with every second that passed and that's why I probably should have sent Any again, but the gangs had to see me with her. It was time to put me out there, to send the other bosses a message, that the Loops had more than one ace. That K.C. had a worthy heir they could follow when Karma struck.

Lynne was already considered the Dutch Beauty in the circles, and they were saying she was the niece of van der Volt himself. As I thought, the rumors developed on their own; you just had to know the right people and plant some seeds. The mere assumption that the Loop Baron had a connection with the inventor of the most powerful drug made me grow and walk even more confidently than usual.

Just like the other benefit galas, this one was over-decorated. Waiters jumped around like buzzing bees, always ready to offer appetizers or wine. As we entered, Lynne held onto my forearm, and threw a few men a fabulous smile here and there, and every time she did, I stiffened without being able to do anything about it. Just like the other benefit galas, this one was over-decorated. Waiters jumped around like buzzing bees, always ready to offer appetizers or wine.

We walked up a marble staircase, into a vast hall, right into the heart of the Museum of Modern Art. People loved to hold fundraising galas here. Alongside the walls stood columns of sculptures that, like Picasso's paintings, had the most impossible postures. A large chandelier hung from the ceiling, giving the high room a soothing yellow light. There were a few bar tables with a white tablecloth, decorated with white Calla lilies.

I walked towards a table next to a makeshift stage. I wanted to show off Lynne and therefore we needed to cross the hall.

Getting looked at by this many people made my heartbeat rise. I would have to take another pill later, there was no getting around it. Fucking shit. I hated the human psyche. My anxiety disorder made me feel like shit right now, especially since Lynne had to do another job for me today—just thinking about it made my stomach churn.

She hadn't even asked me why she had to do all of it.

It was not so much an expression of her naivety as of her being in a hopeless situation. I—the big asshole—had her in my hand because I had hidden the bone and refused to give it to her. She seemed to be in such deep shit that she even did illegal stuff for me, without asking a thing, just so I would finally give it to her. If I were a good man who deserved the way she looked at me right now, I would have given her the bone long ago.

But I was not a good man.

I led her to the stage where all the fine gentlemen and ladies were already gathering and drinking fancy aperitifs. I looked around, faking some smiles. This whole event was pure money laundering and a way for people like me to communicate without attracting the cops' attention or giving away locations and territories.

Everyone had an alibi life here. I was an entrepreneur who

invested in real estate, owned three clubs and several housing complexes. All a sham. A way to make my money clean and to think better of myself while trying to sleep. So did Z-Mexx, Big Al Cortez, and Cockeyed Joe. My rivals and leaders from the other gangs in Chicago. The Black Crowns, the Chicago Roosters, and the Toxic Taipans.

We all laundered money—well, we had to or otherwise we'd all be in jail. There were a hundred ways to do it and my way was called a cash-intensive business. My clubs generated cash revenue from incidental legitimate strip clubs in addition to the illegal cash. That way, I simply claimed all cash as legitimate earnings. My clubs were perfect—and, of course, well-thought-out because of it. They had a large ratio between revenue and variable costs, which made it a pain in the ass for the cops to detect my money laundering. Of course, I had some employees who didn't even exist and just lived to make my money clean, making my pockets fatter and fatter.

But we all had one thing in common. We were hunting after Vernon van der Volt, who was said to be at the gala too, but it was not easy to tell who he was. So, everyone looked at Lynne, thinking she was a link to him, making me even more important.

As we stood at a table, sipping our drinks, and waiting for the opening ceremony, Governor Jenson smiled at me from another table. I frowned. That man had such cold eyes, and his skin was so pale, he didn't seem very alive to me.

I raised my glass and saluted him. He did the same. Lynne turned, looking over her shoulder and then back at me. Her eyes asking me if that was the guy I told her about. I nodded. Yes, that was the man she had to give the drugs to tonight. She straightened herself, ready to head over to him, but I took her hand, stopped her.

I opened my mouth but suddenly my vocal chords didn't work the way I wanted. The heat radiating through her gloves made me sigh. Fuck, it felt so good to touch her. But it wasn't just the sudden contact that I felt. When *our fingers intertwined*, I had the urge to keep her here with me. To cancel my plans— just hold her tight. But then Aria came back to my mind, and I forced myself to keep going.

After I took a deep breath, I said: "Not now. Wait till the opening is over. Then go."

She nodded, glancing at our hands. I quickly untangled mine and was glad when the headmistress of the fundraiser organization started talking.

I looked around. Today there were not only some drug lords present but also other men who made their money with tax evasion or other false machinations. Like I said, health galas were the best for money laundering. Who would ask where the money for sick people initially came from?

No one.

When the music started to play and the first couples did a few dances, I nodded to Lynne. Now she could go to Jensen. And oh, she did, with swinging hips and a smile that made even the ice-cold governor shine. When he touched her with one of his dirty hands on the small of her back, my hand shook, and my heartbeat quickened. I took one of my pills, threw it in and flushed it down with water. I would have preferred a martini, but alcohol often made my symptoms worse, experience had shown.

Jensen talked Lynne's ear off, and I wondered if he had figured out, she was mute yet or if he was just yakking away, hoping she would fall for it as if by magic. Of course, he showed her his fully loaded wallet right away and invited her for another drink.

Drink what you want, beautiful girl, his eyes said, *I have all the money in the world.*

If the bad jokes didn't work, his bank account would do the job, huh? My eyes were glued to them. If he even dared one wrong touch, I was ready to tear off his head in front of everyone.

She wrote something on a napkin, and he raised his eyebrows. Now he probably knew it, but it did not seem to bother him at all that she couldn't speak. Sadly, I had to go about my business too. A couple of investors were waiting for me and soon I had too many people on my hands, who, as usual, were frittering my time away asking for van der Volt. What else. In Chicago, Volt was always number one these days. Especially, since the rumors had it that he was going to sell his recipe and move to the Gold Coast.

I tried to find out who knew what about Volt, and the most important thing: if they knew *more* than me. Here and there I could not help but check out Lynne and in that very moment I saw her giving the C-Wax to Jensen. A taste of the huge delivery that Punchy delivered his men right now. Customers always had to test the goods to make sure they weren't buying punched shit. Of course, he gave it back to her immediately, as stunned and irritated as I hoped. Normally, customers tested the drugs in a corner, somewhere no one could see it.

Ha, he was so blunt.

Snickering, I quickly glanced around, assessing my surroundings.

Big Al Cortez and Cockeyed Joe had watched the Dutch Beauty too, just like I'd hoped, and had seen the little golden packet flashing in Jenson's bloated hands. Trained eyes like ours knew what that was. But they did not see Lynne selling it to Jenson. No, they saw Jensen giving the package to Lynne, confirming their belief the governor was Vernon van der Volt himself and I loved it. A new rumor was just born, and I totally got a kick from it.

Whenever my schemes worked out, I smirked, touching my incisors with the tip of my tongue and at that very moment Lynne looked at me. Our eyes were like magnets, always searching for another. But this time, her nostrils slightly flared. She knew that my plans were working out for me, although, her look was wary as if she didn't trust me, but that made me glad, because not trusting me was the only smart thing she could do. Good girl.

Later, Big Al Cortez and Cockeyed Joe tried to ensnare Lynne as well. They wanted to find out if she was the niece and Jenson her uncle. I snickered and talked to one criminal after another, disguised in a suit and tie.

Fortunately, I had so much to talk about, because my blood pressure would rise if Cortez or Joe stared too much at Lynne's cleavage or pushed her into a corner, touched her inappropriately. Of course, I knew she could fight back. That was always one of my rules when I hired new people. I wasn't a babysitter, not for anyone. However, it didn't do my anxiety any good when I lost sight of her. She probably went out with Jenson so that he could try the C-Wax.

Once she came back, nodding at me and confirming to me that everything was right, I couldn't stand it anymore, grabbed her, pulled her onto the dance floor and did something I shouldn't have done. Again. I danced closely with her, holding her delicate fingers, and didn't want to let her go. To any other man. But she was done with her job tonight, so why shouldn't we celebrate?

I could tell by the look on her face that she was amused by my behavior. In response, I only held her tighter, pulled her closer to me and smiled as she looked up at me with her eyebrows raised and a slight frown on her lovely face. Despite the high heels, she walked like a goddess thanks to Cherry, but she was still so much smaller than me. I felt like I could crush her with my arms.

As we turned, I showed her my waltzing skills—maybe I did learn something at that snobby high school. While turning around with her, I saw Any. He stood in the back, watching us, grinning behind his cocktail glass. Strange, he hadn't said anything to me about this event. But I should have known he'd come. He did own his father's company, a business that manufactured medical equipment. So, of course he was here, at this gala. It was important to make contact with hospitals and their salesmen. After all, in a capitalist society, contacts were everything.

Any smiled at me in a way nobody noticed and when I whirled Lynne, she saw him too, and her smile dropped, changing into a deep scowl. I wondered what the poor guy had done or said to her to get the evil eye.

"A penny for your thoughts?" I whispered against her ear, trying to tease her a little. My skin tingled as I noticed how close I was to her face. "Okay. Ten bucks if they're dirty."

She laughed, shaking her head and warming my cold heart with her beautiful smile.

"You look gorgeous," I said, coming too close to her neck and smelling the beguiling scent of her, mixed with a daring sweet perfume. I asked myself, just for a second, if I maybe could have her to myself after everything was over. After we succeeded. But did I really deserve that, thinking of the way I used her? Like a tool? I glanced down at her, into her dark eyes and noticed her irritated look.

She didn't expect me to say something sweet like that.

I leaned into her and laid my head lightly against her temple. Closing my eyes, I swayed to the rhythm of the live music behind us and felt her hand sliding along my back up to my shoulder. Did a man like me deserve happiness, and maybe even more than that? I looked at her again and prayed to God that she would forgive me, once the truth was out.

Then she smiled at me, and I couldn't help but return it.

I looked deep into her eyes, and I recognized a yellow wreath in the middle of her iris and got curious. I had seen this wreath before. Not many people had it. She had always looked familiar to me but now she triggered a memory that I had buried in the depths of my broken soul for a long time, a memory that I no longer wanted to have and that was partly to blame for my panic attacks.

It made me hate myself, stirred my anger towards myself, and caused the outburst in my body. All covered under the veil of the anxiety disorder. I learned so far that hate, anger, and anxiety were very similar feelings and were often to be mixed up.

The moment I saw the wreath in her eyes, all the feelings came back to me and instinctively, I took her hand, placing it on my chest, calming it on the spot as if her hand were the cure for my disease. That my heart was kept where it should be.

Lynne stroked my chest with her hand, caressing the pressure away and just like that it was gone. My heartbeat normalized. We didn't dance extensively anymore, but rocked to the beat, just looking at each other. I can't even remember the last time I let someone get that close or when I let someone know my weakness at all.

I loved being in control and admitting to a beautiful woman that I sometimes could be knocked out by my own feelings, lying on the floor because I imagined I got a stroke, was not easy for me at all. When it hit me, I was useless. But she was so broken in her own way that it was easier for me to let her see underneath, let her see my weak side instead of holding on to my strength every second.

That's when I pulled her outside.

CHAPTER EIGHTEEN
LYNNE

He was so different now.

Was that what the queen wanted, lust? Pure desire? Not just the need, but a feeling that went deeper, that made both our hearts beat faster and our bellies twist? Did I finally reach my goal?

Rio led me outside, ignoring some of the glances that were following us. First, we crossed a brightly lit stone terrace and raced down into a barely lit garden, my heels making a clacking noise on the stone floor all the way down.

He pulled my hand, eager to bring me somewhere else. We rushed past trimmed bushes, fresh cut grass, and roses that smelled like the perfume I got from Cherry the other day. He squeezed my fingers tighter and pulled me further and further into the darkness. My heels made a clacking noise on the stone floor all the way down.

Rio chuckled and led me towards a huge fountain that was so strongly lit that we both shone in a golden light now, making his eyes gleam like stars. He stopped at a brick fence, turned, and pressed me against it, imprisoning me with his arms. I caught my breath, and my heart skipped a beat as I glanced at his strong biceps next to my head.

Breathing heavily, I looked back up at him. His ice-blue eyes were determined, his breast heaving with his quick breathing. I pushed myself further back into the wall and kept myself from touching him, although my fingers were longing for it. Instinctively, he pressed his body against mine, making my legs feel like butter. He sighed and I could feel his hot breath on my skin.

"You know what happens when I *do* kiss you?" he whispered. The purr in his voice made my knees buckle a little.

He pressed himself further against me, showing me his naked neck. The smell of oakmoss and musk were everywhere and by the Dead, I wanted to kiss the spot between his jaw and ear so much right now. I moved towards that damned spot, and he leaned into my movement.

"If we do that, I'm not responsible for what comes after," he whispered against my neck, making me feel hot and cold at the same time.

I knew he had more in mind for me than to just seduce me. That evening and all the others had a purpose, but I didn't really know what he was after yet. Did I really care, though? Did I care what he was up to, especially when he was looking at me like that? No. I just wanted to screw everything up and kiss that skulling spot between his jaw and ear—and I did. His soft moan made me shiver in delight and I exhaled the breath I'd been holding.

He tilted his head and kissed slowly down my cheek, stopping right at the corner of my mouth. Then he cupped my face with his hands in a rough and demanding way and kissed me, setting off a chain reaction of pure lust. Rio grabbed my chin, forcing me to open my eyes and look at him while he kissed me.

"I may seem calm," he said, "but I've already fucked you a hundred times in my mind since we met."

My breaths came quicker now.

Dear Stix and all the gods there are.

The spot between my legs was pining for him, wanting him to finally touch me. Then he pressed his soft lips against mine once more, making me lean into him and holding his waist with my wanting hands. He grabbed my butt tightly as if he wanted to push me inside him, so we would become one.

Impatiently, I opened my lips, and welcomed his tongue in my mouth and skull. I had kissed men before but none of them had taken my breath away yet. None of them made me forget that I had to breathe at all. Except him.

When the daring touch of his hot tongue made me shiver slightly, the feel of his hands on my naked back made me gasp into his mouth. Grinning, he arched his head and circled my tongue with his. Every single body part of mine was aware of his.

"Fuck," he said, sighing into my mouth. "That won't be nearly enough."

He kissed me harder.

I gasped at the feeling of my tongue mingling with his. When I wrapped my arms around his neck, making him bend over even more, I looked up at Rio as our past settled around us. All those years of watching him and wondering what his kisses felt like passed by. And oh, his kisses felt like something I missed all my life, as if suddenly I needed his kisses to breathe. I pulled him tighter against me, his hands flitting over my body as if they wanted to touch every inch of me at the same time and kissed him.

But at that moment something burned on our lips.

Like fire—not because of the lust we shared. No, it was a feeling that was very different from this world.

We flinched back from each other and I noticed his lip glowing golden for a moment. Skull. I raised a hand up to my mouth. It was swollen and...burning up. That was magic. Rio ran an index finger over his burning lip as well, looking at me, utterly confused.

The Blood Queen.

It was the kiss she wanted—a kiss driven by pure human lust.

I opened my mouth, wanting to say something but the next time I blinked Any appeared behind him, with a gun in his hand and something inside of me died.

As ANY MOVED his finger to pull the trigger all I could think about was Rio. Rushing forward, I knocked Rio over with all the strength I had. We fell to the ground. Landing on top of him, I tried to look for Any, thinking about killing that bastard right away. Just the thought that something could happen to Rio made me want to puke.

When my chin hit Rio's shoulder and his hands pressed me against him to absorb the impact, I heard a sonic boom, like a crack in the air and then a bullet passed us, flying over us, accompanied by a buzzing sound. Rio and I whipped our heads towards Any and he pointed to a man standing behind us on a bridge.

"What—" Rio cried, looking at me, sitting on top of him and then back at Any.

But before anyone of us could have said a thing, a laugh drew us back to the man Any just shot. He now held the bullet between his index finger and thumb. My eyes flitted over his split black lip with severe blood crusts on it.

I caught my breath.

Burns.

In some places the skin came off, showing his red and white flesh underneath. My breath escaped me, and fear rushed in.

His burned skin hung down from several body parts, allowing us to see some of his bones. Rio swallowed, held me by the hips and raised me to my feet.

"Go," he said, trying to pull me away from here but I stopped in my tracks, trying to figure out what was happening. "Please, Lynne. I can't let anything happen to you."

My eyes flicked to Any, he still held the pistol in his damned hand.

"Don't look at me like that," he said, acting like he had tried to save us. Again.

My hands trembled, wanting to touch him and finally kill him, but Rio held me firmly as if he knew what I was thinking about.

"I saw him, and I was going to shoot him," Any lied.

I just squinted my eyes. Right. Whoever that guy was in the back, but I saw Any standing here first.

"What the hell is happening?" Rio asked, pulling me further back now, telling Any to follow us. This time, I let him since the creepy man was getting closer and closer.

We stumbled upon the grass, and the man's laughter grew louder and echoed back to us from the high walls that surrounded us. Glancing over my shoulder, I watched him casually stroll over the bridge and throw the bullet up in the air, catching and throwing it again and again.

"No need to run from me. I'm faster," the man said and the moment he spat the first word, Rio and I recognized him.

We stopped, sucking in air simultaneously. We turned around and his stench of decay hit me like a wall. But it wasn't until I saw his face that I quivered.

That was Fish.

The man my hands had killed, and Rio's men had made disappear.

"Surprised to see me, Barbie girl? Fucked up, huh?" he yelled at us. "Oh, and Baron, don't act surprised, do me the favor. After all, I was dipped in acid, fucker. Bummer for you, I was resurrected in the soup, as you can see."

He held his hands in the air and chuckled. My mouth formed a small o.

That was me.

I made this hell of a mess.

"How... how can you... what—" Rio stammered, clasping my hand until his knuckles turned white.

Any gasped and I turned around, checking on him but he didn't really look surprised at all. It had affected him more to hear that I was related to it, than to see Fish and his gross body. Any should have been more surprised, right? Fish looked terrible! Not like Fish used to look, but... but like he'd just come back from the dead.

"Oh, you haven't told your lover yet, huh?" Fish laughed at me, only some feet between us now.

He looked exactly like a Deadwalker, a creature that I've encountered several times in the Underworld. They were souls stuck between two worlds and punished by it. But why was he here? What have I done?

From the corner of my, I saw Bory hopping down the stairs, frantic.

"Behead him!" he screamed and tore me out of my stupor. Yes!

To kill him, I had to cut off his head...but how? With what? It was the only way he'd disappear forever, but I didn't have a sword or anything to cut his head off right now. Oh, why did my hands have to create Deadwalkers? What the skull? Like there weren't already too many of these idiots in the Underworld?

Fish rushed towards us, black saliva dripping out of his opened mouth and all I could think about as Rio. Fish could hurt Rio. I looked at him and his eyes told me volumes. He was scared too but for me.

"Move, Lynne!" Bory screamed and I freed myself from Rio's grip. I pushed him back, signaling him to run. Praying that he did, I turned around, and tried to find something useful, something to cut Fish's head off with.

"Over there," Bory yelled at me, throwing stones at Rio and Any to make them run faster and they did, trying to hide in the park. "There's a statue with a weapon!"

Oh, for the love of the Dead, yes! My heart dropped into my pants. That was just what I needed right now. As I ran for the statue, Rio shouted something at me and I forced myself to not turn around, to run faster—but I couldn't.

I glanced over my shoulder and saw Fish rushing towards Rio, mouth open and ready to bite him.

I caught my breath, slowed down and just stupidly watched him evade Fish. My body trembled, saliva pooled in my mouth, and hot bile rushed up my throat. That's when I noticed that I couldn't let anyone hurt Rio. I just simply couldn't live with it.

I ran to the statue, swinging myself up onto it and pulled at the sword, trying to rip it out of the stone, but it was impossible. Then I heard another shot and whirled away. Rio had pulled his gun and fired at Fish, which of course, didn't work at all. It only made the Deadwalker laugh, but how the hell was he supposed to know? Skull! I had to hurry up!

I pulled the sword even harder now and used all of my Underworld strength, noticing tiny cracks in the stone figure. When I looked up again, Any stood beside me, helping me pull it as if he knew why I was doing it. I growled, trying to make him understand that I didn't want him here. Didn't want his help.

"Don't be like that," he hissed and pulled at the sword with me. "I saved your life, and you need me."

I wanted to hiss back but there was no time.

We pulled and pulled and then we finally broke the sword out of the stone. Any wanted to take it, but I hit him in the shin and grabbed the sword fast as lightning. Then I ran to Rio and saw Fish trying to touch him. Oh skull, no. Please gods…

"Faster, Lynne!" Bory yelled and jumped nervously back and forth, throwing some more stones at Fish, trying to do something.

I ran faster, sprinted up the fence, hopped towards Fish, and jumped, leaping for him. As I flew through the air, I noticed Rio looking at me with true bewilderment. I tried to ignore it, swung out and cut through Fish's neck. My muscles trembled as I drew the sword through his thick flesh.

As I cut through it, I exhaled in relief. Rio would be safe now.

Then I heard a sly bump and Fish's body fell to the ground. Panting, I watched his head roll beside me, dragging a sea of black blood with him. He finally lay, dead as ever in front of us. By Stix, we really were lucky. Looking at Fish, the man I killed in the park came up in my mind. If Fish was back, then so was he.

My hands were a curse.

Rio gasped and tore me out of my thoughts. I whirled and looked him in the eyes, and it almost broke my heart. His facial expression was a mixture of fascination and pure terror— because of me…because of what I'd done. My stomach dropped and I started to realize what I'd done. I took a gulping breath and didn't cover the hurt in my eyes.

Rio opened his mouth but Any sauntered towards us. Still crouching on the floor and holding the sword in my trembling hands I checked his hands for weapons.

I furrowed my brows, feeling Rio's stare. I didn't want him to look at me like that. I wanted him to look at me like a couple of minutes before and not like this, with all this fright and anger. But now there was no way back, I had just decapitated a Deadwalker in a jump, with a sword. I guess not many humans in ball gowns did that, right?

But we didn't have time to analyze what had just happened, because some guests were already looking for what was causing the stir. From a distance I could see people standing on a balcony, trying to figure out from where the shots came from. Thank God, we hid well in the dark.

Rio came to his senses quickly, starting to order us around again. "Any, take him with you. Take him to Punchy's and meet us at my place."

Any nodded and picked up Fish in no time. Then Rio grabbed me by the upper arm as if he didn't want to come near my hands anymore and pulled me to the brick-wall, not gentle at all. I knew what we were going to do, but I was wearing a shitty ball gown and I couldn't climb with that at all.

Rio sighed at my hesitation, tore the sword out of my hand and shortened the dress until I only had a rag on. A tiny shirt-like cloth that was barely covering my ass. He stood two feet away and didn't dare to look me in the eyes, making me want to cry.

We ran on the roof tops, jumped over ledges and ran for over an hour. We climbed up, down, jumped, leaped, crawled and we did all of it without talking or even looking at each other. He was in front of me and every time I caught up, he accelerated, took another direction. I knew he didn't want me at his side at that moment, so I stayed in the background, running after him.

Then, after a while, we found Rio's BMW.

We got in and he drove away from the event. I wasn't even sure we were still in Chicago anymore, but I didn't know my way around anyway. I felt numb, ashamed, and lost like never before. As I pressed my head against the cold window I just wanted to sleep, lose myself in the dark chasm of my dreams.

The neighborhood he brought me to was a mix of modern houses and tall buildings with apartments. Rio's legs wobbled the whole way, and his hands clasped the steering wheel, beads of sweat adorning his forehead. Even Bory was quiet.

Then Rio pressed a button and a big gate opened and closed again as soon as he drove his car in. He parked in front of a modern mansion, got out of his car, and walked in without paying attention to what I was doing. So, I awkwardly stumbled after him, sighing, and wondering about the house. There were windows everywhere, it wasn't as huge as Reina's house, but it was also much too big for my taste. The lawn was illuminated by floor lamps, almost blinding me.

I followed him into the kitchen, which was connected to a sitting area.

There I stood, shivering, and holding my upper arms tightly around me. Chicago was skulling cold and I've been virtually wearing nothing for hours.

"There's a bathroom to the right," he simply said, rushing to a cupboard and throwing a shirt at me. "You can wear that. Take whatever you need, I'll shower upstairs."

He somehow spat out every word one by one and didn't look at me at all as if he were ashamed of me. Of kissing someone like me. Then he was gone, and I was alone in—apparently—his house. Every heartbeat of mine felt like a knife cutting me inside. Why? Why was this happening to me?

To distract myself from my feelings, I looked around. So, this was where he lived. It was sparely furnished and had the kind of style that I often admired on TV with Cherry. Very clean, straight cut, lots of white furniture, and many windows. Although, nobody could look inside, because the house was surrounded by fences, trees, and bushes as if it were a hiding place. Perhaps it really was.

So, I went to the bathroom, stepping on the heated floor. Standing before the big shower I had to have Bory explain the different functions of it to me until I shooed him out and took a shower. I couldn't talk to him right now. I just wanted to move, to do something, and ignore what had happened. Ignore what his rejection did to me.

And holy Stix! This rain forest shower was quite something. How would I ever get used to the simple life in the Underworld again? I was so spoiled now. Usually, I used a bucket to wash myself. Used a river as my toilet or a lake to wash myself properly. This shower was wonderful. The warm water enveloped me and immediately relaxed me, made me breathe freely again. But nevertheless, things escalated tremendously in my mind. Gasping, I leaned against the heated tiles.

There were Deadwalkers in the Topworld. Because of me.

What if there were more creatures that kept wandering between the two worlds, if monsters were already here and the majority of people just didn't know about them?

I shivered.

That would be counterproductive. The Blood Queen herself said that a former lover stole her book and left it here in the Topworld. Then her lover must be a world-wanderer, too. But she also said she wasn't allowed to stay in this world for long, but why? Argh, so many questions!

All those years I lived down there without knowing anything about the existence of a world like this, about a connection of our worlds. But that was the normal case— knowing everything was the special case. Unfortunately, I had tasted blood now and wanted to know more.

I slipped into Rio's shirt and smelled his wonderful scent, making me want to rip the shirt off right away. It was so big that it was like a dress, hanging down to my knees. The fabric felt like a second skin I didn't want. Burning.

I ran my fingers through my hair to constitute combing it and tried to fix my sad look so I could go and face him again after all this skull.

He was already sitting on his couch, freshly showered in jeans and a hoodie with white socks, pinning me down with his sapphire eyes, arms crossed and the expression distant. I found it very hard to take and simply stood there as if rooted to the ground. He was so damn handsome, and I got tempted to brush my fingers through *his wet hair.*

Although so much had happened, I could still feel his kiss on my lips, on my neck. His hot fingers on my naked, cold back, on my butt, my hair. And just like that his gaze flitted to my naked thighs and I sighed in relief. Good, so he was not that disgusted with me that my appearance was completely ineffective to him now.

"He seems kind of pissed off," Bory said, making me flinch.

He snuggled up in one of the soft blankets on the sofa.

As Rio was still staring at me, I avoided making a face and preferred to just mentally snarl at Bory. Rio wasn't pissed, he was disgusted.

"What are you?" Rio finally said, his deep voice making me shiver.

I sighed and finally dared to approach him. This time he didn't flinch, so, he couldn't be that afraid, right? But I preferred to keep my distance, although I wanted to throw myself into his lap, kissing him again. It almost broke me...the way he looked at me right now and his damned shirt on my skin didn't help either, it smelled of his perfume, his scent all over me. On my body. For a moment I was frozen, my heart seizing. How could I possibly tell him the truth? How?

"She's from the Underworld," I suddenly heard Any say.

I gaped, turning to where his voice came from. He appeared behind me, strolled into the living room, and threw himself casually on an armchair, like it was normal to do such a thing or to say such words.

After no one said anything at all, he just said, "Nice outfit. "

It came to me that I only wore the shirt, it covered my butt, but that was it. It left little to the imagination...

Any turned to Rio, apologetic, but with a hint of remorse.

Did he regret he hadn't killed him yet? While I sat on an armchair across from them, throwing a white blanket over my naked legs, I gave him a very curious look. How did he even know about the Underworld?

"The fuck?" Rio said out loud what I've been thinking, demanding an explanation.

"That girl is coming from down low," Any clarified, pointing with his index finger to the floor. "She's dead."

I winced, noticing that my breath came in short bursts now. I wasn't dead! Even Bory hissed at Any's comment.

"How does he know about our world?" Bory asked me.

I don't know, I said to him through our bond, but my sentence ended in a choke. This was too much. All of it. There it was, life caught up with me.

"You're dead, girl," Any said, giving me the same evil look as before. "You can't fool me. You can create Deadwalkers with your bare hands."

Panting, I looked at my hands, which were covered with gloves as usual. Yeah, I could do that because… because… I really was dead in this world? Was I some kind of parasite because I didn't really belong here, which led to a transference? A death, transferable but not fully, which let me create in-between beings? Oh, by Stix and all Hellhounds. Was this the reason Underworlders weren't allowed in the Topworld?

"Is it true?" Rio whispered after some time. His eyes looked pleading, like wishing me to not say it. But I nodded, making him wince.

None of us dared to speak for a while and the silence stretched between us.

Everything in my head blurred and the question of how I could bring things back into order hammered loudly in my brain. How could I convince Rio I wasn't dead or bad or what-ever he thought I was right now? How could I ever forget the bone-shaking look of his?

Rio, I am real, I am alive, don't you see it? my eyes told him, but he didn't get it, as if we spoke a different language now.

"How do you know about that, Any?" Rio asked, turning to Any instead of me.

Despite the ache in my chest his question was everything I wanted to know, too. Bory nodded as well, though no one but me could see him.

"I made a deal," Any started, and Bory and I sucked in the air.

"A deal?" Bory hissed. "That doesn't sound good."

No good at all, I told him. *Deals are never good.*

CHAPTER NINETEEN
RIO

"What deal?" I asked and took a generous sip of the beer I just fetched myself. In some moments you needed alcohol, and this was one of them. Even Lynne and Any took a beer.

"My father. He, uh, was never around, remember?" Any said, slowly removing the label from the bottle.

"Yeah," I said, still waiting for a halfway decent explanation for all this shit.

Any's father really was never around—just like mine. Only Any lived in a villa, and had nannies, money and more than one roof over his head.

But the absent father connected us back then. Any told me he saw his father once or twice a year and that was it. I always thought his father maybe had another family and that's why he was never there for Any and Aria. According to his father's stories, he had work in China, where his company had another hub, making more profit than in the US. Making the real money. At some point, he bequeathed his American headquarters to Any and he stayed all the way in China, although he was never really home anyway.

But everything was alien right now. Just like Lynne. My God, it's been a shitty day. Barbie girl was a fucking assassin! I've only seen people killing the way she did in computer games and movies, never in real life. She attacked, light-footed like a dancer and lethal like a lioness. Fish turned into a zombie, and she decapitated him. Fuck. Fucking fuck!

But now what?

Now Any talked about an Underworld and about Lynne being dead. I wasn't a fucking necrophiliac! With her rosy cheeks, she looked very much alive. So, she couldn't be dead. But these hands, these fucking hands of hers, I'd seen them in action before. But back then I never expected her hands to be as deadly as they were. No, I took it all as a joke…believed she had a quirk, a tick. A bit crazy, nothing else. It turned me on, actually, but now...fuck. I understood Punchy's suspicions about her.

"Well, at some point I stalked my father and well, he's not from this world and not from below but…from above," Any finally managed to say.

"He… lives in heaven?" I started to laugh. That was insane, like really, who would believe such nonsense!

"Well, sort of," Any confessed, looking away from me. "I don't know how it works, what he is…neither Mother nor he ever told me anything. Then I found old books…and learned how to summon things with runes, tarot cards... blood...you know." Any glanced away.

"No, I don't know," I yelled at him, noticing the fidgeting of my foot. "Are you kidding me?"

Sighing, I ran my index finger and thumb over my eyes. I knew Lynne was staring at me at that moment, but I couldn't look back. I didn't dare. Every time I saw her, I'm reminded of her hands changing Fish to a zombie or God knows what. This wasn't right.

I haven't had many moments in my life when I would have

loved to throw up but smelling Fish had been one. I had never seen nor smelled anything so disgusting in my life and I had seen and smelled a lot. Bodies that were dissolved in acid, people that were strangled, hung, or cut into shashlik pieces. Nothing could compare with the stink and burnt skin of Fish and it was her work. Lynne's work.

"I began to read into this kind of spells. I met with some people and learned how to attend to specific circles and one day I conjured someone up and learned about the Underworld from him," Any said, his voice dropping to a whisper.

Lynne sucked in the air, shaking her head.

Her aversion to Any didn't seem to get any better. Even though he saved our lives. Who knows what Fish would have done to us otherwise! We were so engrossed in each other that we probably would have fucked in the park because we were so horny, a feeling I couldn't stomach right now. Her hands were all over me, the mere thought made me shiver, causing another dichotomy inside of me.

I didn't want to feel that way about her, but I did. Now I dared to look at her. How in the world could someone like her create such creatures? Was I sick for wanting to kiss her despite that? Still wanting her even though she could create zombies and might be dead? What did that say about me?

"One time, I did something wrong and creatures came through the... pentagram," Any said, playing with his sweater.

I narrowed my eyes at the sight of him and as he rose his sweater did too, revealing black scars over his stomach. Lynne covered her mouth, glancing at a chair with a blanket on top. Was she not looking at her shoulder anymore?

I pointed at the scars, and suddenly my eyes felt heavy. "What the fuck is this, Any?"

He shrugged and pulled his sweater down again. "Some critters did that to me. I couldn't let them hurt other people, so I tried to fight them. I travelled to other countries and well, those were the years when I stopped coming to see you. While you were in prison."

So, that's why he cut off contact with me, not because he finally turned his brain on and realized how bad I was, but because he went to see witches, fortune tellers, and charlatans...

"You can't be serious." I laughed, trying to push all the news away from me, to not let them near me. After all, it was a bad joke and nothing else. Underworld? Bullshit. We already lived in the underworld with the worst kind of creatures—greedy and racist people. Why would we go looking for even worse things?

"I'm serious, Rio. You saw Fish, didn't you? You've seen what she can do." He nodded at Lynne. "She's also here because she has to do something for someone down there. I'm sure." Any hesitated before talking again. "If you don't believe me, then ask her."

"Are you from the Underworld, Lynne?" I asked and could hardly believe I was asking shit like that. But then she nodded, and I couldn't breathe properly for a few seconds. The truth was shaking me to my marrow.

Why? Why did she nod? She hated Any. Now would be the perfect moment to make him look stupid, and yet she agreed. She agreed with Any...I got up, shook my head, and got another beer. Man, what was this all about? It couldn't be true, no, it couldn't! There must be some rational explanation for all of this. Opening the beer, I threw the cap over my kitchen counter and took a big gulp. Then I looked back at Any, at his blue-green eyes. The yellow wreath in his eyes glimmered in the dark light. He wouldn't lie to me, would he? Any was my best friend.

"What deal, Any?" I hissed, sitting down again—my feet still fidgeting.

"One day I conjured up a powerful witch," he whispered.

243

"The Blood Queen—" at that Lynne sucked air in again and stood up, to walk up and down my living room. My ears were ringing. Fear creeping in.

"And?" I urged, my gaze following Lynne's every step. My heart beat faster and faster.

"I asked her for a wish. My heart's desire," Any stuttered, tears glittering in his eyes.

I swallowed, breathing against a lump in my throat. Bracing myself for what's to come.

"To bring Aria back?" I whispered, trying to speak through my gasp.

"That's what I wished for at first, but she couldn't do it. Bring back the dead. She wouldn't be herself, the queen said. So, I wished that Aria's killer would be punished."

Now I was the one sucking in the air and my throat tightened up. "D-Do you know who killed her?"

Any hesitated, looking at his feet. The cold air hit me like a slap.

"No," he said, avoiding my gaze again. "I did something wrong then and the queen took advantage of my ignorance. Made up her own rules. Pulling me into deep shit."

I clung to my beer with both hands. My breathing became shallow, my stomach felt like an anthill, tingling everywhere.

"Now I must kill the murderer of my sister. Then he will be punished by her when he arrives in the Underworld. But the Queen never makes a deal without getting something in return," Any said, and stopped mid-sentence, making me even more curious.

"What the fuck does she get from you, Any?" I asked in a thin and scratchy voice.

This time Any lifted his right pants leg and Lynne made a sound which, if she would have the ability to talk, would have been a scream. She rushed to Any, crouched beside him and examined his foot. There was a black tattoo there, growing up his leg, the top sticking out of his waistband. I hadn't seen it before, or was I too distracted by the black scars? I dunno.

Lynne's reaction was so bad that I was immediately worried about Any. What kind of shit had he gotten himself into and how come I didn't know anything about it, about those tattoos? Well, we hadn't gone swimming for a couple of years, actually, we hadn't done that since we were little boys and he hadn't undressed in front of me since... since... *phew!* No idea since when! I wasn't really paying attention…

"Fuck! Any!" I gasped, not able to move an inch. Dumbfounded, I looked at Lynne still touching the tattoo and gesturing wildly to the seat.

"Okay, Lynne, what the fuck?" I asked her.

She winced at my outburst and jumped back to the couch, her eyes filled with tears.

"Why are you talking to my chair? Does it have eyes and ears for you?"

She snorted, pulled out her cell phone and texted me with a deep scowl on her face. A few seconds later, my phone vibrated in my pocket.

I've got a little helper who supports me here because I couldn't do it alone. It is different up here. Very different. But you can't see him. He's enjoying your comfy blanket and I was talking to him.

I exhaled hard, closed my eyes, and massaging my eyelids with my index finger and thumb. What the fuck? Really. What the fuck? I didn't have enough booze in the house for such nonsense. I really didn't. I sat up, glancing at Any. Then back to Lynne.

But Any spoke first, "The tattoo is growing. If I don't kill the killer until the tattoo reaches my heart, I'll end up downstairs and join the queen's court instead of him."

Lynne coughed and she went back to talking to her…her helper. Then my phone vibrated once again.

"She asks if you'll be a slave," I told Any with a scrunched-up face. At that point I struggled to keep my face expressionless.

But he shook his head. "No, I am only to live below, as one of her subjects."

Lynne shook her head, indicating to Any that he was an idiot. I snorted. Well, he was. But then my laugh died, and everything went dark again. "Fuck, Any. Let me...we... I."

"I have to kill him, Rio," he simply said.

The words got stuck in my throat. Yeah, or he'd die, too. My best friend would die. I couldn't live with that, not after Aria died. Not again.

"Let me do the coup. You know how important it is to me. You will kill the murderer afterward. I promise you. I'll help you do it!" I stumbled. "I promise."

Any looked at me for a long time and I suddenly understood that he'd known who the killer was for a long time. My stomach dropped. Maybe that was the problem. Could it be?

"How much time do you still have?" I dared to ask.

He shrugged. "Don't know. It doesn't follow any particular rule. I couldn't figure it out. Sometimes it grows faster, sometimes it doesn't grow at all for months. It took years to get to my knee, but the rest went pretty fast. I think I have around a year, maybe less."

Fuck. My best friend was dying, and I didn't even know!

Any nodded at Lynne, as if he didn't want to talk to me anymore. "And what about you? Why are you up here?"

Lynne bit her fingernails again and I felt sorry for her. What if the fate expecting her was something as bad as Any's? She hesitated and seemed to be talking to her helper. Not able to really think about all of this, I just finished my beer. Fuck it. It was all too much, man. Even for a drug lord like me.

Then, she was typing for a long time.

I lost the bone in your world, and I must take it back. If I don't make it, I'll be enslaved, which is worse than what you'd expect, Lynne wrote.

She looked at him like she wanted to tell him not to kill Aria's murderer. Did she know who killed her, too? What did I miss? Then my phone vibrated once more and I read her message aloud: *They took my voice too, so I wouldn't tell you about the other world. But they didn't think of Any, apparently.*

All I could think about at that moment was that I could help her right away. Do something.

"All right, I got the bone here and you're going back. No slavery, all is well." I spoke so fast that Lynne had to listen carefully, but she started to shake her head.

What now? Didn't she want to go back after all? I couldn't save Any, but at least her.

My hands were shaking even more. Luckily, I had already taken a pill at the event, otherwise all this would have probably knocked me out already.

Lynne sent me another message: *I can't go back just yet. The bone is part of the deal, and another part is to bring the queen a book that I have to steal at the auction you mentioned to me the other day. They never do anything without getting something in return.*

"The auction," I sighed. "That's an oddly perfect fit."

Lynne nodded. It fit like a glove.

"Fine. I'll help you," I managed to say.

Lynne nodded again.

"Well, boys and girls, it was wonderful to have slaughtered a Deadwalker with you and then to philosophize about our messed-up worlds, but I still have to do something else tonight. So, have a good night, guys," Any said and stood up.

With that he left me and Lynne alone.

Damn, now I was facing a dilemma. She had just poured her heart out to me, the whole truth, like an open book, vulnerable. Now she was even more dependent on my help than before and oh, I wanted her. All of her. I really did. But at the same time this information, about a whole world I did not know about, was too much for me. Her hands. Fish. Deadwalkers, Any dying...

What should I do? Ignore everything and pretend it never happened? Yeah, that was not going to happen.

She stood up, and as if guided by instinct I did too and walked towards her. Just like that, Lynne came to me, and we met in the middle. Jerkily. We were acting totally stupid now, neither of us knew how to react, how to start and fill in all the blanks we created, find our way back to our intimacy. But then she looked at me and hit me with her wounded gaze right in the heart. I wanted nothing else but to kiss her, lose myself in her body, feel the silk of her hair between my fingers and take her up to my bed, making my body feel alive again.

But then she raised her hands, wanting to touch me and I shrank back. I drew back as if she was as filthy as Fish. Of course, I regretted it right away, but I couldn't. I couldn't touch her anymore. I blew up everything that could have been blown up.

First, her look was hurt, hurt that I was afraid of her. Then her eyes turned deadly like the eyes of a feline predator. Her nostrils flared slightly, and she showed me her...middle finger. Right up into my face like she wanted to shove it up to my throat. I didn't know whether to laugh, scream, or whatever the fuck else I should in such a situation. But before I could gather my wits, she ran after Any. In my shirt. Naked underneath with nothing but herself.

"Lynne, wait! Lynne! What should I—I just need time! Wait!" But she didn't. I looked at the chair then and laughter bubbled up in my throat. Well, what was I about to do now? Ask her little helper that I couldn't even see to bring her back to me? Fuck!

I buried my face in my hands.

I wasn't just an idiot. I was a fucked-up idiot.

CHAPTER TWENTY
LYNNE

"That skulling bastard," I spat, stomping circles on my bedroom's floor. "He's scared of me, Bory. A man who kills people without batting an eye, runs a drug ring, and whatever else that guy is up to, is scared of me! I can't believe him."

"You've only said that for the hundredth time now," Bory said from the desk, his nose in a few books.

"How can one be so ignorant and narrow-minded! Him of all people?" I yelled. "That man isn't a saint either. Well, maybe he's too good to be considered bad but he's too bad to be considered good as well! So, he shouldn't judge."

"Well, you don't care what I say anyway. Is it normal to have a rhetorical conversation with yourself?" Bory murmured. "Hm. I don't think so."

"And then he messages me this," I threw the cell phone on the bed.

Rio was such an idiot. Such an incredible *ass-skull*! Ever since Any brought me back, I would have loved to smash Rio's skull. What was he thinking? I had this gift of mine—or whatever the hell it was—since he first saw me. But that did not change me, I was still the same girl. He made me feel like I was disgusting. He knew from day one what my hands could do… or had he perhaps not realized it? Then he was even dumber than I thought.

"That bastard has some nerve. *I'm sorry. Give me time.* Time is the one thing I don't have!"

"I don't know why you're so upset now," Bory said a tad louder, so that I finally noticed him. "You got the kiss. It worked. Yay, victory. So, you got the bone, more or less. Just concentrate on the artifact now and everything will be fine! It's almost over. To hell with what he thinks of you, we're here to save your life."

I looked at him with my mouth open and at first, I couldn't decide what swear word I was gonna use now. But he was right. I fulfilled two out of three conditions and there was only one more to get. Still, it felt like a setback. And it was important to me what Rio thought about me…

Falling backwards onto my bed, I reread Rio's messages one more time. I hadn't answered any of them and he had bombarded me with more.

Let's talk, Lynne.

We can figure this out.

Just give me some time.

It made him nervous that I didn't write back, but I was stubborn as hell, so I never would, nor tried to. At some point he stopped and hadn't messaged since.

It didn't get any better over the next few days, in fact it got even worse. Rio wanted to summon me to his office several times, but I didn't show up. He then told Punchy to bring me. So, I asked Punchy if it was relevant to the job, and it wasn't. So, I didn't go. I didn't care what the reason was, I simply couldn't stomach Rio looking at me with such disgust ever again.

Rio made it very clear to me the other night that he had no

feelings for me. But then Rio started sending me messages again, making a hunt out of it. Always the same bullshit: he was so sorry for how he reacted, all of it was so new to him, and he was not afraid of me, but of my power. Not afraid of me, my ass. He wasn't afraid of Any, the stupid moron of all morons. Making a deal with the Blood Queen just to find out who killed his sister. Maybe I couldn't understand that because I never had family, but this was just too much.

It all escalated when I blocked Rio, a feature I found out about thanks to sheer boredom, and I thought it was appropriate, given the number of texts that fool sent me. After blocking him, a few minutes passed, and Rio thundered into my room. I felt like I was being blown against the wall.

"How dare you! What if there was an emergency? Block me again and I'll kill you. I don't care what you are."

Yeah, right. That one was clear. I stared him down. He knew that I wanted to say: *you are afraid of me! You care about what I am. You care too much!*

Then he grabbed my wrists and held me strongly, his breathing uneven. We stared at each other for several seconds. Hating one another but also wanting one another so badly it hurt. At that moment, I wanted to have my voice and ability to scream so badly.

So, I just stood in front of him and wished he would drop dead. Of course, I didn't mean it seriously, but I had to stand up to the hot-headed man, it simply was in my skulling nature. Therefore, I pushed my chin forward, trembling inside and wriggling out of his grip. He seemed to understand but kept screaming. Yelling. Raging and hitting things.

Over and over again.

There may have been a moment or two when I didn't know if we were going to tear off our clothes because of hate or lust but thank Stix it didn't come to that. But oh, if he thought everything was fine between us now just because he dared to touch my filthy hands—which were gloved anyway—then he was very wrong! That was not a sign of trust. Nothing was all right. Nothing. I needed him the other night, I needed his attention, some kind of approval or appreciation, and what did he give me? He backed away from me as if I were death itself.

"Fuck, Lynne," he said, closing the space between us and I stumbled back until I bumped into the wall behind me. His gaze was fixed on my face and a blast of heat shot throughout my body as he splayed *his hands* on *the* wall on *either side of* my *head*. I caught my breath.

"I'm sorry," he whispered, his forehead touching mine.

Before I understood the meaning of his words, we noticed a gathering behind my door. The girls and Dee, gaping like guppies. All of them. The boss very rarely came to Dee's in person, and lately, only did so because of me. But he had never screamed at any of the girls, at least not like that. I wanted to tell him how much he'd hurt me the other night but now we had an audience and even though I didn't give a damn about his skulling gang hierarchy, I knew better. He drew back and pulled himself together visibly before he left, not looking at the other girls for a second.

When he walked down the corridor, all the girls stared at me in amazement, especially Fox, who followed Rio like his little lap dog. Wow, would I never do such a thing. Running after a man when he was in such a mood.

I closed my door and went to my window, watching Rio storming to his car. I saw Fox getting in as well. She smiled at me then. So, he'd found himself a not-so-disgusting replacement. Fine. I didn't care.

I was just going to steal that book and kill everyone who was keeping me away from it. There was no way I was going to end up as a shadow-slave.

"Come," Punchy said the next day and dragged me into Rio's office.

When I saw him, I could swear there was thunder outside. That's how loaded we still were.

Sighing, Punchy put me in a chair across the room so I wouldn't provoke Rio too much. Couldn't promise that, though. There were only ten days left until the big auction and we had to plan how to steal the governor's Van Gogh portrait. They called it Project Raging Bull.

I learned that Rio had registered it as a blind auction, so the buyers did not know what kind of Van Gogh painting they would be bidding for, making it more secure. The painting would be delivered the day before the auction, that was the deal Rio made with the auctioneer, but of course nobody knew that Rio was the seller; everyone thought it was the governor. In order for the governor to not hear about this, everything was top secret.

Neither Rio, nor Punchy, or Slappy explained to me why we were selling a picture of another man, pretending it came from Jenson. But, whatever. Rio had his secrets, always.

"There's only one way we can do it," Rio said, trying to look at me without hissing. It didn't seem to be easy. I folded my hands and glared back him. "A few hours before the auction starts, there will be a preview party where buyers can try to get an initial estimate of what they're bidding on. Barbie will lock herself in the room and wait for the auction to start, replace the book with a replica in the middle of the process, and run away with the original."

"And the cameras?" Slappy said, skeptically.

"We'll check them today; we need a blind spot for her to vanish through."

"How are you gonna *check* that?" Punchy asked, arms folded, cheesecake crumbs on his sweater.

"Barbie and I are invited to a preview party tonight."

"For the auction?" Slappy asked.

"Another one, idiot. These parties are always on the same day as the auction. I signed us up for a different one. So that we can analyze the building, the security, and the cameras," Rio said, smirking at me.

I pouted, not feeling like going anywhere with him, though I wasn't sure if that was such a good idea after all that had happened. Punchy seemed to agree because he looked at Rio as insecurely as I did.

"I'll pick you up at seven. Put some nice clothes on. We are in for a role play, darling," he said and then he threw something at me.

I caught it, frowning.

A little black box.

"Congratulations," he said, and I swallowed at the pleased glint in his eyes.

My eyebrows shot up as if to ask: *For what?*

"For marrying me."

CHAPTER TWENTY-ONE
LYNNE

P unchy played our chauffeur because we needed to appear rich and discreet enough to attend an auction like this. So, Rio and I played—much to my dismay—a recently married and happy couple that wanted to buy some paintings for their new mansion. Rio looked totally different when he picked me up, wearing a wig that made his hair so much longer and straight.

He had tied it in a knot at his nape, wearing a black suit and a blue tie to match my generously cut dress. On top of that he had contact lenses that made his eyes seem dark brown, and he was shaved too, soft like a baby's ass.

When we sat in a car I never saw before, Rio put a ring on my finger, smirking like hell, his grin as fake as the wedding ring. "I do, honey. Oh, I do," he said.

I growled. All I wanted to do right now was headbutt him. Hard.

"Don't look like that, Barbie girl, we are going to invest in some pretty paintings tonight. You can even choose." Rio laughed, a full rich sound, making Punchy join in.

Ha, ha. Very funny. I rolled my eyes and was glad when we

255

finally arrived at the auction house. Rio opened the car door for me with a big smile, offering me his arm. I held on to him, flipping my now short brown hair off my shoulder, and let him lead me inside.

The auction house was at the outskirts of Chicago in one of the many skyscrapers I had admired a few days before with the girls. Even from the ground those kinds of buildings were breathtaking.

"Remember," Rio said, whispering in my ear. His breath was hot on my skin, forcing me to close my eyes for a second. "We are happily married, so smile a little."

I tilted my head back. Yeah, he'd like that, huh?

Oh, I'd give him what he wanted, he could count on that. He should never have misled me. He'd get it all back double, and quick. That jerk.

He was desperately trying to get a chance to continue where we had left off. But was *he* ready for it? I held him tighter with my *disgusting* fingers and looked at him for a long time, batting my wonderful fake eyelashes and telling him everything I was thinking of through my gaze. He just smiled. *Let him smile while he still can.*

We entered the house, and a man led us into a back room with a huge sign: THE VIEWING. It was a preview of the property held in advance of the upcoming auction. I was quite amazed when I saw the beautiful artwork in front of us.

Rio and I, though, focused more on the showroom itself just like he told me to—on the architecture, shape of windows, doors, closets, emergency exists, ventilation shafts, and most importantly, the video cameras. There were five of them, one in each corner and a round one in the middle, which I learned later was called a dome camera. The objects themselves were also secured accordingly, and no one was allowed to touch them. A mere touch would set off an alarm.

Then Rio pulled me towards him, whispering against my

earlobe. "See that cleaning cupboard over there?" He held me close, our bodies touching.

Before I could wriggle myself out of his grip, he slightly caressed my neck with his lips. Not knowing which cleaning cupboard he was talking about exactly, I squinted over his shoulders and saw a green one, with an iron door loosely opened. I'd have plenty of room in there. That would work.

"Exactly in the blind spot of the camera," Rio whispered, biting my earlobe.

I gasped and breathed against his skin between neck and shoulders, clawing my hands into his hard hips. Now he gasped. I tipped my head back and smiled at him, just as he liked it, starting to touch him provocatively with my hands. But this time he did not flinch. No backing away anymore?

I went on, touching his face. My blue satin gloves went over his nose, mouth and he bit my finger softly—

"Oh, it's so nice to be *so* in love!" I heard an old lady croak behind us towards her companion, a young lady who threw me a judgmental glance. At that, both of us winced. We drew away from each other.

"Oh, so nice. So beautiful! I want to be in love like that too!" the lady sang and waved to me and Rio. We stood there, looking at her as if we'd just been splashed with ice-cold water. In love? Us?

Rio and I made a face and walked on, trying to ignore the thought that came up in both of us. But a few seconds later, he took my hand again, as if he had just remembered our little role-play and that we did want to make it look like we were in love. Unfortunately, what happened just a few moments ago wasn't intentional, wasn't just a role-play.

So, we played our little game further and pretended to be interested in some paintings. Rio asked the staff many questions, sounding a lot like an art collector. I was impressed. Could it be that he was indeed interested in such paintings and the painters? It had to be, because he was able to discuss forgeries, price range, market value, art form, and the like. I noticed when he talked to people other than me, he had a different accent, and his voice was a bit distorted. I didn't know which accent he was imitating but everyone seemed to buy it. After a while, I really felt as if we were a married couple trying to get rid of a few bucks. Wouldn't that be nice?

But I honestly think it would be too boring for people like Rio and me. We needed adrenaline. The feeling that we were doing something forbidden. People like us liked to tease, to pretend, to play. That's why we were in the skull we were in—whatever Rio's skull was, though it had to be at least as big as mine.

"Honey, this picture would make a great addition to our living room. For your hideous fireplace, don't you think? Where your mother's awful cat pictures hang." Rio smiled at me, and I couldn't help but grin back. Cat pictures? What the skull?

Then he poked my cheek with his nose, and I felt his breath on me again. Just like that I stopped and held his face in between my hands, testing him. I noticed the employee behind Rio look away, embarrassed by our closeness.

"We'll do the same thing on the day of days. We will kiss and make the guards feel weird. Then I will push you gently into that cleaning cupboard and our dummy will run into the hall with me. As soon as everyone is out, your little helper will swap the original book with the replica and you'll vanish through that ventilation shaft above the cleaning cupboard, okay?" Rio whispered, turning my gaze to the shaft.

Well, it was a decent plan. No one and no cameras in the world could see Bory but unfortunately, the book was too heavy for my little helper to steal all by himself, so I had to come along as well. But with this hiding place and the suitable escape route, it should work anyway. Rio whispered some more instructions into my ear, and I had to grin at that. All the people around us probably thought he whispered sweet nothings into my ears. But no, we were planning how to rob them.

When he said "dummy", Rio meant Any. That probably was the most hideous part of Project Raging Bull. We needed someone who would pass as me, and Any had exactly the same skin color as me. His bad. When I wore very high heels, we even were almost the same height. With the right wig and a thick fur coat, no one would notice—at least Rio said so. Of course, Any protested at first but eventually he agreed. He couldn't resist Rio's puppy eyes and had agreed to help me too. It didn't make any difference to me. I wouldn't like the guy more just because of that.

"Come on," Rio said, pulling me outside.

As soon as we made it through the showroom, we entered the auction room, where all the art objects would be auctioned.

"Luis Porter and my beautiful wife, Fiona," Rio said and registered us with a fake address, fake number, and fake passports. I gaped when I saw the passport photo of me. When did he have it taken? I was really surprised; could people do something like that on the computer? Bory already told me that the computer was a miraculous thing and made almost anything possible.

Ignoring my uneasiness, Rio put the passports back in his jacket, kissed me on the cheek, and led me to our seats. He was able to throw me completely off track with his touches, kisses, and whatever he was doing right now, which was of course only for show. I hadn't even noticed that he had a bidder card with the number 22 in the other hand—the hand that was touching my hip right now.

We sat down in the back row and Rio put his free hand on my knee, stroking my kneecap with his thumb. Sighing, I turned my other leg over which made his hand wander upwards. And just like that he caressed the crease where my hip and thigh joined. I blushed and pushed his hand away, but it only made him smile even more. Bastard.

I took out my phone and wrote, *You're enjoying this too much.*

Rio pretended to listen to the auctioneer's opening speech, but wrote back in passing: *Why can't I enjoy something I want?*

That made me blush even more, my cheeks feeling hot like lava. I couldn't even look him in the eyes.

If you are embarrassed that easily, how would you react if I told you that I would like to touch the spot where my hands were just now with the tip of my tongue? Rio pinned me down with his eyes.

By the Dead, what was he thinking! I quickly hid the phone screen, glancing to the man next to me. Thank the Hellhounds he didn't pay attention to me and my phone. Rio chuckled. He liked to tease me! My phone vibrated once more. I glanced at it. Damn it.

I've always wanted to be the reason you hide your phone screen from people. He smirked.

I gave him a nasty look but then the auctioneer rang a bell. The auction had started, and within seconds the people held up their bidding cards one by one with eager expressions. All I could hear was numbers. Numbers, numbers, and numbers over numbers.

My phone buzzed.

Wouldn't you like it if I kissed you down there? Kissed your breasts? Your nipples?

This time not just my cheeks turned red, every body part of mine was getting hot. And Rio was just getting started. I jabbed him gently in the chest and gave him a look that should make it more than clear he shouldn't write such things.

But instead of putting the phone away he turned his face towards me, giving me a crooked smile. Without even looking to the auctioneer once, he bid for an utterly expensive painting on the side.

Shaking my head, I wrote back, *I wouldn't know whether I*

would like that sort of kissing. I have never been intimate with a man before.

When he read the message, he choked on his own spit and looked at me with his eyes wide open. He accidentally bid again and bought the painting. Seemed like he didn't want to after all.

You are a virgin? he quickly texted.

I nodded and frowned.

"Fuck," he said, appearing to be distracted for one second longer and then he looked at me again.

What? I wrote back.

He kept looking at me. Oh, did he remember that my hands weren't the way he wanted them?

You can't be a virgin, don't joke about something like that, he wrote.

Why not? I texted him.

You don't seem like one.

I snorted and typed faster this time. *What do virgins look like to you? Do they wear a sign that's saying, 'I've never had sex in my life'?*

He coughed once more and wrote back: *The way you kiss. That's not how girls who have never had sex do it, Lynne.*

I said I was a virgin, not entirely innocent. I shot him a glance.

So, just because I had never wanted a man so badly before as to invite him into my cave, meant that I was a complete fool? It just meant that kissing had been mostly enough, or maybe something was indeed wrong with me. Don't know. I even thought I liked women, but I hadn't met one yet with whom I really wanted to take the next step either. Just like I hadn't met a man who I wanted to do it with. Well... not until *he* touched me.

Rio started fidgeting with his foot and it seemed he had a problem with touching me once again.

What is it now? Am I grossing you out again? I texted.

He squinted his eyes and shook his head in disbelief.

261

"What? Is that what you're thinking? Why you're still angry?" he asked a tad too loudly.

All the people in front of us turned back. We smiled and Rio reached for his phone.

I am just telling you this once, his text said, *you're wonderful. I never found you disgusting. Never. You almost drive me crazy because I want you so much.*

I grunted and put my phone back in my bag. The conversation was over. Of course, he didn't like that, but he put his cell phone away too and then he leaned into me, his breath tingling against my ear again, and I couldn't help but think about where he said he wanted to kiss me a couple of minutes ago. My breathing became faster, making my chest rise and fall noticeably, much to his liking. He smiled when he glanced at my breasts.

"If I could turn back time, I would, Lynne," he said, took my hand in his, squeezing it tightly.

I couldn't overlook the symbolic power of this gesture but all I learned today was that he still couldn't admit he really was afraid of me. He could deny it as often as he wanted, but I wanted to hear the truth from his mouth. No meaningless excuses. I wanted an honest apology that told me exactly what he was feeling sorry for, and why. The only thing he did was prove to me was that he still triggered feelings in me. Even though I couldn't get away from him, it didn't mean that I forgave him. He hadn't trusted me and that still hurt. Maybe it was because he meant more to me, than I did to him. After all, I had some kind of strange connection with him. I felt like I had known him since he was a kid.

I knew him all my life and somehow, I had imagined what he might be like, why he was so sad. But I was kidding myself, I just realized. All this time I thought we had an intimate relationship, a connection that only we shared, because I was able to see him on Storm Day. But he didn't know me.

THE BONE THIEF'S TALE

I just stalked him for years... there was nothing more behind it.

Skull, Bory was right again.

The remaining time we watched the auction like normal people did, and when everyone started to leave, Rio said he had a few corners to look at and escape routes to think about, so I should wait for him outside. Just like that he took off and forgot his cell phone on the chair. I rolled my eyes and was about to call after him, but I remembered I couldn't do that. Shit. I had no voice, duh.

Then I shrugged, put his phone in my pocket and decided to just give it to him later. How could he be such an important gang leader and forget his phone like that? What if the wrong people found it? He really wasn't that smart actually, was he?

I started to find my way out when I felt a firm grip on my upper arm. I whirled and saw Z-Mexx. How the hell had he recognized me?

"If that isn't the Dutch Beauty herself! It must be my lucky day! Are you here with van der Volt?" he asked, glancing around.

I shook my head and pointed at my outfit, confused.

"How did I recognize you? Well, I could never forget your face, darling. Did you get anything nice at the auction?" Z-Mexx asked, his snake eyes slightly narrowed.

I nodded and went to the exit, but he followed me.

"Thanks again for your advice the other day," he said, trying to keep up with me.

No idea what he meant but he probably was referring to the envelope Rio made me give him. Then my phone rang, and I reached for it, only later did I realize it was Rio's. I glanced around quickly, but he was nowhere to be seen. I noticed the surprised look of Z-Mexx. He immediately tried to pull himself together, but it was too late. Seeing his look, I glanced at Rio's display myself and was startled. Skull, what had I just shown him? Governor Jenson was calling! I tried to not get too upset and put the phone back. I smiled, embarrassed, and wanted to leave as soon as possible, but Z-Mexx pulled me back.

"He's van der Volt, isn't he? The governor?" he asked with a thin but urgent voice.

I rolled my eyes again. That phantom was the most important person for everyone here in Chicago, wasn't it? Why did everyone think that I of all people had something to do with him? I just wished that guy would show up and tell everyone who he was, just to make them shut up.

"Which of his paintings is he auctioning off? The van Gogh?" Z-Mexx asked, still holding on to me, too firm for my taste.

I hesitated and realized what I'd just done. Why did I do that? Rio said it so often, everyone could read my face like a book, and so did Z-Mexx. I just told him about the painting…

"Ah," he said, still grinning sheepishly. "The van Gogh, of course. He keeps it in his office where anyone who negotiates with him can see it. All his clients know that painting. I should have thought of it myself. Van der Volt and Van Gogh. Of course. Thank you, Dutch Beauty, I hope to see you at the auction."

I tried to smile but failed terribly and stumbled out. Rio was already waiting outside, and I quickly pressed the mobile phone into his hand, noticing my trembling fingers.

"Oh, God. I'm a fool, thank you," he said, put it in his pocket and directed me to the black car Punchy was waiting in.

Actually, I wanted to write a message to Rio and explain what had just happened, apologize, and prepare myself for arguing with him…but the way he acted, like everything was okay while it certainly wasn't, put me off. Rio was hiding something from me again. I glanced over my shoulder and saw Z-Mexx, smiling triumphantly and talking to…to the cop. My mouth hang open. The same cop who followed me after the incident at the Pie Factory. Farid. Did Mexx not know that he was a cop or was he not a cop at all, and just a member of the Black Crowns?

What the hell was going on?

Then I glanced up to Rio and I finally got it.

He hadn't lost the phone—it was one of his schemes. I was supposed to take it with me, and I was supposed to get that call as well. That was his plan all along because he wanted Z-Mexx to approach me and see the call. I clawed my fingernails into his arm, but he didn't respond, knowing that I'd figured it out by now.

"Bye, wifey. I have some more work to do after our pleasant night," he said, opening the car's door for me. He gave me a kiss on the cheek and pushed me gently inside.

As Punchy drove away I watched Rio walk in a completely different direction. For skull's sake, what was that man up to?

CHAPTER TWENTY-TWO
RIO

Lynne climbed up the wall of the governor's mansion, making my fucking stomach squirm. This was exactly why I didn't want any relationships between my gang members. As planned, I sat on the roof opposite of Jenson's mansion, and watched her steal the painting.

The nightly chill wrapped me up like a straitjacket. My leg fidgeted, and I noticed my hands sweating. I knew Jenson was not at home tonight, so it was the perfect day to go through with my plan. The lucky guy had actually won a romantic weekend for two, although he had not even taken part in a raffle. Who was stupid enough to fall for that?

I had to admit, we had staged it well.

Slappy, our hacker/photoshop guru was able to produce mockups better than some advertising companies. He had so much talent, but of course he didn't use it well. No, he wasted his time and made fake coupons for me. Well, he was better off now. The idiot really did propose to Cherry last night.

Anyway, Fox played my secretary as usual and called Jenson with a cheerful voice congratulating him a hundred times on his win. The fool cheered with happiness. What a prize! A whole weekend in one of the most expensive wellness hotels in the States. He could have easily afforded it himself, but stingy people like him loved to get expensive things for free, and above all he loved to win, even if it was only a raffle. My wallet was still hurting from the loss but, well, sometimes you have to invest to maximize your profit.

I didn't have a good feeling when Lynne broke in, she was all black and silent like a wraith, but deadly as a weapon made flesh. Like planned, she tried to reach the windowsill and swayed for a second. My heart stopped and I cursed under my breath. I already felt sick, seeing her at those heights, without me being below her to catch her if she messed up. So, when she caught herself again and finally stood in the bastard's bathroom, I exhaled in relief and massaged my chest. The sting went away slowly.

Man, I was stupid. Stupid because I let her get close to me, because I let her get under my skin eventually. What good came from all of this for me? None. She would soon be gone and not just overseas or to another state, no, to *another world*. To the fucking Underworld. And I wouldn't have a chance to see her again, not until I died…if she still wanted to see me after all this madness was over.

The mere thought of her hating me forever tightened my throat, making the air I breathed feel like shards of glass, cutting me from inside.

Trying to breathe more steadily, I looked at her once again. The streetlights lit up the apartment wall, allowing me to see Lynne's shadow. I asked her to leave the bathroom window open so that if anything went wrong, I could get to her—something else I'd never done before. Playing the babysitter.

After I couldn't see her shadow in Jenson's office for a few minutes, I was about to run to her, jumping over the joined roofs. Fortunately, I pulled myself together. Fuck. I couldn't work properly with these feelings. She shouldn't mean anything to me, the fact that she could die should be meaningless. Lynne should be a tool, an investment, not a real person. It endangered everything. And yet I needed her, there was no way back, and she needed me too, as if our lives were intertwined. I was actually thinking about running away with her. Leaving everything behind. How could that have happened?

Both my feet shook unsteadily now, and I couldn't calm down. My fingernails pounded on the dirty roof tiles I was sitting on, and I kept my eyes on Jenson's office window. Only when Lynne's shadow was visible on his desk did my feet stop shaking.

She had the picture; the jerk really wasn't guarding it any more than we thought. A real van Gogh? I would've thought he had other alarms, but no, it was just as we thought. Moron. He used a typical alarm system that could've been knocked out by a twelve-year-old—or, in our case, by a girl from the Underworld.

I watched Lynne take the painting off the nail. I ran over the rooftops to Jenson's, jumping over a gap. Then, as we agreed, Lynne stuck her head through the bathroom window and held the painting up for me. And then, well, we found out that Jenson did have another alarm system after all. It went off and Lynne shimmied down from the mansion's façade and jumped onto the street below. Like planned, she ran immediately, not directing anyone to me, since I had the picture now.

After a few minutes the cops were there. How else could it be, when the governor of Illinois himself was being robbed in his fancy mansion? In such cases, they moved quickly and actually did the work they were supposed to do. They chased Lynne as if she were the prey and they were the bloodhounds. I hesitated, thinking about stupid things, but thank God I remembered that Lynne could take care of herself. So, I ran over the roofs to my escape route, where Punchy was waiting for me, ready to drive.

"What happened?" Punchy asked me, concentrating on the street.

I was breathing fast, too fast, when I sat in the car.

The picture was safe in the trunk, but my blood pressure was beyond what was safe, and everything was pounding inside of me. There was this fucking pressure in my ears, making me gasp. This pounding! Make it stop!

Boom. Boom.

Boom. Boom. Boom.

Clasping my left breast, I wondered if I had taken the pill today. Yes, I remembered, I had taken it. But, apparently, it was insufficient for my current level of stress. Lately, my panic attacks were getting worse, and I had to increase my doses. I should probably visit Dr. Meinhard again.

So, I took a deep breath. Exhaling, inhaling. I tried to concentrate on the things that were touching my skin, to feel my surroundings. My feet were touching the bottom of the car and my back was pressing into the cold leather seat. My left hand was on top of my chest, feeling the fast beating of my heart. Everything was good. Lynne was fine, she knew her way around.

"Where's Slappy?" I asked, trying to speak through my rumbling breath. "Tell me he is waiting for… Barbie."

"Slappy couldn't make it, he's with Cherry, her—"

"*Who's picking up Barbie, then?*" I shouted.

There was nothing I hated more than when my plans were interrupted. I told Slappy to wait for Lynne to pick her up and save her in case she triggered an alarm. No one else. Slappy was supposed to do it! Nobody had the right to change my plans because of some nonsense!

"We—Cherry's mother—" Punchy started.

"I don't care!" I screamed, still massaging my chest.

Everything was tight and throbbing and I just couldn't breathe. I was trapped in a straitjacket. Trembling, I fumbled with my backpack on the floor, looking for the pillbox. It slipped from my wet fingers. Fuck. My heart was beating faster and faster and faster. The drumming in my ears got louder and the blood pressure hammered in my head.

Then I found the tiny orange box, opened the lid, and took a pill. Sighing, I fell back into my seat and tried to breathe evenly, to let the lump in my throat go. Find my way back into this world and not let the creeping fear win over my body and sanity.

"Who. Will pick up. Barbie?" I spoke through my teeth and tried to fight against the black wave that had almost hit me. Punchy said something, but too softly. I couldn't hear him; my heartbeat was louder than his voice. At least in my head.

"Fox is waiting for her, we couldn't get anyone else on short notice and she was there, and she offered herself and—"

"Fuck," I cried out, hitting the dashboard. "Fox? Are you nuts?"

"What? She'll do almost anything for you."

"She ain't a gang member, Punchy. What did I tell you about that?"

The adrenalin that had just kicked in made my anxiety fade, and my heart rate slowed, and there was no thumping or drumming inside of my head anymore. I don't know if it was the effect of the pills, or because I already knew what was ahead of us, but I could finally think clearly again and was able to talk without any problems.

"I'm sorry, boss." Punchy clasped the wheel tighter. "The truth is, Cherry's mom got into a shootout. The Taipans attacked us when a group took a new batch of C-Wax. They meddled in a park, in front of civilians. There were a lot of casualties, boss. We're in deep shit and Slappy... is fixing it right now."

"Fuck," I shouted, and hit the dashboard again. It's going to take us weeks to sort that shit out.

"How many got busted?"

"Thirteen of us, twenty fucking Taipans," Punchy explained.

"Fuck."

So, we drove home.

Every time I saw the blue and red lights flare up, I cringed. At the club, we tried to work out the worst things first, see who had to stay in jail, to keep up appearances, and who we could bail out right away. Which residents and tenants we had to bribe to not make statements to the cops or journalists, and how much hush money was needed. What the victims wanted. What contacts I could rely on.

It was fucking bullshit and the responsible lieutenants were punished extensively that same night. I was so loaded that I beat them up myself in front of a bunch of my gang members, just to remind them what I was capable of. Every tooth I broke was a win for me. With every second that passed while Lynne didn't rush into my office, grinning at me with her wonderful lips, I got more and more angry and wilder. Eventually I sent Punchy out to look for her and when he came back with the information that she was in jail, I smashed up my office.

Now there was no denying it anymore. No negating that I had overwhelmingly strong feelings for my Bone Thief.

I had to get her back, now.

CHAPTER TWENTY-THREE
LYNNE

"Where have you been?" I asked Bory and ran up and down the little chamber they called a 24-hour-cell. Until now I had to talk to two extremely ugly men who stared at my cleavage more than they really wanted to talk to me. Skullholes, all of them were skullholes. Especially Fox!

"I was with Cherry, I'm sorry," Bory said.

What? Was he serious?

"Bory, I can't believe you. She can't even see you," I yelled back, pacing.

The cell was small, though, so I was more or less running in circles like a locked-up animal. Damn, I was so skulling angry. I could have ripped anyone's head off, preferably Fox's.

I had been running for my life, jumping over benches, climbing stuff, and just as I had finally come to the place where Slappy was supposed to wait for me, I had seen Fox. Of course, I'd hesitated at first, because Rio had not mentioned her to me before, but I'd ran towards her anyway and what she had done then, had been absolutely horrible. She was such a bitch. Fox had seen that the cops were on my heels, that they had been already storming out of the cars, pointing their guns on me. Oh, she'd known she could have saved me. But instead, she'd smiled at me and left. Just like that.

Well, nobody could say she hadn't been there. Oh yes, she had been there. She had been there to watch the cops take me away. So that she could have her precious Rio just for herself. How jealous could one be? Thanks to her, the cops surrounded me, aimed their laser pointer guns at me and kept yelling the same thing. "Hands above your head!"

One read me my rights, another handcuffed me and dragged me to their car. Of course, Rio already had a plan if I got caught. He always had more than one plan. They couldn't prove a thing. Since Rio had disappeared with the painting and I was wearing gloves, my fingerprints weren't anywhere to be found. The video cameras of the governor's cameras were pointless too, because I wore a mask the whole time and despite my hurry, I had managed to change my clothes while running for my life.

When the cops saw me, I pretended I was afraid of them. Fear of guns and all of that. I played the good girl that had gotten into a possible gang conflict and was scared to death now. I made it look like I wasn't running from the cops after all. So, I tried to cooperate, and played the part Rio gave me. No one could prove anything, I was sure. But I'd never forget Fox's face. Oh, she'll regret this. That bitch will regret messing with me. Maybe she won this fight, but in the end I would win.

"Why were you even with Cherry, Bory? You should've been with me. You could have helped me!"

"Her mother was shot," Bory yelled back at me.

"What? Skull."

Bory had developed an unhealthy affinity for Cherry. Could it be that a ball of fur could fall in love with a human being? It was even more insane than my attraction to Rio.

273

"There's a gang war going on, or it's already over. I don't know. Apparently, the Loops were involved. Big time."

"Skull," I gasped.

Then Rio was in deep shit, too. And what could I do? I had to wait, talk to cops, lawyers, cops again. In those situations, it was good that I could not talk after all. I told them nothing. Just that I was on my way to the movies, and they scared me. Rio gave me an identity card, and that night I was Sara Longbeat, a CU student of English literature. Hopefully, they didn't ask me about my studies, because I knew less about literature than I did about mobile phones.

Just before I had spent twenty-four hours in this narrow cell, a guard came and told me someone had posted my bail. That someone was none other than Rio, who was waiting for me outside in a leather outfit and was involved in an intense talk with one of the guards. My heart skipped a beat at the sight of him and my pace quickened. When Rio heard me approaching him, he turned around and pure relief was obvious on his features, relief that I was well and alive. But then neither I nor he knew what to do. Hug? Kiss? Shake hands? Nod? How the hell were we supposed to greet each other?

Everything felt wrong at that moment, and we quietly agreed on a smile that looked more like stomachache than joy.

While approaching him, I noticed the wary and reddish eyes of his, with red and blue circles under them. I gasped at the sight of his split lip and the many scratches and barely healed wounds on his neck and hands. Under the thick pitch-black leather outfit, I couldn't check the rest of his body, but I was sure he had more injuries there. If he noticed my concern, he didn't say anything, but rather examined me to see if I was all right, if they had hurt me.

He came closer, stopping in front of me. I knew instinctively that if he saw even just one injury on me, the guards would have one more problem. But I wasn't hurt, unlike him. Bory told me he had been in a fight but not that he looked like this...

"Everything is fine." He cupped my head with his hands, checking for injuries once more. "Have they done *anything* to you?" He suddenly sounded lethal.

His touch took me completely off guard, but I shook my head and pointed to his wounds instead.

"We had an argument, nothing serious." Rio ran his thumbs down my cheeks and I wanted to touch him too, but the police had demanded that I take off my gloves. As if he had been prepared for this, he pulled another set of gloves out of his pockets and waved them in front of my face, making me smile like always.

Gratefully accepting them, I slipped my hands inside.

"Because of... Fox," he started.

He checked the guards and continued speaking in a whisper. "I took care of her. She is somewhere else now and won't bother you anymore."

When I heard her name, I could feel the bile rising up to my throat. I was so angry, and I would have loved to strangle her by myself, although I honestly did not believe that Rio hurt her. Rio was different with women, he treated them differently, as if they were more vulnerable and less dangerous. But that wasn't true—at least I was more dangerous than most people around here, more than Rio even. I wondered if he knew that once I fully unleashed my strength, I could kill him without any issue. Well, after the show with Fish, I was sure he did.

He nodded to the bathroom of the police station and gave me a bag with clothes in it. The same kind of black leather clothes he wore.

"Please put these on. We're going for a ride." He winked at me, and I learned what motorcycle gear was. I put on the thick gloves, pants, jacket, and heavy boots that were inside the bag.

OUTSIDE CHERRY and Slappy were waiting for us, and I beamed to see that they were doing well. Slappy's face looked about the same as Rio's, but Cherry was fine and I was so grateful for that, so I hugged her.

They were waiting in front of two motorcycles—as Bory called them. Two devilish vehicles with which one could flit through the world even faster than with cars. I was so excited! I would have loved to jump right on and ride to the end of the world. Rio took two helmets off the motorcycle and threw one towards me. I caught it with an excited look on my adventure-loving face.

"We're going to ride for quite a while," Rio said and helped me put the helmet on. While he fumbled for the clasp, we didn't do anything but stare at each other, the blue of his eyes capturing me.

Slappy and Cherry turned away from us, as if they couldn't stomach seeing Rio this gentle. "We're not going back to Englewood, at least not until we finish Project Raging Bull. I'm taking you to a hotel where you'll need to check in. Slappy and Cherry will be there, too," he said.

I looked at him with my eyebrows raised. *And you? Where will you stay?*

He pulled his lips into a crooked smile and finally closed my helmet and stroked the short strip of my uncovered neck that peeked under it. "I'll sleep in another one; it's safer that way."

I nodded, the fear of endangering others was always his biggest problem, wasn't it? Somehow, he was as trapped in his life as I was, as if we were always in a cell like the one behind me. Then I felt Cherry hugging me from behind.

"Safe ride," Cherry said. "Slappy and I will leave Englewood after the coup, too."

I turned and smiled. Oh, I was so happy for them! Cherry finally had her degree and could start another career, start working with flowers, just as she wanted her whole life, and Slappy could use his computer knowledge. Away from gangs and drugs.

"I'm pregnant," she added, grinning from ear to ear.

Oh, I wished I could cry, just once, to show her how skulling happy I was. But, well, I guess she saw it in my eyes, because hers glittered the same way as mine felt.

Then Rio put his helmet on, folded down his visor and swung himself onto his motorcycle. When he started it, my whole body fidgeted with excitement. The deep roar made my heart beat faster. Oh, yeah, I wanted to ride that thing!

"Do you think that's a good idea? I don't have any protective clothing at all," Bory said and folded his arms in protest.

Stop whining! I opened the pocket of my leather outfit. *Just hop in, Bory.*

He mumbled once more and then, thankfully, was finally silent.

Rio reached out his hand and lifted me onto the bike behind him. "Hold on to me. I'll be going very fast, so, try not to fall down."

I smiled and grabbed his waist with my hands, hugged him as tight as I could and then he drove. Oh my, I just wanted to cheer loudly and scream joyfully at the passing wind. It felt like Soothie was taking off, just on the ground and not in the air. The pressure I felt made me happy and I loved every second he rode through town with me and yes, Rio was going fast. With him everything was fast, extreme, and dangerous and that's what I liked so much about him. With him, there was nothing impossible, unattainable, or unthinkable. His thoughts were just as dirty as mine and I was sure that he wouldn't last a day in Cave Town without starting some nonsense—just like me. When I clasped him tighter, pressing myself against his cold leather jacket, I put my head on his hard back. He took one hand and squeezed it as if to tell me that he enjoyed it as much as I did.

We drove for quite a while. At every turn he leaned in, so I did the same, adapting myself to his movements. That night I felt the road under his motorcycle, felt the centrifugal forces in every curve, and felt as if we could turn the whole world with the throttle.

When the journey was over, I wanted it to go on. On and on. I wanted more cities flashing past me, more of the cold wind on my heated skin, more of the adrenaline. But we had arrived at our destination and checked in.

As Rio escorted me to my room—which was actually three rooms and much too spacious for just one person—he said that all of my things were already here, thanks to Punchy. Cherry and Slappy would only be a few doors away in case I needed anything and then he stopped in front of my door. We were acting weird again, as if we were not able to communicate with each other anymore. We danced our little dance where he took a step forward and I took one back, with me reaching out one hand and him hesitating until we stopped.

"See you tomorrow," he finally managed to say, hesitating once more, looking at me from top to bottom. I thought he wanted to say something else—but he left.

When I closed the door, I leaned against it, sighing deeply. I heard Bory say something, but I couldn't quite listen right now.

"I'm going to see Cherry," Bory repeated louder.

"Do that," I said, closing my eyes and tilting my head back again.

I would have loved to open the door, run after Rio and yell at him, ask him to stay. Here. With me.

But before I could come up with something stupid there was a knock on the door.

I opened my eyes.

Skull.

And just like that my heart was pounding up to my neck, my stomach tingling, my knees shaking. Without thinking, I opened the door and saw Rio standing there. Looking at him, my heart sank into my pants. He was breathing as hard as I was, holding onto my doorframe, as if he had to hold himself back from something.

His expression was determined, dangerous, lethal.

I opened my mouth but all I could do was stare and form a small o with my mouth. There he stood, backlit from the wall lamp behind him. His eyes flitted to my mouth and my stupid thoughts were suddenly spinning around the question of whether or not I was still mad at him.

Well, I was, somehow.

A little.

Or, rather, almost not at all.

Oh, I didn't know or care anymore! All I could think of now was that look in his eyes. No, I wasn't angry anymore. There was another feeling boiling up inside of me at that moment…lust.

"Lynne," he said in a drawn-out voice that made the blood in my ears roar.

But there was nothing more to say or do, because then we fell into each other's arms, kissed, and longed for another. Totally consumed by pleasure, Rio pulled me inside, slammed the door shut with his foot, and pushed me slightly against the wall, making me gasp against his hot lips. Our hands were instantly everywhere.

"If we cross that line, Lynne," he said while kissing me,

breathing the words rather than saying them. "We are fucked up."

I nodded under his kisses, started to unzip his jacket, and exhaled when his hands touched my breasts, cupping them. Smirking, he threw my jacket on the floor and pushed me back into the suite without letting go of my lips even once. I pulled the jacket off his shoulders. As if he couldn't wait any longer, he took off his shirt by himself, fast as lightning, making me impatient just with the sight of his bare, muscular chest. He was every woman's naughty fantasy for sure.

My eyes flew up to his, meeting a challenging grin.

Slowly, he took off my shirt and kept pushing me towards one of the two big sofas in the middle of the room. As he pressed me against the cold leather, he got rid of my pants and my bra. He bent down, kissed me again, and his hot fingers cupped my breasts, squeezing a little as I shuddered.

"God, you're beautiful," he breathed, his fingertips brushing my hardened nipples, tugging, and twirling.

Rocking against him, I put my hands up to his neck, pulling his face down to mine while at the same time I was aware of the growing ache between my legs.

He parted my lips, his breathing full of desire as his tongue swept in. Only the fabric of his pants and my panties separated us now and my body ached to be touched by him, seeking relief.

I wanted all of him at once.

Rio drew his lips into a smile and put his hands on my ass, firm and demanding. He picked me up then, pushed me against his naked body and something hard pressed against me. Just kissing wasn't enough anymore. As Rio gave a throaty laugh, he threw me onto the big leather sofa, and in the span of a moment his fingers were twisted in my hair.

I gasped but he swallowed the sound with a forceful kiss.

When he pulled out of the kiss I wanted to complain but he

started to brush his lips against my collarbone, my breasts, my belly. Suddenly he took my panties' seam between his teeth and his hot breath met my most sensitive spot. Shudders raced through me. I held his head with both of my hands, shoving my fingers into his hair, tangling them with black strands of hair. He chuckled and with the edge of my underwear in his mouth, he slid down my body, freeing me.

And there I was.

Naked.

At his mercy.

He put my panties on the floor, his gaze sweeping over me, from my face to my bare breasts, my hardened nipples, my stomach, my impatient gloved hands, my thighs which I rubbed together in anticipation, and then he started to undo the belt of his trousers, slowly, drinking me in all the while and my eyes never left his.

"Do you want me to stop?" he asked.

My eyebrows shot up. Stop? Was he insane?

As I shook my head vehemently, he smirked and threw his belt into a corner of the room. Then he unzipped his pants and let them slide to the floor, his face illuminated by the dim light, golden like in a portrait we were likely to steal. "And now?"

I shook my head once more, biting my lower lip. By Stix, no, he should never stop. Never.

My eyes flitted over his defined muscles, his strong arms, the shaped V of his hip muscles and my mouth went dry at the sight of him. Slowly, he got rid of his boxershorts and his socks. The moment could have lasted days. I couldn't get enough of watching him undress. My eyes flitted from his long and strong legs, his skin so even and tanned, to his best feature.

By the Dead, there wasn't a single inch of him that I didn't love.

And he was mine. For now, all of him was mine.

Smiling and undoubtedly loving the way I looked at his body, he crawled over me, assessing me with his wanting eyes.

Oh, I wanted him.

Needed him.

To claw at him and never let go of him again.

When his face was just a handbreadth away from mine, his hot breath tingled on my lips.

"If you don't want this, I'll stop," he ground out, "I will never sleep with a woman who doesn't want me."

I grinned and indicated to him through my glance: *Then what do you want?*

"I want you," he whispered, kissing the tip of nose. "And I want you to want me."

I could hardly breathe as my hands went over his muscular back, down to his butt and squeezed. Just as his hands did with my breasts, making me moan. By the Stix, this man was a force of nature. Hard, stiff, and smelling like heaven.

"Relax," he said, "I will not slide into you. Not yet."

I raised my eyebrows.

Did he not want to sleep with me?

What was wrong?

"First, I'll show you how beautiful it can feel for you and kiss you...maybe here?" he grinned and kissed me on the neck.

His smell was everywhere, daring me, luring me in. Gently, I bit his neck, and he bit mine, as if we were animals claiming each other.

"You know—" he went down my body, kissing my nipples, making me twitch under him as he continued, "—there's something about you that I don't want to lose because I know I can never find it in another person again."

I moaned in response, grabbed his head with both hands and pulled him up to me again, to kiss him once more.

Rio's kisses were wild, demanding. They left me almost no room to breathe but I didn't want that room. I wanted him to

THE BONE THIEF'S TALE

take any kind of space from me and replace it with himself. I probably could have kissed him for hours, could have gone to war with his tongue for days, and could have celebrated reconciliation for months. But then, he bit my lower lip and tugged it between his teeth. My body tingled and I curled my toes.

He kissed my neck, went down to my breasts, sucking my nipples—A tremor ran through me, and I arched my back towards him, clawing at the soft fabric under me. The sensations that hit my body when he went further down were unbearable and I wanted to scream. He kissed me right between my legs, but the tingle wouldn't stop. It increased, making my head spin.

But what he did to me then was from another world.

I breathed faster and faster as he licked me like ice-cream. I wanted to pull him up to me, but he didn't let me, he was stronger now and did everything to make me happy and oh, he did. My whole body burned with impatience and need. I had never experienced anything like this before and then he said three little words that made my head feel dizzy.

"You're mine," the rumble in his voice made me scream and my body clenched. My breaths came in short bursts now.

Moments later, I lay broken under him and beamed over both ears, my body alight.

"I could watch you climax all day, month, year. Do you know how beautiful you are, Lynne? How special?" he said, lying beside me and tracing the outline of my jaw, the shell of my ear...

I sighed.

I pinched him lightly in the chest and grinned as he took my hand in his and kissed up to my shoulder.

"Shall I tell you a secret?" he whispered, looking me right in my dark eyes.

I nodded.

"I was scared to want you. To want you so much. But now, here I am anyway… still wanting you."

Once I again I was glad that I couldn't talk. I had no clue know what to say back to him. So, I kissed him again but this time I rolled on top of him. He stroked my back and grabbed my ass with both of his hands. I gasped into his mouth and could feel how much he still wanted me, but I didn't know what to do. How should I start?

He made that guttural sound again, grabbed my back and just like that he lay above me again. He didn't like to lose control at all, huh?

"If we do this, there's no going back, Lynne. Once we're like this we can only fuck to get over our feelings."

I nodded, pinning him with my eyes. Making it clear how much I wanted this. Him. We'd already kissed and slept with each other in our mind. So, what was he afraid of? Maybe that's exactly what he was trying to tell me…that he indeed was scared. Afraid of wanting me more, maybe even loving me.

Do it, my glance told him. *We're lost anyway.*

And so, he did.

He slid into me, and I felt a sharp pain, making me cry out. He slowed down then, but my movements told him that he had to go faster. Faster, not slower! *Skull the pain, Rio, skull it.* And he did. Holy Hellhounds and skulling Stix. I cried out, in pleasure, not in pain, pressed my nails into his back and wanted him to never stop, wanted to be one with him forever.

Rio and Lynne. No one else.

" I could kiss you for hours, Lynne, but fuck you for days." He said and just like that everything that was going to doom us started.

CHAPTER TWENTY-FOUR
RIO

Every smile, every move, every attempt to get up from the hotel bed made me pull her back to me, onto me. I was like an addict who couldn't stop, a starving man in front of a banquet.

And all those times, I thought about what I should do now, what I could do. I wanted to grab her, run away, leave my life behind, and make sure that what was about to happen wouldn't happen. So, every time I looked into her eyes, I feared she might hate me, that she would never forgive me when she saw my true colors. Still, I couldn't tell her. I couldn't lose her.

No, I couldn't tell her my plan, because I needed the element of surprise; the adrenaline pushing her for spontaneous decisions. Lynne had to be authentic for my plan to work, there was no other way, and yet I cursed myself every time one of her silken strands of hair slipped through my fingers, every time I kissed her soft body, every time I felt her gloved hands on me, every time I made her giggle and glanced at her little dimples. Of course, I didn't set foot in the other hotel once, I stayed here the whole night like the fool I am.

We lived in a bubble all the while, even though the Project

Raging Bull was on our doorstep. Actually, I used to think these last days would be the worst because I had already planned everything, greased everyone, calculated all escape routes and only had to wait for the shit to go down. Wait until the hour struck and everything ended, and a new era began. Nevertheless, it was exactly these hours that made my heart jump with joy—because of this delicate creature, with light hair like a star, dark eyes like the night itself, and the most daring, dirty smile there ever was.

Lynne couldn't tell me about the Underworld because she was under a spell. Of course, I still had problems getting used to the fact she was really from another world, that the myths and fairy tales I always found so exciting were kind of true, like in all the Hollywood movies.

Still, she could tell me about the feelings she had down there. So, Lynne told me about the feelings that ran through her body when she was stealing for the queen. Sometimes she wasn't able to type certain words because a spell stopped her, so she avoided those parts and told me about other vague things, about her friends. About the dragon Soothie, about Mal and Bory, the little helper who apparently kept hanging around in our or Cherry's room.

Then she asked me the most delicate question she could.

What happened to Aria, Rio? she wrote at some point between a shared shower and spaghetti that we ate on the floor.

It wasn't easy to read Aria's name on Lynne's phone, to think about her, let alone talk about her to anyone but Any.

Aria.

She was everything to me back then.

I lowered my eyes, taking a deep breath before I started. "When I was fourteen, thanks to my middle grade teacher, I won a scholarship to graduate from the University of Chicago Laboratory, *the* school in Chicago if you wanted to make something of yourself. The school with the best chance of getting into Yale or another good college," I said, kissing her shoulder, but she pushed me away, wanting me to continue.

"I noticed her the first day of school, " I continued, my voice dropping to a whisper. "Aria was Any's twin sister, but she was born a few seconds later, so he always called her his little sister; she looked much younger than him too. Her eyes were the first thing that fascinated me about her, they were green like the grass outside, like emeralds." I smiled at the thought of it and laid down on the carpet, staring at the ceiling. Lynne meandered along my body and laid her head on my arm, looking at me from below.

"Aria was the only one who dared to talk to me. Everyone else kept their distance. I was the outsider, the poor boy among all the rich, and they made me feel that, especially because I was Italian too. In the area we lived, all Italians were considered mafia or drug lords." I sighed and stroked Lynne's soft back. "So, I was considered scum, the one boy without money. The scholarship only came along once every four years."

I could hardly breathe. After all these years, I had problems talking about her. Her laugh was bright as a bell, but her way of thinking was a reason to be jealous. She didn't have a photographic memory like me, but she could see through people, she could sense when something was right or wrong, could understand things that were too deep for others—sometimes even for me.

Lynne nudged me slightly with her nose then and put one of her warm legs over my stomach, making me want to touch the spot between her legs again. I turned to her and pulled her closer to me. Then I took her hand and intertwined our fingers. I imagined how it would look without the gloves, my olive-colored hand, and her white fingers. Together.

"Aria always waited for me in the hallway after class, asked the teacher to assign me to her as a lab partner and somehow forced herself into my life. From there, I couldn't stop thinking about her. Anwyn Wadden, Any's full name, came along soon, and then it was just the three of us. For my whole class it was unimaginable why the most popular girl in the school wanted to hang out with me. Well, I asked myself that same question until the end."

I cleared my throat. "But after seven months, my life started to go downhill. I couldn't afford the things the others in my class had. I had to rely on donations if I wanted to go on class trips and I was happy about the school uniforms, wore them even outside of school, at Aria's. I didn't have anything like the other kids' clothes. Eventually Any made me wear some of his, but I hated it. Hated that I couldn't buy such things for myself. And then my father and Alba left. They left me with two small children and abuela got sick. Fucking cancer. We had no money, so it meant either abuela got no treatment or we'd starve. We already ate plain noodles and rice only."

My eyes felt heavy and burned. Back then I was ashamed of my story, that I was poor once but now, I was proud of what I had achieved. "I couldn't understand why the hell people had to choose between being fed, paying the rent, or getting a treatment. In the States, your wallet decides whether you can live or not."

Lynne seemed to sense my inner conflict and kissed me, taking away the weight of the words that would follow. "I started selling drugs, and in no time, I was swimming in money. I told Abuela that Any's father gave me a job...that I would earn so much that I could pay for the treatment for her. That way, I could buy us a few years with her. I needed a quick way, and there is no faster money than drug money but it's also the way right into hell."

Lynne took my face in her hands and kissed my forehead, my nose, my cheek, my chin. Then I pressed her against me, pulled her up and had her on me.

"Eventually I got greedy, I started wearing the nice clothes, giving Aria presents she didn't really want and buying my family a flat in another, better neighborhood. But then, of course, I messed up. I was with the Taipans at the time since I spoke Spanish and not a single word of Italian. But they knew my father and they remembered he had fooled them once as well. When I showed up at their place, they saw in me the chance to take revenge on my father through me. I didn't get behind their schemes."

She smiled faintly, telling me to continue but I felt strange. I never talked this much about myself, to no one.

"Until then," I started, "I never wanted to carry a gun, only made small deals. But they forced me to work in a quarter that belonged partly to the Taipans and partly to the Black Crowns. I wanted to get out, but I had to make one more delivery. They threatened to kill my family if I backed out. The problem was that the Black Crowns hated my father too, he fucked up their former gang leader. I had no choice but to make the delivery."

Lynne put her chin to my chest and hung on my lips, but the words cut my throat. Could I really spit the words out? The words that haunted me for a lifetime?

"Then Aria and I got into a fight because I'd been so different lately, because I stopped laughing, because I didn't want to do anything with her, for fear the gangs would threaten her too. I...I—" My words trailed off and I inhaled deeply.

"I did the stupidest thing I've ever done in my life. I told her everything, all my problems, and she offered to help me. Eventually I agreed, and she offered to make my last delivery. Nobody knew her, nobody would accuse a girl her age of being a drug mule, and I was in the bushes to protect her, ready with a gun."

The last words I said so softly, I wasn't sure if she heard them. But from the look in her eyes, she did. She knew what was coming, didn't she?

"That night... I killed Aria," I said.

For a moment she froze, still as a mannequin, and her look was startled.

Afraid she would judge me, I stood up.

My heart raced, my hands were covered with sweat, and I could feel a slight shiver rush through my body. Whenever my feelings hit me that hard, I needed to physically do something. To walk. To work. Anything. So, I stood up and walked to the window, avoiding her broken gaze.

Only seconds later, I felt her tiny hands on my back, turning me towards her and forcing me to look right into her beautiful face, telling me it was okay but no, it was not.

"I've never," I started but my breath came in short bursts now, "I've never told anyone that before."

She nodded understandingly and caressed my burning cheek with one hand. Then she waved to the bed, and I followed, laid down, and watched her reach for her cell phone that she had left on the bedside table. Eventually, she reached her phone out to me. I read it with interest.

Let me tell you something. A secret for a secret, okay? I grew up with a woman who picked up children and raised them with her. She was everything to us. I helped her, took care of the younger ones, and became her helper. Then I got older, and I was just…full of crap.

She took her phone again and wrote another message, typing while I watched her.

I made a mistake out of arrogance. One day, I took a boy with me on my tours because he wanted to, and I wanted to show off. To show how brave and adultlike I was. That day he was eaten by a Sircha because of me, because he couldn't keep up, because I thought I needed to prove something. I couldn't save the boy and then I saved a Sircha. So, I came home with an animal everyone in my town feared to death but without the boy. A kid I promised to watch over. Nana threw me out that night, because I killed the boy.

So, she knew how I felt.

"Thank you," I said, taking her hand in mine. "For telling me."

While I was still lost in my thoughts, she typed again.

How did Aria die?

I took a deep breath and picked up the dropped thread of my story. "She stood there with the package hidden under her coat, shaking and shivering. I saw it, but I hid behind a tree. Then I realized Z-Mexx set me up."

She raised her eyebrows.

"Yes, Z-Mexx was the new leader of the Black Crowns after my father got the previous into jail. He teamed up with the leader of the Taipans and wanted to send me to jail or kill me. So, all kinds of gang members waited for me in the park, but they found Aria delivering it for me, so the men grabbed her, grabbed her breasts, touched her inappropriately. A 15-year-old girl. Then I pointed my gun at a fucker that touched her and…accidentally shot Aria…instead of the man."

My voice broke, and I saw Aria standing in the hollow dead-end street, spitting blood, eyes rolling back, sagging in the bastard's hands. Dying in another man's arms.

My heart shattering into pieces.

At that moment, Lynne held my stare. I found those words so hard. So, fucking hard. I loved Aria, all that time I had been in love with her, and I was her killer.

"Then the police arrested me, just me, none of the Black Crowns and none of the Toxic Taipans. Me, the son of Enardo '*Sniper*' Renero. But I wasn't blamed for the death of Aria. Another man was. He was sent to jail with me, but I said nothing to set the record straight. I was a coward and claimed it was him, told Any the lie too. A short time later, that man was killed in a cell. In the normal prison, it was different from the juvenile prison, although it was no walk in the park either."

It was an accident, Rio, she wrote, and I sighed.

"Yes, I know, but it was my fault, Lynne. I shouldn't have

had a gun in my hand. I couldn't shoot back then, and I had little practice. I shouldn't have fired. She would still be alive."

She would have been raped and maybe her life would also have been over after. You don't know what would have happened, Rio. Your thoughts count and they were good. Badly executed, but your heart is good! her text said.

I laughed and put her cell phone down, but she took it again and wrote another message.

I understand you, Rio. I understand you and I'm here with you.

I avoided her gaze, looking at my hands. "I shouldn't have let her help me. Shouldn't have told her a thing. She never should have been there that night."

Then you'd be dead, and she'd be miserable.

"It's not fair."

Life isn't fair.

I read the message and kissed her. She picked up the phone again, but I got impatient. I didn't want to talk anymore, I wanted to kiss her and do far more with her right now. While she was writing I kissed her neck, but she hit me in the rib with her elbow, making me wince.

"Fuck," I hissed and got the phone shoved back in my face.

Any will kill you.

I nodded. "Yeah, he knows."

Then she typed again, trying to keep me away from her with a pointed elbow. But I stroked her butt, only to get another evil look that made me smirk.

Why was he even looking for the killer, you said someone was charged for it.

Yeah, that was one of those things. "At some point it came out that the guy wasn't even there. He was in the supermarket next to the street where it all happened. He came out and the Black Crown gave the cops phony evidence, a scheme. He must have been intertwined in all of this too. Maybe he ratted them out once."

292

Who was the man? she wrote.

I shrugged. "Never found out who he was, but it's thanks to him that I'm here... not in jail anymore. I was only charged for drug dealing and I was a minor. But yeah, why him...this question has killed me all my life as well, though."

Another reason why I couldn't look at myself in the mirror in the morning. Why I didn't want to be Rio anymore.

"So, eventually I will follow you into the Underworld."

Now she looked at me with pure horror for the first time, as if that sentence had been the worst over the last hour. "If Any kills me after all this."

She shook her head and quickly reached for her phone once more. *No, he won't kill you. I won't allow it.*

"You won't be here, Lynne, and I can't watch over myself forever. I had promised him, I owe him. With all the shit I've done, I won't go anywhere but your world after dying anyway."

She shook her head again, her brow furrowed, her eyes narrowed, and her cheeks turning red.

You can't come to my world, Rio. It's not like this one.

"What else can I do? I am too bad for heaven."

Not yet. You're not going to the Underworld yet.

"I owe it to him. I can't let another friend of mine be killed. It was my fault."

Now she was angry, I could tell by the look in her eyes, the flaring of her nostrils, her flailing hands.

No. It's his own fault. Nobody who's smart makes a deal with the Bone or the Blood Queen.

"You did it."

I'm not smart.

"You are," I said, tired of fighting.

I kissed her, put the phone away, and kept her hands busy all night long, trying to brush away the thoughts about the inevitable that was yet to come. Once I'm done with what I have planned all my life, I'll let Any kill me.

CHAPTER TWENTY-FIVE
LYNNE

"I don't have a good feeling, Lynne," Bory said, sitting on my shoulder, restless as usual.

I snorted. *Stop being so pessimistic. It will be alright.*

Cherry had once again done a great job styling me. I wore an off-shoulder top, a tight skirt, and short pants underneath so I could take off my skirt to climb if necessary. Rio was wearing a suit, a tie, and his finest shoes. Under his waistband were two pistols, which I had put there this very morning. When we left the hotel room, we were both deadly quiet and hadn't said anything until a few seconds ago. It felt as if we had to say goodbye to a life, we never had in the first place. A feeling of being stuck somewhere and not being able to dig ourselves out of it.

When I looked up at him, I felt utterly naked.

Not because we slept with each other so often—I didn't even know how many times, in truth—but because he knew so much about me now, like I did about him. Underneath his hard and lethal shell, Rio was thoughtful and hurt, hurt so badly throughout his life that he may never recover from it.

It all felt like a dream when we walked back up those stone

stairs to the auction house. If I wasn't feeling the solid ground under my stilettos, smelling the scent of various human perfumes, or feeling Rio's firm grip on my hand, I would have thought I was imagining everything.

As we went through the revolving door and waited in a line to be taken to the showroom, I wasn't nervous or excited. Somehow, I felt dull and numb today, which perhaps should have been a warning to me.

I looked around to see if I knew anybody—but no. Nobody from the other gangs were there yet, or at least only unimportant foot soldiers. The van Gogh would not be taken out of the vault until the auction started at seven o'clock sharp.

"Lynne," Rio said with a calm tone that I didn't like at all. "Remember that I'm going to hold up my end of our deal, no matter what will happen today."

I didn't know what he meant by that but nodded. By now I trusted him blindly. Maybe the sex made my judgment worse. Our two days in that bubble—which had nothing to do with gangs, plans, the Underworld, or any kind of deadly deals—blinded my intuition.

When Rio took me back to the showroom, I noticed the same staff as last time, standing in the same positions. I didn't have to turn around to know that Any was behind us. Cherry made him up with everything she had. Make-up, contour, rouge, all to make him look a little bit more like me, and frighteningly, she managed to do it quite well. With the wig on, we even looked so much alike that Rio didn't feel comfortable with Any standing next to him.

Just like the last time, there was a walk-through before the actual auction, and bidders were able to view the goods. Only then did the actual auction take place. As planned, we had to distract the officer and I needed to hide while Any would take my place next to Rio.

We strolled to the back room, Any trailing us. Again, many

different works of art were on display in here. People were scurrying around, talking about the art, and considering if any of it was worth bidding for. We knew everyone was waiting for the van Gogh, but that one was in another room, safely guarded. My eyes immediately fell on a book in the corner. Holding my breath for a heartbeat, Rio noticed my stiffness and followed my stare. There was the book the queen wanted. I could hardly mistake it, because the magic that emanated from it was so strong, I felt a slight vibration. It was dark and framed with red and golden flowers and berries, in the middle of it a white skull stared back at us, it wasn't a normal skull, though. Somehow, it seemed alive. A light shimmer surrounded it as well and I wasn't sure if humans could see the shimmer too.

I shivered slightly and forced myself to glance away. Just before we arrived at the cleaning cupboard, I took off my coat and put it over Rio's arm, kissing him on the cheek, inhaling the fragrance of his aftershave. Oak moss and musk—a feeling of timelessness invaded me, making me dizzy once again.

Rio pulled me towards him, but not like during the rehearsals. No, much more seriously, as if he wanted to say goodbye to me, and just like we wanted, the staff turned away, embarrassed about us celebrating our feelings. But my body tensed up. This felt more like a goodbye, though.

His haste would have been almost too much for me if the closet handle hadn't pricked itself in my back. Now we only had two minutes left but I wanted to ask him what was wrong, what he didn't tell me…

When he grazed my nose, sighing, I knew it was too late for that.

The prudish guard turned and sighed in disgust, and I grasped the handle with one hand, just as we had rehearsed in the hotel room a few hours ago. Rio, however, cupped my face with his trembling hands and looked into my eyes like a fire breathing dragon gleaming out of a cave. I stiffened up, what was he doing? This wasn't part of our plan.

"I'll keep my deal," he said again, and I started to feel queasy about him saying that again.

Rio, what did you do?

"It was real, okay? Last night was real."

I nodded in confusion, opened my mouth but before I could have done anything, Rio gave me the sign. So, I opened the cupboard's door, Rio whirled around with the coat, and hidden behind the thick, black coat, I hopped into the cleaning cupboard and just like that Any was wrapped into the coat instead of me and I was gone.

Afterwards—as if nothing had happened—Any and Rio went arm in arm into the auction room and I waited in the closet, shaken to the core, high on adrenaline. My body felt hot, my heart was racing in my chest, and my thoughts circled over and over again. I kept thinking about Rio's cryptic words. I knew where the bone was, he gave it to me in the hotel room. I had admired and cursed it. That stupid thing. So, what the hell did he mean by keeping his side of the deal? I already had the kiss, the bone, and the book soon, too. What would he need to keep on hold?

"Rio is acting weird today, huh?" Bory said, sprawling on the floor.

"Yes…maybe he is nervous?" I tried to calm myself.

Bory had it easy in here, tiny as he was. I, on the other hand, had to bend halfway over in this cupboard, bend my feet and shift my weight oddly so that I could stand in it. The cupboard was full of cleaning things and not as spacious as I thought. My butt troubled a vacuum cleaner and my hair hung in a feather duster. Nevertheless, I had to bear it for some time, for better or worse.

The preview took more than an hour, while Rio and Any drank champagne and tried not to laugh at each other. For me it was incomprehensible that Rio kept talking to Any after everything, pretending that nothing was wrong. Laughing, joking like there was no death threat between them.

But watching Any from the thin slits of the cupboard, I knew why. The way he looked at Rio, how he smiled at him...

Any wasn't into women but into men.

He loved Rio, probably always had, considering the story of the two. That's why he hadn't killed him yet, because he was fighting with himself, with his feelings for his sister and Rio. Everything made sense. That's why his other murder attempts were only half-hearted, badly thought-through, because he couldn't carry them out anyway. So, he let the Blood Queen's mark grow up to his ribs. I had seen it when he had stripped down back in the hotel and slipped into the same top as me.

I've wondered what would happen if I just killed him. Could Any die before the tattoo reached his heart and if so, would his mission be considered a failure then? Did that mean he still had to be part of the Blood Court when I killed him? Probably. Rio would hate me for it but by now I had reached the point where I was even willing to accept that, just to keep him from following me into the Underworld.

Who knew where he would go? By his deeds, it would probably be further east, near the Tartaros. If he was lucky, it'd be the Gate of Shades, or the Hall of Nights, maybe the Lake of the Dead. For skull's sake! I didn't know and never would, and one thing was for sure, I would never see him again once he entered the Underworld. A Cave Town dweller like me had almost no access to the other courts of the Underworld. So, if Any wanted to kill Rio today, I'd beat him to it, that was for sure.

"I think they're gone, Lynne," Bory said shyly, after a few minutes that felt like an infinity.

"Then go," I whispered, though no one could hear me anyway.

I pulled out the little book, which was an exact replica of the book Bory was about to steal, and pressed it into his hand. He had a hard time holding it, but for a few minutes he would manage. I knew it, he was stronger than he seemed.

"Put it down before you jump up," I said, worried that he might not make it.

"Who's the mother hen now?" Bory grinned.

I nodded at him; well, he was right this time, but even a broken clock is right twice a day.

So, I pushed the door open slightly so it didn't make any noise. Then Bory jumped out, holding the book convulsively between his hands, and tapped carefully to the podium across the room, to the real book. My heart was beating up to my neck as I watched him. Not knowing what to do with my fingers I kneaded each finger one by one, desperate to do something, anything. My inner restlessness got worse and worse the closer Bory got to the podium, then he paused and put the book down, shook his hands out, and grabbed it once again. With an elegant leap he stood on the podium. I exhaled the breath I was holding in. Burlocks could jump several feet high, and this jump was a cinch for him. Though he usually didn't jump around with a book in his hands.

He quickly switched the two books and jumped down with the real one. He rushed towards me, carefully using the way we told him to, because of the cameras. Rio had made sure the cameras couldn't get a glimpse of him. They might have seen a short flicker when he changed the books but otherwise, they wouldn't see anything. Only when the new owner held the book in his hands would the exchange be noticed. By then, though, I would no longer be here. I squatted expectantly and held my breath once more when Bory was only a few feet away. As he stood next to me, I sighed.

"Thank the Dead, Bory," I grinned, and stuffed the book in my bag.

We searched for a long time until we found a bag that was elegant enough for a believable outfit, big enough to stow the book, and also good to carry while climbing. This bag was perfect. I could throw the short handle over my head and carry it over my back, it was elegant, and thanks to the square cut, perfect for the book.

Then I took off the skirt and hid it in the closet. Rio said it wouldn't matter if they found evidence of me because I would soon be in the Underworld anyway. Then, I had to act fast because I didn't know when the auctioneers started preparing the items for the auction.

Stepping out of the cupboard I climbed up on it and opened the ventilation shaft. Then Bory and I climbed in, heaved ourselves up and closed the shaft from the inside. The shaft constricted me from all sides, and I suddenly had a very good feeling of what it felt like to be locked up in one of those human coffins. The air was stuffy, and the light dull, but that didn't bother me. It actually gave me a feeling of home. Since I was not the biggest, I still had enough space here.

I crawled along the shaft, further and further until I came to another opening. *I must* have been *somewhere in the auction room now*. When I looked through the ventilation slits, I could see the hall, which was paneled with wood, the stage with the auctioneer, who had already sold the first painting and was starting for the next. He was shouting the numbers so loudly that they echoed back to me. I searched and found Rio sitting in the front left, seeming cold and calculating. Very different from yesterday or the day before. That man was the head of the Loops, not Rio. There were always two sides to him.

The other gang bosses were all there, too. Z-Mexx, the leader of the Black Crowns, was surrounded by a bunch of Crowns. Big Al Cortez, the leader of the Chicago Roosters, had only two foot soldiers next to him, but probably had others elsewhere. In the back sat Cockeyed Joe and his Toxic Taipans.

No one met the other one's gaze, as if one look alone was enough to have a reason to kill the other. It was quite possible, considering all of them were armed and each had several men scattered around, incognito.

Surely, there were also some civilian cops here, a reason why everyone pretended to be sinless. I was curious to how they would act when the van Gogh was brought to the stage. Who would give in? Would the buyer become a target afterward? Was that what Rio wanted? Everyone believed that the painting would contain the recipe for C-Wax. But I stole that painting, so it definitely wasn't from van der Volt. So, where was this miraculous drug recipe then?

I glanced at Rio again, wondering why he couldn't tell me about his whole plan. Knowing that he had trust issues, I tried to blame his past for his lack of trust. He certainly would explain it to me later. There must be more to it.

So, was there another picture here with the real recipe, only Rio knowing about it? He had contacts to van der Volt, that I knew. If someone knew where his legacy was, it was Rio. It had to be somewhere in this auction house though, hidden in another artifact, because that way he could quietly and secretly buy a picture that everyone dismissed as unimportant, while the others fought about the van Gogh, blinded by Rio with cleverly used false reports and rumors. No one but him had any real contact with van der Volt and so only he knew where the recipe really was.

Smart, smart move.

The whole thing dragged on forever. So, I huddled with Bory in the shaft and watched the auction, which couldn't have been more boring. I couldn't get out yet because it was broad daylight and there were lots of people outside who shouldn't see me, and could have been ferrying Rio's mission, whatever it was. Sometimes I really wondered if I should have been pushier and maybe forced him to tell me his whole plan, but he was so intent on the idea that he couldn't tell anyone, that I probably would have had to threaten him with death to get him to tell me. That would have been fun, though, and would have ended in having sex with him again.

Just like that, I remembered how his soft lips kissed me awake this morning, how he looked at me as if I was everything to him, how I lost myself in his blue eyes. The eyes that now stared at the stage as if he wanted to blow it up.

Slappy and Punchy flanked him, as well as a few others. The various parties bid for art objects that were not important to them. Rio bought a painting that almost nobody else was interested in and I wondered if it contained the C-Wax formula. If so, his expression didn't tell anything.

Cold. Meaningless. Bored.

Then it happened.

Rio stiffened, slightly but he did. It was time for the van Gogh painting. The auction helpers pushed a big canvas on rolls, a white cloth over it, into the room. They waited a few moments to stir the drum of tension and the helpers tugged at the cloth and Vincent van Gogh's self-portrait appeared. A murmur went through the room and the auction visitors moved beneath me like ants in a heap of earth. Now, the first bidding signs went up, numbers were yelled, and I wondered who was part of the drug scene. Probably all of them. Everyone belonged to some gang in Chicago for sure.

It seemed like the bidding wasn't going to ever stop. But Rio wasn't bidding at all. He was on his cell phone, talking.

What the skull?

Well, why should he bid? He knew the recipe wasn't inside the painting. Every now and then he would raise his hand to give the appearance that he wanted the painting, but it was just a scheme. No one seemed to notice it, though.

Skull. I didn't know how to sit anymore. At some point I laid in the shaft like a dead fish, on my belly, peering down to watch the madness while all hell was breaking loose down there. After quite some time and a lot of shouting, Big Al Cortez stood up and pointed his index finger to the stage. He was so much smaller than the others that I only recognized him because suddenly there was a hole in the crowd. Cockeyed Joe was easy to spot since he wore a white cowboy hat. He pushed one of his men in response and his long hair flared up under his hat. He pointed vehemently at the security guards. They were getting impatient, and I pricked my ears. What was happening?

Everybody wanted the picture, and the price was getting into swindling heights. Only Rio stayed calm like a rock in the middle of a turmoil, he was the only one who kept the overview here.

Then the door opened, and I forgot to breathe for a few seconds. Governor Jenson came in, with two policemen in tow, pointing to the van Gogh, *his* van Gogh.

"That's my picture and it was stolen—"

But he didn't have time to finish his sentence because one of the men from Cockeyed Joe jumped up, pulled out a pistol and held it into the crowd.

It was Farid. The policemen I met that one day…

I caught my breath.

"What is it?" Bory squealed next to me, trying to see what I saw.

"Something's wrong," I said, my heart racing in my chest.

Screams. Some people cried out, ducked. I was getting hot and cold at the same time. Everything was getting too tight, and I suddenly wanted to get out of here, dig myself out, wishing for some air.

Then, realization hit me like a slap.

It was all planned that way.

They had all fallen into Rio's trap.

Why hadn't I understood it before? Farid, the man I met at

the pie factory, was an undercover cop, an FBI agent. My eyes shot to Rio, who looked as alarmed as the others, but I knew deep down he was happy. He was glad because everything he had planned worked out. Then the cops behind the governor nodded at Farid, one of them grabbed Jensen's joints from behind, twisted his arms back and handcuffed him. The governor yelled, screamed at the officers. But no one gave a shit about him.

"Rat!" I heard someone scream.

"Vernon van der Volt! That's van der Volt," screamed another one, jumping over a chair, only to get tackled by another one.

"*Scarpe grande*," cried an Italian member of the Roosters, which I later learned that it was a code word to alert the others. *Big shoes*, it meant, because the FBI agents apparently had such big feet. But I had no time to observe the feet at that moment because one of the Rooster's gang members suddenly shot at Big Al Cortez.

The sound of the shot went through me like an explosion. I ducked and hit my chin. When I raised my head again, Cortez was lying dead on the floor, and his gang members jumped over the chairs, over men whose butts were stuck to the chairs in shock as if suffering from a sudden rigor mortis.

"Raid," cried another one. "Run! Fucking, run!"

"Get out!" I heard them screaming, panic written over their faces.

It was a mash-up of screaming, shouting, and rushing. Then suddenly the Taipans shot at the Roosters, aiming for Cockeyed Joe, seeking revenge. Most ducked under the chairs, others ran towards the exits, but the FBI had already stormed the action house, blocking the doors.

"*Down!*" they screamed, encircling the gangs, and hitting one after another. I didn't know where to look anymore, people were jumping over people, beating each other to get free. Z-

Mexx and a few of his men, and many of the Roosters were already arrested by the FBI.

But the police were outnumbered. There were far too many gang members. Again and again, I heard: "The *Dutch Beauty*! It was her! Her!"

Then I saw Rio taking the van Gogh, running towards a window, shooting at it, and slamming it with his elbow until the glass shattered, giving him another escape route. Slappy and Punchy waved to the other gangs, showing them a way to get away. They played the heroes. Rescuing everyone from the cops.

"Follow me! I know a way out! Follow me!" Slappy yelled.

"Come!" Rio shouted. His voice gave me goosebumps.

Punchy and Slappy pointed their guns at the cops who were following them, shooting already. One of the cops aimed and... he shot Slappy. I held my breath.

The bullet went right through his chest, and I knew he couldn't survive a shot like that. Slappy's lips trembled, and his glance went to the wound, to the cop, and then... and then...to me?

How'd he known I was in this shaft? That I was waiting here? His eyes told me to tell Cherry he loved her.

My skin felt like I'd just been splashed with freezing water. Frantic, I watched Slappy going down on his knees, and that's when I figured out what Rio really was up to.

Who he really was.

Rio was Vernon van der Volt.

And I had driven all the gang leaders into a dead end with the little games I played for him. I was the link between them all. I led them all here today to seal the hour of their death. On one of my first days here, I had to go to the governor's house to meet Big Al Cortez. Rio probably spread the rumors that the governor was van der Volt to distract everyone from himself.

To finally get back at the governor.

Rio told me once he wanted his revenge. Play Karma. Revenge for all those silly laws that favored white supremacists, that made sure that money won over love, that made sure that injustice prevailed, and enhanced a war against their own people. The governor was the law, and now he was gone, probably jailed under the name of Vernon van der Volt. How often did he tell me that the politicians here were the real criminals and that no one ever stood up to them? My eyes flitted to Rio, watching playing the hero.

What else did he do without me noticing it?

I had to leave drugs and a document in Jenson's office the night I stole the van Gogh. Did I plant the proof he was Volt?

Suddenly everything played before my eyes, like a movie. All the little things I did for Rio, which now formed a bigger picture for me. A spider web that drove me into its clutches. Cockeyed Joe saw me at Jenson's and so I became the Dutch Beauty. Rumors spread by Rio and his men. I always wondered why they called me that, but the Dutch connected me with van der Volt, an assumption that we came from the same country.

Joe probably spread the wrong truths about me afterwards, and in the opera, I met Z-Mexx, who I gave the drugs and information about the auction to—who knows, I never opened the letter…and Punchy? Was Punchy involved in all this shit too? Was he not a cheesecake fanatic at all but rather set me up to meet Farid and Big Al Cortez so he could see the C-Wax bag and just by chance the flyer for this skulling auction? I swallowed, watching Punchy leading someone out of the window.

Yes. We had to go there every single day because Rio knew Big Al Cortez would possibly be there. Maybe he had appointments with the shrink there and by visiting the Pie Factory every other day the chances that I met Farid or Cortez were high…it was all staged. Everything.

Rio and his foot soldiers have probably been spreading

rumors since my arrival that I was their fancy contact to van der Volt, that I was the one who could give all the gang leaders the much-desired recipe, that's why they all talked to me, that's why they were so fond of me. All just to take their mind off Rio.

To distract them.

Whenever the two of us were outside, he wore a disguise, except today, and the benefit gala, where he talked to me about as much as anyone else, to show the others he was in the game, that he was important, and that he might get the recipe before anyone else. So, they only got more curious about me.

And now?

Now I was the only name, the only person they connected with C-Wax and van der Volt besides the governor, the only person they could tell the police. The only suspect who left her skirt in an auction house closet as evidence because she trusted her lover. The only one who was probably on all the cameras, because she was always there when it came to C-Wax and Van der Volt.

My stomach sunk.

It had been three minutes while I had deciphered all the riddles, three skulling minutes. The ventilation shaft was rustling at the other end with the sound of someone opening the shaft vibrating from all sides. The hammering I heard from all directions had only one reason behind it, only one reason why Slappy looked at me the moment he died. Only one reason why Rio said this skulling shit to me before we started the mission. They had betrayed me. The police considered me a prime suspect and they knew where to get me, because he had ratted me out. Rio had teamed up with the cops to get back at the other leaders and threw me to the dogs.

Panting, I pushed myself backwards with my forearms, towards where I came from.

I cursed and noticed on Bory's face that I more or less

voluntarily sent my thought processes through our bond. He trembled all over his body and looked about the same way I felt.

"Come!" I yelled at him, but he was stiff like a pillar, still watching the confusion down there, the mass panic.

Rio wanted to be the king of Chicago. For that to happen, he had to take out all the gang leaders and to gather the other gangs under one, his own. And to do that, he had to come out as the good guy, the one who saved all. Well, of course the prick was the hero for them now, because all the fingerprints led to me and not to him! I grunted spitefully as I crawled back and dragged Bory with me.

"That ass-skull!" I rasped.

"Slappy," Bory whimpered, slowly coming to himself again, able to walk and follow me. The beads of sweat ran down my forehead and mixed with the dust underneath me, causing my hands to slip again and again. These skulling gloves!

"Damn it!" I hissed and pushed myself further back, as the noise in front of me became louder. They were coming for me now, searching for me because Rio told everyone where I was. Told the police my exact hide out. Cursing, I took off my gloves in a rage and pushed myself back even further, my heartbeat raced, and I felt sick, but I had to suppress this feeling. There was no time for feelings.

"Cherry..." Bory whispered, still in shock about the betrayal, the murder, the danger behind us.

"That's all you have to say?" I nagged. "Seriously?"

I felt sorry for Cherry, too. After all, she wanted to build a different life with Slappy, away from here, away from crime. Death itself was no big deal to me. I knew what came next and that was what Slappy should be afraid of now. That's what worried me, not the fact he was dead. The sound of hard shoes that kept hitting the metal surface with their tips made me crawl even faster, sweat dripping from my forehead. I couldn't go to jail, I couldn't. I didn't have the bone with me, it was in the hotel. I couldn't get imprisoned, because I had to go to the graveyard with all the goods I had to bring back. When they imprison me, I lose everything.

I jerked up as a pair of hands hammered through the shaft with an annoying staccato. I need to speed up! I need to!

"I'll kill him!" I moaned, crawling for my life.

When I reached the shaft opening from where I came from, the one in the backroom, I saw two policemen through the shaft. Already examining the room, checking my skirt…

Damn it. I pushed myself further, hoping that I would somehow get out at another shaft, and then suddenly Rio's cryptic sentence made sense to me. The shit he whispered into my ear several times.

I'll hold up my end of the deal, Lynne.

A cry escaped me as I crawled and crawled. I wasn't supposed to come out here as a free woman. No, I was supposed to be captured as a pawn, to draw the attention away from him. But, not with me. I looked at my hands. If necessary, I would fight my way free, no one will deny me the chance to go back to the Underworld. No one. Not even Rio. I won't end as a freaking shadow-slave.

A tear streamed down my face as I pressed myself to where I thought the exit was. When I found another ventilation opening, I pushed it open, crawling out into the fresh air and sighing with relief. But my smile dropped the minute I set foot on ground again. I was right. There were two cops already waiting for me, guns pointed at me. A large black man and a white woman with red hair and a scrunched-up face.

"We've found her, over," said the woman into a little black device as the other cop rushed at me, making me duck and whirl around—starting a fight.

I kicked the man in the face, then punched the woman, kicked the guy between the legs while she screamed, and grabbed him by the shoulders. Without a blink I knocked him out with a headbutt, using all my Underworld strength. The tears came while he dropped to the floor like a fly, his head crashing against a stone. Unfortunately, the second cop was already behind me, grabbing me by my waist and holding the pistol against my temple. I closed my eyes, damned Rio with all my heart and thrust my ungloved hand into her face. With a burn on my skin, she fell over, thumping like a lump of earth to the ground. My stomach dropped at the thought of what I had just created.

She'd become another Deadwalker soon.

But I didn't falter.

I simply had no time.

Bory jumped over the dead onto my shoulder, sighing as if he had just done all the work. I felt so hot that even my pants and top were too much fiber for me right now, despite the icy wind. The hair on my neck stuck like freshly washed and my breathing was so rapid and heated it formed steam clouds in front of my face.

How could he?

How could Rio betray me after all we've been through?

After all the truths he told me?

The trust we shared.

I used the short time to look around and found myself at the back entrance of the auction house. Across from me was a canal, the moonlight lighting me the way.

"They are running! There they are!" Bory screamed, pointing at the tunnel.

All the gang members and foot soldiers ran for their lives, using the canal to escape the police.

Without thinking, I ran towards the fence across the street, grabbed the cold stone and hoisted myself over it. I landed on all fours and barely missed a running man. Ten more came towards me, almost running me over, but they managed to evade me, running for their lives as well.

Breathing heavily, I got up and saw Rio.

He was a little further ahead, showing the men a way out of this neighborhood, an underground tunnel that we had already used on one of our night tours. When he saw me, his facade crumbled.

Our eyes locked and I clenched my fingers into fists.

My stare was cold.

Hard.

Merciless.

Rio didn't expect me to be free, to have used my hands, because I was so afraid of the power I was unleashing. But I wouldn't risk my freedom.

Never.

Instead of running away with the others, Rio gave Punchy the van Gogh and came jogging towards me. All the men he passed by were patting him on the back, thanking him for saving them from the raid. I snorted. He was the one who put them into danger in the first place, but in their eyes, Rio was the only gang leader that survived, and saved everyone from the cops, got everyone out of trouble. Soon everyone would join him because he had the C-Wax recipe. But he always had it.

Rio was skulling Vernon van der Volt. C-Wax was his drug.

For years, he had created a story about the mysterious van der Volt, about the drug to make everyone addicted to it, to make everyone dependent on the possession of his invention. But he couldn't fool me anymore.

In the distance, I could see Any waiting for him. Rage filled my body. Of all people, he had to cheat on *me*. And to the one who really tried to kill him several times, he entrusted his life. All of a sudden, my body felt dirty. Well, it really was dirty, covered with dust and sweat, but the filth I felt was triggered by his touches and his betrayal.

I had given myself to him, slept with him, shown him the weakest side of me. Like a dog that offered its throat to the stronger one and got bitten, deeply. For the first time, I felt the urge to wash myself in holy water.

"Lynne," he said and stopped in front of me, eyes wary, broken.

I stepped back. He had no right to look at me like that. I wasn't his. Not anymore.

"Please, listen to me," he said, trying to reach for my arm, but I slipped away from him, keeping my gaze steady, showing him exactly what I thought about him.

He winced and my lower lip trembled, my eyes were burning, feeling hot. Especially as I looked at him. My heart wanted to be with him again, to be wrapped up by his strong arms, to feel him kiss my forehead, my lips—but no, there was no way back.

He betrayed me.

All those words were pinned to my forehead, ready for him to be read. I was so disappointed in him, so incredibly disappointed. He might as well have stuck a knife in my back. *Leave your skirt there, they won't find you! Just wait in the shaft. You just have to wait outside the house, flirt with the man, give him an envelope.* It was like writing a text all over my body saying: *I'm your number one C-Wax contact! Arrest me now!*

Rio tried to approach me once more, saying something, but his voice dropped to a whisper. He wanted to confuse me again with his touches, but at the same moment something hot ran down my cheek. His mouth opened, but he said nothing. Scared, I touched my cheek and felt something wet.

I cried…I've never cried in my life…

Rio winced, touched my his wrist, trying to pull me into his arms and comfort me, but I kept him away again. I was acting too naturally, too instinctively in front of him. I was not fully aware of what I was doing, and stopped him from nearing me.

"No, Lynne..." Bory cried and only then did Rio and I realize what I had done.

"Lynne," Rio gasped, eyes wide open.

My chest tightened like someone crushed the air out of my lungs.

We both stared at my hand on his hand, on his skin, grasping him desperately. My naked fingers touched his skin...

"Fuck," Rio coughed, trembling.

I shook my head, staggered back, watching as he fell to his knees, blue eyes pinned on me. His eyes widened at something behind me. He opened his mouth as if he wanted to say something to me, but it was too late. Someone hit me on the back of my head, and I started to lose my conscience.

Bory, I said with all the strength I had left, closing my eyes. *Give... him... Mal's cream.*

I swayed and my eyelids closed. Falling, I was falling. *Stay... with... him. Bory.*

"I'm sorry... I'm so sorry," Rio croaked and went down next to me.

CHAPTER TWENTY-SIX

RIO

"What do you mean you can't get her out?" I yelled, leaning on my desk in my office.

Punchy reared up behind Farid, making it more than clear he had to answer me. To me, the King of Chicago. Ah, it felt good to finally have given everyone back what they deserved. Playing Karma instead of being played by it. After a decade of inventing a drug, a phantom, and a new world. Finally, I got what I wanted.

"Not yet," Farid started over, staring me down with his golden eyes from a chair in the corner. For seven days, Lynne had been in prison. Seven fucking days and we only had four left until her 99 days were up. I had to get her out. I had to honor my deal with her even though she almost killed me. I promised.

After seventy-two hours of deep sleep, I woke up with Any by my side. Actually, I thought he should be glad I was dead— or almost dead. I thought, he would kill me eventually, but no. Any was howling like a locked-up dog when I woke up, inhaling all the oxygen on earth at once. I wasn't a Deadwalker, I wasn't like Fish, and I wasn't dead. The only thing that changed was a new mark showing up on the spot where Lynne touched me on my upper arm. The edges were frayed and a bit darker than the rest of my skin, but it looked like a tattoo, one I couldn't decipher.

Any kept saying that me being alive was not possible, after Lynne touched me. I had read too much and watched too many movies in my life, so it occurred to me that maybe it was Lynne's feelings for me, because she cried when she touched me. I knew it sounded stupid and I didn't want to think this thought through, but I needed an explanation. A reason I was still alive.

The mark looked strange. It was a line at the end of which were three other shorter lines, like a kind of broom drawn by a child. It didn't hurt. I was alive and felt exactly as alive as before.

My plan worked like a charm. The rumors that the Taipans were interacting with the police spread quickly and more than three quarters defected. Others came to me because I had the recipe. I now ruled over all 9 districts of Chicago, over 77 community areas. They all belonged to me. Of course, in the long run I would have to control the remaining smaller gangs, which had now split off from the big ones, refusing to be led by me, but I didn't care. My goal was revenge and I had achieved it. Maybe Any would kill me after all, although I doubted it since my little accident. Meaning I had to find some way to save his life instead, but first I needed to save Lynne's.

The one thing that didn't work out like clockwork and the only thing I could think about ever since. I drove to the jail immediately, but they didn't let me in. There was no other way to contact her. Those pricks stole her phone, and everything else. But I needed to see her. Just once, to apologize. I had to tell her all of it. Why I had to do it.

"She was only gonna be in jail for two days," I snarled at Farid.

He nodded. "I know, but she killed an agent, Rio. We didn't agree to that! All the statements, the materials, and the evidence suggest that *she's involved with Vernon van der Volt.*"

Farid stretched the latter part unnecessarily. Farid was into all this shit as much as I was. He gave me the idea to invent a new drug in the first place, connected me in jail with Alexander DeWinther, the actual inventor of C-Wax. But DeWinther was already living in a villa in Andalusia, far away from us and any connection to his criminal past, Farid, and me. We had a bigger agenda. He was the only one who could give me the most important thing of my life: getting back at the chairmen. I wanted it so much I even got involved with the FBI.

Lifetime immunity, was there anything better?

All that for bringing down the governor and taking out the drug lords.

"I want her out today, Farid!" I said, rocking back into my chair.

"Don't talk to me like that!" he shouted back, and by God, he was the only man here who was allowed to. After all, he got me out of jail that time. Without him they would still be beating the shit out of me there.

"We were able to use the evidence you gave us against the governor. Everything is going as planned, Baron," Farid reassured me. "I'll see what I can do about her."

"No," I yelled and stood up, firmly gripping the ends of my desk, "you do something! You get her out. I don't want her in there another minute, or I swear to God, I get her out by myself."

"I'll say it again in case you didn't hear me. She murdered an agent, Baron," Farid said.

"You can't prove that."

"Montgomery is missing. What else could she have done? She knocked Carlson down. We already have a statement. How shall I undo that?"

"You can't believe that," I said, snorting. "Did you see her? She's as petite as a fairy. She couldn't have done that."

Farid drew his mouth in a straight line. He didn't believe me. Not at all.

"There isn't a body anywhere, so leave it at that," I growled, knowing all too well there was no body to be found. That woman was walking around like a zombie right now doing whatever the hell she was. "Get her out."

"How, Baron? How?" Farid said, sighing.

I slipped him a flash drive, making him raise his eyebrows. "There's a confession on it from Jenson that he's van der Volt and he forced her. It'll support her alibi. I'll pay the bail. I'll pay everything you want me to."

"This will only get her a temporarily release. This is bogus."

"It'll take them weeks to figure that out," I said.

"And then what?" *Then she'd be in the Underworld, and no one would ever find or bother her again.*

He rubbed his chin. "Maybe she can only get out for a few days…I'm sure we'd have to lock her up again, though but if that's all you want for now—"

"Just get her out... please. I saved your brother, now I am calling for my life debt."

Farid sighed, looking at me as if I were the devil himself, but I had to bring his brother up. Ajay would have been dead if it weren't for me. An inmate wanted to kill him, but I didn't let him. That's when Farid became aware of me, and we started to plan Project Raging Bull. Several years ago.

Farid approached the USB. It's amazing how much a little word can do if you don't use it a lot.

"Fine," he said. "It's the last thing I'll do for you."

"Fine."

"Did you know Cockeyed Joe killed K.C.? Yesterday? During dinner?" Farid asked while pocketing the USB.

I tried not to smile, but I couldn't. This moment, when the

plans worked out, was everything. Now, all the former gang leaders were either dead or in jail.

"You knew this would happen, didn't you?" Farid looked at me again like I was the real trash in here, and maybe I was. I'm pretty sure I was.

"I'm not God, Farid. How could I know such a thing?" I said, rocking in my chair again.

"Why does Joe hate K.C. so much?" Farid always dared to ask direct questions. He probably was the best cop there will ever be, and for sure the only one I would ever really trust.

"K.C. was banging Joe's wife just before he went to jail. Joe was always trying to get back at him." Farid shook his head and was about to walk to the door. "Um, Farid?" He turned, looking at me.

"Bring her to my house."

Meanwhile, we had to go to Jamie Jones' funeral. To Slappy's funeral. To pay our last respects to my brother. It shouldn't have happened, and I took all the blame, one reason why I was going to offer to adopt Cherry's child today. Without Jamie, she had no one, and looking after his child and fiancé was the only thing, I could do to try to make things right again.

Because of me, Cherry and her unborn child were on their own now.

WHEN MY DOORBELL rang later that day, I didn't quite know how to act. I wanted to have her out of prison, wanted her back with me but how would we continue? I gave the FBI her name, or at least her face and DNA. She probably would have done it for me if I explained it to her, but I couldn't. I couldn't take any risks.

When I opened the door, I braced myself. But this time it

was different, nothing tied up my throat. I had no high blood pressure, and nothing was pounding against my forehead ever since I almost died. In fact, I hadn't had any panic attacks since the accident, since Lynne's hands killed me.

I even skipped the pills to find out if the panic attacks were coming back. They didn't. Usually, the anxiety attacks got worse when I just stopped taking the pills without reducing the dose day by day. I knew what I was talking about. I had tried it six times in my life and six times I had worse attacks than before. Not this time. No, this time I was healthier than ever, wondering if this was a good sign.

I didn't remember how I was able to regain consciousness. The only thing I remembered when I woke up was that strange smell in my nose and the spot on my chest that felt oily, as if someone had applied cream to me. Any swore he didn't touch me.

Now, I looked straight into Lynne's face and there I was, frozen. Mouth open. I couldn't make a sound because I saw the thing. That thing. Her little helper. He sat on her shoulder, right where she used to look at. It was as big as a hand, with puppy eyes and lots of blue feathers everywhere. Kind of chubby, to be honest.

Lynne lifted her gaze, piercing me with her eyes, pure anger lighting up inside of them.

"And now he dares to look at me like a sheep too, can you believe that?" she nagged, pushing her way past me into my house.

Only when Farid honked at me did I gather my wits again. Her voice. I had heard Lynne's voice, didn't I? My chin dropped. She sounded so lovely, although the content of her statement was perhaps the opposite, but her voice! Fuck! I waved at Farid in confusion and followed her, barely remembering to close the door.

Startled, I strolled into the living room, fearful of what it meant for me, for her. Why could I hear her voice?

Her soft, fragile voice?

I put one foot in front of the other, reminding myself of every step to actually keep on moving. I could see *Bory* and hear Lynne *talking*.

As I came around the corner, I noticed she was wearing the clothes she was imprisoned in. Her long white-blonde hair hung down her shoulders and her dark eyes watched my every step, arms folded and nostrils flaring.

"What is he looking at?" she muttered at Bory again. "Do you think he's lost his mind now?"

"Would be better for him," Bory said, crossing his thick, furry—well, he had a lot of fur for such a small thing—arms.

"Does that look like a heart attack to you?" Lynne asked Bory, tilting her head.

"More like a stroke," Bory said, mimicking her.

"I'm not having a stroke," I said, buzzed, still bothered with the fact that Lynne was talking to me, that her beautiful pout was actually moving, that I heard her voice, her all-American speaking voice!

She had no accent, none at all, she sounded like she was straight from Chicago, and her voice was so unique, she blended each sound with the next one, sliding into higher pitches, then moving her pitch smoothly, like rolling hills. Damn. She sounded so damn sexy.

"Did he just—" Lynne asked, her mouth falling open.

"—answer you?" Bory completed her sentence, almost as dumbfounded as me.

"Skull," Lynne whispered.

I turned around, looking for a Deadwalker or whatever but there was none.

"What skull?" I asked.

"By the Stix!" Lynne cried, stepping towards me but then

stopped, covering her mouth with one hand, looking alternately to me and Bory.

"You can hear me!" she said, opening her mouth and closing it again, not knowing what to say, or how to react.

"I can hear you..." I said, more for me than for her.

It was as if we were just seeing each other for the first time, really seeing each other. She dropped her bag, which she had held on tightly to until just now. Then she rushed towards me and out of a naïve stupidity I thought she would fall into my arms—but no, it was Lynne and she hit me. She slapped me so hard that I gasped. My skin burned.

As she raised her hand again, I fended off her blows as they grew stronger by the second.

"You damn skullhole!" she screamed, hitting me even harder. I slapped her hands repeatedly away until it was enough, and I grabbed both of her wrists.

"Why? Why? I—" she screamed but suddenly we both looked at her hands, frozen.

"What the fuck Lynne?" I screamed this time, but I didn't let go of her hands. "Are you trying to kill me again?"

"I thought you were dead!"

"Sorry I'm not!"

"Five days, you skulling idiot!" She withdrew her hands from me, turning away. I saw her back moving under her heavy breathing. She ran one hand over her face and then continued calmly. "I thought you were dead for five days, Rio. And I was in *jail*! Because of *you*!"

Lynne turned again and I saw her eyes were watery. Rio. She said my name. With a light rolling *R*, not too strong but gentle like a cat's purr.

"Five days Rio. Do you have any idea what that felt like to me?"

I swallowed, not able to answer her.

"Why?" she asked after a moment of silence.

"How about you explain why you tried to kill me?" I asked.

"I didn't!"

"Then what is this," I said, showing her the mark on my arm, "and why can I see Bory? Hear you?" Lynne looked at my mark and the little ball of fur peeped up, brushing its fur in an uncomfortable way.

But Lynne just shrugged, nudging her chin forward. "I don't recognize this mark."

"Oh, of course, so everything is fine?" I said without hiding my sarcastic undertone.

"No. It's not."

I winced and found myself closing up the little space between us. "I'm sorry, Lynne." She avoided my gaze, biting her lip.

"Look," I said, taking her hand.

I could have held her hand forever. How long had I been wondering what it felt like? Then I brought her hand to my lip and kissed it, closed my eyes, and enjoyed the feeling of her skin against my mouth. "I couldn't tell you."

"Because you still didn't trust me," she nagged.

I held her gaze, wanting to pull her even closer to me, to hug her, but she was so angry that I feared I would cross a line if I did it, pushing her further away from me.

"It had to look authentic, Lynne. If I told you, you wouldn't have acted like I needed you to, and maybe you'd have run away before we achieved anything...I couldn't risk it."

She closed her eyes and took a deep breath.

"You're a skulling idiot, Rio! I wouldn't have left! I would have done anything for you!"

"Yeah?" I asked with a sly smile, but then she took her hand away, stepping backwards. My smile dropped. I didn't want that.

"Lynne, I would have gotten you out of prison myself. You had to be there, authentic and angry, answering the cops' questions. I have no idea how talented you are in acting and I didn't want to put it on the map."

"Was it worth it? Risking losing me instead?" she said, her eyes glittering in the dim light.

"I'm gonna lose you in four days anyway." My voice seemed fragile and not as strong as usual. And fuck, I didn't want to say that at all, at least not in the way I did. "Darling, I am not a good man—"

"Don't darling me! Stop luring me in with your sweet talk," Lynne cried and her little helper seemed uncomfortable as he walked straight to the pool. Knowing exactly where to go...

"Can I tell you something?" I asked carefully as she wanted to snarl something at me again, stopping her from even getting started. Then she threw her hands up in the air, falling on my couch in a very dramatic way.

"Spit it out."

"Z-Mexx and Big Al Cortez fucked Dad and me over and were responsible for Aria's death. Cockeyed Joe raped my mother, killed her while fucking her, and K.C. betrayed me to the FBI. That's why Farid knew my name, but Farid liked me and so offered to help me if I was willing to help him in getting at the chairmen. I took over K.C.'s gang as compensation but for me to be released I had to help Farid. I needed that, Lynne. I lived for revenge," I said, hoping to find some kind of forgiveness, some kind of understanding in her eyes, but her expression was cold.

"I was in prison for seven years, Lynne," I started over. That seemed to worry her more. "Not seven days. Each of the fucking 2555 days I spent in there was spent killing those four men in my dreams, getting revenge, giving them what they deserved. Fighting back for my mother, for Aria, for abuela, and my brothers and sisters. I know I'm not a good person but —" The word stuck in my throat. Forgive me. Please.

"Why did you let me believe that you were dead? If Bory

hadn't found a way to—" she said, suddenly looking empty. Had she cried? Has she been crying for me?

" I couldn't foresee the accident thanks to your touch…so, I slept for three days and then I tried to come to you but…the fact that you killed an FBI agent messed my plan up. I'm so sorry, Lynne. I didn't think of contacting you. I just wanted to get you out of there."

She nodded, drawing her full lips into a smile that didn't reach her eyes and punched her disappointment right into my face, like a hard fist. Then it was enough for me. I walked up to her, sat down next to her, and grabbed her by the upper arms.

"Lynne—" I started but being close to her took my words away. I never apologized, nor begged to be forgiven. It was definitely a first. "Forgive me, please."

CHAPTER TWENTY-SEVEN
LYNNE

Ever since I was here. All these 95 days, I've felt like an emotional wreck. I was angry, in love, happy, sad, and angry again. All because of this man who held me in this very moment and almost cried because I didn't forgive him for turning me over to the police to achieve his selfish goal.

Actually, I wanted to kiss him, roll around in his bed with him until none of us could talk anymore. Then there was the thing with my hands and my voice. I could touch him, talk to him! I really didn't know what Mal's cream did to him and I hoped that he was okay, but hearing me and seeing Bory couldn't mean he was, right? There had to be something wrong...was Rio dead now?

No, he couldn't be...he was alive, wasn't he?

I wanted him to be alive so much that I couldn't stand it any longer. Couldn't stand to not kiss him, hold him. Instead, I chose to express two feelings at once: desire and hate.

So, I threw myself at him, slapped his stupid muscular stomach while doing so, kissed him under his wince, and tore his shirt from his daring body. I wanted to bite, punch, kiss, and fuck him at the same time.

Then he threw me on my back, jumped on me like an animal and held my hands up so that I couldn't scratch or hit him anymore, kissing me like he was drowning, and I was his air.

"You can spank me all night," he breathed while kissing me, pulling my hair, "maybe I'll learn something."

I didn't laugh, pulling his face towards mine once more, pushing the thought away that I could kill him right away for making me feel all the things I did. We kissed like two cats of prey who hated each other, like two soldiers who were ordered to kill the other and couldn't because they liked each other too much, like two madmen who would be even more insane without each other. His lips filled mine, his hands flitted over my body, and then I pushed him off the couch.

Sighing, I laid back, straightening my hair, and looking at the ceiling. Smiling at the loud thud he made when the bastard dropped.

"I haven't forgiven you yet."

Rio rubbed his head and I almost drooled at the sight of him. He was lying under me, *look*ing up at *me* through his *thick*, black *lashes*, supporting himself with his elbows. Rio's abdominal muscles were tense and his mouth about to shout or laugh at me. Who knew? With us everything was possible.

"I think I liked it better when you couldn't talk," he managed to say.

I grabbed one of his useless pillows and slapped it into his skulling gorgeous and traitorous face. He laughed then, but the laugh died when he grabbed my feet and my hands and pulled me down on top of him. I fought back with everything I had and I landed on him again.

"I am truly sorry, Lynne," he said with a rough, gravelly voice, cupping my head with his hands like he always did.

Then, I let him kiss me again, my own feelings betraying me right now, not playing along like they should. I should hate him. I should tell him off and go home. I had everything I needed but...when his lips were on mine, I couldn't. I didn't want to go. My heart seemed to lose the battle against my brain, and I didn't know if I loved or loathed it.

Damn it. I was so glad he was alive, that he was here, that my anger faded with every second I spent with him. He was here. Not in the Underworld, somewhere in Tartaros where I could never find him again. No, I held him tightly. He was with me.

"Rio," I said, parting my wet lip from his, and tilting my head away from his, just enough that I could talk into his open lips, "you hurt me."

Sighing deeply, he put his forehead against mine and spoke in such a calm voice that it gave me goose bumps. "I am so sorry. You're right that I put my goal above your well-being but please believe me, I would have bombed that prison to get you out, I would have killed everyone, I would have—"

"Shh," I said, putting one of my index fingers on his lip. The feel of his skin, touching him with my bare ungloved fingers still felt incredible. As if it allowed me to see him differently, more intensely.

"I wanted the truth," I admitted, "There's nothing I hate more than meaningless excuses."

"Then you'll forgive me?"

"No," I said with a scowl on my face. "I am not stupid. You cheated on me, Rio, for that I'll be mad at you for a long time. You did it for a cause but I'm vindictive. You should have told me, should have made me your ally. So, I want something in return."

"What?" he asked, raising his eyebrows.

"Don't let Any kill you."

He pulled his head back from mine and looked at me closely, as if to make sure I was serious. Hell yeah, I was.

"What?"

I sighed and jabbed him in the hard chest. "When I'm back in my world. Don't let Any kill you."

He frowned and tried to kiss me, but I stopped him.

"Do it for me," I whispered. "Live first." *Because* it will be *over for you down there.*

He put his forehead back on mine and I could feel his warm breath on my cheek.

"You are asking me to let my friend die?"

"He brought it on himself," I said in a firm voice. "He should pay for his mistake, not you."

"I don't think he will do it anyway," he confessed.

"That wasn't the answer I was looking for."

"Okay, but what about my sins? I should pay too. I killed his sister."

"Believe me, you paid enough already."

He sighed. "No. I didn't. Someone like me shouldn't be alive, Lynne. Any is better. I hurt everyone, even you."

"Any made a mistake and he's no better than you. You may have a lot of stupid ideas but deep down you're good, Rio. It's about intentions, about feelings, about admitting that you've done something wrong. You want to help. I know you'll help Chicago in some twisted way. What's he gonna do? Keep playing daddy's boy?"

He grunted and buried his face between my neck and shoulder, holding me as if he feared I would vanish any other second.

"I can't promise you that but—"

"—at least until I have to go back?"

"Yeah, I won't be killed until then." He smirked but it was my turn to smirk now. I got what I wanted and instead of outplaying me, I outplayed him. We were even now.

Rio would live because by the time I need to go back, Any will be dead. His tattoo was almost finished, and he wouldn't make it any longer. Rio was not paying for Any.

"I will only be there for you, Lynne. For the next couple of days, you won't be able to get rid of me for even a second."

"What about the gang?" I asked, smiling as he took my top off.

"Punchy."

"He will spend all your money on food."

"He will," Rio chuckled.

I caressed the mark on his shoulder and had to think about Mal's gift again. I was hoping that it'd save him, that it would really work. I never thought his gift could stop him from transforming into a Deadwalker. So, what the skull was Mal really capable of?

"What should we do for the next four days, Lynne?" Rio asked and gently took off my bra.

"I want to ride the hell vehicle for the whole four days!"

"What?" He laughed and stroked my breasts, claimed them, kissing my neck. "Ah the motorbike. Where should we head to?"

"Anywhere. I want to see something of your world, show me something human, the most human thing you can think about."

AND OH, he showed me.

For four days, I rode with him, taped to his back through American cities, villages, lake towns. We ate burgers until we had bloated bellies, sang in bars, and kissed. Oh, we kissed. I held my feet into countless parts of Lake Michigan, we slept in a hotel in Greenbay with lake views, bed breakfast, and countless massages, and sex—lots of sex. It could have gone on forever.

When we returned to Chicago, I spent my last hours with

Cherry and the girls, thanked Diva Dee for everything and then Rio took me to the cemetery.

My 99 days were up.

CHAPTER TWENTY-EIGHT
RIO

When I accompanied her to Oak Woods Cemetery, I wanted to run away with her again. I was getting cheesy, huh? But after our short break, it was time to grow up. Time to take things into my own hands. What do people always say?

Time wasn't measured by the clock, but by memories. Maybe I should learn from such sayings. Every step we took, passing the graves, the oaks, I thought about what I could do to keep her here with me. Could I make a deal, too? What if she took me with her? But there was no other possibility then simply letting her go. Lynne would never let me make a deal.

As a child I used to cut out the phrases I liked best from books and stick them on the wall, driving my father crazy. But I did it until my wall was wallpapered with sayings from Winnie The Pooh and co, covering all the cracks and holes. Today I remembered the following: *Don't walk behind me, I may not lead. Don't walk in front of me, I may not follow. Just walk beside me and be my friend.* So, I did. I walked beside her, heart-pounding, sweating, and sad as fuck. I would never admit it, of course.

"Don't look like that," she said and managed to smile.

"We'll meet again on Storm Day. Next time you might even see me."

"Ah, you mean The Day of the Dead. Funny that it's that day, actually. My abuela always told me that on Día de los Muertos the dead would be able to visit us."

"Your abuela was a smart woman."

I nodded. "So, it's going to be something like an annual one-day affair?"

She shrugged her shoulders. "Maybe."

I smiled back, shaking my head. "What if I have a wife until next year?"

"Then you bring her along and I'll be happy for you."

"You're just saying that."

"Yeah." She grinned and pulled me to Aria's grave. "Don't bring her."

I sighed as I passed by. It was a little easier today because I finally felt I had given her tormentors what they deserved. I was the only one missing, but I wasn't worried. Karma would eventually give me what I deserved, even if it was only some place in the Underworld.

Lynne stopped in front of a tower I had never seen before.

"When was this tower built?" I asked stupidly, looking at it closely now. The tower was made of dark, dusty, black bricks that actually looked like bones.

She didn't answer. So, that thing wasn't built at all. It was an Underworld thing I could see because... because of Lynne killing me?

"Have you got everything?" Bory asked next to Lynne. I would somehow never get used to him. A blue creature that was more conservative than the pope.

"The book," Lynne said, checking her bag, "and the bone." Then she kissed me, and I didn't quite know what she was trying to tell me, but I kissed her back just as quickly. Man, would I miss kissing her, her sweet pout, her cheeks, her dimples, her smell...I never thought I'd think like this ever again.

"Day of the Dead," she said again.

"I'll be here."

The tower behind her was glowing in a way I didn't like. I wanted to spit on it, kick it, shoot it down—destroy it.

"The last few days with you were so—" Lynne started but Bory interrupted her.

"Oh, guys, nobody can stand it! You can't extend the time with lulling," Bory growled.

Lynne and I gave him such an evil look that he voluntarily went to the tower. I held Lynne's hands once more in mine and pulled her towards me, but the glow of the tower seemed to spill over her as if calling her back home. If someone had told me that three months ago, man, I wouldn't have believed it.

Then, I ran my fingers over her face. As the glow continued over her body, covering her head, the moment it hit her face, her eyes changed to...green. Emerald green. I almost knocked her over, that's how startled I was.

"A—" I stuttered and went through all my memories again from the beginning when I saw her for the first time. How she looked and... how she talked. How she said my name... how she laughed, how...

"Do you know who she is now?" Any's voice almost gave me another heart attack.

"What is *he* doing here?" Lynne said.

I let go of her, still beside myself.

"Good to see you, little sister," Any smiled. "I'd give you a hug, but I think you and I just need to grow back together in our new home, downstairs."

"What—" Only then did we both seem to realize that Any could talk ... to... Lynne... Aria.

"I—you—you," I stammered stupidly and ran my hand through my hair. What the fuck?

"Yep, my curse caught up with me, and you managed to fall for the same person twice."

And lose her twice.

"Aria?" I groaned, looking back at Lynne.

Yeah. Her eyes. I realized that her face had changed a bit, too, as if I had previously seen her in a blur and wore glasses now. I saw her clearly now. Aria was in front of me... damn it... Aria was in front of me the whole time! Lynne was Aria…and she was with me every year I spent crying in front her grave.

"Fuck!" I didn't know where to put my hands, but she moved back to me, hugged me, squeezed me.

"I—I can't be—" she stammered confused. "I died young. I was just a kid. Not fifteen…"

"You always looked much younger than you were, and you know time runs differently in the Underworld," Any said, avoiding calling her *sis* as he used to. Then my eyes flitted to Any's tattoo. He wasn't wearing a shirt, as if he was suddenly too hot. The tattoo now circled the area where his heart had been. I ran to him and touched him.

"Any—" I gasped. "How—"

"When you left for your little trip and said goodbye to me, I heard her talking to you and that's when it hit me. The closer the tattoo got to my heart, the clearer I saw her. It was her all along. A spell clouded our minds, so we couldn't recognize her."

I couldn't stomach it. No, I couldn't…

Any hugged me. "I'm with Aria now. Everything's fine," Any said and whispered in my ear. "I forgive you. You didn't do it on purpose. I forgive you, my friend."

At that moment, it felt like a layer of rock fell from my heart.

"I forgive you," he said again, and my eyes were wet.

"I'm so sorry. I should have died, instead of you—"

"No. This is my path to follow. It's all right. I'll see you on the Day of the Dead, right? Once a year is enough for us, don't you think?"

"It's Storm Day now and no, I want to be alone with Rio. I won't share the day with you," Lynne hissed, grabbing my hand.

"We'll see about that," Any teased.

I kissed her, long and hard, until Any and even Bory groaned. She released herself from my fingers, one finger at a time, smiling at me like when I first saw her at school, sitting on her table with her legs crossed and playing hangman on her math book. Killing the teachers she hated.

Now, I looked at her, walking to the tower with Bory and Any in tow and suddenly there was no tower anymore.

No Aria.

No Any.

I couldn't wait for the next Day of the Dead.

It had always been my favorite day of the year.

THANK YOU FOR READING!

Thank you so much for reading and taking a chance on this series. If you enjoyed The Bone Thief's Tale, please leave a review on Amazon and Goodreads, and don't forget to follow me on social media so you'll be notified for every new release or preorder.

ABOUT THE AUTHOR

Heleen Davies is a 29-year-old teacher with a passion for writing and creating different worlds. Her debut, THE BONE THIEF'S TALE, is the first in a planned trilogy. She writes Fantasy Romance, set in magical worlds with fierce heroines and broody, morally gray heroes you'll fall in love with. Heleen is a mother to a little girl and a Golden Retriever, lives in the mountains and usually sticks her nose in all kinds of books. Find her on TikTok, Instagram, Twitter and Facebook!

Acknowledgments

Writing a novel doesn't happen overnight, and there are several people who supported me, and I'd like to thank you all! Especially the readers, you make all of this happen! Thanks a million.

I want to thank my best friend Sarah, who is always my first reader and loves my books like she wrote them herself. I couldn't have done it without you. My sweet daughter, who had to wait because I had to quickly read through something or write something down. Granny and Mom, who believed in me from the very start. My aunt Beate, who made me this amazing cover. Karen, who was my earliest writing collaborator and my bookipedia, she knows everything about publishing and I'm glad I can ask you thousands of questions every day, and plot with you. She was also the reason I started the selfpub journey! Also, a big shoutout to Franzi, she always finds a glitch that even my editors have missed. Thank you!

And last but not least, thanks to my beta readers, whom I can always count on for an honest opinion. Thanks for reading all the books I wrote before I decided to publish them.